The Door

by

Richard de Montebello

THE DOOR

Doors are physical barriers between two environments. God's Angels used them to travel from Heaven to Earth and ***through time*** knowing *"Only the good may pass."* But during the infamous *"**Witch Trial**s"* in Salem Village, the **Devil** did come to Massachusetts and he was invited into a holy Puritan Church, through one of these doors, breaking the safe guards. Now Heaven itself and all of humanity are threatened by the ultimate evil of the universe.

And *he* wants in...!

Photographs
by Eric Jenkins

THE DOOR

SaberCat Comics
The Door

Warning: The following material may not be suitable for minors.

THE DOOR

SPECIAL THANKS
Nancy Holt - Chief Editor
James "Kelly" Osborne - Editing
Thomas Richardson for front cover pictures of THE DOOR
Bill Plaskon for the picture of the Northern Lights
NASA for photo of "The Eye of God."
Dr. Don Correll for his medical advice.
Charlie-Bill Totten for his Civil War historical and technical advice.
John Olbert for his Civil War historical advice and proofreading.
De Land Police Commander (retired) Steve Dovi for special ops advice.
Eric Jenkins for Civil War (Saltville, VA) reenactment photos.
John Stramiello, Mary "Liza" Peters and Rei Massanet for proofreading
Richard de Montebello, dust cover design and page layout.

Their long and arduous voyage across the Atlantic is
finally over. William Brewster and his Puritan followers
stand, behold and give thanks to the Almighty
upon their arrival to their new home in America.

THE DOOR

For the Nineteen

THE DOOR

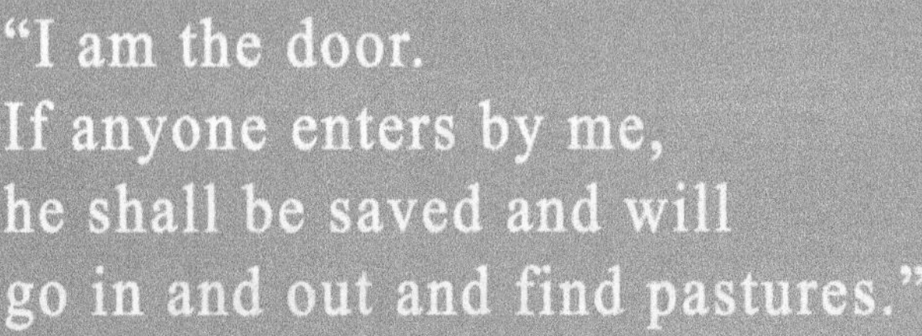
"I am the door.
If anyone enters by me,
he shall be saved and will
go in and out and find pastures."
Jesus Christ
John 10:9

THE DOOR

TABLE OF CONTENTS

PART ONE: ⊕ DANGER CLOSE ◎

(c) **The Door** 2011-2014 is a work of fiction. Any resemblance to real persons, living or dead (with the exception of recognized historical figures) or any Native American tribe is purely coincidence. Any resemblance to any law enforcement organization, military units, towns and town governments or federal agencies in both the United States and Canada and their dedicated and sworn personnel is purely coincidence.

* The Mayflower lands at Plymouth Rock in 1620 with nineteen Puritan families.

THE DOOR

CATHOLIC FICTION BOOK REVIEW
THE DOOR
Review by Jody Rakis

The Door is a real page turner! Excitement in every sentence. The story-line is familiar, about good and evil. The author takes that storyline and raises it to the level of suspense throughout the book, from first page to last. It is a story of a family of door manufactures, who were the descendants of the very Puritans who came to America in 1620. It is the awesome power of a Puritan church door and the craftsman who made it and who entered into a nefarious covenant with the Lord of Darkness himself that leads the reader through history like you have never experienced before. The doorway has a purpose, some for good and some for bad, the suspense builds as each time someone goes through it. From Hitler, to Einstein, conversations are serious, funny, or dramatic in content. Stories from the Civil War are most prevalent with the door-makers' family and they are warm and touching. But though the story soars through time, and characters in history, it is connected and easy to follow. Each page brings suspense, sometimes scary happenings, but definitely excitement. I recommend this book for kids of all ages that enjoy a good, exciting story of good and evil. It's even kind of fun to see the devil knocked to his knees once in a while! And, who can pass up a story of victory from Archangel Michael? Good work!

MIDWEST BOOK REVIEW
James A. Cox Editor-in-Chief

THE DOOR is a grim, fantastic novel about connections between our world and Heaven - Hell. Angels have long used mysterious "doors", through which only good is supposed to pass, but the Salem Village witch trials revealed that the Devil is also quite capable of traversing them! The Devil's invitation into a holy church nullified safeguards, opening the way for incalculable evil and corruption. Will the Devil's scheme to not only enslave Earth to his worship, but also enact a coup upon Heaven itself, come to fruition? The Door is a riveting read to the very last page.

The Door is filled with witty situations. Lighthearted at times, and filled with suspense. A must read for anyone who has even the slightest belief in God and the devil. Richard has an amazing way of weaving multiple scenarios and tying them up into one awesome story.

John J. Stramiello
Executive Direcfor
Behind the Stone Ministries

THE DOOR

X
The Puritan Church door
is this the one???
CONFIDENTIAL
PART ONE:
DANGER CLOSE
CIA
PROJECT DOOR
File LOMAX 616 Submission Date Jan 15, 05
Diciembre
Signed
THE DOOR

Chapter One

KNOCK! KNOCK!

SOME PEOPLE NEVER GET A BREAK IN LIFE.

Ever! Unfortunately, it was that way from the very beginning for Israel and Mary Pilgrim's first child. Today, July 23, 1997 was his birthday, but nobody was celebrating. Hurricane Danny was roaring through the Appalachian Mountains of western North Carolina and Southwest Virginia. The Pilgrims lived in the little town of Marion, Virginia where most folks would say, "Nothing ever happens" and they liked it that way.

The baby wasn't due for another month, so the would-be parents took an opportunity to kick back and relax. Mary Pilgrim was half asleep as she watched the weather reports on television. A commercial came on and the narrator said, "Some people will do the dumbest things at the most important moments of their lives."

The TV commercial showed a group of people walking through a brightly lit white corridor. The old man in the middle of the crowd appeared nervous. "*Ohhhh,* I've got a lot to answer for."

The camera pulled back far enough so that the audience could see two doors on either side of the corridor. The door on the right had red light pulsing out of it, while the door on the left had bright white light coming out. A tall, lean man in a white suit called the "Welcoming Man" appeared with his arms held high. "Brothers and Sisters, such a joyous day. I have wonderful news for you. You're all going to Heaven!"

The crowd of people appeared relieved, some yelped and the old man pumped his right arm as he did a little dance. When he stopped, he stared at the door on the right with curiosity in his eyes. Others did the same.

THE DOOR

The smiling Welcoming Man was gesturing to the door on the left, but when he noticed that nearly everyone in the group was gazing and even pointing at the other one, he swept his hand to the right. "You want to take a little peek? It's okay. Everybody does it. Go ahead! It's no big deal."

The people in the crowd look to one another for guidance, but it was the old man who led the way to the Hell door. He gazed into the doorway, but apparently couldn't see anything. Several others joined him at the doorway, turning their heads every which way to see what should not be seen. Several turned to the Welcoming Man with disappointment written all over their faces.

"Step inside for a better view," he said presumptuously, flashing his pearly white teeth. "Don't worry. All of you are supposed to go to Heaven, so what are you worried about. Trust me!"

It was all these people had to hear. They entered and the others in the group followed. Some were even giddy and laughed.

The commercial cut to a dirty city street corner, where the Welcoming Man, now wearing filthy clothes, confronted a little boy. The Welcoming Man rubbernecked to see if anyone was watching him, then he held out his gloved hand with exposed fingers in front of the boy. In the middle of the glove was a piece of crack cocaine. "Hey, kid! Got Heaven for *ya* right here!"

In the next shot, the camera focused on the face of the little boy and the narrator said, "Why would anyone trust someone we don't know with our lives and future…when we know better?"

The commercial cut back to the hallway as the Welcoming Man started to close the Hell Door. He stopped when he noticed that the boy, who was the same one on the street corner, had remained behind. He gestured to the Hell Door. "Don't you want to go with your friends?"

"*Nope!*" With that, the little boy bolted to the Heaven Door.

The Welcoming Man turned towards the camera, his eyes blazing red. "Kids! You *gotta* love them." He gave a big smile. "I know I do!"

"Don't be stupid," said the announcer. "Say: '*Nope*' to dope."

Mary screamed. Her water broke. It was unexpected and not supposed to happen until late August. Israel Pilgrim, her husband, wasted no time in putting her into the car and driving her to the hospital. What Israel didn't notice was that directly across the

THE DOOR

street the garage door—of a neighbor he had never met—opened and out came a black utility van. It followed the Pilgrims through the town without its lights on. Not even the brake lights came on.

When they drove by a parked stretched limousine, the driver pointed to the clock on the dashboard and said to his passenger in the back seat, "Right on time, sir."

The female driver of the van clicked on the light to her wrist watch. "Ten oh five exactly. How did he know? How did our unseen, *'If I tell you my name I'd have to kill ya'*, client...suddenly know that Mary Pilgrim would go into labor at this precise time."

"When she wasn't due for another month..." added the male passenger.

"I don't like it," she said. "I don't like it one damn bit."

The sky was full of streaking lightning bolts that occasionally found their way to the ground. Many of the stately oaks that lined the streets and made the town look so beautiful were being struck by lightning or knocked down by the high winds. The roadways were covered with at least a foot of water and scattered with all kinds of debris. Israel not only had to contend with the most dangerous driving conditions he had ever encountered in his life, but a screaming wife who was about to have her first child. A yellow pickup truck came out of nowhere and t-boned the Pilgrims on the driver's side, sending their car crashing into a power pole. Both Pilgrims were knocked unconscious. The power pole came down and struck the Pilgrim's car, lacing it with cables. The damaged pickup left in a big hurry. The female driver of the black van pulled to a halt some thirty feet behind the Pilgrims' car. The male passenger activated a portable red emergency light—the same kind used by local volunteer firefighters and placed it on the van's dashboard. But the two people in the van weren't volunteers; they were professionals on a covert mission. The male passenger put on a set of rubber gloves used by power utility pole workers and got out of the van. First, he pulled all the power cables off the Pilgrims' car. Next, he hooked up a metal cable to the rear axel of the

THE DOOR

Pilgrims' car and activated the portable winch on the van's front bumper. While he pulled the car away from the fallen power pole and cables, the female driver opened the rear doors of the van and laid a blanket over the coils of power and coaxial cables that covered the floor. The coils weren't as soft as a mattress, but they would be far more comfortable than the metal floor. The male passenger had to use a long crowbar to open the car's front passenger door. It took both of them to remove the Pilgrims from their car and carry them to the van. They worked like a team, fast and efficient and hardly saying a word. Once the oblivious Pilgrims were safely on board and the winch's cable was recoiled, the unknown couple got back into the van. From that moment on, the lightning storm seemed to grow in its intensity as dozens of stately oaks crashed down onto the power lines that crisscrossed the streets. In an instant, the power grid shut down, casting the town and most of the county into darkness. "Now, the power goes out!" he said to the driver. With the hurricane still raging, the absence of street lights made it a more perilous drive to the Smyth County General Hospital entrance.

The hospital's emergency generators had a long and respected history of working properly during power outages, since it was such a common occurrence during the winter months. *But not tonight!* An electrical fire broke out in the maintenance department and the Halon fire suppression system failed to activate. Patients were calling for their nurses or wandering out into the dark hallways where they collided into one another.

Both the van driver and passenger donned the jackets of Washington County Volunteer EMTs and went into the emergency room. They came back with the only gurney they could lay their hands on. Both Pilgrims were rolled into ER on that gurney. The unknown EMTs from another county gave an ER nurse a quick rundown on the medical condition of the two unconscious patients and disappeared into the darkness and confusion.

Flashlights were brought in to the operating room and to the horror of the attending nurses and the physician, they flickered constantly and gave off very little light. Just as the baby entered the world, a massive barrage of lightning bolts crisscrossed the sky, creating quite a sight and almost lighting up the emergency room at its most critical time. The thunder was deafening. One of the young nurses screamed, but the older and more experienced Maggy Hamilton reached out to her and said, "Get a hold of yourself!"

Dr. John Edwards, a very young physician, still in his twenties, gave the baby a strong tap on the rump.

"Did he cry?" asked Maggy.

"I'm not sure. It's so noisy in here." The hospital seemed to rumble from all the thundering. The doctor hit him again, but the baby didn't cry.

"Let me have a crack at him, Doctor," said Maggy.

The doctor knew better than to argue and handed the newborn to the hospital's best and most experienced operating room nurse. She gave the baby a good rap on the rump. This time the baby cried and took his first breath.

"That was a nice shot you gave to the kid," said the young doctor.

"You're new here, Doctor and its common knowledge that I beat my husband regularly." She smiled. "We call it foreplay...."

As Maggy wrapped the newborn in a blue blanket the baby stopped crying. The baby seemed to be content just staring at her. She had always wanted a child, but instead spent a career presenting newborns to their mothers. And tonight she would do it again. "Mary, here's your little pride and joy!"

As they were wheeling Mary and the newborn to room 19, the hospital's emergency generators came back online, restoring power and lights. There was a collective *"Ahhh!"* heard throughout the first floor.

Israel, who had been treated for cuts and bruises and a dislocated kneecap in the emergency room, had to ride in a wheelchair to his wife's room. He arrived as Dr. Edwards was visiting Mary and the baby.

Dr. Edwards glanced over his shoulder and spotted Israel. "Well, all together at last." He gestured to the baby. "Your boy sure picked one heck of a night to come into the world."

"I'll say," said Israel. "Thank you, Doctor."

THE DOOR

Dr. Edwards gave a gentle rub on the head of the newborn. "I gave him quite a shot on the rump. He didn't flinch or make a sound. Real lion-heart *y'all* have here."

Mary exchanged a glance with her husband and grinned. "We've been trying to agree on a name. I think we should call him…Richard."

"Ah, your love of history," said Israel. He agreed with a nod.

Knock! Knock!

All eyes turned to the bathroom where the knocking seemingly originated.

"Someone in your bathroom?" asked the physician as he took two steps towards the closed bathroom door and grabbed hold of the doorknob.

"Dr. John Edwards, you're needed in OR One, STAT!" the voice said over the public address system. He released the doorknob and exited the room forthwith, giving a goodbye wave to the Pilgrims.

"So," said Mary, "our son is a tough guy."

"The way things are in this world, he better be…." Israel rolled the wheelchair towards the bathroom door and reached out his arm.

"Excuse me," said a nurse, who just walked into the room. "Dr. Morgan wants to have a look at your baby."

Mary gave Richard to the nurse, who promptly left the room.

Israel grabbed the door handle and gave it a good twist and pull. The bathroom was dark. He then turned on the lights and found it unoccupied, clean and in good order.

"I heard it knock," said Mary.

"Me too," said Israel as he closed the door.

*   *   *

That same night, over the frozen waters of the Canadian Arctic, a Canadian Geological Survey helicopter was racing south—almost skimming the ice. The two engines were running rough and by the way the airframe shuddered everyone on board thought the old CH53 was about to shake apart. Above them was a raging electro-magnetic storm known as the Northern Lights that got its energy directly from the sun. Scientists refer to it as the Aurora Borealis. The magnetic storm reeked havoc on the helicopter's electrical systems, overheating them and causing them to shut down. They

THE DOOR

were on a heading that would take them to a place on Ellesmere Island the Nunavut Indians called Revelation Fiord. It was the northernmost human community in North America.

A Royal Canadian Mounted Policeman named Seacrest was standing on the tarmac of Revelation Fiord's tiny airport with a village tribal holy man and his six wolves. The two men stared out into the open and vast expanse of the frozen arctic, under a sky that sparkled with the ebb and flow of the Aurora Borealis. To the Indians who lived in this hostile world and their ancestors, the Northern Lights were thought to be the spirits of those who once lived. Seacrest noticed that while he and the elder looked north, all the wolves were laying on the ground in an almost penitent manner, facing south at the burned out foundations of the original village that bordered the runway. If Seacrest wasn't so stressed out he might have wondered why they were staring at the old village. Not much of the place remained except for the foundations of the half dozen houses and one tough, seemingly defiant house door that stood there still attached to its door jam. But he did notice something odd about the wolves. Instead of their constant barking, growling and snarling, the wolves were quiet and occasionally broke their silence by letting out a whimpering cry. They were definitely not acting normal, but then again, nothing at Revelation Fiord was. "I've never seen the Northern Lights so active," said Seacrest. He pointed to several places in the distance. "It looks like it's touching the ground!"

"A bad sign," said the elder, who was both the tribe's Shaman and the town mayor. "Very bad. The spirits are angry." He raised his arms and started to sing a religious chant.

Just then the transformers to the town's power grid overheated and shut down, casting not only the town but also the airport's runway into darkness

Some twenty miles out into the Arctic Ocean, the CH53 was in bad shape.

"I'm losing avionics!" shouted the pilot.

A middle-age female geologist came forward and put a hand on the pilot's right shoulder. "How far to Revelation Fiord?"

"About thirty kilometers. We're close, but we lost our radar and I can't see any lights up ahead." He glanced over his shoulder at the woman laying on a gurney, moaning in pain. "How's our patient?"

"Her contractions are five minutes apart."

"Where are the flaming nurse and doctor that are supposed to be with you, *eh?*"

"She's the nurse and her doctorate is in Climatology, not medicine."

"Bloody Hell!" shouted the pilot.

The geologist glanced out the window and noticed that they were flying no more than a hundred feet off the ice. "Can't we fly higher?"

The pilot seemed to fight even harder with the controls and replied in a stern tone. "No!"

The wolves turned towards the ocean and started to stir and howl.

"They hear something," said the elder.

"The chopper!" said Seacrest. "Quick, light your flares!"

Seacrest and the holy man lit their flares and placed them in a long line about twenty feet apart, just off the runway.

The co-pilot pointed to the windshield. "There! At eleven o'clock!"

"I see it," said the pilot, seeing the flares. Just then all the indicator lights winked out and the main jet engine started to whine down. "Oh, no! This is not good! Not good at all! Brace for impact!"

It was a hard and dangerous landing. As the engines sputtered out, the pilot was forced to fly the helicopter in a manner that it wasn't designed for. Instead of hovering before making its final descent, the CH53 came in like an airplane and made a dead stick landing—bouncing off the runway then skidding on the tarmac until it struck a pile of dirt.

Seacrest drove the pickup, which was the town's ambulance, close to the helicopter and got out. He confronted the pilot. "You call yourself a pilot? What kind of landing was that, *eh?*"

"The best, you asshole" replied the pilot. "The kind everybody walks away from."

The gurney and the pregnant woman were pulled out of the helicopter and rolled to the cargo bed of the pickup.

"I'm driving!" demanded Seacrest as he climbed into the pickup's cab.

THE DOOR

The holy man and geologist climbed into the cargo hold to ride with the moaning patient.

"Hang on, Thunder," said the elder. "You're home now."

Seacrest gunned the engine. The old pickup made a lot of noise as it charged towards the dark arctic township. As he approached the spot where he and the elder had placed the flares, he noticed that the wolves hadn't moved. They were still facing the old village.

Knock! Knock!

The elder heard the knocking and so did his wolves. They sprang to their feet and started howling. Seacrest heard it too, but thought it was an engine knock. When the wolf pack's alpha male crossed the pickup's path, Seacrest had to slam on the brakes and bring the vehicle to an abrupt halt to avoid hitting the animal. He was shocked to see the rest of the wolves silently trot in front of the pickup just like they were in some kind of a trance.

The geologist banged her hand on the rear window and shouted, "For goodness sakes, hurry!"

Seacrest responded by giving a kick to the gas pedal.

As the pickup raced off, the Indian elder watched his alpha male lead the other wolves to the ruins of the original Indian village at Revelation Fiord. To him and all the members of his tribe, it was a place of sadness and bad history and shame. The Canadian federal government had built the old village for the Cree Indians that they had forcibly removed from northern Quebec. The elder noticed that the Northern Lights were reaching down from the sky with long shafts of sparkling red lights and actually touching the ruins and the only free standing remnant remaining there: a door. It had been standing there for decades, in what could only be described as the harshest environment on the continent. Even though it looked brand new and there wasn't a scratch on it, it was a real old oak door. It was thick and heavy and designed to keep out the cold and the polar bears. For years, the hunters would use it for target practicing. But no matter how many bullets

THE DOOR

they fired at this door or the size of the caliber, the door remained standing and undamaged. When Revelation Fiord and especially the old village became a tourist destination for Native American history buffs, the town council enacted a local ordinance prohibiting any shooting within town limits, and thus protected the door.

The elder had taught his alpha male wolf how to open doors. He watched the alpha male walk up to the door, get up on its hind legs and twist the doorknob with its mouth. The elder was both a down to earth politician and a realistic religious leader, which was the reason he got elected to both posts. He didn't believe in curses or most of the wild old camp fire tales spun by his uncles and grandfathers about spirits and demons. But when he saw the Northern Lights descend upon the old village and opened door, his heart started to race. What really got his attention was the appearance of a dark figure of a man, who stood in the doorway, silhouetted against the sparkling and swirling Northern Lights. In an instant, all those old tales seemed to have a ring of truth to them. As the pickup drove by the old village the dark figure turned his head as though he was watching them. The elder was surprised to see his alpha male face the door and the dark figure and sit down, as though waiting for a command. The other wolves had by this time joined their alpha male and sat down, panting and tails wagging excitedly. A cold feeling ran down the elder's spine, the likes of which no Arctic wind could ever create. His mind was not playing tricks on him. What he was seeing was real. A powerful gust of wind came roaring in from the ocean, rocking the pickup with its force and slamming the door shut. The wolves remained where they were, but started to howl.

When the pickup arrived at the town hall, which also housed the town's only medical clinic, a group of native midwives hurriedly came out to meet them. The gurney and its patient were taken inside. The men were told to stay out.

The holy man confronted Seacrest, who appeared exhausted by it all. "I have seen the face of Evil this night. It will not be an easy birth."

Just like with Mary Pilgrim, the birth was done under the glare of flickering flashlights and the light of a roaring fireplace. As the Indian woman named Thunder gave birth, she cried out in pain and

THE DOOR

joy and the fireplace erupted with flames. A moment later, the magnetic storm faded away and the town's power and lights were restored. The baby was a girl. They named her Allison.

*   *   *

Back in Marion…

A few minutes before five in the morning, Maggy Hamilton had called it a day. She had worked a double shift and was tired. But first, she wanted to check on the Pilgrim baby. She stopped at the nurse's station on the first floor and asked, "How's the newborn doing?"

The other nurse grinned. "Well, they sure named him right."

"Oh?"

"Yes. Little Richard is as hungry as a lion. He's already drained Mary dry twice. I swear if we fed him a steak, he'd eat it."

Maggy chuckled. "I thought I'd check on them before I went home."

The nurse pointed to room 19.

Maggy entered the room and found Mary asleep, with Richard cradled in her arms suckling. What a beautiful picture it would have made. Having never had children, she was envious, but happy for the Pilgrims.

She quietly pivoted on her heel, not wanting to make any sounds that would awaken Mary—.

Knock! Knock!

Maggy turned to the closed bathroom door, where the knocking originated. Her eyes narrowed. This was a private room. No one should be using this bathroom except the patient and/or her visitors. Some of the male orderlies had the idea that they could use any bathroom in the hospital and she didn't go for that. "Who's in there?" she asked with a stern voice.

She stepped towards the bathroom, grabbed the door handle, turned it and flung open the door. She was startled by the burst of bright light that blinded her and the vacuum that lifted her off her feet and pulled her through the doorway.

Later, the nurse at the nurse's station would tell the police that she heard a "thump" coming from room 19, but nothing else. That thump was the grand total of all the sound generated when nearly

THE DOOR

everything in the room that wasn't nailed down was sucked though the doorway in less than three seconds.

The bright light winked out and the door closed.

When Mary Pilgrim awakened, she found herself and her baby lying on the floor. Only the mattress she laid on and the sheets and blankets that covered her and Richard remained. All of the furniture and all of her and Richard's personal items and gifts, were gone. All the windows were smashed. Her eyes widened when she gazed up at the ceiling. All of the ceiling tiles were gone and the aluminum track that held up the tiles was bent and twisted and pointing in one direction, towards the bathroom door.

She screamed.

THE DOOR

Chapter Two

THE ROGUE

What a perfect time to break into someone's house. The hurricane was still raging and the Pilgrims were hospitalized. Most of the county and especially the town of Marion were without power. Old trees and utility poles had fallen all over the place. The neighborhood was as black as pitch. Traffic on the roadways was limited to emergency vehicles and anyone dumb enough to venture out.

But Lomax was anything but dumb. He had a job to do and a high paying client to please.

And his name really wasn't Lomax. It was his code name in the government.

The lightning prompted a flashback for Lomax, the first of several.

A man named Diciembre handed Lomax a memo. He read it. "Lomax? Why Lomax?"

"It's an oxymoron," replied Diciembre. "Low, Max. Good and bad, thief and Samaritan. It suits you."

"Well, I hate it."

"I figured you would. That's why I picked it. Welcome to the CIA."

When Diciembre reached out his hand, Lomax didn't shake it, marking the beginning of their tumultuous relationship.

Lomax was a complex man with a sordid past and upbringing. He never met his father or even knew who he was. His mother raised him until his fourth birthday, when he asked. "Mommy, who's my daddy?" She never answered. She started to cry and didn't stop for hours. She went out that night and never came home. Years later, he would learn that she went to a bar where someone had given her a narcotic known as meth amphetamine. Days later, a police K-Nine found her body in a hastily dug grave in a wooded area, not far from the bar. She had been brutally raped and murdered. Lomax would spend his early years being shuffled from one bad foster home to another until an unknown party paid the fees for him to attend a military boarding school. His teachers considered him intelligent, but prone to violence. He liked to fight, especially the big fat bullies who picked on him. He may have been half their size, but he could beat the crap out of them. His teachers also found him totally undisciplined and resistant to authority. He would not be fit for the military. He knew it, so one day he didn't show up for roll call.

For the next couple of years, he lived on the streets, cold and filthy and doing whatever was necessary to stay alive. His first big break came when a construction foreman hired him as a laborer. Yes, he was shorter and thinner than the Mexicans who worked on the site, but he was strong for his size and could fit into tight places—an attribute that would serve him well all his life. He also was not afraid of heights or doing hard work. He was also a fast learner. He built everything from houses, to banks, to commercial towers, to government buildings. Oh, he loved building them, especially police stations and courthouses.

Lomax's life changed again when a local utility company recruited him to be a lineman. He jumped at the chance and graduated from electrician school first in his class. This was the area in which he shined the brightest. He was in love with electrons! But after two years of repairing power lines, he hung up his utility belt and went to work for a telephone/cable company. For him it was the same poles, different job, same utility belt, but lower pay. On the other hand, it was a way for him to get his *foot in the door* and he knew he wouldn't be climbing poles forever. Eventually, his talents were recognized and the telecom offered him a job in one of their communication hubs. They sent him to several computer tech schools where he discovered he had a knack for writing computer codes. It became a passion. While writing codes and fighting viruses on a daily basis for the telecom, he learned how to be a hacker from the best in the business. Many of his fellow co-workers were convicted felons who now worked for the same telecoms they once played havoc on. Their job was to thwart the efforts of the next generation of hackers who were doing the very same things they did before they got caught. *What a world!* He called it "Cracker Tech" and he was their best student. Before long, he surpassed the abilities of his convicted teachers.

Prior to tonight, Lomax had spoken to his mysterious client only once. He and the female driver were on the run, literally running through a forest in Kentucky. Their stolen car had broken down and barking hound dogs from the local sheriff's department were chasing them. They had no money, no weapons; they were cold, hungry and bone tired. They had been on the run for days. They happened upon a dirt road, but kept to the trees bordering it. A four-door Ford drove by them then skidded to a halt. The window on the front passenger door came down and a man called out, "Lomax, get in the trunk." The window went up and so did the trunk.

When Lomax stepped out onto the roadway, his female companion grabbed him by the arm. "Wait—he knew your code name!"

"Yes he did and the hounds are getting closer."

She was too tired to argue and threw up her arms in defeat. "Okay."

They ran up to the trunk and looked inside. A mattress with pillows and blankets covered the floor of the trunk and there where reading lamps on both ends. They also spotted the water bottles and sandwiches wrapped in plastic.

"All the comforts of home, my dear," said Lomax as he gestured for her to get in. They climbed into the trunk and Lomax closed the lid.

The car sped off and didn't stop until it arrived in Marion, Virginia. During the trip, the man who would become Lomax's client spoke to him over a speaker. "I need a man of your expertise for a long term deep cover case. I will pay you handsomely for your time and efforts, say high five figures a year."

Lomax opened an envelope marked "petty cash" and found a thick wad of twenty-dollar bills. He held it up for her to see.

Her eyes widened.

"And that's some spending money," said the client.

How did he know Lomax had opened the petty cash envelope? In the coming days, Lomax would tear the trunk apart in search of a camera, but would not find one. Another mystery!

"Deep cover, you say." said Lomax. "How deep and for how

long?"

"The deepest and for seven years..."

"How do you know how many years—?"

"—I just do. Leave it at that."

"Who's the target?"

"Open the file marked **PILGRIM**."

The Pilgrim File was on top of a small stack. Lomax opened it and pulled out photographs of Israel and Mary Pilgrim. He quickly read their bios and studied the blue prints of their house.

"They're just common people," said Lomax.

"They are...for now. And they're good people. But they will become involved in the biggest national security threat this country will ever see. Your job is to observe, record and report to me on their welfare on a regular basis. But you are not take any action that might compromise your cover. Is that clear?"

"You expecting trouble?" Lomax never got an answer.

The client changed the subject and advised that they had two months to prepare and go operational. Mary was in her seventh month of pregnancy, which gave them plenty of time to prepare for this long deep cover assignment. As Lomax relived this moment, he wondered if the client knew then that Mary would go into labor a month early. The client then informed Lomax and his companion that as part of the compensation package, the two houses they would operate out of would be theirs to keep.

Lomax's companion went foraging through the stack of files that lay on her side of the trunk and discovered one that contained the deeds to the two houses with names she did not recognize printed as the owners. She also found a second set of keys, a Virginia Drivers License with her picture on it, a car title to a four-door Ford (the one they were riding in) and car/house insurance policies and a personal checking bank book all in the name of Daphne Simmons.

"Who's Daphne Simmons?" she asked.

"That's you, my dear," answered the Client.

Lomax shot her a glance. "Daphne? I like it. It suits you."

Daphne handed the file with the name **EDWARD DANE** stenciled on the cover to Lomax. It contained all kinds of official documents, such as birth certificate, high school diploma and report cards. There were also copies of Commonwealth and

Federal tax returns for the past ten years, Virginia Drivers License and so forth. There was also a business license, and personal and business bank checking and savings books showing years of activity and collectively a total of ten thousand dollars in their accounts. She also found a deed to the other house. "Oh, wait until you see what your name is...."

The client drove by the two houses to check on the progress of the carpenters he hired. The two houses were to say the least, eyesores and had been for years. "I'm going to pop open the trunk lid for you to get a glance at your new homes," said the client. He then pressed the button to open the trunk lid.

When Daphne saw the houses she said, "They're wrecks!"

But when Lomax first laid eyes on them he smiled and said, "No, they're perfect!"

Both were two story wood-framed houses built when Eisenhower was President. The house that would be Daphne's didn't have an inch of paint on it. The other, which stood directly across from the Pilgrim's, had most of its second floor burnt away by a fire. Some twenty or so Mexican carpenters were building a new second floor. About half that number was busy pulling out all the old drywall from Daphne's house. No one had lived in either house for years and they looked it.

When the client turned onto another street, Lomax closed the lid.

"I want you to make a list of everything you will need," the client said to Lomax. "Put it into the addressed envelope that I've provided. And be advised that the PO Box will only be used once."

Lomax found a piece of paper and wrote a message to Daphne. It read: "This guy is or was a Fed."

"I hope you've got deep pockets, because you're going to need them," said Lomax. "Put a used white utility van at the top of the list. Both houses are going to need to be rewired and I'm going to do it." Once again, the client didn't give a reply.

THE DOOR

The sound of the car brakes being applied was heard. Next, the driver door was opened and closed. The motor was left running.

When Lomax opened the trunk and got out, the client was gone. They were now in the parking lot of a hotel, next to a white utility van with the following printed on the side. "Hot Diggity Dog Electric Man" and "Eddie Dane – Owner."

Daphne handed him a file that contained the utility van's keys, a notarized house title and car and house insurance policies. She had a big smile on her face when she climbed out of the trunk. "Here are your van keys, Doggie! Yes, it suits you."

Lomax raised a hand. "That's Eddi…not Doggie." He then glanced at Daphne's house title and noticed something odd. "Hey, wait a minute. This house title was notarized ten years ago with your alias." He gestured to the date on the notary seal, then to the signatures of Daphne Simmons and the Notary on house titles. "Don't ask me how he did it, but that's your signature."

"He bought that house ten years ago?"

Lomax checked the other house title. "This one too. But it's in my alias's father's name. Edward Dane senior." He then discovered the Death Certificate for Edward Dane Sr. and a Last Will and Testament. "He died ten years ago…and I'm the only heir to his estate."

"How convenient."

Lomax frowned. "It's all too convenient…."

Three days later, Lomax parked his van on the cracked driveway of "his" house. He was now sporting a moustache and wearing a T-shirt that said in Spanish: "Yo no pago contribuciones asquerosas". Translation: "I no pay no stinking taxes". He had learned enough Spanish living on the streets and in his travels for the CIA to quickly win over the Mexican carpenters. While they framed out the second floor, Lomax rewired both houses and redid all the plumbing and drywall. A local painting company was hired to paint both houses inside and out, and their garages. The front and backyards were covered with new sod along with bushes and a row of medium-sized evergreen trees planted in the space between the houses, which separated the newly paved driveways. Lomax packed the walls and floors with standard insulation. After the building inspectors gave their approval, he repacked some of the walls and floors with lead foil and the material that stopped infrared scans.

The very last problem Lomax had to contend with was his electricity usage. With all of the surveillance and computer systems he was going to install in the basement, he knew that his house would stand out like a sore thumb if it got a higher power bill than his neighbors. Once again, his work experience as a utility lineman would come in handy. It was nothing for him to hot-wire a second power line directly to his basement from behind the house's meter box. Now he had access to all the power he needed for free and more importantly, no one would be the wiser.

Every business day an unmarked van would arrive with heavy boxes or wooden crates with furniture store markings. But only some contained furniture. The client would provide the best computers and surveillance equipment on and off the market and everything else he would need for this long-term surveillance.

For the next month, everyone involved worked real hard to refurbish the two houses. When all the work was done, both houses were the cutest on the block. Daphne was so happy with her house she grew a flower garden.

Lomax and Daphne would live in one house and operate in the basement of the other. That was the plan.

But all plans change....

Daphne drove through the township, carefully avoiding all the fallen trees and power lines. This time, however, she drove with the van's lights on...until they reached their street. That's when the van lights were turned off and she put on the night goggles. She then drove into Lomax's garage so that he could load up the van with his gear and all the equipment he was going to need.

After Lomax loaded the van, he changed into a black outfit that made him virtually invisible outside. Next, he put on his night goggles. The only negative feature about wearing night goggles was that lightning flashes were greatly intensified and would momentarily blind him. ***They also hurt!***

Daphne went into the attic and started feeding the rope lead line that was tied to a long coaxial cable through the same vent as their TV cable came through. She had to work in a tight space because most of the floor space in the attic was taken up by an assortment of satellite dishes, antennas and surveillance special devices. A lot of it was fresh out of Research and Development. To Daphne, the attic resembled a dark and foreboding jungle with all power cables and wiring that lined the walls and hung down from the ceiling.

As the rope lead line came outside of the attic, the high wind took it and whipped it around wildly. Lomax had to leap into the air several times to catch it. Once he had the lead line, he tied it to his utility belt. This would allow him to use both hands to climb the wood utility pole on the front corner of his house. The only error he made on this side of the street was when he kicked over the *For Sale by Owner* sign that was on the front lawn. His utility pole stood directly across from the power pole on the Pilgrim's sidewalk and there were several cables and power lines running between them. Once again, he put on the rubber gloves before climbing up the utility pole—just in case the power came back on. Even though he was only thirty-five years old and in great physical shape, it still wasn't easy climbing a slippery pole during a raging storm, trailing a rope and cable line behind him. At one point during the ascent, the wind reached speeds upwards to eighty miles an hour and he almost fell off. When the wind finally subsided, he used a battery-powered drill to screw an eyebolt into the top of the utility pole's crossbar. He untied the rope from his utility belt and inserted it through the eyebolt. He pulled on the rope line and the cable that followed until the line became firm. He then climbed down the pole, crossed the street, pulling on the lead line. Upon reaching the other side of the street, he once again tied the end of the rope to his utility belt and went up the Pilgrim's utility pole. The wire he would run to the Pilgrim's house was a custom made coaxial cable that also included a power line, all wrapped together in black synthetic rubber. Once the second eyebolt was installed, he inserted the end of the lead line through the hole and pulled until the cable was firm once more.

He came down the pole and pulled the cable up the Pilgrim's driveway to the garage. He then used a flashlight to flash a signal across the street.

Daphne started up the van and without lights on, slowly and expertly backed the van across the street. She parked the van in front of the Pilgrim's garage and turned off the motor. He opened the rear doors of the van and removed all the tools, electronics gear and coils of wiring he would need and piled them under the overhang at the rear door of the house. The last items he removed were two ladders that were tied to a utility rack on top of the van. Both were painted black. He used the long ladder to get on the roof of the Pilgrim's house, pulling on the coaxial cable for the last time. He inserted the cable into the same metal conduit the telecom used to enter the attic with their wires and cables.

When he turned and stepped towards the ladder, a powerful gust of wind kicked up and he lost his balance and slipped and fell down hard on his buttocks. He slid off the roof and one of his outstretched arms managed to grab hold of one of the ladder's rungs. It broke his fall, but it felt like he pulled every muscle in his arm. The pain would linger for days. For a moment, he hung there, staring down at his partner, wincing in pain.

She opened the driver side window, stuck her head out and called him a: "moron!"

He got onto the ladder and climbed down. After he put the long ladder back on top of the van and tied it down, he tapped the side of the van twice, thus giving the signal for her to drive home.

It was now time for him to do what he did best: break into the house. It was something he learned living on the streets, breaking into people's homes for food and whatever he could pawn. He never liked doing it, but when you are hungry and alone you will do anything for your next meal. The first thing he learned, after almost getting caught by the homeowners was that he needed to case the place before he burglarized it. In his youth, he did it with his eyes and ears. Now he did it with cameras and bugs. But the most significant change in Lomax was that he never again targeted the common citizens, the working class who were trying to make ends meet. No, he went after the drug dealers and especially the meth amphetamine makers. Not because he had some romantic notion of being Robin Hood and stealing from the rich crooks to give to the poor. It was because he hated them for all the lives they destroyed, especially his *dear mother's!* He also knew that meth dealers had plenty of cash and that the bastards deserved to get ripped off. All capable criminals have specialties. Lomax's specialty was stealing from criminals without them knowing about it. He left nothing behind that could be traced directly back to him. That is unless they tore down the walls of their houses or trailers looking for the pinhole cameras and bugs he installed. Even after the bad guys realized they had been screwed, who were they going to call, the police? So, in one sense it was a perfect crime! But there was always the danger that he could get caught in the act or identified. If that happen he would end up dead. But Lomax took comfort in the knowledge that the dopers who were making meth were usually too high to notice they had been hit by a real pro. Lomax was also known for his coup de grâce or his finishing blow. After stealing from the dealers, he would covertly inform on them to the Feds, providing copies of videos and even samples of their product.

Ironically, it was the federal agents who were staking out meth labs that started to take notice of the fast-talking and fast moving "Cable Guy." They saw potential and stood back and watched and waited. Why? They knew all good things come to an end and even the best screw up…eventually.

Lomax would later admit that he got greedy and sloppy and made the mistake of burglarizing a bank where the meth dealers kept millions of dollars in their safe deposit boxes. He thought he had silenced all of the alarms and blackened all of the surveillance cameras, but a redundant system he didn't know about went off and he was caught red-handed. Now the meth dealers he had preyed upon were on to him and they wanted him dead. This was when the government stepped in, offered their protection and recruited Lomax for the CIA. He never wanted to be a spy, but it was either join them or get whacked by the meth dealers. Agent Diciembre, Lomax's first "handler", knew that the meth dealers would never stop looking until his new recruit was dead, so he killed him. Lomax was allowed to make a spectacular jailbreak, but during the high-speed police pursuit his car crashed into a gasoline tanker and exploded. It was a rather expensive way to secure his services, but what the government got for their money was a man who was good with electronics and computer software. The CIA made him better than good. They gave him the best training and access to the most sophisticated hardware in the world and made him an expert. One of his teachers commented, "Lomax was like a sponge. He absorbed it all in." For about a year, they put him in Research and Development where he wrote a lot of programs and invented all kinds of neat little gadgets. His superiors liked him because he always thought out of the box. It was probably the most secure and happiest time of his life. If they had left him alone in Research and Development, he'd probably still be there now. But the powers that be thought he would do more good for the Agency as a field operative. *Big mistake!* After another year of the most intensive training he would ever have and working two years in Black Ops, he failed to report to work one day and just simply disappeared.

That was then. This was now.

Even though it was dark outside, he stealthily went around to the front door. He froze when there was a bright flash from a lightning strike, knowing that even though he was a black shadow any movement in light could be noticed. The flash momentarily illuminated the small business sign planted in the grass, near the front door. It read: *Murals by Mary*. When he started casing the Pilgrim house, Lomax came to appreciate the fact that Mary Pilgrim was a professional artist, who specialized in painting wall murals. Examples of her talent could be seen in a number of local homes and businesses, which Lomax checked out and photographed. Her artwork would fit right into his plans.

With one hand he reached into a pocket for the small case containing his lock pick and with the other he grabbed the doorknob and turned it. Next, a simple push and the door opened. He shook his head. No need for his special talent on this job! Since home burglaries were rare in Marion, many town residents didn't have deadbolts on their doors. They knew that their neighbors were watching and would call the police if they saw anything suspicious, but not tonight with a hurricane roaring. The Pilgrims did have a deadbolt, but Israel was too busy rushing his wife to the hospital to engage it. Lomax just walked right in.

Not wanting to leave any evidence of his illegal entry, Lomax used a towel he brought to wipe the wet footprints he made, as he traveled through the house. When he opened the back door, he brought in the short ladder, his gear and all the coiled cable and piled them onto the mudroom floor. He was soaked to the skin, so he stripped off his clothes and wiped himself down with the towel. He changed into a black jumpsuit and sneakers, and hung his wet clothes, towel and boots on the patio's clothesline to dry. He would need them again for the return trip home. He took a moment to catch his breath and drink a few sips from a small bottle of Coca Cola he stored in one of his bags. He referred to the blueprint of the Pilgrim House, illuminating it with a small flashlight. It designated every room and gave their dimensions. However, the blueprint didn't show where the cameras and microphones were to be installed. That he would have to do tonight.

Unfortunately, the green glow of the night goggles didn't pay justice to the colorful wall murals Mary Pilgrim created. In a sense, the old Pilgrim house was her studio and showplace for her little business. A lot of people and potential customers came there to check out her handiwork. Each room had a "theme", whether it be the Revolutionary War, Civil War or in the case of little Richard's bedroom, a traveling circus. Even his bathroom door had a mural of puff white clouds and an Angel playing a long horn painted on it.

It was Lomax's job to plant at least one camera and microphone in every room in the house, save the bathrooms and the basement. He was told that it was to be a long-term surveillance, thus requiring the need for electric power, not battery for the cameras and audio systems. Since secrecy was paramount and signals from wireless systems could be intercepted, the only option left was using coaxial cable, hence, the need for a coaxial cable with electrical lines connected to a stationary power source. This was the reason Lomax lived and operated out of the house directly across the street from the Pilgrims. He had to bug every room in a house that was built at the end of the Civil War that had wood floors, old windows, and fireplaces on both floors and in the basement and post-World War II wiring system that had passed its prime and should be replaced entirely.

When Israel brought his new bride to the house to live, the first thing she asked for was his permission to paint murals in all the rooms. Israel happily agreed because he wanted this house to be Mary's home and she wanted to brighten up the old gloomy place. However, he did hold his ground when it came to keeping his beloved grandfather's office exactly the way it was.

Lomax would use Mary's murals to his advantage. He had to position the cameras and audio bugs in places where they wouldn't be noticed, painted over, or blocked by a piece of furniture. The client wanted each camera to have a wide-angle view of all the doors in the room. Lomax didn't understand the reason the client wanted him to watch the Pilgrim's doors, but his was not to reason why, his was to do what his high paying client demanded. This meant that the cameras had to be positioned in the walls, close to the ceilings. So, he went from room to room on the first and second floor with the small ladder. He would select a spot on Mary's mural that was black or brown in color and no more than a foot from the ceiling. He stood on the ladder and drilled two thin holes in the mural, one for the camera and the other for the super sensitive microphone with high-gain pre-amp that would pick up and record sounds from distances up to fifty feet away. Both systems were digital for highest quality.

He inserted a metal rod to mark the spot. He then used a battery-powered vacuum to leave no trace behind. The only room that had no murals was Israel's office. It was lined with beautiful cherry wood paneling. Lomax selected two dark knots in the wood and drilled the holes.

Once all the targets were marked he went up to the attic. It took him about ten minutes to prep each room on the second floor, making measurements, splicing cables and soldering and crimping connectors. He made quick work of inserting cameras and bugs for the second floor. All he had to do was go to the end of the attic where there was a thin space, about two inches wide, between the house exterior wall and the room's interior wall. It was called a vapor barrier and it was wide enough for him to reach down and insert the long aperture of the camera. He then housed each camera in a lightweight metal cage to protect them and their wiring from house mice, which might gnaw on it, and screwed it to the drywall. The microphones also had a long aperture to reach through the thick wall and he protected their wires by liberally applying drywall cement over them. Once each unit was installed, he called out on his headset to his partner, standing by across the street. She would check the signal strength of each bug and the clarity of the video stream the camera sent. When she gave the okay, he would then cover up the works with some loose fiberglass insulation. Exactly one hour had elapsed since he rolled the cable coil out of his garage to the power pole on his sidewalk.

"How am I doing on time?" he asked Daphne.

"Oh, you're good. Fast and furious," she then uttered, "as usual." She was thinking about sex with him.

He left the attic and went down to the second floor to inspect

THE DOOR

his handiwork, pushing on the end of those apertures that stuck out of the wall too far. The second floor was done. Placing cameras on the first floor would prove more difficult and take three hours to accomplish. To plant cameras and bugs on the first floor, he had to work on the second floor and use a hammer and crowbar to gently remove the wall molding on one side of each room. This gave him access to the vapor barrier and the rods he placed in the walls on the first floor. Only once did he have to pull up a floor plank to reach a rod. Once the cameras and bugs were installed, he used some drywall cement and paper to patch the holes on the second floor. He even put a dab of paint over the nail heads to completely cover his tracks.

Lomax managed to finish the job about a half an hour before first light. The hurricane had reached the Atlantic and the winds had all but stopped. He merely crossed the dark street with the ladder and all his gear and replanted the for sale sign on his house.

He even dead bolted Pilgrim's front door.

The last thing he wanted was some crook to break into his neighbor's house….

Chapter Three

THE BABY SHOWER

Just before leaving for work, Mr. "Ham" Hamilton called the Smyth County Hospital to check and see if his wife, Maggy Hamilton, was still working. He knew she had worked a double shift and was concerned that she might pull a triple. One nurse had checked her time card and found that Maggy had clocked out just before five.. It wouldn't have been the first time Maggy had crashed out on one of the available hospital beds that doctors used during their long shifts, instead of coming straight home. On the other hand, she would have left him a message on his work phone machine and said "I'll be bunking out at the hospital." Of course, there was a hurricane and a blackout last night. He really wasn't too worried because he knew that his Maggy was a tough broad who in her youth was a U.S. Navy Corpsman. He knew she could handle just about any situation.

Hamilton was then advised about the incident in room 19….

Patrolman Dewey Mitchell had been dispatched to the Smyth County Hospital to investigate a "suspicious incident". He had been on the road for four years now and had grown tired of the dispatcher's constant use of that term. He knew that the dispatcher had spoken to someone on the phone and had an idea of what had happened. Instead of being a little informative and preparatory, which was part of her job, the dispatcher just called it a "suspicious incident" and let it go at that. Most of the time these calls were bogus and led to nothing. He arrived at 07:12 AM and like many cops he gauged how well his day was going to be on how well the first call went. A security officer met him at the elevator on the second floor.

"Officer," said the security officer, "I'll take you to the room."

"I know my way around," said Mitchell. "I don't need an escort."

THE DOOR

"Well, you're on the wrong floor. It's Room 19."

"My dispatcher said it was Room 219," said Mitchell.

"No, it's room 19...on the first floor."

Mitchell didn't appreciate his dispatcher's inaccuracy or the security officer's little dig. He sighed. "My favorite number." They rode the elevator down to the first floor.

A slightly older second security officer with Sergeant chevrons on his collar devices was standing guard at the door to Room 19.

"So, what's going on here, *Sarge?*" asked Mitchell.

"At 03:00 hours," reported the SO (Security Officer) Sergeant, "when the patient was admitted to this room," he gestured to room 19, "it was a fully equipped and functioning hospital room with furniture, diagnostic equipment, drapes, ceiling tiles and properly working windows. At approximately oh five hundred hours, the nurse on duty at the nurse's station heard…and I quote, 'a distinct thump'… followed by the patient screaming." He gestured to the room again and stepped aside. "And this is what she found."

Mitchell gazed into the devastated room and his eyes widened. What he saw truly surprised him. "My God…!"

Only the mattress and bottom sheet were left on the floor. The floor was wet from all the rain that had come through the open windows.

"Is this some kind of joke?" asked Mitchell.

"No joke," said the SO Sergeant as he stepped aside. "And we left everything exactly as it was."

"Left what? It's an empty room…and it's a wreck!" When he turned his attention to the mattress, he became concerned about the patient's welfare.

"Where is the patient?" asked Mitchell.

"We moved both mother and newborn to the emergency room to be checked out."

"They okay?"

"Yes, sir. They're doing fine." The SO Sergeant handed a printout to Mitchell. "Here's the patient's name."

Mitchell read the printout and said softly. "Oh, no. Mary Pilgrim!"

"You know her?"

"I played football with her husband in high school."

"He's also with her in the ER. They both got pretty banged up from the car crash." The SO Sergeant made a face. "They had a rough night."

Officer Mitchell would remain quiet for a time as he stared into the room 19.

"What are you doing?" asked the SO Sergeant.

"Something I learned from an old Evidence Tech I know. He always stood at the door and did a one-eighty of the crime scene…to form a mental picture of the place…before people went in and started stepping on everything and moving things around."

Three things struck Mitchell as odd. First, even though all the windows were smashed, there was no broken glass on the floor. Second, the wall mount for the TV was hanging upside down by one screw, and was bent forward towards the middle of the room, in the direction of the bathroom. *What force could do that?* Third, all the ceiling tiles were gone and the aluminum ceiling track was all mangled together and pointing towards the bathroom. All the furniture was gone, including the gurney, the visitor's couch and chair, the TV, all the medical monitoring and display equipment. There were long gouges in the drywall on three sides of the room and fresh scratches on the floor tile, all converging at the bathroom. "Did anyone hear or see anything unusual?" he asked the SO Sergeant. "Anything at all?"

"Nothing." He turned and pointed to the nurse's station. "Even though we were short handed, there was a nurse at that station…"

"No, no. That's impossible. Another nurse, a patient on this floor, a passing orderly—somebody heard those windows shatter?"

"Negative. I did make inquiries."

"—And Mrs. Pilgrim?"

"She said she was sleeping with the baby."

"Is the nurse still on duty?"

"Yes."

"Get her." He did.

The hospital's Chief of Staff had just arrived at the hospital and was informed about the incident in Room 19. He had a worried look on his face. He and the SO Sergeant escorted the nurse who was on duty at the time of the incident to back Room 19 from another location in the hospital. She was shook up.

As gently as he could, Mitchell asked her a few questions and basically let her talk. She stated that she had been busy doing

THE DOOR

paperwork at the station. Even though they had just experienced a hurricane, it was a quiet shift. No hassles and the phone hardly rang. He gave her a polite nod and said, "Thank you. That will be all." As she turned away, a thought flashed through his mind. "Nurse, did anyone visit Mrs. Pilgrim after she was admitted to this room?"

"No, sir. Visiting hours don't start until eight—."

"—Not family or friends. I mean hospital personnel?"

First, she shook her head and said, "No." A moment later, her eyelids shot upwards. "Wait! Maggy!"

"Maggy Hamilton?" asked the Chief of Staff. He was surprised.

Mitchell noticed the Chief of Staff's startled reaction.

"Yes, sir. She stopped by my station just after five and said she was going to check on the Pilgrim boy." She turned to the Chief of Staff. "She helped deliver him."

"That sounds like Maggy all right," said Mitchell, who just happened to be a friend of the Hamilton family. Marion was a small town and everybody knew just about everybody. "Where is she?"

"She told me that she had clocked out," said the nurse, "and was going home."

"She didn't," said the Chief of Staff. "I just spoke to her husband. One of my SO's found her car in the employee lot, engine cold. After a storm like this, I'd be more surprised that she did go home. She must still be in the hospital. I've got my SO's checking every room. If she's here, they'll find her."

"Let me know when you do," said Mitchell.

The Chief of Staff gave a nod.

Mitchell backed up and scanned both sides of the hallway. He spotted the security camera that was no more than thirty feet from Room 19. "Please tell me that camera works."

"It had better," said the Chief of Staff. "That system cost me a fortune."

"Good, because maybe it can shed some light on what the hell happened here?"

Mitchell pointed to the SO Sergeant, who had been so helpful. "I want you to go to your security office and stand guard over the video recorder to this camera." He pointed to the camera. "Guard

THE DOOR

it with your life. Let it run and don't touch it until I get there. You got that?"

"Yes, sir!" The SO Sergeant turned and bolted down the hallway.

"Good SO you got there," Mitchell said to the Chief of Staff.

"He wants to be a low paid and unappreciated cop…just like a certain former SO Sergeant I know."

Mitchell grinned and appreciated the complement. "He'll make a good one."

Mitchell radioed his shift commander and requested that the Crime Scene Investigator be dispatched ASAP. The shift commander replied with a phone number that he could be reached at so that he could discuss the case further with his patrolman.

Within twenty minutes, the Police Chief, the shift commander and half the patrolmen on duty were standing outside Room 19 waiting for their Evidence Tech to arrive.

"We found the Pilgrim's car," the Police Chief said to Mitchell. "They're lucky to be alive!"

"The doctor in the Emergency Room said that two Washington County EMTs brought them in."

"I checked with Washington County and they said none of their people were up this way."

"Then who dropped them off?"

"They must have been Angels because the Pilgrims hit a power pole so hard that it broke off its base and landed right on top of them."

*　　　*　　　*

The Evidence Tech stepped out of the elevator, pushing a tool cart covered with boxes of equipment. He met up with Mitchell at Room 19. "What do we have here, Dewey?"

"A real weird case," replied Mitchell, as he swung open the door.

The Evidence Tech took a look inside and did a double take. "Okay, what am I looking at?"

"Last night, this room looked like all the rest. Around five this morning, something happened."

"Yeah, yeah…?" The Evidence Tech waved his arm indicating that he wanted Mitchell to continue with his report.

"That's all I got." Mitchell withheld a few facts.

The Evidence Tech studied Mitchell's face and realized that the young patrolman was not being serious. *"Hmmm!"* He opened the case containing an eight-millimeter video camera and turned it on.

"What happened to you standing on the edge of the door way of a room and sweeping your eyes to make a mental picture in your head?" asked Mitchell.

"I've gone high tech. Now **shhhh!** This video camera makes both visual and audio recordings. If you're overheard on the tape, then you may be called to testify. So, if you don't like going to court, shut your trap and let me do my job, okay, wise guy?"

Mitchell backed off, knowing that he had pissed off the Evidence Tech by not reporting everything he knew. He didn't want to prejudice the man with too much information. In other words, he wanted to see what his old friend could dig up on his own—*acting just like the dispatcher he detested!*

The Evidence Tech started off with an exterior shot of the hospital room, making sure the number "19" was clearly seen. He then took one step inside the room and swept the camera from left to right with the widest possible angle, forming a total video picture of the scene. Afterwards, he entered the room and shot close ups of the scratches on the floor and the walls and ended up facing the closed bathroom door. He reached out and opened the bathroom door to find it in pristine order. The Evidence Tech only spoke while the camera was running when he wanted to point out something for the record. But when he opened the bathroom door, there was something that he noticed the camera never would: an unexpected odor. He sniffed hard. "I smell cordite." He sniffed even harder. "Cordite and burning wood." Then: "Mitchell, come here."

Mitchell entered the hospital room and tiptoed over to the bathroom.

"Do you smell something?" asked the Evidence Tech.

Mitchell sniffed the air. "Yeah, I do?"

"Like what?"

"Burning wood. Oak and something else…Cordite!" The

THE DOOR

burning of gunpowder produces a hot gas known as Cordite. If there's one smell that was near and dear to all cops it was Cordite.

The Evidence Tech turned the camera to focus on Mitchell. "Officer Mitchell, has anyone opened this bathroom door?" He closed the bathroom door.

Mitchell referred to his note pad. "One of the security guards did at around 06:00."

"For how long?"

"Don't know. But I'll find out." Mitchell went back out into the hallway to get the security officer who escorted him earlier.

The security officer followed Mitchell into Room 19.

"You're the one who opened this bathroom door?" asked the Evidence Tech.

"*Uh,* yes sir, I did—."

"—How long did you keep it open?"

"Not long. Just a few seconds—."

"—What did you smell?"

Mitchell noticed that the security officer wasn't surprised by the question.

"Burnt gunpowder," replied the SO.

"How do you know it's gun powder?"

"I'm a hunter. I'd know that smell anywhere and it was fresh…real fresh. And lots of it too."

"Like after target practicing with your friends," asked Mitchell.

"Yeah, buddy!"

"Nobody opens this door unless I say so," said the Evidence Tech. "Understand?" He closed the door.

The security officer nodded, then left the room.

"So," asked Mitchell, "what do you think?"

The Evidence Tech stared into Mitchell's eyes, studying the man. "What do I think? I think that if Nurse Hamilton wasn't some how involved in all of this, I'd say it was a very elaborate joke pulled by the Chief and some of the old timers in the Department to trip me. But since this isn't a gag, I don't know what the hell to make of it." The Evidence Tech unpacked his equipment and promptly started bagging samples.

Mitchell left the evidence tech to his work and went directly to the hospital room where Mary Pilgrim had just been admitted. The door was closed. He knocked on it and said, "Mary Pilgrim? This

THE DOOR

is Officer Mitchell, Marion Police Department. May I enter?"

"Come on in, Dewey."

He opened the door and stepped inside. He gave the room the once over, even though he promised himself that he wouldn't. He tried not to be too obvious about it. "Well, I wish this was under better circumstances."

Israel Pilgrim, Mary's husband was also in the room, sitting in a wheelchair. He had a bandage wrapped around his head and a brace around his injured knee. He had great difficulty climbing out of the wheelchair, but he wanted to stand up like a man to shake Mitchell's hand. After all, he took bigger hits than what he got last night playing football for Marion High.

"They took my drivers license and insurance card," said Israel, as he sat down.

"I'm not investigating the crash. A traffic officer is handling that and will probably come to see you later in the day."

"Why are you here?" asked Mary.

"I'm conducting another investigation and I've got to ask you some questions."

Mary tilted her head to one side and became defensive. "If you think I had something to do with what happened in that room—?"

"I'm not here for that. I'm here on another case."

"Busy guy," said Israel.

"How many cases are there?" asked Mary.

Mitchell was taken back. "They didn't tell you…?"

"Tell me what?"

"Maggy Hamilton is missing."

Mary's mouth dropped. "Missing?"

"Maggy?" said Israel. "Are you sure?" A sharp pain went shooting through his head. He touched his forehead and winced. "And you think we know where she is?" He too started to get defensive. "Dewey, look at us." He gestured to his wife. "She just had a baby and we were both involved in a car crash, for Christ's sake!"

"The last person to see her was the nurse at the first floor nurse's station. Maggy told her that she wanted to check on '*the Pilgrim boy*'."

"I never saw her," said Mary. "I was totally out of it."

Mitchell made a notation on his pad. "*Gotcha.*"

THE DOOR

Mary became very emotional and tears started to flow down her face. "Oh, my God! Something happened to Maggy." She turned to her husband. "She helped deliver Richard, you know. Oh, Israel, this can't be happening."

A sad expression grew on Israel's face as he moved over to the bed to console his wife. "Hey, hey, come on now. You know Maggy. She's probably out there doing first aid for somebody." He worked for Maggy's husband and they were close friends. So was Officer Mitchell. He turned to Mitchell. "I'm sorry I yelled at you, Dewey."

"No," said Mitchell, "It's okay. I mean, after what you guys went through last night—"

"—I never saw her," said Mary. "I was asleep. When I awakened, I was laying on the floor with Richard in my arms!"

Mitchell put away his pad and thanked her with a nod.

Israel went out into the hallway with Mitchell. "Dewey, what is going on around here?"

"Heck if I know."

*   *   *

Marion Police Chief Grayson was standing at the nurse's station when Maggy's husband, "Ham" Hamilton arrived. They were close friends.

"Chief, have you found her?" He looked like he was about to have a stroke, pale as a ghost and frazzled.

Grayson raised his hands and spoke in a low tone. "We're doing everything we can to find her, Ham."

"This is not like my Maggy."

"I know."

Hamilton was part owner of one of the largest factories in the county and was well liked by his workers and the community. He was a great manager and businessman, with strong political ties to both parties. He was no nonsense and no bull. His friend, the Chief, knew that. So when he asked, "What do you have so far?" the Police Chief gave him a quick rundown.

They went to the Security Office where Mitchell was standing by a TV monitor. The Chief gave him a nod.

"Okay," Mitchell said to the security officer seated at the

control panel. "Play the tape."

The hallway camera showed Maggy stepping away from the nurse's station opening the door to Room 19 and going in. She left the door partially open. Some ten seconds later, there was a brilliant flash and the door slammed shut. It was a typical hospital door, big, heavy and made of solid oak. And no hands were seen closing the door.

"You see the flash?" asked Mitchell.

"What could cause a heavy door like that to close like that?" asked Hamilton.

"One mother-sized vacuum," said the Chief.

The SO Sergeant fast-forwarded the tape to show the first nurse who went rushing to the hospital room and pulled open the door. She then raised her arms as though she had seen something that shocked her. She turned and appeared to be calling out to someone. The video showed two other nurses coming out of the rooms down the hall and running to Room 19.

"You can stop now," said Mitchell. The security officer did, then popped out the tape and handed it to Mitchell.

"Maggy went in and didn't come out," said Chief Grayson.

While the tape was being played, the hospital's Chief of Staff entered the security office and watched in silence. He had already seen what was on the videotape. He put a hand on Hamilton's shoulder. "Maggy is one of my best operating room nurses."

The police chief faced Hamilton. "I'm going to have her car impounded for the FBI to go over."

"Do we have to bring them into this?" asked the Chief of Staff.

"No choice. She's a missing person."

Hamilton started to weep. He left the office.

"The news media is going to have a field day with this," said the Chief of Staff.

They did.

But even before the newspaper was released, a half-dozen unmarked and black colored semi trucks arrived at Marion. Two of them went to the hospital. The rest took up positions on hilltops or at the highest parts of the town. They either had domes on their roofs or were festooned with long antennas. A caravan of black SUVs and utility vans drove through town and parked at the

THE DOOR

hospital. The FBI had arrived in Marion, Virginia...and they brought friends.

*   *   *

Two days later, a meeting was called in Chief Grayson's office.

Chief Grayson remarked to Mitchell that he had never seen the FBI respond to a missing person report so fast and with so many resources. He counted forty agents. They spent most of their time removing and bagging pieces of the floor tile and drywalls. Mary Pilgrim was questioned for more than an hour and they weren't as cordial as Mitchell. Maggy's car was inspected and promptly returned the next morning. They determined that it had not been used nor had anything to do with her disappearance. The Evidence Tech had to turn over the tape he made of the room and all the security tapes he got from hospital security to a Special Agent of Hispanic descent named Diciembre. He described him as "*A real creep!*" The Evidence Tech admitted to the Chief that he lied when the FBI asked him if he had made any copies. It was an accepted fact in the law enforcement community that when a local agency was told to turn over all the evidence they had acquired to the FBI, they rarely got them back. But what got the Evidence Tech's attention was the fact that even before reviewing his tape, the FBI had arrived at the scene with some very sophisticated air sampling devices.

"How did they know about the cordite in the bathroom?" the Evidence Tech asked the Chief. "The ink on Mitchell's incident report hadn't dried yet and they show up with gadgets like this."

"I have no idea," said the Chief. He nodded in Mitchell's direction. "When I handed them your report, they didn't even read it. That...gave me the distinct impression that they already knew what they were looking for."

But it was Mitchell who made the keenest observation. "Chief, something ain't right here. Some of those guys weren't who they said they were."

"Then who were they?" asked the evidence tech.

"Don't know. I just know that they weren't from the FBI. Especially that Diciembre *fella*."

"How do you know that?" asked the Chief.

"Because of the way he was telling the FBI techs what to do and those tech guys didn't like it...at all!"

The Evidence Tech made a face at Dewey. "What, four years on patrol and you think you got cop eyes?"

The phone rang. The Chief answered it and spoke for less than twenty seconds, then hung up. "That was the hospital's Chief of Staff. The Feds have packed up and left." The others started to say something, but he raised a finger and the room fell silent. "He said that they tried to remove the door from the bathroom."

"Tried?" asked Mitchell. "What does that mean—tried?"

The Chief made a face. "You got me. But they sealed up the room and said they would be back for it."

"Why would they want the door?" asked the Evidence Tech, shaking his head in disbelief.

Exasperated, Mitchell brought a hand up to his face and rubbed his eyes. "Nothing about this case makes any damn bit of sense. And I got a gut feeling that this is only the beginning...."

*　　*　　*

For the Pilgrims, life went on. Israel's injuries were such that he was released from the hospital the day after Mary and the baby. His doctor had confined Israel to a wheelchair, but it got folded up and put in the corner the moment he passed through the front door of his house. He did obey his doctor's orders about staying in bed. That was easy. Israel was exhausted and in a lot of pain. Also, the meds he got from the hospital knocked him out cold. One of Mary's sisters lived a couple of blocks away and pitched in to give a helping hand.

August was a better month. It was actually a happy time for Israel and Mary Pilgrim. They had tried for five years to start a family. They had been a loving couple and tried vigorously to keep the romance alive in their marriage. When nature didn't work, they sought professional help, but the only thing the drugs that were prescribed did was make Mary sick and irritable. Usually, an argument would ensue resulting in Israel sleeping on the living room couch, thus defeating the purpose. The Pilgrims dropped the doctor and went back to the old fashioned way of baby making, but there was something unromantic about how big the

THE DOOR

"X" was on the calendar—designating "Ovulation Day", which went from one edge of the paper to the other. Mary even commented that it made her feel like her husband was a World War Two aviator on a bombing mission. All seemed lost except for that cold winter night when the spaghetti was spicy hot and the White Zinfandel flowed like a mountain stream and somebody put on Luis Miguel's Grammy award winning *Segundo Romancea* (Second Romance) CD. **OLA!** Now they had a bouncing baby boy! Israel was now walking with the aid of crutches and well enough to go back to work. Mary was up and about and no longer required any help from her sister.

Since Richard was born prematurely and on the eve of the intended baby shower, it was rescheduled for the second week of August. Friends from the factory and family from as far away as Roanoke came to meet the newest member of the Pilgrim Family. It was a beautiful moonlit night. The barbecue was all fired up and burning ribs and steaks. Every light in the house was on, even the Christmas lights Israel was too lazy to take down after Christmas. The festive mood was accentuated by Tony Bennett music. They removed all the living room furniture to make room for some wild dancing. It wasn't long before the dining room table was covered with bone covered plates and empty champagne and beer bottles. As the night wore on, Israel dimmed some of the lights to mellow the mood. But what really got the folks slow dancing was the introduction of country music. They were all happily married middle-aged couples, but maybe it was the way the moon shone or the warm August air or all the alcohol they had consumed, but they were acting like horny single teenagers with all the butt grabbing and slapping that went on, sometimes with each other's spouses.

When it came time for the gifts to be opened, the dancing stopped and all the women gathered in the living room while the men went out on the front porch to drink and have a few laughs. They were carpenters and they liked to drink and get noisy.

But nobody drank more or raised a ruckus as much as Parris Good, who was their vice president of sales and marketing of the company they worked for. He raised an empty glass and cleared his throat. "A toast, to the son of the best carpenter…and to all you guys. You *guyssss* are the best…you *guyssss* are the best…"

"How can you make a toast," one of the guests said, "with an

empty glass?”

Good lowered his glass and stared at it. “He’s right. Pilgrim, damn you, my glass is empty.” He reached for a bottle of champagne and tipped it over in the direction of his glass. It too was empty. The other men laughed.

Pilgrim popped open a new bottle. “Here you go, Parris.”

“*Ah*,” said Good, “now that’s the sound I like.”

Everyone took a drink.

“You know,” said Good, “our ancestors would have been up in arms if they saw us drinking like this. They would have had a holy fit…!”

Williams spoke up. “In those days, they were stringing them up for all kinds of vices.”

“No wonder they were so poor and miserable,” said Green.

“They weren’t so miserable,” said Pilgrim. “They had plenty of kids. They were doing something with their wives!”

Some of the men laughed.

“You mean wife,” said Green. “If you even looked at another woman—they hung ya.”

The other men grumbled collectively.

“*Ah*,” said Good, raising his empty glass, “the yearning to be pure and sanctified.”

“Look who’s talking,” said Williams.

They all laughed, but when it ended, Green took the floor.

“Okay, I know that we all agreed not to talk shop—.”

“—*Ah*, come on,” said Williams.

“*Na*,” said Good, “its okay. What is it now, Green?”

“There’s a rumor floating around the plant,” said Green, “about Maggy.”

Good seemed to sober up almost instantly. “You mean the one where people are saying she ran off with some other guy?” Green nodded. “Don’t believe it. I know the Hamiltons better than all of you. I was a snot-nosed young buck when he recruited my parents and all your parents and brought them all down here from Massachusetts. Ham and Maggy were as tight as glue then and they’re the same today. They’ve been married for what, twenty years? Hell, I’ve been married for half that long and there are times I wish someone would send my old ball and chain to the gallows. I was born in the wrong century!”

THE DOOR

"He hasn't been back to work since she went missing," said Green.

"Ham has three passions: Maggy, the Civil War and the business. He'll die at his desk." He glanced at his empty glass. "Hey, thanks a lot guys for getting me drunk!"

"Your welcome!" they replied.

Good then said to Israel, "If you don't show me the way to the men's room, I'm going to show you my appreciation for inviting me to this wonderful party in a way you may not appreciate."

Israel took Good by the arm and guided him towards the half bathroom on the first floor, which was at the end of a hallway.

"Hell of a party," he said to Israel. "And you've done wonders to this old place."

"You helped, don't you remember, *ole* buddy?"

"Some ole buddy you turned out to be…getting me drunk like this."

They trotted by the pile of torn gift paper and baby Richard in a crib.

"Cute kid you got there, Israel. You know, I shouldn't say this, but he can't be yours."

"I think you're right, but I think I'll keep him."

Good stopped in front of the bathroom door, turned to Israel and patted his employee on the shoulder. "You're a good man. Have I ever told you that?"

"Never."

Good turned around and touched the bathroom door. "To be honest with you, I never thought we get this door to fit."

"They all seemed to give us a hard time…being stored in the basement for so long. Maybe a hundred years…."

"Whose dumb idea was it to remove all these well-crafted doors in the first place?"

Isreal shook his head. "One of my great-grandfathers did it, but no body ever told me why."

"I mean, look at'em, Israel. They're beautiful…and they're ancient!"

"You know my wife. She's partial to old things, especially old wood."

"Just remember one thing, ole buddy. Wood is like fine wine…." The alcohol was really starting to affect.

THE DOOR

"It gets better with age?"

"What does?"

"Old wood?"

"*Na!* What idiot told you that crap?"

Good went to the bathroom and threw up in the toilet. About five minutes later, he came stumbling out and closed the door. He went up to the crib and looked at the baby.

Knock! Knock!

He turned and stared at the bathroom door. Did he hear a double knock or not? He knew he was drunk. "*Na!*" He turned and took a few steps into the living room.

Knock! Knock!

This time he was sure that he heard it.

His wife came up to him. "Honey? You okay? Oh, my God! Did you throw up?"

"Yupe!" He then shook his head. "No.... I don't know." He had an odd look on his face. He gestured in the direction of the bathroom. "That door."

"What's wrong with the door?"

"I heard knocking...I'm sure of it." He reached out his hand and took two steps towards the door.

"Parris," she said in a strong tone, "it's time for us to go home."

He grabbed hold of the doorknob and started to turn it, then stopped. He released it and turned to his wife. "We better get out of here."

"You think?" She was being sarcastic.

"I think I did something not so nice in the bathroom."

"Oh, Parris!" She grabbed him with one arm to steady him.

As the Goods stood there, the bathroom door started to shake violently as though someone on the other side was rattling the doorknob with great force. They stood and stared at the door with their mouths wide open. It ended a few seconds later. With the loud music and all the talking and laughter, no one else heard it.

The Goods exchanged a glance, then left the house without saying goodbye to anyone.

They would never, ever, come back to the Pilgrim's house again....

The guests left about a half an hour later.

Israel was cursing loudly.

THE DOOR

"What's wrong?" asked Mary.

"Some a-hole pissed all over the walls in the bathroom!"

"Oh, no—not on my mural!"

*   *   *

The next morning, CIA Deputy Director Blackburn was shown a video clip that got his attention. "The hospital's emergency generators had broke down," said Diciembre, "but the old battery in this security camera had just enough juice to capture this."

Blackburn leaned forward in his chair to study a granny wide-angled shot of a man and a woman pushing a gurney with two people on it into the Emergency Room entrance. He barely got a glimpse of the man's face as he glanced up and smiled at the camera. The edited video stopped and zoomed in on the male's face.

"Lomax!" said Blackburn. "What the Devil is he doing in Marion, Virginia?"

"Playing Good Samaritan again. He rescued the Pilgrims from a hit and run—."

"—Pilgrims? Where do I know that name?"

"It was Mary Pilgrim's hospital room where the incident took place."

"Oh, yes. What about the door?"

Diciembre hesitated. "Sir, we would have had to tear down the walls and dig the jam out of the concrete floor to get it."

Blackburn shook his head. "No, no, don't do that. It would raise a lot of suspicion. We've got to try keeping this under raps. Recall your people."

"But, sir? Your standing orders are to secure all doors the moment they are identified."

"I know. But this is a hospital. We have to wait until things cool down, then go get it. The hospital can seal up the room till then."

"What about Lomax?"

Deputy Director Blackburn leaned back in his swivel chair. "Yes, what about Lomax?"

Chapter Four

RICHARD'S BEDROOM

Still walking with the aid of crutches,

Israel Pilgrim, accompanied by his wife and newborn son, slowly made his way through the hallway at the hospital. What made it creepy for the Pilgrims was the way the hospital personnel stopped, stared and even pointed at them. Even though it had been seven weeks since Richard's birthday, what happened in Room 19 was still the talk of the town and the hospital.

Parris Good met the Pilgrims in the hallway.

"We came as soon as we heard," said Israel.

"How bad is it, Parris?" asked Mary.

"No heart attack is good," he replied, "but the doc said he'll pull through."

"Thank God!" said Israel.

"This is so terrible," said Mary.

"Poor guy," said Good. "I don't think he will ever get over Maggy's disappearance."

"Is she alive, dead or what?" asked Mary.

"Not a peep from the FBI and Chief Grayson told me that his people have turned over every rock to find her."

"And they were such a happy couple," said Israel.

"He wants to see all of us," Good said to Israel.

They went into Hamilton's private room.

Hamilton was sitting up in his bed, surrounded by an oxygen tent. He had to wave his left hand at the visitors because the right arm was immobilized with IV drips.

"Ham," said Israel, "you old lazy bum! You don't look so bad."

Mary, with the baby cradled in her arms, managed to elbow her husband and utter, "You jerk!"

THE DOOR

"I don't know what's worse," replied Hamilton, "lying here, hooked up to all these confounded bags—with stuff either going in or out—or having to put up with all of your sick, idiotic and perverted jokes **PILGRIM!**" His face turned blood red and the diagnostic equipment started sounding alarms.

Israel gulped and thought. ***Oh, my God! He's going to fire me!***

"You've been working for me for what—fifteen years?" said Hamilton.

"*Uh*, yes, sir!"

"You never complain. You never asked for a raise or a bonus. You're the first one to clock in and the last one to leave on your shift. And you're one of the best carpenters I ever had. In short, Mister Pilgrim you are a screw-up and I for one am not going tolerate it anymore!"

Israel was frozen with fright until Hamilton shot a wink at Mary.

"Now let's have a look at your boy," said Hamilton with a smile.

Mary held Richard closer to the oxygen tent.

"Is this the baby my Maggy helped deliver?"

"Yes, he is," said Mary.

"Good looking little *fella*," said Hamilton. He leaned over to Mary and whispered, "Any idea who the father is?"

"I don't know," she whispered back, "but he must be a carpenter."

"How do you know that?"

"From all the splinters he gave me. I still can't sit in a chair."

That made Hamilton chuckle. He knew Mary was a good sort and had a sense of humor and right now he needed some laughter. "I envy you two. Your youth, your baby and the love you have for each other."

"Thanks, Ham," said Israel, putting an arm around his wife's shoulder.

"If I could go back in time and start a new life, I'd still be a carpenter. We're the guys who cut down perfectly healthy trees, slice them up into pieces and make beautiful furniture for people to use and enjoy for many years, sometimes—even generations. But some scientists have said that plants and trees actually feel pain.

THE DOOR

They even cry out. So, I guess we deserve to be punished for our sins against nature.”

“Ham,” asked Israel, “everybody back at the factory is wondering when you’re going to stop slacking off and come back to work.”

Mary was shocked and embarrassed by what her husband said. She pulled away from him and said, “Israel…!”

“We may work for you,” continued Israel, “but we’re all family and when one of us hurts, all of us hurts.”

“Here, here,” said Good.

Surprisingly, Hamilton wasn’t offended or troubled by Israel’s brashness. Actually, he was impressed. He had watched Israel Pilgrim grow up into a man and he liked the result. “I can’t. This thing with Maggy is more than I can handle.” He let out a long drawn exhale and his eyes wandered off as he thought of Maggy. “But I and my silent partner have made a decision and it involves the both of you. For the good of the company, we need for someone to take over as CEO.”

Parris Good was a vice president of sales and marketing and next in line for the job. Israel Pilgrim was a director of manufacturing and considered third in line. Good stood a little straighter, expecting a promotion.

“I will stay on as Chairman,” said Hamilton. “Parris, you’re the best at what you do. Your marketing skills have kept us afloat even during the hard times. And we need for you to stay right where you are.”

The blood ran from Parris’ face and his shoulders slouched slightly. He was surprised.

“Israel,” said Hamilton, “I want you to be the new CEO.”

Israel and Mary were shocked.

Hamilton raised a hand. “Now don’t rush to thank me. You’ll probably end up in this same hospital room and under the same oxygen tent.”

“I…I don’t know about this,” said Pilgrim, turning to his wife and shaking his head. He was content being a department head and working with his hands. To him, a CEO pushed a lot of paper and talked on the phone. Not for him.

“When have you ever heard me take no for an answer?” said Hamilton. “You either take the job or you’re fired. What’s it going to be?"

Knock! Knock!

It came from the hallway door.

"That was rather loud," said Mary.

Pilgrim turned, took two steps towards the door and reached for the door handle.

Suddenly, the door swung open, almost striking Pilgrim's hand, and a middle-aged nurse with huge breasts stepped inside. With a big smile on her face, she sang the following words. *"Good morning, Mr. Hamilton! And how are we feeling today?"*

The nurse spotted the baby. *"And who do we have here?"*

"His name is Richard," said Mary. "Richard Pilgrim."

"Oh, he's such a beautiful baby!"

"Thank you," replied Mary.

"And now I'm going to have to ask you all to leave," said the nurse. "I have a patient, a creaky old fart whose plumbing needs attending to."

"You see what I have to put up with?" said Hamilton. He then said to the nurse, "By the way, I love it when you talk dirty."

"You carpenters are all alike. That's why I married one…*and divorced him.* It's all about…the wood!"

"Why did you divorce him?" asked Mary.

"When I hit forty, I suddenly realized that I preferred saplings to old growth forest. What can I say? They seemed to grow on me!" She flashed her eyelids at Mary, who chuckled and winked back. "Okay, folks, visiting hours are over."

The Pilgrims and Parris Good said their good-byes and left the room.

Mary noticed the facial expressions on her husband's and Good's face. She knew that they needed to talk and jerked her head in the direction of the elevator. "I'll wait for you at the elevator."

"Thanks, honey."

Pilgrim and Good went into a small waiting room, just across from the nurse's station. "The old man has really lost it," said Pilgrim. "Me? CEO?"

Good didn't like the idea of being passed over, but Hamilton was right. He knew marketing but right now what the factory needed the most was a steady hand to run the place. Israel ran the

line better than anyone and was the man for the job. "I'm okay
with it. Look, you make it, I'll sell it and we'll both have a
paycheck at the end of the week."

Pilgrim never reported for work later than 7AM. Today, he came
in around eight, the time Hamilton usually showed up. He was still
walking with crutches and was warmly greeted by the office staff.
Hamilton's personal secretary poured him a fresh cup of coffee,
just like she did every morning for the boss and followed him to
his new office. There was a brand new nameplate on the door. It
read: Chief Executive Officer Israel Pilgrim. He stopped and
stared at the nameplate. The secretary opened the door for him and
stepped aside. When he looked inside he remembered the first
time he came to this very office. Hamilton's name was on the
door. He was eighteen years old and fresh out of high school. His
father was at his side. Hamilton was sitting at his desk, talking on
the phone.
    "Is that Israel?" asked a younger Hamilton. "I'll call you back,"
he said to the party on the phone and hung up.
    "Step inside in my office, young man. My God, look at
you—all grown up!" They shook hands. "Your father said you're
looking for a job. Well, we have an opening in janitorial services.
It means you'll sweep the floors but who knows, one day you may
end up running the place!"
    He went into his office and looked around. The walls were
adorned with Civil War paintings and artifacts. Hamilton loved the
Civil War.
    "We haven't had a chance to remove Mr. Hamilton's things…"
    "Don't. Leave them right where they are. This is his office and
it wouldn't feel right without them."
    The secretary liked what he said.
    Pilgrim met with all the employees out on the factory floor. All
the machines were turned off so that he could be heard. Folding
chairs were lined up in an open area facing a long table covered
with donuts and coffee makers. After everyone got a cup of coffee
and a donut, they took a seat and waited for Pilgrim to speak.
"I've asked *y'all* to meet with me, here on the floor. Not because I
am your new CEO. I've asked you here because this is the floor
I've worked on since I was a kid and found my first true love:
THE DOOR

carpentry. I didn't expect or ask for this job." He shot a glance at Parris Good, who was looking down at the floor. "But it's what Ham wanted. This company is Ham Hamilton's dream and I'm going to do my level best to see that it thrives in his absence. When he's feeling better, he'll come back. Until then, I'm in charge and it's business as usual. When I'm not wearing out my ass on Hamilton's old swivel chair, you will find me right here, working on the floor, where I am the happiest. We're a small company, but we're efficient and profitable. My number one job is to keep it that way. Questions?" There were none. "All right then, let's get back to work!"

It was Parris Good who started clapping. Before long, all the employees of Hamilton-Pilgrim were applauding and some even cheered.

* * *

The hospital Chief of Staff entered his office to find a man he didn't know standing by his window, looking out at the front lawn. The man wore hospital greens, a white lab coat and a stethoscope. For a moment, the chief thought he was one of his new doctors.

"Well, hello, Doctor?" said the Chief of Staff, with a smile and extending his right hand.

"I'm not a doctor," replied Lomax. He continued looking out the window and did not shake the Chief of Staff's hand. "I heard that you were looking for an investigator, someone who could work discretely, for a special case."

"I did," said the Chief of Staff, his smile diminishing. "However, nobody seems to understand what the word *'discrete'* means."

"Does this case have anything to do with Maggy Hamilton's disappearance and the incident in Room 19?"

The Chief of Staff closed the door behind him before he answered. "Yes, it does. I don't believe I heard your name."

Lomax turned and faced the Chief of Staff. "I didn't give it. Who I am is not as important as what I can do for you."

The Chief of Staff's eyes widened when he got a good look at the man in the window.

Lomax saw the look and knew that he had been recognized.

"And what can you do for me?" asked the Chief of Staff.

THE DOOR

"Find Maggy Hamilton."

"You sound expensive."

"I am."

The Chief of Staff's shoulders sank. He and his hospital were now the laughing stock of the medical profession. Some newspapers were saying that his hospital had a time-space portal. Others were saying Maggy Hamilton was kidnapped and murdered. It was all bad news anyway you looked at it. On the other hand, he truly wanted Maggy found. "Look, the FBI is looking—."

"—They'll never find her."

"And just how do you know that?"

"If they can't find me, how are they going to find her?" Lomax held up a picture of himself, the one supplied by the FBI. "I found this in your center drawer." He then lifted his other hand, showing a small broken device. "And they bugged your phone." He tossed the bug to the Chief of Staff. It had been crushed like someone had stepped on it.

The Chief of Staff was not pleased. "Son-of-a—! It's Lomax, right?" Lomax didn't reply. "Well, sir, I'm a doctor. I don't have the luxury of time to play in this cloak and dagger game. I have a hospital to run and I don't think I can afford to hire you."

"You don't have to. My client is paying for everything."

"And who's that?"

"Never met him. Don't know his name. Is that discrete enough for you?"

The Chief of Staff nodded. "Yes, it is. But why are you here? If you already have a client, why bother me?"

"I need to know whose side you're on: the Hamiltons or the Feds?"

"I'm for both and I'm not going to break any laws."

"I'm not asking you to. Just don't call the number they gave you every time you see me walking the hallways."

"And if I refuse?"

"I won't be able to do my job and you'll never see Maggy Hamilton again." Lomax headed for the door.

"I need time to think about this. Do you have a number where I can reach you?"

"Not necessary." Lomax smiled at the Chief of Staff. "I'll

know when you need to speak with me."

"How's that?"

"I bugged your office too."

Lomax took the elevator down to the first floor and strolled past Room 19. Strips of yellow police evidence tape still crisscrossed the door, which was padlocked. His cell phone rang. It was his partner in crime.

"Honey?" she said.

"Yes, sweetheart."

"Our little boy just used his secretary's phone to call you know who…just like you said he would." Lomax lied to the Chief of Staff when he said he had bugged his office. Instead, he bugged the secretary's office.

"And so it begins…."

It was a brilliant tactic. As soon as the CIA found out that the hospital's Chief of Staff *"had made"* Lomax, they swarmed into the area like an army of worker ants, setting up surveillance cameras on the rooftops of every government building, dozens of power and light poles and a host of unsuspecting homes and businesses. A rundown old house on a hundred-acre farm, halfway across the county that was in foreclosure was suddenly leased. The first thing the happy new renters did was put a fresh coat of paint on the old house and parked a recreational RV inside the barn. It was actually a Mobile Command Center for all the surveillance cameras that either beamed a signal to CIA HQ by way of a satellite antenna in the hayloft of the barn or by landline.

Special Agent in Charge Diciembre entered the Mobile Command Center and addressed the agents who were at their posts, gazing into monitors and working the controls. "People, this is a Priority One Hard Target Search. Our target is a former agent code name: Lomax." Lomax's picture and classified information were projected on the wall monitor. "We believe he is operating in or near Marion, Virginia. You can expect him to be in more than one place. Be advised, he's a technical genius. We can expect him to be using the same surveillance equipment we are using." That revelation made several agents shoot a glance at each other. "He also knows how to jam them. He'll be using a lot of electricity, so hack into the local utility and start checking for houses and local businesses that suddenly use higher than normal usage. Stay extra tuned to all police frequencies. If they run a DL or tag, I want to know about it. Be on the lookout for any stolen vehicles, especially utility vans that have been returned. He likes doing that. Check with the local realtors to see if any houses in the area have been rented or sold recently. Check with the county to see if any repos have been bought within a one-mile radius of the Pilgrims. Now remember one thing people, no matter how good he is at hiding he has to sleep somewhere. And even a rat comes out of his hole when he's hungry enough. And we got a big rat to find. So, get on it."

*   *   *

Lomax knew his former employer was looking for him and would go to great lengths to capture him, especially now that he was somehow involved in the Maggy Hamilton disappearance. So, it was important for him to have them operating out in the open rather than in the shadows. To the locals, these people were hardly noticed. But to the trained eye of a former field agent, they and their activities stood out. The most important result of using the hospital's Chief of Staff in such a way was that the CIA didn't remove the door from Room 19. The Director himself issued the order to keep it there and use it as bait for their rogue agent. The problem was Lomax wasn't biting. He didn't have to. He knew they were going to do a 24/7 electronic surveillance of the bathroom door. Sure enough, they wired the room with the latest motion detecting cameras, equipped with night vision devices—because the lights were kept off in the room—and microphones and all kinds of sensors which sent signals to their Mobile Command Center on the farm via a landline. Lomax tapped the line the night after they parked the RV in the barn. The plan was that once the field agents edited the data that came in from Room 19, it would be laser beamed to a secret satellite orbiting in space thousands of miles away, then sent to CIA head-quarters in Langley, Virginia. The problem with that plan was that in its first month of operations, not a single signal was land-lined, edited or sent to Langley. All was quiet in Room 19.

*   *   *

Later that day, Police Chief Grayson called Dewey Mitchell's wife and asked her to come to the PD to observe the ceremony he had planned. It was all a big surprise. Coffee and donuts or what cops consider "*blood and manna from Heaven*" were served in the squad room. The ceremony began after the newspaper reporter and photographer arrived. It was short and sweet.

"You earned this," said Chief Grayson, as he handed Mitchell his silver detective shield. "Ladies and gentlemen, allow me to introduce to you Detective Dewey Mitchell." One of the patrolmen let out a whistle, followed by a loud cheer and a short applause from the other officers present. Grayson and Mitchell then shook hands and posed with Mrs. Mitchell for a picture for the county newspaper. His wife gave him a peck on the cheek and then scooted off to her job.

Grayson went to his office and bade Mitchell to follow him in. Once they were alone, the Chief told Mitchell that, "Even though you have a personal friendship with the Pilgrims, I want to assign you to oversee their…unique situation."

"Isn't that against department policy…assigning officers to cases where they may have a personal bias?"

"Damn it, Dewey," he said softly, "name someone '*straight*' in this town you aren't friends with? So, consider yourself on the case." He turned to the window and gazed at the small parking lot in the rear of the PD. A black SUV rolled into the parking lot. "And, there's someone you need to see…."

Detective Mitchell went out the back door and a black SUV with tinted windows pulled up along side of him. The rear driver window came down and Special Agent in Charge Diciembre called out to him. "Detective, may we have a word with you?"

Mitchell turned and glanced over his shoulder at the Chief, who was gazing out his office window. The Chief gave him a nod, then stepped away from the window. Mitchell took the nod from the Chief as a sign of his approval to the meeting with Diciembre. He got into the SUV and was whisked away.

"What," said Mitchell, "you're not in the FBI anymore?"

"Chief Grayson told me that you figured that one out…before anyone else." He then handed Mitchell a file. It had the following printed on the cover: Top Secret: **LOMAX.**

"You write good reports," said Diciembre. "I'm surprised you haven't transferred to a bigger police department."

"This is my hometown. It's a small, safe and nice place to live and I want to keep it that way."

"So do we, but we need your help."

"Oh? Who or what is Lomax?"

"He's a rogue agent we're looking for. We believe he's operating in this area. What I am about to tell you is to be considered Top Secret...."

Mitchell held up a hand. "If this guy is a threat and he's in my town, I want to know about it. And I can keep my mouth shut."

"I would recommend that." He placed an electronic device in the Detective's hand. "A device similar to this one was found on your unmarked police car. We didn't check, but he's probably planted one on your private vehicle as well."

"I've seen bugs before, but nothing like this."

"It's our new special issue with GPS and all the bells and whistles and they're very hard to get."

"Then *how'd* he get his hands on these?"

Diciembre grinned and didn't answer the question. "If I were you, I'd leave them alone. If you remove them, he'll only replace them. We can expect that all the phones at your PD are tapped and all of your cell phones are being monitored. Your Chief has been briefed on all of this."

"You want him to listen in on us?"

"Yes, we do."

That completely surprised Mitchell. But then again, he was a cop and not a spy.

Diciembre tapped his finger on the cover of the top-secret file and Mitchell opened it and glanced at the pictures of Lomax and the thirty or so pages of documents. "Lomax worked for us in both R&D and as a field operative," said Diciembre. "Even though he has no prior military experience, he's handy with a gun and should be considered armed and dangerous at all times. He's pretty good with disguises, but there are two areas where he is a master: surveillance and working deep cover. And right now he's down right invisible."

"It says here that he's a technical genius with an extensive criminal past."

"Let's just say, with certain things, we didn't teach him. He taught us."

Mitchell leaned back in the seat, his mind running a million miles an hour. "*Hmmm!* Why do I have the gut feeling that you're really not looking for him?"

That question caught Diciembre completely off guard. "Excuse me?" He was not convincing.

"No, you want him to know what's going on because you're looking for someone or something…and you think he's going to lead *y'all* right *to 'em*."

Diciembre studied Mitchell's face for a moment and decided to come clean. "Detective…your powers of deduction are excellent."

"Spare me the compliments, sir. What do you want from me?"

"We need for you to be our eyes and ears in this town. Our operatives attract too much attention, whereas everybody around here knows you, especially Israel and Mary Pilgrim."

"They happen to be friends of mine—."

"I know and they are in grave danger. You can help them." Diciembre presented Mitchell with a cell phone that had no brand name like AT&T or Sprint. "This cell can't be intercepted."

Mitchell was dropped off in the parking lot of the county library, which was across the street from the PD.

*   *   *

Wearing surgical gloves, Lomax drove the black utility van late that night to an abandoned gas station, on a lonely country road, near Mountain City, North Carolina. He turned off the motor, but left the keys in the ignition. He also left a large envelope with a typed report, an assortment of still photographs and a DVD containing clips of each camera he installed in the Pilgrim House. All of this was for his client.

His Jeep Cherokee was parked in front of the garage. As he approached the Jeep, he noted all the unmarked cardboard boxes and ammunition crates and the stack of rifle cases in the cargo area. "Well, looks like things are about to heat up." The keys were in the ignition and a sealed letter and a large envelope were found on the passenger seat. He opened the letter envelope first and found thirty crisp 100-dollar bills. It was his pay for the past two weeks. He would pocket a thousand and give the rest to

THE DOOR

Daphne. He then opened the large envelope. It contained his bonus for bugging the Pilgrim House, two rolls of American currency totaling twenty thousand dollars. There was also a one page typed letter of instructions. This was one of several ways the client occasionally communicated with him.

The letter confirmed Lomax's suspicions that this would be a well-paid and long-term stakeout, which was exactly what he needed. But in the letter, the client made a new demand. Previously, he just wanted the Pilgrims to be watched, followed and recorded continuously. Now he wanted Lomax and Daphne to protect the Pilgrims "*at all costs.*" To that end, he provided Lomax with the means to start a little war. A list of all the weapons, explosives and types of ammunition was included in the paper-work.

The envelope also included several deciphered communication intercepts from Diciembre to Deputy Director Blackburn about the cameras Lomax had placed around the Pilgrim House. "This is clearly the work of Lomax," said Diciembre in one of the intercepts. "The house was covered on all sides with expensive wireless cameras with signal strength that could be picked up for a distance of three miles or more."

As soon as Lomax drove home and parked the Jeep Cherokee "in Daphne's garage," he went down to the basement "of the other house." Wood and cardboard boxes and an assortment of home improvement items such as sheets of drywall, rolls of insulation and bundles of two by fours filled one side of the basement. The other side only had a control desk setup in front of a wall of monitors and audio speakers. Each monitor displayed the real time video stream of each camera he had set up in each room of the Pilgrim House. A hand written piece of tape was placed under each monitor, identifying each room. The sound of a baby crying echoed through the basement.

"Its feeding time!" his partner in crime reported. Daphne was twenty-five years old and a whiz with computers and electronics. She had just taken a shower and was wearing a towel over her head, a robe and slippers.

"Where's mommy?" asked Lomax.

Daphne pointed to the monitor showing Mary moving around in the kitchen. "She's in the kitchen, warming up a baby bottle."

THE DOOR

Lomax grinned. "I thought she was breastfeeding?"

She shot an angry glare at him. "She is. That is, when she has some. That kid is insatiable."

"Someone once said that about me."

"In your dreams...." Daphne then snapped her fingers. "Okay, let's have it."

Lomax handed her the large envelope. "He now wants us to protect the Pilgrims."

Daphne froze for a moment. "Did he supply us with any guns?"

"More like an arsenal."

"That will work."

She removed the single roll of currency wrapped in a ribbon that read: $10,000. "This is the bonus? A little light for all the work you—I mean, we done."

"Well, he did change the oil and tires on the car."

"I don't know why. You're not going anywhere."

"I can't. They know I'm here and they're looking. But you can come and go as you please."

"So," she swiveled the chair towards him, "this is what you spies call 'deep cover'. What did your wife say about all this?"

"My wife?" He turned away and brought a hand up to his face. *"Uhhh!"*

Daphne stood up and dropped the robe, exposing the sexy black lingerie she wore. She took off the towel and shook her head to make her hair fall evenly onto her shoulders. She then went over to him, brushing her body up against his.

The look of surprise flashed over his face. "What are you doing? And do you think what you are wearing is appropriate for this kind of work, young lady?"

"Did you tell her about...me...working here...with you?"

"Who? My wife?" He shook his head. "No way. Are you crazy?" He pushed her away. "Look, the less she knows, the better. And put some clothes on, will *ya!"*

"She doesn't suspect anything?"

"She suspects everything and everybody! That's why I married her."

"Including you?"

He exhaled deeply. "Especially me." He turned away and became defensive. "You know, she treats me like I'm not a good

THE DOOR

provider. I just bought her a new house—."

"It's old and she doesn't like it."

"Yeah, but it's paid off and it's located in a nice subdivision."

"Subdivision, Hell! It's a hood! It's so bad the cops don't patrol it."

"Hey, it's a working class neighborhood. The streets are lined with trees. The schools are clean and the sewers only back up every time it rains. What more can you ask for?" He opened his arms wide. "But *nooooooo!* It's not good enough!"

"*Ah*, but you're so generous..." she said mockingly.

"How can you say that when I even got her the best job in the world. She doesn't have to leave the house. All she's *gotta* do is watch TV and answer a phone...that never rings. I mean, when I met her she was slinging hamburgers at a local Burger Queen and her hair had so much grease she could lubricate the ball bearings on my car with it!"

Daphne's eyes widened. Her face turned flush red. She lunged at Lomax and knocked him off his feet. "I'll lubricate your ball bearings!" They rolled on the floor and knocked over a nightstand that displayed their Las Vegas wedding picture—their only wedding picture. They kissed hard and passionately and Lomax's shirt flew through the air.

Everything stopped when the sound of a doorbell ringing came over one of the speakers.

"Where did that come from?" asked Lomax. "Here?"

"No! It's from the Pilgrim house!"

They quickly dressed, then took a chair at the control desk.

Lomax pointed to the monitor marked "Front Foyer". Mary Pilgrim had opened the door and stepped aside to let a blonde haired young man enter the house. "Who's this guy?"

"Maybe it's her lover?" She gave a devilish smile.

"Oh, no don't tell me that! WOMEN!"

Daphne made a face and pointed to the monitor. "What are you, going blind? He's wearing a tool belt. How many lovers wear a tool belt?"

He cocked an eyelid. "I know of one."

"*Hmmm!*" went Daphne. "Say, he's cute. I'd like to see his tools. Look at all those muscles. He must work out. *Oooooh! He's so hot!*" She fanned herself.

She worked the controls and focused a camera they had standing in the second floor bedroom window that faced the Pilgrim House. She zoomed in and focused on the writing on the side of the utility van, parked on the street. "He's with the phone slash cable company…whatever they call themselves these days."

That brought chills down both their backs.

"Something wrong with their phones?" asked Lomax.

"Not that I am aware of?"

"I would like to have an extension put in my son's bedroom," said Mary. "So, when I'm in there I can use the phone."

Daphne gave a sigh of relief, but it was only momentary.

"No problem, *ma'am*. Just point me to the room?

"Was there a phone jack in that room?" asked Daphne.

"No." Lomax was as stiff as a slab of marble.

"That means he'll have to install one...

"...and go up to the attic."

"Do you think he'll spot your handiwork?"

"If he's real good…he might."

"We're dead!"

As they climbed the stairs to the second floor, Mary spotted the name tag on the phone repairman's jumpsuit. "Sparky? That's an interesting nickname for a telephone repairman."

He smiled. "Actually, it's my legal name."

"May I ask why your parents named you Sparky?"

"Cause I was born during a lightning storm."

"So was my son." She gestured to the door with the name RICHARD engraved at the top.

"Well, if he's anything like me, he'll have an interesting life."

They went inside. Richard was awake and going, "*Goo goo!*"

"Oh, no!" said Daphne pointing to the monitor showing the front of the Pilgrim's house. An unmarked four-door car parked behind the van and Dewey Mitchell got out. He was wearing a suit and

THE DOOR

tie. "That's Dewey Mitchell! What is he doing here? And why isn't he driving a patrol car?"

"He was just promoted to detective."

Mary heard the doorbell ring. "I better go see who that is."

Sparky was moving a handheld stud finder on the walls of the bedroom. "I'll be done here in a minute." When little Richard laughed out loud, he stopped what he was doing and went over to the crib. "You're a cute little *fella*." He gave a big smile.

Knock! Knock!

Sparky was surprised to hear the knocking. He turned to the bathroom door, which was closed. "Hello? Is somebody there?" He reached out and grabbed the doorknob.

"Dewey!" Mary said with a smile. "I read in the papers that you got promoted! I'm so happy for you."

Dewey showed off his Detective's badge. "Thanks Mary. Hate to bother you, but I *gotta* few questions."

"Sure. Come on in—"

There was a brilliant flash, followed by a strange sound and a vibration that shook the whole house.

Mary screamed.

Dewey charged into the house, rubbernecking. "Where's the phone guy?"

"Upstairs in Richard's bedroom!"

Dewey dashed up the stairs.

"My baby!" shouted Mary as she charged up the stairs.

The "Richard" door had slammed shut and wouldn't open. Dewey had to place his foot on the wall and pull the doorknob with all his might to get the door open. Normally, he would have charged in, gun in hand, *but not this time!* Both he and Mary stood there at the threshold with their mouths and eyes wide open.

Only Richard and the crib's mattress were left undisturbed. He wasn't even crying. Everything else in the bedroom was gone and it looked like a cyclone had run through the place. Both windows were smashed, but no broken glass was found anywhere.

Mary lifted her son out off the floor and cried for joy.

Once again, there were streaks and gashes in the walls and floors and they all led to the bathroom. The bathroom door was

THE DOOR

closed. After Mary had left the room with the baby, he cautiously opened the bathroom door. Everything inside was okay.

When Dewey exited the bedroom and met up with Mary in the foyer he had an odd expression on his face. He didn't know what to say.

Daphne was frozen in fright.

They, thanks to the camera Lomax had installed, saw everything that just happened in Richard's bedroom. The bright flash was followed by an enormous vortex of energy that drew almost everything that wasn't nailed down in the bedroom through the opened doorway. The whole event was over in a matter of a few seconds—three to be exact and ended with the closing of the bathroom door. She slowly turned to Lomax, who appeared unmoved by it all. He flashed a smile. "Make a copy ASAP. He's going to need to come up with a better bonus for this one."

THE DOOR

Chapter Five

WHO THE HELL IS THAT LITTLE GIRL

Units from both the town Police and Fire
Departments were dispatched to the Pilgrim's house with
emergency lights flashing and sirens blaring. Neighbors from three
blocks away came to the Pilgrim's house to see what was going on.
A K-9 unit from the sheriff's office was dispatched after Mitchell
and the patrol units failed to locate the telephone repairman. TV
news media vans with large satellite dishes and antennas on their
roofs parked in front of Lomax's house and started broadcasting.
When it started to get out of hand, Marion Police cordoned off the
street to stop all traffic. The last thing they needed was for
someone to get hit by a driver who was minding the goings on at
the Pilgrim's and not the roadway in front of them.

Lomax figured that at least one of those news vans with a big
antenna would be sweeping for him, so he had Daphne shut down
every system except the camera recorders.

Lomax went to the second floor bedroom of his house that faced
the street. For once, he was more interested in the action outside
the Pilgrim house than what was going on inside. Besides, all of
that was being recorded. With a still camera and a very long lens
on a tripod, he peered out the small openings in his Venetian blinds
at the crowd that had gathered on the street. Sure enough, he
"made" some of his former colleagues. "Well, well, well, if it isn't
Señor Diciembre!" Special Agent in Charge Diciembre was clad in
jeans and a John Deere cap—trying to fit into the local population.
What gave him away was the long sleeve shirt he wore and how he
kept raising one arm up to his mouth to speak into a push button
microphone.

Daphne joined Lomax a short time later. She was out of breath.
"Do you have any idea how many buttons and switches I have to
press to shut everything down?"

THE DOOR

"Sorry about that. I'll rig a master shutoff switch that you can use in either house. I don't want you running down to the basement every time a black van rolls past the house. Remind me to put it on the "To Do List.""

"I thought you said all the junk we have just received signals and can't be pinpointed."

He shook his index finger in the air. "Now, now. The word "can't" isn't in the CIA Dictionary." He turned to Daphne and noticed that her face was very pale. "You okay?"

"I feel awful."

"Is it morning sickness?"

"No, it's not that!" She started to weep.

He stepped away from the camera tripod and gave Daphne a hug. "I know, baby." He wiped some of the tears from her face. "I know that it seems like you and I are only in this for the money."

"And we're not?"

"No. When the cops and Feds leave, the only ones who will be looking out for the Pilgrims will be us. Remember that."

She pulled away. "Don't give me that! We've been together for over a year now and I know when you're trying to con me."

He raised his hands in defeat. "Okay, you got me. But you have to understand that when I take a job, I finish it."

She was shocked. "You just don't get it, do you? You think you're on a spy mission against some terrorist group or the Russians. Lomax, this is beyond all that. We're dealing with something here that none of us should have a hand in. That horrible video of the phone repairman says it all. We're dealing with strange powerful forces which neither you nor I can explain. And if we don't watch out, we could be victims too." She touched her stomach. She was starting to show. "We got another one whose safety we have to think about."

He gave a nod. "I know, Daphne. Trust me when I say that I won't let anyone or anything hurt the most important people in my life."

"I may not be a Bible thumper, but I do believe in God and the Devil and what's been going on in this town is very outer-worldly. Lomax, it scares me to death. I don't want to do this anymore. Please, let's just leave and be done with it."

THE DOOR

"I can't. We can't. Whether we like it or not, we're stuck here."

She studied his face for a time. "All right." She turned and took two steps towards the door before stopping. "Just promise me one thing," she said with her back to him.

"Maybe...." *It was typical Lomax!*

She slowly turned and gave him an angry scowl. "When the time comes, you will help those people."

"Yes."

After she left, he went back to his camera and clicked a few pictures of Israel Pilgrim arriving home. Pilgrim didn't arrive by car. He had to walk quite a distance with his crutches.

"Oh, Israel...."

*   *   *

A rookie patrolman was standing guard at the front door of the Pilgrim house. He held up his hand and said, "I'm sorry, sir. But I can't let you in."

"My name is Israel Pilgrim and this is my house!"

Mitchell was in the living room and recognized Israel's voice. He went into the foyer and called out to the rookie. "Let Mr. Pilgrim in."

The Patrolman stepped aside and allowed Israel to enter.

"Dewey, where's my wife and boy?"

Mitchell raised a reassuring hand and spoke calmly, trying to defuse the situation. "They're both fine. They're in the kitchen."

Israel was oblivious to the happenings in this house because he had driven home without his car radio on. "What's going on?"

"It happened again." It was the only thing Mitchell could think of to say.

"Again? What again?" A terrible thought raced through his mind. His eyes widened. "You mean?"

Mitchell gave a nod. "This time it was with a telephone repairman, who came to install an extension line in Richard's room."

The blood ran from Israel's face and he almost fell over. Mitchell grabbed his old friend. "First Maggy, now this. Why is this happening...?"

Mitchell shook his head. He had no answers.

THE DOOR

*   *   *

By the time Dewey Mitchell arrived home, it was dark.

"Your dinner is cold," his wife said.

"I'm not hungry."

"I saw you on TV…at the Pilgrims'. First, the news media was running the story continuously, then nothing."

Mitchell smirked. He, like Lomax, could spot a Fed a mile away and Marion was swarming with them. The only question he had about the news blackout was why it wasn't implemented before any reports were made. Something told him that error would not be repeated.

"Dewey, what's going on over there?"

He shook his head. "All I know is two adults, a man and a woman disappeared under the most extreme circumstances. Is it murder, kidnapping or an elaborate prank? There's no evidence of foul play, unless you overlook the fact that two tornado-like events occurred within two rooms, across town from each other, sucking everything out except a newborn baby and whatever he was sleeping on. Try to explain that one! No suicide notes, no ransom notes, no nothing. But hey, lucky me! My last unsolved case as a patrolman becomes my first case as a detective. And I *gotta* figure it all out by 08:00 hundred tomorrow morning, or the Chief will probably yank my shiny new badge." He snapped his fingers. "I know! The baby did it!"

*   *   *

It was midnight and every light in the Pilgrim house was on and all the windows were open. Little Richard was crying and Lomax didn't need his sophisticated listening devices in this instance. He could hear the baby loud and clear across the street. But when he saw Israel answering the phone, he wanted to listen in. So he put on a headset and aimed a coned shape device at the room where Israel was located. Richard's crying blasted his ears. "*Gees*, will somebody give the kid a bottle." Israel had been on the phone virtually non-stop since he came home from work, trying to convince both family and friends that they were well. He put up a good front, but the truth of the matter was, the Pilgrims were not

THE DOOR

well. How could anyone go through what they had experienced and be well? The tension reached its peak when Ham Hamilton arrived at the house, just after midnight and rang the front doorbell.

"Ham?" said Israel, who answered the front door with a radio-phone still stuck in his ear. "What in blazes are you doing out this late in the night?" He bade his company chairman to enter the house. He then made an excuse to the caller and turned off the radiophone.

"I thought I'd see more news media here," said Hamilton. He also noticed that Israel was no longer using his crutches to get around.

"They were here *en masse* then all of a sudden, they were gone."

"Well, I had to see for myself all the ruckus you were causing," said Hamilton. "Not only did the six o'clock news mention your name and address, but they also said that you were the CEO of our company."

Israel brought a hand up to his face. "I'm sorry, Ham."

"Don't be. None of this is your fault."

"What makes you so sure about that?"

Hamilton jerked a thumb out the doorway. "Haven't you noticed all the black semi trucks and vans parked nearby? The same feds who came here when Maggy disappeared are back, but in force. They're sniffing around like sailors at a whorehouse."

"Can I offer you a drink?"

"No, I've stopped drinking, remember?" He reached out and put a hand on Israel's shoulder. "Now show me the room."

Police evidence tape crisscrossed Richard's door just like it did at Room 19.

Israel opened the door, activated a flashlight and handed it to Hamilton. "You'll need this."

Hamilton stepped inside and swept the room with the light. "Good God! It's Room 19 all over again."

"Those were the exact words Dewey Mitchell said to me."

Hamilton picked up some of the broken drywall off the floor. Part of the balloon Mary painted was still distinguishable. "Mary's mural is ruined."

"She'll paint another."

"How…how could the kid survive this…twice?"

THE DOOR

"I've asked myself that same question." Pilgrim's shoulders sank and the look of despair flashed all over his face.

Hamilton saw it. "Son, you look like you can use a drink."

They went downstairs to Grandfather Pilgrim's office, where Israel kept a bottle of Kentucky whiskey. It was unopened.

"I sent you that bottle the day you took over as CEO," said Hamilton.

"Actually, I kept *that* bottle in the office. This belonged to my grandfather." He opened it. He then lifted two glasses and Hamilton gave a nod, indicating that he wanted a drink.

After what Hamilton just saw, he needed one. They both did.

"He was a good man…like your father. The Pilgrims' have always been good people."

"Not always. We did some shameful things in the past."

"That was over four hundred years ago. The Hamiltons' and the Pilgrims' were guilty of nothing more than being caught up in the moment, just like the rest of the people in that accursed town." He waved his index finger at Israel. "At least you didn't change your name, like the town did. I don't care what they call it now. We all remember it as Salem Village."

"They had to change the name. Nobody would go there. Bad for business."

"*Ahhhh!*" He held out the empty glass and Israel poured him a drink. "Now throngs of tourists go there to get scared. Go figure!"

"Ham, our ancestors were pioneers, fishermen, carpenters and merchants. They laid the foundation for this country and helped make it great!"

"They were also stupid. Falling for all that witchcraft crap those little girls spewed. Hundreds of innocent people were arrested and some died. It was your great, great, great, great grandfather who started it all when he built the first wood mill in the old village. My great, great, great, great, great grandfather cut down the trees and yours made them into furniture and goblets and even the gallows they hung those poor people by. Did you know that? Did your father ever talk about it?"

A cold feeling ran through Israel's body. "Never. Dad wasn't the talkative type and he had a thing against history. He preferred sanding wood. He once took me to a baseball game and all he talked about was how they sanded the bats."

THE DOOR

That made Hamilton chuckle. "*Ah*, your old man was a top rate carpenter! But your grandfather…now he was a businessman! When he came home from the Korean War he found out that his grandfather had started a mill here after the Civil War. He decided to do the same. He ran it well and business boomed in the seventies. But when he got old and found religion, he sold it to me because I had the money to introduce automation. And he had other interests…."

"You mean his wood carving?"

Hamilton smiled. "He carved and your old man sanded and painted. They were a pair!"

"Have you ever seen any of the religious carvings they made?" asked Israel.

"Can't say that I have. They never sold any."

"That's because they kept them all. The basement is full of them."

Israel poured himself a drink and chinked glasses with Hamilton.

"To hot women and cold nights!" said Hamilton.

"Hot damn, I'll drink to that!"

They drank.

"I hear the transition went smoothly," said Hamilton.

"Well, I haven't fired anybody… yet."

"Don't. If anything can be said about our company…it is that we're a family. We work like a family. We play like a family and we fight like cats and dogs. But at the end of the day, we're all carpenters and we love what we do and we make the best damn doors in America!"

It was around two-thirty when the phones stopped ringing and the crowd of spectators went home. Even the black vans and semis left as quickly and quietly as they came.

Israel climbed the stairs to the second floor. When he reached the top of the stairs, he stopped and stared at Richard's door.

"Israel?" said Mary. "Come to bed. You must be exhausted."

He turned, went down the stairs and into the master bedroom. He closed the door behind him. "I am. What a day!"

"How's Ham holding up?"

"Good. A little heart attack isn't going to put him down. He'll

THE DOOR

be here when Maggy comes back."

There was a pink colored crib positioned in front of their bed.

"Pink for a boy?"

"My sister brought it over."

"That was nice of her. I'll make a new one." He leaned over and kissed the baby.

He moaned as he lay down next to Mary on the bed.

"Why is this happening to us?" she asked.

"God only knows."

Mary started to massage Israel's shoulders. He loosened up and moaned again. "Oh, that feels so good —."

Knock! Knock!

Mary and Israel turned to their bedroom door.

"You heard that right?" asked Israel.

"Yes! Is someone in the house?"

Suddenly, the doorknob to the master bedroom started to turn and rattle violently as though someone was forcibly trying to gain entry. What followed truly terrified the Pilgrims. Someone started pounding on the master bedroom door.

"Call 911," Israel shouted as he slipped out of bed and opened the closet door. He pulled out a shotgun and racked a round into the chamber.

"Who's there?" he called out, taking aim at the door.

No response.

Mary picked up the telephone receiver and listened for a dial tone. "No dial tone!"

Across the street, Lomax was awakened from a deep sleep when Daphne came into the bedroom and shook him hard.

"What is it?" he asked.

"The Pilgrim's bedroom door just knocked!"

"What?" He jumped out of bed and bolted up the stairs to the second floor bedroom. The surveillance systems in the basement were still deactivated, but Lomax had setup a folding table with a laptop in the second floor bedroom so that he or Daphne could access any camera he had installed in the town. "You mean Richard's bathroom door—?"

"—No, the master bedroom!" She sat down and ran her fingers across the keypunch. "Let me show you." She rolled back the

THE DOOR

tape and showed the horrible sounds of the master bedroom's door.

"It means that they got more than one active door in their house."

"Lomax, if they open that door they'll all die!"

"It will be interesting to see if the kid survives this one."

Daphne became furious. "NO! We can't let that happen—!"

"—And what would you have me do? Call them up and say, *'Good morning and for God's sakes don't open your bedroom door'!*"

Daphne opened her cell phone and started dialing. "I have to try!"

"I'm sorry, but the number you just called is out of service," said the computer-generated voice.

"Oh, no!" said Daphne, as she closed her cell phone. "I can't get through! What do we do now?"

"We watch," said Lomax. "That's all we can do." As cold as that statement was, he was worried about the Pilgrims. If something happened to Israel and Mary Pilgrim and they mysteriously disappeared like Maggy and Sparky the telephone repairman, then there would be no reason for the client to finance for a 24/7 surveillance. Lomax and Daphne would be out of a job.

Mary panicked and started to scream uncontrollably.

Daphne went over to Lomax. "Please don't let them die. Please do something!"

While Israel aimed the shotgun at the bedroom door, Mary pushed the crib out of the line of fire and next to the window.

With his free hand, he reached out, grabbed the doorknob and slowly started to turn it.

"Hey!" shouted Lomax from the street. "Hey, you folks in the house!" He came stumbling across the street carrying a liquor bottle. "Where everybody go? What kind of party is this, *huh?*"

Daphne ran out onto the street and gave Lomax a hard slap on the arm. "You're going to wake up the whole neighborhood, you drunken fool!"

Mary stuck her head out of the bedroom window. "Please call the police! We think we have a burglar in the house!"

Daphne flipped opened the cell phone and called 911. "Hello, police? This is an emergency…!"

THE DOOR

"Am I good, or what?" Lomax gave a slap on Daphne's buttocks as he strode by her on the way home.

Once again, the street was all lit up with flashing emergency lights. The police arrived, opened the front door and released the K-9. After the dog swept the opened rooms on both floors, it returned to its handler and sat down and barked once, giving the "all clear" signal.

The rookie cop who wouldn't allow Israel to enter his house was the first patrolman to reach the master bedroom.

"Mr. Pilgrim?" asked the young patrolman.

"Yes!"

"This is Officer Heath, Marion Police Department. May I open your bedroom door, sir?"

"Hold on a second. Let me put down this shotgun. Okay, come on in."

Officer Heath, with his nine-millimeter Beretta at the ready, slowly opened the bedroom door. Nothing happened.

"Officer," said Israel, "am I glad to see you."

"The feeling is mutual. May I have your shotgun, sir?"

Israel handed it to him butt first.

"Was there a burglar in our house?" Mary asked Officer Heath.

"We are checking, but be advised that your front door wasn't locked. Anybody could have come in here."

As the police checked the house, the Pilgrims went outside, where Daphne introduced herself to Mary. They hugged each other and became fast friends.

About an hour later, after all the emergency vehicles had left, Daphne exited the Pilgrim's house, crossed the street and met up with Lomax in his basement. He played and replayed the tape from the camera in the hallway on the second floor, showing the master bedroom door being pounded by an invisible force.

"Look at that," he said to her. "Is that spooky or what?"

"Thank you," she said in a low voice. Lomax's quick thinking and unique action may have saved the Pilgrim's lives.

"It's the kid," he said, pointing to the bank of monitors.

"What do you mean?"

"Maggy Hamilton goes into Mary Pilgrim's hospital room and puff...she disappears along with everything else in the room but

THE DOOR

Mary and the kid and the mattress they were laying on. A telephone repair guy comes to the house, hears a door knock, opens the door and puff…he's gone along with everything in the room …except the kid and the crib's mattress. Mary Pilgrim sets up the crib in their bedroom and the door knocks. I'm telling you, these phenomena have something to do with the kid."

But Daphne noticed something Lomax didn't. "And something else. The doors. They were all closed when the knocking occurred."

Lomax cocked an eyelid. "You're right! Not bad, *kid-oh!* Your observational skills are improving."

"I have a great teacher."

Lomax changed the subject slightly. "So, I see that you've made friends with Mary Pilgrim?"

"Yeah, any problem with that?"

"None. Just do me one little favor. When you go over there to visit and you hear a door knock…don't answer it."

They turned their attention to the Pilgrim's master bedroom. Even though the camera wasn't focused on the king sized bed, they knew Israel was in bed because of the way he snored. When Mary checked on the baby for the last time, she closed the bedroom door, turned out the lights and joined her husband.

A few minutes passed. Lomax and Daphne waited silently.

Knock! Knock!

It awakened Israel. "What happened?" He turned on the lights.

"I don't know?" said Mary. "I just closed the door."

"Oh, no!" said Daphne. "Why did she close the door?"

"They don't know," said Lomax.

"What do we do?" asked Mary.

"Look, we can't call the police—." said Israel.

"Why not?" said Mary and Daphne in unison.

"They were just here. They checked the house. There's no burglar."

Mary was breathing hard. She was scared. She tried to calm herself by controlling her breathing. She raised a hand. "I'm okay."

Knock! Knock!

Mary screamed and awakened the baby. Richard started to cry.

Once again, Israel went into his closet. The police had taken his shotgun, so all he had left was a baseball bat.

"No, no, no!" said Lomax. "Think, Pilgrim. Think!"

The door handle started to rattle violently and it seemed as though someone was actually kicking the door from the other side.

Pilgrim went up to the door, pulled back on the bat in preparation to strike whoever entered his bedroom.

Suddenly, and for no apparent reason, the rattling stopped.

Israel looked to Mary with a perplexed expression on his face. "Why did it stop? If there was somebody out there, why didn't they just come in?"

"Aha!" shouted Lomax. "He's figuring it out."

"What are you saying?" asked Mary.

He lowered the baseball bat. "Honey, none of the doors have locks on them."

"Holy cow!" said Daphne.

"Even I didn't notice that…" said Lomax.

"There's nothing to stop anyone from opening that door and walking right in," said Israel.

"You mean," said Mary, "there's nobody out there?"

"Well, there's something out there. And it wants us to open the door."

"If we do, then what happens?"

"We end up like Maggy and the phone guy."

"Bingo!" shouted Daphne.

"Give that man a cigar!" shouted Lomax. "He figured it out. You know, I like this guy!"

The door would continue to knock and rattle until Israel used the baseball bat to bash a hole in the wall large enough for him to climb through to the hallway. Once on the other side, he opened the door and the knocking stopped. He also opened all the other interior doors of the house too.

The next morning, Israel removed all the interior doors and their jams from the house. He piled them up—with Richard's bathroom door on top followed by their master bedroom door—in an opening in the backyard and doused them with rubbing alcohol. He then set them afire. Or so he tried. The doors didn't burn. Next, he resorted to using gasoline and the flames went two feet high. But when the fire died out and the smoke cleared the doors were still there, seemingly unblemished by it all. He got so angry, he took a few swipes at them at with a sledgehammer. Nothing.

He went down to the factory and borrowed the company pickup truck. He loaded all the doors onto the pickup truck and drove them down to the county landfill. One way or another, Israel was going to get rid of these doors.

At the county landfill, people unloaded their unwanted garbage. Dale Bonham was a sanitary worker at the county dump. His job was to crush and cover whatever people brought in with a bull-dozer. He loved his job, because he was a scavenger. To his surprise, the dozen interior doors and jams someone left off wouldn't crush. He ran over Richard's bathroom door four times and then got off the bulldozer to check. It didn't suffer a scratch.

"Look at these doors," he told a co-worker. "Where did they come from, Fort Knox?"

That evening, he arrived home with the dozen doors. Bonham was the next-door neighbor of Israel and Mary Pilgrim.

"Anything to report?" Daphne asked Lomax. She had slept all day.

"The place sure looks different without doors," he replied, gesturing to the wall monitors displaying the interior of the Pilgrim's house.

"Israel took down all the doors?"

"Yes, he did. Would you believe he tried burning them and they wouldn't burn?"

"You're kidding?"

"Would I kid you?" They made playful faces at each other. "So he told his wife that he was taking them to the county landfill."

"Well, I guess we'll all be sleeping better tonight." Daphne was happy about that.

"But of course, it also means we're probably out of a job."

Daphne stopped smiling. "Oh...."

Just then, one of the exterior cameras on Lomax's house that was programmed to focus on movement in the street, turned and focused on an old banged up pickup truck as it pulled into the Bonham's driveway.

"Hey!" said Lomax. "Zoom in on that pickup!"

She worked the controls and zoomed in on Bonham's pickup truck. They saw twelve doors and their jams piled in the cargo

THE DOOR

bed. "Oh, no!"

"Oh, yes."

"I thought you said Pilgrim dropped them off at the county landfill?"

"He did. That's Dale Bonham. He works there. That idiot picked them up and brought them home."

"Don't call him that. He doesn't know what he's got there."

"You think maybe we should go tell him? Of course, it would blow our cover."

Daphne didn't want that. Her silence answered his question.

"*Ah!* So, you don't want to walk away from this sweet deal we have here and lose this house you hate so much—?"

"Stop! Is there anything we can do to warn him?"

"Daphne, will you relax. Those doors only knock when Richard is in the room and if the doors are closed. Now the odds are good that neither will ever happen at the Bonham's."

"I see your point," she said. "But, I'll keep an eye on him."

"You do that. It's your shift. You do what you want. I'm tired and I'm going to hit the sack." With that, he went upstairs and went straight to bed.

Daphne gave the basement the once over. Lomax had been working hard to set up all the equipment the client had provided. He had also done some framing to break up the basement into two soundproof rooms.

Dale Bonham also worked real hard to replace three doors in his house before he called it a night.

At around three in the morning, a bright flashing and flickering of lights occurred at the Bonham house, activating the light, sound and motion detectors that Daphne aimed in that direction. She had nodded off and was even snoring in her swivel chair. A flashing red light and buzzer awakened her. When she gazed into the main monitor and realized that all the arrows were pointing at the Bonham house, she sprang into action. She raised the tubular shaped periscope that came out of the eave air vent on the roof that was on the side of the house facing the street. It came out about a foot and was indistinguishable in the darkness. She activated the night scope, panned it towards the Bonham house until the cross-hairs were centered on the bright light shining on the second floor

THE DOOR

bedroom. Similar in design to the Pilgrim house, where two of the three second floor bedrooms faced the street, this bedroom was on the west side of the house whereas Richard's bedroom was on the east side. This allowed Lomax and Daphne to observe and record what was about to happen at the Bonham's. One other disguised device Lomax installed on his roof to observe the Pilgrims was a round power air vent containing special long-range microphone. Daphne now trained it on the Bonham's house. Her timing couldn't have been better. The bathroom door (formerly Richard's bathroom door) to the second floor bedroom suddenly opened, filling the room with light.

A seven-year-old girl, wearing a Little Red Riding Hood costume stepped out of the light and bathroom.

"Who are you?" asked Daphne. She sounded a buzzer to awaken Lomax.

"*Huh? What now? What is it?*"

"Do the Bonham's have any kids?"

"*Nooooooo!*"

"Then you better get down here cause one just came out of a door."

"Is it Richard?" He was still half a sleep and not very witty.

"No, stupid, it's a little girl."

That motivated Lomax. He came racing out of the master bedroom and nearly tripped and fell down the basement stairs to reach the control desk in ten seconds flat. He gazed into the bank of monitors on the wall and noticed several were displaying the movements of a little girl wearing a red costume at the Bonham house. Daphne had all the exterior cameras focused on the Bonham's house windows, giving them a limited view of the interior.

Daphne had rolled back the tape and placed it on pause for Lomax to observe. She hit PLAY when he arrived.

Just as soon as the little girl stepped across the bathroom door's threshold and entered the second floor bedroom, the bright light winked out. She proceeded to exit the bedroom, then stopped in the hallway to survey her surroundings. She then stealthily made her way down the stairway to the first floor. The only time Lomax and Daphne could see the little girl was when she crossed or stood in front of a window.

THE DOOR

"Was that Richard's bathroom door?" he asked.

"Uh, ah!"

Dale Bonham had stacked the remaining nine doors in the first floor hallway. The little girl spent sometime looking them over and even caressing the one on top before going off to explore the rest of the first floor. From that point on, the little girl was out of the video camera's view. Lomax and Daphne listened as the little girl opened closets and drawers.

"What is she looking for?" asked Daphne.

"I don't know, but you better switch to infrared so we can see."

The periscope had all four types of cameras: normal light, nightlight, spectral range (which some animals use to see at night by utilizing UV and electromagnetic radiation) and a long-range thermal imaging camera.

Unlike your everyday normal light video cameras, the thermal imaging (infrared) cameras could see through walls. The rooms and furniture of the Bonham House were viewed as cool green outlines on the monitor. When a hot blooded human little girl appeared on the screen, her heat signature was fiery red and yellow in color. Daphne used a joystick to lock on to the little girl with the crosshairs and manually followed her movements. The little girl went into the kitchen, opened the refrigerator, removed a covered plate and ate ravenously.

"She looks hungry," said Daphne.

Knock! Knock!

"Hello," Lomax said mockingly.

The suddenness of a door knocking startled both the girl and Daphne, who was jolted in her seat.

The little girl screamed and dropped the plate. It smashed to a dozen pieces on the floor and made a lot of noise. She let out a yelp as she bolted out of the kitchen.

"Make sure the recorders are online," said Lomax.

"You check...I'm busy!" She had to fight the joystick to maintain the crosshairs on the little girl.

A red warning light started to flash on one of the new monitors.

THE DOOR

It lit up and displayed a computer generated architectural design of the Bonham's house and greenish glow around the two active doors.

From the corner of her eye, Daphne noticed the glowing from the unmarked monitor. She jerked her head at the monitor. "What is that?"

"Electromagnetic scanner. I just installed it."

"You told me that the doors only knocked when Richard was in the room!" There was more than a hint of anger in her tone.

The sounds of a doorknob being rattled violently came out of the speakers. It was followed by the sounds of the door being pounded on.

Lomax gazed at the monitor and noted two glowing doors, one on each floor of the Bonham house. "It's coming from one of the doors in the stack. It's probably the Pilgrim's bedroom door."

"How can a door go active when it wasn't installed and closed—?"

"—Daphne, all the doors in the stack are closed. One of them must have gone active when the kid got close to it."

Daphne's eyes widened. "That makes her—!"

"—Another Richard."

Lomax sat down and started working the controls on the second control desk, situated next to Daphne's. He was mesmerized with the new monitor. "Look at the way those two doors pulsate with energy!"

"Why are they doing that?"

"I don't know but I think we're going to find out in a hurry."

The little girl raced passed the stack of doors and the stairwell.

"She's heading for the front door!" said Lomax.

"You better get over there and grab her!"

Lomax started to rise out of his chair.

Suddenly, the little girl stopped at the front door.

"Wait—she stopped!" said Daphne.

"Why?"

They watched as the little girl turned around and looked upward.

"What is she looking for?" he asked.

Silence. Then:

THE DOOR

Knock! Knock!

It came from the bedroom door directly opposite the bedroom the little girl came in by on the second floor.

Daphne gasped and Lomax sank into his chair.

"What?" asked Daphne. "Another active door?"

The electromagnetic monitor that got its signals from the spectral range camera projected three glowing sources in the Bonham house.

Lomax raised three fingers. "That makes three!"

The little girl bolted for the stairway.

"Lomax, she's going upstairs!"

"Stay with her Daphne."

Daphne worked the joystick. "She must have known it was going to knock."

"No—you're crazy!"

"For marrying you—yes! But not with this!"

"But how? How did she know? She was downstairs in the foyer."

"She stopped at the front door—remember?"

Lomax rolled back the tape and stopped it when the little girl turned and gazed upward. "And looked upstairs."

"Maybe she sensed it…?"

Lomax made a face. "Oh, please…."

The next voices they heard came from Dale Bonham and his wife.

"What was that?" Dale Bonham was heard asking his wife.

"Someone is in the house!" shouted Mrs. Bonham.

Lomax made a face. "Now they wake up?"

"You call the police!" said Dale "I'll get my gun!"

"He's got a gun!" said Daphne.

"I heard!"

All three doors started to rattle violently creating a wave effect that ran through the house—and shook everything—right down to its foundations. The little girl had to stop and grab hold of the stairway's wooden handrail until the shaking stopped. Daphne and Lomax watched with their mouths open. Unknown to everyone a propane line to the stove in the kitchen ruptured, as did the one to the fireplace in the living room, spewing flammable gas into the air.

THE DOOR

Daphne made the thermal imaging camera pull back for a wider shot so that all three human heat signatures could be seen in the Bonham house.

Lomax pointed to the monitor. "She's going back to the bathroom!"

Dale Bonham dashed out of the master bedroom on the first floor with a pistol in his hand. His wife was right behind him, holding a radiophone. Dale gazed up and got a glimpse of the little girl reaching the top of the stairs. "Stop or I'll shoot!"

Knock! Knock! went the active the door in the stack.

Dale, with his terrified wife right behind him, went up to the stack of doors. With his free hand, he shoved off the three doors that lay on top of the glowing one. "What the…?"

"Oh, no!" said Daphne. "He wouldn't!"

"Oh, yes he would. Here we go again!"

Dale reached down, grabbed the doorknob, turned it and gave a mighty pull. A bright flash blinded both him and his wife. A very powerful vacuum lifted him and his wife off their feet and drew them into the glowing void along with everything that wasn't nailed down in the foyer and the first floor. His gun went off, igniting the propane gas that lingered in the air. The force of the vacuum was so great that most of the burning propane was drawn into the open doorway. But some remained.

A split second later, the flame that streaked through the air in the foyer met up with the cloud of propane in the living room and ignited.

As the little girl pulled open the bathroom door—which now acted as a portal to another place and time, she glanced over her shoulder at the streak of flame that seemed to follow her into the bedroom. She leapt through the opened bathroom doorway. It was the force of the propane explosion that forced the bathroom door to slam shut behind her.

"*Uh, oh,*" went Lomax.

Suddenly, the whole house exploded. But it was not like any explosion Lomax or Daphne had ever seen before. First, the burning gases and flaming debris roared outward, shooting high into the sky and across the street—almost hitting their two houses. Then, everything just stopped and hung there for a few seconds, motionless and silent before it was all pulled back into the house and through the doorway Dale Bonham had opened. The incident ended with the closing of that door.

Lomax and Daphne left the basement and went outside to watch what was left of the Bonham house burn. Basically, it was nothing more than a burning skeleton of a house. Even though they had the periscope camera focused on the burning house, there was something about seeing it with their own two eyes. And yet, Lomax walked outside with a small video camera in his hands.

Daphne pointed to a spectator, who was standing across the street in front of the Pilgrims. "Who is he?"

When Lomax spotted the man in a black suit, he instinctively grabbed Daphne's hand and pulled her into a shadow. He then pointed his camera at the man in black.

"He looks like a priest," said Daphne.

"*Ah*, your Catholic upbringing again. But there's something about this guy. I don't think he's a priest. More like an agent."

The man in black turned, faced and starred right at Lomax and Daphne.

Both would later say that their bodies went totally numb.

A second explosion occurred at the Bonham's house. Sparks flung out along with arcs of electricity. The concussion wave knocked both Lomax and Daphne off their feet. When they got back up, the man who had been staring at them was gone.

The town sent every fire engine and firefighter they had to fight the fire that completely consumed the Bonham's house. But by the time they arrived, the fire was completely out.

The next morning, Israel Pilgrim stood on the front lawn of his house, wearing a robe over his pajamas. Fortunately, his house was undamaged by the explosions or the house fire. He stared with a solemn look on his face at the black skeleton of charred wood that was once his neighbor's house. Only the wall framing of the second floor remained. The floor had caved in. What an eerie sight it was to behold. There were only two undisturbed and unburned objects on the second floor: a bedroom and bathroom door. He realized that they were his interior house doors when he spotted the door with the name Richard carved at the top.

Mary joined her husband on the front lawn. "Honey, you okay?"

"No."

THE DOOR

"What's wrong?"

He gestured to the bedroom door on the second floor, then to the stack in the foyer. "Look familiar?"

She looked, recognized them and gasped. "It can't be. But, how? You dropped the doors off at the landfill."

"Dale works there. He must have taken them home."

She reached out and hugged her husband. "What does this mean?"

"We're cursed."

Across the street, Lomax and Daphne were watching from the second floor bedroom of her house. Lomax had pulled up the blinds so that they could gaze out the window.

Daphne was rewinding the tape on the video camera Lomax had used when they went outside. "That's odd."

"What is it?"

"The man in the black suit…he's not there."

"What do you mean he's not here? I took dead aim at him…even zoomed in on his face. I swear to you, I saw it on the monitor…"

He took the camera, rewound it, pressed the play button and gazed into the little monitor. The Pilgrim house was clearly seen from all the light the fire at the Bonham's created. Suddenly, there was an explosion with arcs of electricity shooting through the air. He stopped the tape.

"Maybe he's our mysterious client," she said.

Lomax let out a sigh. This was one time technology had failed him. *But how?*

"And I'm absolutely certain that the Bonham's had no kids."

"Then who the hell is that little girl?" asked Lomax.

THE DOOR

Chapter Six

PROJECT DOOR

The twelve doors that either stood

erect or were stacked inside in a charred skeleton of what was the Bonham's house were unscathed by a fire that consumed everything else. For safety reasons, a bulldozer was brought in to knock down the charred wood frame of what was still standing on the second floor.

"Why didn't those doors burn?" Dewey Mitchell asked the Fire Marshal, pointing to the two doors on the second floor. "Everything else did."

The Fire Marshall, a man well into his fifties, stood awe-struck at the sight of the two doors standing erect on the second floor of the burnt out house. "I have no idea, Detective. They're solid oak." He pointed to the stack of doors. "What probably saved those was the fact that they were stacked tightly together in one corner of the foyer. No gaps between them." He then waved his free hand at the doors on the second floor. "I have no logical answer for those two. I've never seen anything like this. But one thing is for certain. This was a hot one." He picked up a piece of charred wood and sniffed it. "I've worked my share of propane explosions, but none that snuffed itself out after *only* a minute and did this kind of damage."

"How do you know it snuffed itself out?"

"Look around. No water damage. The FD got off easy with this one. The fire was out before they arrived." He tossed the piece of wood aside. "Who lived here?"

"Dale Bonham and his wife."

The Fire Marshall jerked his head back as he recognized the name. "Oh, yes! The bulldozer guy down at the county dump."

"That's him." Mitchell gestured to the bulldozer that was being off-loaded from a trailer. "And that was his bulldozer."

"A fitting gesture….Well, I didn't find any skeletal remains. Who knows! He might show up for work today." The Fire Marshall stepped through the debris, taking pictures along the way. "Something is missing. As a matter-of-fact, a lot of things are missing." He swept his hand over the debris piles. "You can see the remnants of bedroom furniture—a couple of beds, night stands and bureaus—all from the second floor, but nothing from the first floor. No living room furniture. No TV. No stove. No plates. No silverware and no toaster. Everybody has a toaster. Where is it?"

"The neighbors said they heard two distinct explosions. Could a bomb have done this?"

"A chemical bomb leaves residue, which I will test for. But bombs generally scatter debris outward." He flung both arms outward to demonstrate. "The propane lines that fed into the stove and fireplace were severely ruptured and probably caused the fire…and most likely the reported explosions. Now fire needs a lot of air, so it usually expands outward. In this case, everything seems to have been pulled inward, not out." He gestured to the highest pile of charred debris—around the stack of doors—and then swept his hand to the area where there was much less ash. "Most of the ash and debris is piled in this area of the foyer, as though it was drawn to this very spot. By what, I don't know."

"A vacuum?"

The Fire Marshall turned to Mitchell and stared at him for a moment. "More like a…firestorm. But that doesn't happen in houses." The Fire Marshall looked off and smiled as he reminisced about his firefighting career. "You ever see one? A firestorm, I mean?" Mitchell shook his head. "When I was a young buck like you and full of myself, I fought forest fires in the Rockies. There was one particular fire in Idaho that damn near killed me. Our fire team screwed up and let the fire surround us. Next thing we knew a firestorm appeared, sucking the air right out of the atmosphere. I could barely breathe. We tried to outrun it, but it caught up with us. All I could do was lash myself to a tree root and hang on. It lifted me right off the ground and pulled so hard I lost one of my boots." He used one of his hands to show how he went from a horizontal position to vertical. "It was a ghastly sight…one straight out of Hell. Hope you never have to see one.…"

THE DOOR

Mitchell turned his gaze away from the Fire Marshall and focused on Israel Pilgrim, who was watching from the front yard of his house.

"That bull dozer guy must have buried those doors deep," said Diciembre as he entered the surveillance van in the barn, "because we couldn't find any of them." He was tired, dirty and angry. He and several agents had been up all night scouring the county dump for the doors. He then asked for an update from the Lead Agent, who for all practical purposes "ran the farm" but who was in fact his second in command.

"Sir, we just learned that Dale Bonham—the bull dozer guy took them home and apparently installed several of them in his house—"

"—He did what—?"

"—before it blew up."

Diciembre was shocked. "His house?"

"Cause: an accidental propane leak. Did you know that Bonham is *or was* Israel Pilgrim's neighbor?" Diciembre shook his head. The Lead Agent then pointed to a monitor, which displayed a wide angle of the street at night that included the Pilgrim's house and the two houses on either side. A moment later, the Bonham house exploded.

"Where did you get this video footage?" asked Diciembre.

"From a wireless camera on a power pole and we didn't put it there." Three more monitors lit up showing different angles of the Pilgrim house. "However, these three we did know about."

"Lomax..." said Diciembre.

"Definitely his handiwork. Nicely centered. The man knows how to block a shot."

The Intelligence community used wireless cameras to covertly monitor people, places and things. It's a safe and effective way to keep an eye on the target from afar. However, they do have their drawbacks. They run on batteries and emit a signal that can be intercepted. Diciembre's people had discovered the frequencies the four cameras were using and they were tuned into and watching everything they were sending out.

"What about the doors?"

"MPD and the Fire Marshall were told to leave them."

THE DOOR

"Wireless cameras are battery powered and only good for temporary use," said Diciembre. "Lomax wouldn't use them…unless." He slapped his hands. "Call our friend at the utility company and arrange for a power out tonight, around 3 AM. Then have one of our people check the farthest pole out and see if the camera has a battery charger hot-wired to one of the power lines."

"That's dangerous! Who would do a dumb thing like that?"

"Someone who worked on power lines for a living."

"Everybody keeps saying he's a pro. But then why go wireless? He must know we would be monitoring all frequencies."

"This is just his way to let us know… he's here and he's watching."

"The signal strength on those cameras are pretty high. He must be using a booster. He can be ten miles away and still pick it up."

Diciembre shook his head. "Oh, no he's much closer than that. I wouldn't be a bit surprised if he was across the street."

Diciembre left the van and was followed out by the Lead Agent.

"Sir?" asked the Lead Agent. "May I ask you a question?"

"Go ahead."

"Is the rumor true…that you trained Lomax?"

"Negative….I tried to get him fired."

Back in Marion, Daphne met up with Lomax in the attic. He was busy working on the switch and motor that raised and retracted the camera periscope in the eave air vent. The periscope was only half way down.

"The street is crawling with agents," she said.

"No surprise there. They want those doors."

Amidst the huge crowd of spectators on the street were clean cut, lean men and women who were dressed in an assortment of neutral colored shirts and blue jeans or jogging clothes in an attempt to blend in. The problem was that the locals, who had a habit of being suspicious of anyone they didn't know, spent more time looking and pointing at these unknown people than the burnt out Bonham house.

"You're not going to let those SOBs take them—are you?"

"Not if I can help it. We need to figure a way to get the heat off Israel Pilgrim and draw *them* (meaning the agents) off this street."

THE DOOR

"And how do we do that?"

"Oh, a little diversion. I'll think of something."

"Well, when are you going to finish working on that thing?" she asked as she tapped the clear plastic pipe containing the periscope Lomax had been working on. "Cause I *gotta* go do number two and your toilets won't flush."

"Almost there…." He worked a handheld control and the periscope dropped a few inches, opening the airway, causing a slight suction.

Every house has an air ventilation system for the toilets. Toilets don't flush without it. A source of air must be allowed to enter the system behind the water flowing through the pipe, otherwise a vacuum would form behind the water and slow everything down. Lomax had installed three new commodes in the house, replacing the old ones on both floors and adding one in the basement. Each vent ran through a system of hidden pipes that went through the walls and came together in the attic. Lomax placed a freestanding clear plastic tube to the floor of the attic and connected it to the exterior vent for both the toilets and the periscope. The only problem with this system was that they couldn't use the toilets while the periscope was up and blocking the vent.

"Why are you using the toilets vent for the periscopes? Why don't you just install another air vent on the roof? Nobody will notice it."

"The local *yokels* won't. But the people who are looking for me, will. This house has to look like it's for sale and a bachelor occasionally lives in it. It can't stand out in the slightest." He reached out and touched the drywall he just screwed to the ceiling. "Like my handiwork?"

"What's there to like, Lomax? It's drywall."

He sighed. "Last night we used infrared cameras to see through the Bonham's house."

"Sure came in handy."

"Well, if we can look through a house with infrared cameras…"

Daphne's shoulders sank. "So can they?" Meaning the CIA.

He held up a piece of thermal material he got from the client. "This stuff is made out of wool and polypropylene wick and acrylic and it stops infrared scans dead in their tracks."

"Is it the same stuff you put into the ceiling and walls in the basement?"

He nodded. "Yes, except I also put in a layer of lead foil."

"Why lead?"

"Everything that uses electricity generates a magnetic field. The more you use the bigger the EMI footprint. Believe me, we're putting out a lot. The lead will absorb the EMI and act as a shield against X-rays."

Daphne touched her abdomen. She didn't like the idea that the government would X-ray the whole neighborhood to find them.

He pointed to the sky. "Orbiting the Earth, hundreds of miles away, are satellites that are scanning us right now. That's why I packed the walls and ceiling of the basement with this stuff the second week we were here. So, when they do comparison scans, they wouldn't see changes. The trick is not to over use it. If they find a house where everything is blacked out— "

"—Then they would have us."

"Right. So, I only blacked out the basement," he waved his hand at the ceiling of this side of the attic, "and this side of the attic and left the two floors in the house alone."

"So, they have been looking for us?"

"You can bet your life on that. Now that they know I'm watching the Pilgrims, they'll be beating the bushes to find me." He tapped a foot tall tubular device that was anchored to the floor. "But now that I've had a chance to install this little baby, the next time they do a sweep, we'll know about it."

"What about all the electricity we're using?"

He smiled. "Very good! You're learning! It takes a lot of power to run all those gadgets downstairs. If we use ten times more electricity than our neighbors—as we do, we will stand out. This is one of the reasons this house is for sale and we run the lights day and night."

"Won't all that extra energy usage show up on the electric bill?"

"Oh, I know how to tinker with power lines so that we can get all the power we need without anybody knowing about it. And, for free." He raised his arms and smiled. "Am I good or what?"

She rolled her eyes skyward. "You got it all worked out, don't you?"

"Actually, I'm just following the client's plan. He laid it all out for me. He's good. Better than me. I got a feeling he's been on

THE DOOR

the run for a *loooong* time."

"Who is he?"

He shook his head. "I don't know, baby. But we need to find out. As rule, when you're a spy, you never, ever work with or for anyone you don't know everything about. That's how you get killed in this business."

Lomax spotted the newspaper Daphne had under her arm. "Let me have that."

"*Ah*, come on! I was going to the bathroom with it."

He breezed through the pages until he reached the section he wanted. He backhanded the article that was topped off with a picture of a B-24 Bomber. "God Bless America! The Confederate Air Wing just arrived for an air show. Honey, I feel so patriotic right now I think we should go out tonight and get bombed!"

*　　　*　　　*

The Confederate Air Wing was a collection of young and old military pilots who owned vintage bombers and fighter aircraft and spent years and small fortunes restoring them back to their former glory. One way to help pay for the upkeep of these very valuable collectibles was to go out on tour at air shows. It was an annual event in Abingdon, Virginia, a town thirty or so miles south of Marion.

Daphne dropped Lomax off at the highway entrance to the Washington County Airport. Thanks to the air show, it was a hub of activity with cars and trucks coming and going. Wearing a flight suit and Air Force cap, Lomax gave a wave to the sleepy security guard at the main gate as he went in. He trotted down to the hanger where the Confederate Air Wing had setup their displays and parked their aircraft. Expensive motorized RVs surrounded the hanger and housed the owners and mechanics. It was a few minutes past midnight and a boisterous poker game was going on in one of the RVs. Even though the aircraft and displays of World War II, Korean and Vietnam memorabilia were hard to come by and expensive, there were no security guards posted. Situated on the flight line, between a B-24 Liberator and B-26 Marauder was a trailer containing a twelve thousand pound blockbuster bomb. The old bomb had long since been defused and the explosives removed. The fifth wheel vehicle that transported the blockbuster bomb was still attached to the trailer. They didn't even lock the driver door.

Lomax opened the driver door and found the keys in the ignition. A Lear Jet just landed and he waited for it to pass by before pumping the accelerator a couple of times and starting the engine. The jet engines masked the engine startup and his prompt exit from the flight line.

*   *   *

Even though the entire county was blacked out, the emergency generators were producing the power needed to maintain operations and run all the lights at the farm.

An armed agent was patrolling the grounds at the farm. There was only one because they had installed a system of infrared cameras and motion detectors that scanned the farm in all directions. It was 4 AM in the morning. Physically, it was the one-hour of the day the human body ran at its lowest rhythm. Productivity was at its lowest ebb, thus for people who worked nights, this was the time when they were the most tired.

It was the armed guard who heard the sound of a truck engine moving in the cornfield. He activated his flashlight and shined it into the cornfield. It wasn't long before he spotted a reflection from the windshield. "Hey," he called out on his radio, "hey, we got something here! Parameter breach!"

"Are you sure?" replied an agent in the RV. "We got nothing."

Steam spewed out of the engine compartment of the fifth wheel truck as Lomax drove it out of the cornfield at a hurried pace and turned on the high beams to blind the armed guard. The armed guard fired a short burst from his machine pistol before throwing himself out of the way of the speeding truck. Lomax parked it next to the barn, got out and sprinted into the cornfield.

A loud Klaxon went off at the farm.

Special Agent in Charge Diciembre came out of the bedroom where he had been sleeping, wearing slippers, an overcoat and carrying a pistol. "What is it?" He shouted in his headset microphone.

"We found a bomb next to the barn!"

"Evacuate all personnel! NOW!"

THE DOOR

As the agents fled and put some distance between themselves and the barn, Diciembre went over to the fifth wheel pickup truck, which was still running and spewing steam out of its engine compartment. He opened the driver door, reached in and turned off the motor. He then pulled the release latch to open the hood. He was not at all surprised when he discovered the truck engine covered with ice, topped off with plastic bags of ice. The steam was produced from the engine vaporizing the ice. He knew exactly who did this. "Lomax…."

"What's the big idea of using ice bags?" asked the patrolling agent.

"To cool down the engine block and foil the infrared detectors. He employed a low-tech solution to thwart a very sophisticated scanning system. Smart. Pure Lomax."

He went to the trailer containing the blockbuster bomb. He knew that the old bomb was nothing more than a museum piece, but he hesitated when he spotted the box with LED lights flashing, counting down. Ten seconds to detonation. There was a small box wrapped in Christmas paper and red bow, with a Christmas card attached. Without hesitation, he opened the envelope and pulled out the Christmas card.

There was a brief hand written message. "Merry Christmas!" There was also a cell phone number.

Diciembre turned his attention to the LED lights as they flashed to zero. There was no explosion.

He pulled out his cell phone and called the number.

"Ola, amigo," said Lomax, watching from a hill some distance away. *"¿Cómo está?"*

"Bien."

"I'm glad to hear it, Diciembre."

"If you turn yourself in now, Lomax, I'm sure we can work out something…"

Lomax laughed. "Come on. I'm not going to do that. I'm having too much fun."

"Bull. You're as scared of the doors as we are."

Lomax stopped laughing. "Doors? What are you a kid now? The next thing you'll be telling me about is your fear of closets." He winced. He knew he wasn't convincing.

Diciembre knew that he had hit a nerve. "We could use your

THE DOOR

help on this one. All your sins would be forgiven."

"The sins I've committed you can't forgive. And I've got to go…"

"Lomax, do you know what all of this is about?"

Field operatives were taught to think and say the words in their head before letting them come out of their mouths. Speaking your mind can get you killed. Lomax hesitated, said several different replies in his head, but none of them sounded good so he made no reply.

"The doors," continued Diciembre, "are portals. They are also death traps for anyone who enters them."

Lomax decided not to play stupid anymore. And it was time for him to see what Diciembre knew. "Not everybody…"

"Are you referring to the little girl in the red dress? We've been tracking her for years. Whatever you do, don't follow her into the door. It's a one-way ticket to Hell and I mean it, Lomax. We've lost some good people—."

"—My, my. Do I detect concern in your voice, for me? I must say, I'm touched!"

Diciembre decided to level with Lomax. "We've known about the doors since Hiroshima."

Lomax made a face. "You mean the A-Bomb attack? That long ago?"

"We had a consulate there before the war. It was near ground zero. The building was vaporized. Only the door remained standing. Take a guess who made the door?"

"The Pilgrim Door Company?"

"Good guess!"

"How? Israel is only thirty years—."

"—Not him. His family. The Pilgrims have been carpenters since they came over from England four hundred years ago. There are thousands of these doors all over the world. Once they're used and activated, they become virtually indestructible. We don't know why."

Both men heard the whaling of sirens in the distance.

Lomax pressed a button on a device he was holding in his other hand. It activated another device that he had thrown into the cornfield that created some sparks and ignited a small fire, followed by some fireworks shooting off into the air.

THE DOOR

When Diciembre spotted the fire and fireworks, he realized that it was Lomax who set it and called the county fire department.

"Thanks for the history lesson," said Lomax, "but I still don't trust you."

"There's a man, we call him *the Traveller*...."

"Who?"

"Your client. Be weary of him, Lomax. He has a dark past and a darker future. Some say he's the Devil himself."

Lomax could read body language like a book and tell by the inflections of their voice if someone was telling him the truth or handing him a pile of bull. Diciembre's tone was as sincere as he ever heard it. And he was scared. No doubt about it.

"You're *"danger close"* right now," concluded Diciembre. "Don't wait until you're in the lake of fire before calling us." He closed the cell phone.

The fire engines arrived and extinguished the fire in the cornfield. Units of the county sheriff and satellite vans from the local news channel followed.

The Lead Agent approached Diciembre and pointed to the cars and vans that came racing to the farmhouse from another entrance with no lights on. "That will be the door retrieval team the Deputy Director sent to us." He glanced at his wristwatch. "My, my! They work fast. I didn't expect to see them for another hour."

The Lead Agent for the retrieval team got out of his vehicle and reported to Diciembre. "We were unable to secure the doors."

"Why? Didn't the blackout take place as planned?"

"It did. But someone got to them first. I'd bet my IRA it was Lomax."

Diciembre shook his head. "No, he was just here. He couldn't have done it."

The patrolling agent spoke up. "I even took a shot at him."

The Lead Agent gave the young agent an angry stare.

"No man," said Diciembre, "not even the infamous Lomax can be in two places as the same time. It was someone else."

The retrieval team's Lead Agent pointed his finger at Diciembre. "Let me tell you something, Diciembre, the Deputy Director is not going to be a happy camper." He went back to his vehicle and left the farm with his team.

"Sir," said the farm's Lead Agent, "we've been compromised."

THE DOOR

"You think?" Diciembre let out a sigh. "Start packing. Time we said *adios* to Marion."

The only way to get the news vans off the farm was to have a deputy sheriff drive the fifth wheeler and the trailer with the blockbuster bomb back to the Abingdon airport. By sun up that morning, the Mobile Command RV, all the vehicles and all of the field agents had left the farm.

Lomax hid in the backseat of the Cherokee as Daphne drove into the garage. She electronically closed the garage door. "You're awfully quiet."

"We need to find out who our client is."

"Well, it's about time."

"We may have to leave all this."

"I don't care. First it was Maggy Hamilton, then the phone guy, now the Bonhams. Four people are gone. For all we know, they could be dead. We could be next."

*   *   *

It was Dewey Mitchell who, the very next morning, would discover that the doors at the Bonham's house were missing.

"They're gone," he told Israel and Mary Pilgrim.

"You mean, the doors?" said Mary.

"Oh, my God!" said Israel. "Will this ever end?" Israel appeared so distressed that Mitchell thought for a moment that he was going to keel over.

"Who would take them?" asked Mary. She turned to Israel. "Honey, you okay?"

Dewey was studying his old football buddy's face. Israel appeared as surprised as he and Mary were. "I don't know. But if they aren't careful, they will be in a world of hurt."

Israel straightened up and went toe to toe with Mitchell. "You have no idea...."

A few hours later, Israel went to the mill and held out the keys to the company pickup truck to the executive secretary. "Thanks for letting me use the pickup."

She walked up to Pilgrim, but instead of taking the keys, she grasped his outstretched hand. She had a strong grip. "Mr. Pilgrim, that pickup was used by Ham, because he was always

THE DOOR

going to the hardware store or Walmart to get whatever we needed. He's retired. You're the boss now. That truck is yours." She let go of his hand and gestured to Hamilton's office. "And that...is your office."

"All right," he said softly. When he went into his office, he noticed immediately that all of Hamilton's Civil War Memorabilia and personal effects had been removed. For the first time, Israel truly felt as though he had been accepted as the CEO of the company.

* * *

Diciembre entered the office and stood almost at attention in front of Deputy Director Blackburn's desk.

Blackburn was on the phone, talking to the Director of the CIA. He ended the phone call by saying, "Consider it done, Mr. Director." He hung up and shook his head. "You really screwed up this time, Diciembre. The Director is furious with you. He really wanted those doors!"

"Someone got to them before we did."

"Lomax?"

Diciembre shook his head. "I doubt it. He was involved in another action."

"So, I've heard." The Deputy Director leaned back in his chair and exhaled deeply. "I don't understand it, Diciembre. Your service record to this point has been exemplarily. Your missions have all been successful. You're one of the best tacticians in the Agency. You know how to handle yourself in dangerous situations and the agents who work with you respect and rely on your leader-ship abilities. These are the reasons you were promoted. In every way you have demonstrated how good you are in the field, except in one area...."

Diciembre cocked an eyelid. "Lomax."

"Yes, Lomax. If any man had a nemesis, yours would be Lomax." The Deputy Director stood up. "You may have compromised everything by telling him top secret information about this project!" The Deputy Director's voice got real loud at the end of the sentence.

"I beg to differ with you, sir. Whether the old man likes it or

THE DOOR

not, Lomax is involved in this." Diciembre's voice also started to get loud. "Now we can either dick around with Company policies and procedures and blow this thing. Or…"

"Or, what?"

"Or, we can give Lomax the room he needs to see this through."

Blackburn was shocked. "Haven't you learned anything in all the years you've been with us? You don't give a rogue agent anything. Especially, that bastard you trained."

Diciembre raised his index finger. "Sir, I didn't train him."

"Oh, yes!" Blackburn realized his error. "That's right! You wanted us to fire the very man you just revealed our most sensitive secrets to?"

"He may lead us to *the Traveller*."

"I doubt that."

"But sir, before we go any further, there's something I need to report to you."

"I have a feeling that I should sit down first." He did. "All right, what is it?"

"Our efforts in Marion may not have been a total loss. My people may have found a way to locate the doors, and not just the ones from the Pilgrim house."

That got Blackburn's attention. "Oh?"

Diciembre reached into the brief case he was carrying and removed original electromagnetic scans that were done both on the ground level and by satellite. "As you know, we've been using satellites to locate Lomax, but instead we noticed something odd." He laid the plastic scan sheets on the desk before the Deputy Director. "Note the bright electromagnetic discharge in these scans. They're from the bathroom door in Richard Pilgrim's bedroom." He laid another scan sheet to show a comparison. "This scan was taken just hours before the Bonham house exploded. Note the hot spots." He placed another scan on the desk. "This is after the fire."

"This scan has three hot spots!"

"Yes, sir, it does. One additional door had gone active— "

"—because of the fire?"

"No, sir. The fire had nothing to do with it. It went active because someone made contact with them."

"*The Traveller?*"

THE DOOR

"*Uh*, yes, sir. But not the one you're thinking about. The other…the young female we call Little Red Riding Hood."

"Her again?" A thought rushed through the Deputy Director's mind. "So, you're saying that we can now locate the active doors by their electromagnetic discharge?"

Diciembre answered with a nod.

That was a revelation! Any other time, he would have given an: "*Atta boy!*" to Diciembre for uncovering such an important piece of information, something even his own techs at CIA HQ hadn't noticed. Thanks to Diciembre, the Agency could now locate the other doors wherever they were. But what was he to do with Diciembre? Yes, he had violated several security protocols by revealing top-secret information to a wanted former agent. Yes, he allowed Lomax to make a damn fool out of him and the Agency in Marion. Diciembre also knew too much about the doors. *What to do with Diciembre?*

"You may have just saved your job, Diciembre. No, we're not going to fire you! And I will not accept your resignation. You're going to be reassigned…to a lovely little facility where the Director and I believe your special talents can be properly utilized for the good of the Company and the nation."

Diciembre's face started to turn pale. "Where, sir?"

"In God's Country! West Virginia."

Diciembre winced. It wasn't the mentioning of West Virginia that made him react in such a way. It was the CIA installation he would be assigned in West Virginia that was so displeasing to him. No wonder they wouldn't accept his resignation! It was the last place in the world he wanted to be posted. "Thank you, sir." He didn't mean it.

THE DOOR

Chapter Seven

A MEETING WITH THE DEVIL

Late one night, the telephone rang

and Daphne answered it. "Hello?"

"Oh, excuse me," said the male caller. "I got the wrong number." He hung up.

Daphne recognized the voice. "That's him! That's the client!"

Lomax was sleeping in bed next to her. He woke up and glanced over to the clock on the nightstand. "Oh, God! It's three in the morning. Doesn't this man ever sleep?"

"One, two, three," she said. "Third letter in the alphabet. A, b, c and c means the Chilhowie Cab Company. What a crazy system he's having us use."

"He's the boss..."

"But what if he isn't a man? What if Diciembre is right and..."

"...he's the Devil?"

She looked away to hide her fear.

They got dressed and Daphne drove him to the bus and cab station in Chilhowie, Virginia. She left him off and drove home.

As he walked towards the door to the bus lobby a car horn sounded. A set of car lights came on. The taxi pulled forward, then stopped along side Lomax. The old driver lowered his window. "What time did you get up this morning, sir?"

"Three AM and I'm not happy about it."

"I feel your pain. Now, get in."

Lomax was driven to a stately mansion north of Bristol, Virginia.

The front gate electronically opened even before the taxi pulled off the road and headed up the long driveway to the mansion. There was a "For Rent" sign posted by the front gate, leading Lomax to believe that the client didn't own this mansion. He counted four very visible cameras on tall poles.

The taxi pulled to a halt under a portico and the driver turned off the motor. "See you in a couple," he said.

Lomax took the brief case he carried with his DVDs, pictures and reports into the foyer with marble floors. He was awe struck by all the religious paraphernalia that covered the walls in the foyer and in the connecting rooms. A Gregorian chant was being played over the house speaker system. For a moment, he thought he had entered the Vatican.

"I thought this guy was supposed to be the Devil," he uttered.

The Gregorian chant stopped and a voice came echoing through the hallway.

"Be glad I'm not, Lomax." Once again, the client would speak to him over a speaker.

Lomax recognized the voice as the man who rescued him and Daphne in Kentucky and hired him for this long termed surveillance.

"Well, I for one don't believe in the—."

"—Devil? You should. Trust me. He exists and he's truly evil. Make a left face and go into the dining room."

Lomax entered the dining room where a large table and a single chair were waiting for him, along with a camera on a tripod.

"Have a seat," the client said, "and let's have a look at the goods."

Lomax opened the brief case and laid out the contents on the table. The camera pivoted on its stand and turned its lens on the pictures and stack of typed pages.

"Your reports are very detailed, but concise. I appreciate that. Believe it or not, there's nothing I detest more than wasting time reading reports."

"And here Daphne accused me of "cutting to the chase" too often."

"As you grow older, you will learn that time is a valuable commodity…one too precious to waste."

The camera lens rose upward and focused on Lomax.

"Now tell me where are Pilgrim's doors?"

"We weren't home when the power went out. My emergency generator didn't kick in so all of our systems were down. I have no idea who took them."

THE DOOR

"You created an interesting diversion with that blockbuster. Are you aware that they almost fired Diciembre because of it?"

"Really?" Lomax gave a smile. "Well, that is good news!"

"Now, now," the client said, allowing some of his old English accent to emerge. "What was it my sainted and departed mother would say to me? Oh yes, *'never speak ill of others in trouble and in need because their misfortune might turn out to be yours as well'*. In light of the disappearance of the Pilgrim's doors, I'm afraid that I will no longer require your unique services."

Lomax was shocked. "But you said this job was for seven years."

"As you will see, I have provided you with a substantial severance pay. And you get to keep the houses. So, don't complain."

Lomax stood up and gave a kick to the table.

"Careful…that's very old French provincial," said the client.

"Why the mystery book routine?"

"You're not the only one they're looking for."

"Diciembre called you a…*Traveller*. What did he mean by that?"

No reply.

Lomax walked around the table and gave the room the once over. The furniture was very old and very expensive. He found a brief case on the floor that was the same color and style as the one he brought to the house. He picked it up and placed it on the table. He opened it and found several bundles of currency. He closed the brief case and headed for the front door.

"Lomax?"

Lomax had had enough. "I'm done here!"

"I just want you to know that I will think of you and Daphne in my prayers," said the client. "She's due in about six months, right? People don't pray enough and in this business that could prove eternally painful."

Lomax stopped and turned to the camera. "You know where you can go….eternally!"

*　　*　　*

Special Agent in Charge Diciembre was left off in front of an old,

THE DOOR

rusted warehouse, somewhere in the mountains of West Virginia. No one was there to greet him. He was provided a key that opened the door to an unoccupied office. There were no desks or chairs, just old litter. He went into the warehouse and flipped the switch to the overhead lights. One out of a hundred came on, barely shedding any light on the empty giant room.

"This is Project Door?" His voice echoed off the walls. No one was there to hear it.

He would allow himself this one time to let his emotions get the better of him. He shouted, **"I HATE YOU LOMAX!"**

Sparks flung out from the one operating overhead light and it winked out, casting Diciembre into total darkness.

THE DOOR

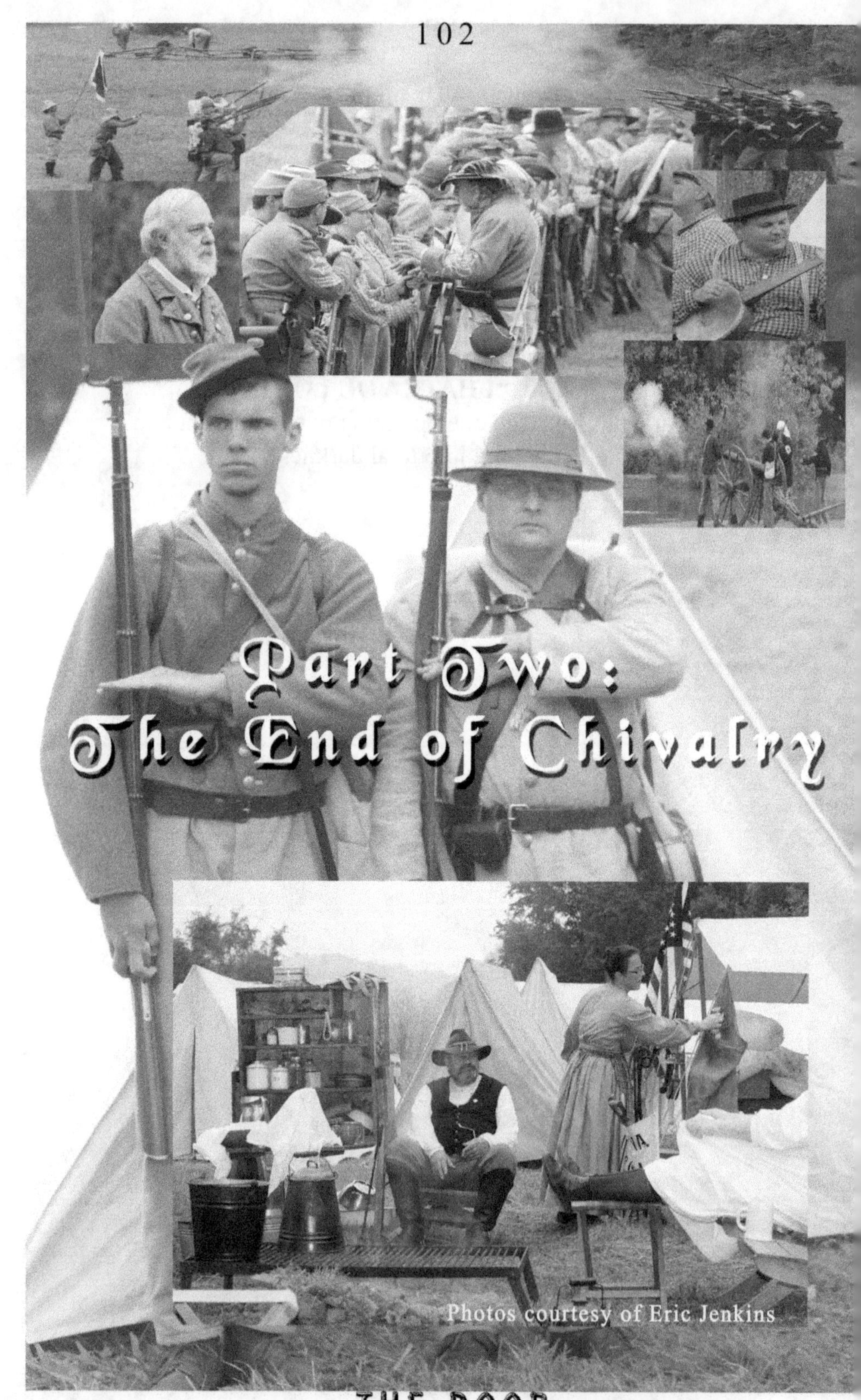
Part Two:
The End of Chivalry
Photos courtesy of Eric Jenkins

Chapter Eight

THE BATTLE OF SALTVILLE

The town of Saltville, Virginia hosted a Civil War reenactment the third weekend of every August, on a plot of land called the Wells Field. This was the place where the infamous Saltville Saltworks once stood and where some twenty-five hundred Negro slaves, men, women and children, worked around the clock processing salt for the South. A hundred and forty years ago, salt was the only form of preserving meat save for smoking and Saltville was the Confederacy's Salt Capital. Towards the end of the war it became the South's last saltworks and a prime target for the Union Army. Napoleon said it best that "*An army marches on its stomach.*" Without salted beef, the Rebs would starve and the South would lose the war. The Battle of Saltville was one of the most important but least recognized series of battles in the Civil War.

For hundreds of costumed reenactors it was time for them to dust off their wool uniforms, polish their brass buttons, shine up their boots, clean their muskets and pistols, erect their tents and report for muster just like they had done every year without fail. Sergeant Major "Ham" Hamilton of the First Virginia was there bright and early, saluting and shaking hands with old friends, telling jokes and organizing his old command. Even though he was born in Massachusetts, he was gray through and through. No doubt about it, if he were given the option of which time and place he would live, Virginia in the eighteen sixties would have been his answer. Ironically, he was not a man of violence. Actually, he abhorred it. What drew him to the Civil War was the chivalry he thought existed between combatants and the yearning for states rights and self-determination. It was something that he thought

America had once again lost with all the crime in the cities and the political correctness that was being flushed out of Washington D.C. Oh, how he he yearned for a time when men were men and women acted like real ladies.

Many of his reenactment friends were genuinely surprised to see him this year, wearing his shiny new uniform and boots and acting as though nothing had happened to Maggy. But he was putting up a brave front. The man was dead inside and overwhelmed with grief. Were the rumors true that the love of his life had run off with another man? After all, they had been married for a long time and the novelty had long since worn off. Both worked hard all their lives. There were no kids to fight with. No grandkids to spoil. Maybe she wanted more? All these thoughts nagged at him, night after night. He needed a break. He could always find solace on the battlefield in Saltville the moment he heard the crash of musketry, a rebel yell and the roar of cannons.

The news media was usually at the event as well as hundreds of local residents and tourists.

For Israel and Mary Pilgrim, it was a chance for them to get out in the sun and show off their newborn. Not surprisingly, many workers from the factory had been bitten by their boss's Civil War bug and were participating in the reenactments here and at other towns. It was a family affair with their wives and kids standing with the other spectators cheering them on in this fantasy. Grown men, playing war and at the end of the day everybody went home. *It doesn't get better than that!*

Hamilton was truly in his element as he commanded an artillery company and firing off an old cannon half a dozen times. It was all smoke, no projectile, but the old gun gave a good kick when it went off and it was music to his ears.

After the battle, the crowds converged on the little tent city where some reenactors sold all kinds of memorabilia. There was plenty of good barbecue and beer to go around. Everybody seemed to be having a good time.

With a beer in his hand, Hamilton called out to his new CEO. "Israel!"

"Ham—I mean, Sergeant Major Hamilton, how goes the war?"

They shook hands. "*Ah*, the damn Yankees got me again!"

"But I thought you were from Massachusetts?"

THE DOOR

"I am." Hamilton belched. "I'm a traitor." He took Pilgrim by the arm for support and they went for a little stroll through the tent city. "You know, Israel, I was born in the wrong time."

"I know," smiled Pilgrim. He had heard this a hundred times.

"If I had to choose, I'd live in the 1860's…when life was simpler…and…when life was simpler." Hamilton was a little drunk.

"*Hmmm!*" replied Pilgrim. "1860's, you say. America was divided, there was slavery and a civil war and you think life was simpler?"

"Yes, sir, I do. My boy, it was a time when men were men. And men were men and things like honor, loyalty and love of God and country meant something. Now if you say 'God' out loud you might offend somebody."

A nerdy looking teenager with zits on his face interrupted their conversation by asking Hamilton a question.

"Sir, are you an expert on the Civil War?"

Pilgrim grinned, but Hamilton was not so amused.

"No, young man. I consider myself a student of history."

The teenager sized up the middle-aged man standing in front of him, and would later describe to his teacher and classmates as this "ancient guy in a costume", then referred to a pad that had a score of questions. "Me too! Now what can you tell me about Champus Fragg?"

"*Uh, oh,*" uttered Pilgrim, rolling his eyes skyward. He knew what was coming!

"He was a Reb Captain. A Calvary Officer—."

"—You mean, a bushwhacker," said the kid, "who murdered injured black and white Union soldiers."

Hamilton raised a hand. "Now hold on there, boy. Watch how you use the word '*murder*'. It was war and people get killed in wars. None of it is pretty. And history is written by the victor."

The teenager made a notation on his pad. He then gave Hamilton a respectful nod and said, "Thank you, sir. That uniform of yours makes you look like a General."

Hamilton turned his body to one side to show off his red Sergeant Major stripes. "Those are sergeant chevrons."

"I stand corrected. You're still very impressive looking." With that, the teenager trotted off.

THE DOOR

"What a respectful young man. You know, I always wanted a kid."

"Ham, are you going to need a ride home?"

"*Naaaa!* Not me. I'm staying put…right *cheer!* Got me a tent." He gestured to a tent with a cot and all kinds of furniture then to the portable toilets lined up by the roadway. "Even got me an outhouse." He raised both arms up high, spilling his beer on Israel. "This, my boy, is Heaven. But you…you need to take that beautiful baby and pretty wife home." He leaned closer to Pilgrim and whispered, so that Mary would hear. "And for God sakes don't let her out of your sight."

The Pilgrims went home and Hamilton got very drunk. So drunk, that he passed out and hit his head on a tent peg.

When Hamilton awakened the next morning, he realized he was lying on a hospital bed. His head hurt from both the hangover he had and from falling on the tent peg. A thick bandage was wrapped around his forehead. His vision was blurred and it took time to focus. When the blurriness subsided, Hamilton spotted the little girl, dressed in a red dress, standing at the foot of his hospital bed.

"Who…who are you?" he asked.

"My name is Allison."

She carried a haversack, one that soldiers would use during the Civil War to carry personal effects. It looked half full and heavy with alcohol pads, gauze pads and rolls and Betadine. She grabbed him by the hand and said, "You got to get up. We have to go. I can't stay here too long."

He resisted. "Go where? No, no, no. I need to stay here."

"You don't understand…"

"Okay, explain it to me."

"Maggy asked me to find you."

Hamilton's eyes widened. He leaned forward in the bed. "What did you say?"

"She needs your help."

"Maggy? My Maggy? Maggy Hamilton?"

The little girl held a piece of paper in her hand.

"What's that you got there?" he asked her.

"A list of things she wanted me to get." She handed it to

THE DOOR

Hamilton, who gave it the once over.

"That's Maggy's hand writing all right." He kept the list. "Why didn't she come back here with you?"

"She said she had a lot of work to do."

Hamilton shook his head. "That's my Maggy!"

Allison kept looking over her shoulder and appeared very nervous. "Yes, now can we go? I can't stay here too long." She headed out the door and wandered off down the hallway.

"Why can't you stay…?" He climbed out of the bed and followed her out into the hallway. He watched Allison creep up to the nurse's station and quietly remove items such as boxes of gauze, little bars of soap and latex gloves from the shelves. One of the cabinets was left ajar. She had to use a step ladder that some of the shorter nurses used, to reach into the cabinet. She found a treasure trove of supplies: bottles of Tylenol, Ibuprofen, aspirin, antibiotics, and syringes, needles, Lidocaine for injection, narcotic pain killers, sutures, suture kits with hemostats and scissors, scalpels and suture removal kits. All the while, a nurse was sitting at the table, writing a report, occasionally glancing at her wrist-watch. Her relief was late and she was tired.

Hamilton went back into his room and opened the closet. He gave a sigh of relief when he found his Confederate gray uniform in the hangers. He dressed quickly and put on his pistol belt and sword scabbard even though both weapons had been confiscated for safekeeping. Once fully dressed, he tucked his Kepi hat under his right arm strutted out of the hospital room.

Allison was waiting for him at the elevator. They rode down to the first floor, then stepped out and lively strode past the nurse's station. She took Hamilton by the hand and directed him to Room 19. "Come on!"

"Where are you taking me?" When he looked ahead, he spotted Room 19. The room his wife entered the morning after a hurricane and never came out.

"To Maggy!"

"Mr. Hamilton?" asked the nurse who was on watch at the nurse's station.

"Yes, I'm Maggy's husband." He entered the nurse's station, grabbed a black garbage bag and started tossing boxes of medical and cleaning supplies into it. "And we need a few things."

THE DOOR

The nurse was stunned. "You…you can't do that—!"

"It's okay. Just put it on my bill."

"Hey!" shouted a security guard, who had just exited the elevator.

"Got to go!" Hamilton said to the nurse as he bolted into Room 19.

Allison had opened the door and Hamilton just walked right in.

The room had undergone a complete renovation with new paint, new windows, roof and ceiling tiles, but no furniture.

"Stop!" shouted the security guard. "You can't go in there!"

Hamilton closed the door and pressed his body against it. The guard started pounding on the door.

"Open the door!" said the security officer

"Now what do we do?" Hamilton asked Allison.

"We wait," said Allison.

"Wait for what?"

It came about ten seconds later.

Knock! Knock!

Hamilton was surprised. "Is somebody in the bathroom?"

Allison went up to the door, but instead of grabbing the doorknob, she tapped the door twice. She then opened the door and stepped a side.

Hamilton beheld a sight he thought he would never see. A dashing young Confederate Calvary Officer, wearing a slouch hat and feather, was sitting on an impressive horse, smoking a cigar. Filthy, poorly clad and often shoeless Confederate soldiers and Home Guard were marching in front of the Calvary Officer and a smoking 4.4.0 locomotive pulling four boxcars filled with troops rolled into a train depot behind the Calvary Officer, screeching its brakes, sounding its whistle and releasing jets of stream. *"Gone With The Wind"* had nothing on what he was witnessing.

"Come on," said Allison, waving him to go with her into the open doorway.

Hamilton stepped away from the hallway door, took Allison's hand and together they stepped into another place and another time.

Both the security officer and the nurse entered Room 19 just in time to witness Hamilton and Allison leave the twentieth century. They stood there in silence, mouths and eyes wide open, watching an event that took place over a hundred and thirty years ago.

THE DOOR

Hamilton stepped off the wooden planks of a front porch to an antebellum house that he had walked on many times. It was the old house owned by William Alexander Stuart, who was Confederate General Jeb Stuart's brother. It was located just off Route 91 in Saltville. But in 1864, there was no Route 91 and the W.A Stuart House wasn't old, but it was war weary. The soot from the trains that stopped at the depot and from the furnaces at the saltworks that was situated to his right, blacked the white paint of the Stuart house.

"I know this place. The train depot! The saltworks! This is Saltville!" He dropped the garbage bag and raised both arms into the sky. **"There is a God!"**

The Calvary Officer came along side Hamilton, noted both the ultra clean gray dress uniform and red Sergeant Major stripes, but thought the wearer was member of the clergy. "Get a hold of yourself, Reverend," he said. "You'll frighten the men!"

"Begging your pardon, sir. I am not a Reverend."

"Then who the blazes are you? And why in God's name are you wearing your dress uniform to battle?"

Hamilton was still a little groggy from all the painkillers he had been given and wasn't as sharp as he usually was. His instincts came into play as he stiffened to attention and gave a snappy salute. "Sergeant Major Hamilton, at your service, sir!"

The officer returned the salute and identified himself. "Lieutenant Barrett." Even though Hamilton's Kepi had the artillery insignia, the young Lieutenant thought this impeccably dressed soldier was assigned to a staff officer. "Are you from General Breckinridge's personal staff?" Breckinridge was a former Vice President of the United States under President Buchanan. He actually ran against Lincoln for President and lost. He was now commander of all Confederate Forces in and around Saltville.

The Lieutenant just gave Hamilton the best explanation he could ever get for his sudden arrival to the 19th century. He needed one because with his northern accent and lack of orders or proper identification, he could be considered a spy and shot on sight. *So much for a simpler life!*

"*Uh*, yes, sir!" He picked up the garbage bag. "I'm to personally deliver these medical supplies to a nurse named Maggy—I mean Margaret Hamilton. Do you know of her, sir?"

THE DOOR

Lieutenant Barrett appeared unsettled by the question. "By thunder, I most certainly do. That confounded woman barks more orders and *cusses* more than a *Gaul dern* General. And I swear if I hear **'snap to, sailor'** one more time—!"

"—A bad habit she picked up in the Navy."

"Navy?"

Hamilton quickly recalled his history. Prior to or during the Civil War there were no female Medical Corpsmen. He came up with a better answer. "Her father was an Admiral."

"Oh, well, that explains that." He pointed to the northeast. "She's at the Sanders Farm."

"That's on the front lines!" Hamilton was shocked and became instantly angry. "Whose stupid idea was that…sir?"

"Hers! Believe you me, if Hugh McClugg's cannons don't send them blue-bellies high tailing it back north, she will! If she's expecting you, you best get up there and in a hurry, or they'll be hell to pay!"

It was then he realized that Allison had laid the haversack on the ground next to him and left without saying a word. "Allison?" he called out. "Allison, where are you?"

When Hamilton turned around and faced the Stuart house, the look of surprise flashed across his face as he realized that the bathroom door to Room 19 was still open and a nurse and security officer were gazing right at him. The nurse even gave a wave. Without any warning, the door slammed shut, breaking the connection between the two centuries.

"Well," he said to himself, "there's no going back now."

Something else caught Hamilton's eye. Soldiers had removed an old double door from one of the boxcars that had the markings of the US Post Office on it. Even though the North and South were at war, the postal service still delivered the mail between the combatant states. It was one of those oddities of the Civil War. It was made of sturdy oak and when the soldiers let it fall to the ground, it remained undamaged.

"Where in blazes did you get this door?" asked Lieutenant Barrett.

"It was shipped all the way here from Massachusetts. A place called Salem Village."

That really got Hamilton's attention! He picked up Allison's haversack and followed Barrett to the side of the boxcar.

"It's addressed to a Cornelius Pilgrim of Marion," one soldier reported, gesturing to the mailing slip still pasted to the door.

"Pilgrim?" asked Hamilton. "Did you say *'Pilgrim'?*" When he noticed all the inquisitive looks he was getting from the men around him, he realized that he should not have asked that question. Here he was, an unknown man asking about a large parcel that was shipped from a Northern state to a town in Virginia that was about to be attacked by the Union Army. It made him look suspicious.

"Do you know this Pilgrim *fella*?" asked Barrett.

Hamilton shook his head. "Only if he is a minister." He reached out and touched the door. "This door is for a church!"

It was a good answer. The soldiers looked away from Hamilton and went on with their business.

"What do we do with it, Lieutenant?" asked one of the soldiers.

Barrett glanced over his shoulder at all the wood the slaves were burning at the saltworks to fuel the stream engines that pumped fresh water underground, and then pumped the brine water back to the surface and to a system of iron kettles that were heated by furnaces. For as far as the eye could see, the hills and mountains surrounding Saltville had been denuded of trees so that they could keep the steam engines and furnaces of the saltworks going.

"Chop it up for firewood."

"No wait!" shouted Hamilton. "Don't do that, sir. Look at the craftsmanship on that door." He quickly realized that his statement meant nothing to a man who was fighting in a war. "Besides, we're going to need all the doors we can get after this battle."

"What for?" asked Barrett.

"Operating tables." His wife may have been a nurse, but he didn't know any other way to say it.

Barrett nodded in agreement. "Quite right, Sergeant Major." He turned to two teenaged home guardsmen standing by the train. They couldn't have been more than fourteen years old. He pointed to them, then swept his arm in the direction of an empty wagon. "You two privates, put this here door on that wagon and see that it is brought to the hospital at Emory and Henry College. See to it personally."

Hamilton instantly liked this officer. By giving them this task, he may have spared those kids from possibly getting hurt or killed. However, the two boys didn't like the idea that they would be out of the fight.

Hamilton stepped in. "You boys want to be soldiers, right?"

They nodded in a nervous manner.

"Then obey the Lieutenant's order and be quick about it!" He turned to a group of privates who were standing near by. "And you boys help these privates load this door and tie it down good. You hear?"

In no time at all, the wagon was loaded and driven away.

"Shouldn't you be on your way?" Barrett asked Hamilton.

Hamilton gave another snappy salute. "Yes, sir!"

Hamilton had no idea the significance of what he and the Calvary officer had just done. However, historically speaking, it was recorded that a double church door had arrived at the Saltville train depot just hours before the battle and was confiscated by the Saltville Home Guard. The church door was later used as an operating table at the Emory and Henry College. Unknowingly, Ham Hamilton had just become part of Virginia Civil War history.

To the raggedly clad Home Guard and regular enlisted soldier, seeing such a clean and bright uniform made them think that Hamilton was a high raking officer. Even some junior officers stiffened to attention and one even saluted him until they spotted the red chevrons—which were obscured by the bags he was carrying. He had been a CEO of a company for years and walked and talked like a leader. He also participated in many reenactments, so he fit right into his new role as a Reb Sergeant Major.

But there was one place he would not be saluted. The salt-works. He had read all the published literature about the two Union raids on Saltville and had heard all the horrors about the day-to-day happenings at the saltworks. Seeing it for real was much more horrible. Being born in America in the twentieth century, he had never witnessed the cruelty and depravations of slavery. He actually liked and respected black people and was credited with hiring a higher percentage of African Americans than any other employer in the county. As he made his way passed all the wood burning furnaces in the Wells Field, he took it all in and he didn't like what he saw. It made him sick to his stomach. Quite frankly, it made him angry. "No human should be treated like

THE DOOR

this," he uttered to himself. When he saw a white filthy looking taskmaster cracking a whip in the direction of a group of black males, who were unloading firewood from a wagon, he stopped and said. "You're very powerful with that whip in your hand. How *bout* you grab a musket and join me at the front line?" The taskmaster recoiled his whip, turned and walked away.

"*Thanke massa*," said a slave named Joe.

"You're welcome...."

Hamilton continued his two-hour hike to the Sanders Farm. He passed through the small downtown district that was made up of a handful of commercial buildings surrounded by a few houses and farms. At one point, he stopped and gazed out into a beautiful green meadow where in the future the town proper, with the town hall, post office, town swimming pool and even the high school would one day stand.

His pace quickened the nearer he got to the Sanders Farm. First, he had to cross Chestnut Hill, which would become the front line of the battle that was only hours away. A sophisticated system of trenches had been built along the hillside, which looked down at a flat piece of land called Broady Bottom. There, the Union Army would assemble and unleash a storm of rifle and cannon fire at the Rebel defenders.

When he spotted the Sanders Farm, situated high on top of a hill, his heart started to pound hard like a boy on his first date.

"Maggy!" he shouted, but got no reply. "Maggy!"

He hurriedly descended the steep slope of Chestnut Hill, allowing gravity to do most of the work for him. His ascent up the inclined pathway of Sanders Hill wasn't as easy but he was running on pure adrenaline. Once he reached the top of the hill, he stopped for a moment to catch his breath. He then charged through the opened front door of the two-story colonial style house, startling the middle-aged daughter of the owner and her children. The children screamed and ran to their mother. They were building a building a barricade in the middle of the living room with all the furniture.

"I'm sorry I startled you," he said, respectfully removing his hat. "I'm looking for a nurse. Nurse Hamilton."

The mother of three pointed in the direction of the back door. "She's fixing up the barn."

THE DOOR

Hamilton glanced into the living room and noticed the barricade. And in that moment. an historical fact came to his mind. "Oh, that's right! You're going to build a barricade in front of the fireplace and hide inside. Good idea! No bullets will get through all that rock." He put on his hat and charged out the backdoor.

The mother of three glanced over her shoulder at the fireplace and studied it for a moment, then she slapped her hands and said to her children. "I think we should push all the furniture in front of the fireplace...."

Hamilton came out the backdoor and spotted a woman, facing the opposite direction, standing over a boiling pot and stirring the rags that would be used as gauze with a broom handle. Even though she was wearing Civil War era clothing, he recognized her immediately. He was so happy and so excited. As he made his way to Maggy, he thought of a hundred things he should say. Unfortunately, he picked the wrong one.

"Hey, lady. *Wanna*-fool around?"

Maggy was shocked. She dropped the broom handle, turned and threw herself into Hamilton's arms. They fell to the ground. She kissed him all over the face, then stopped and rolled onto her back to catch her breath. He got to his feet first and being a gentleman, he reached out his hand. She took it and after he pulled his wife to her feet, she gave him a hard smack on the jaw with her fist. "Where the hell have you been? I've been waiting three days for you—!"

Hamilton staggered about but remained standing. "Three days! You've been gone damn near three months."

"What?"

"That's right. Three months!"

"How can that be? I've only been here three days!"

"Well, Toto, I guess we're not in Kansas anymore." He rubbed his jaw and moaned.

Maggy realized that she may have hurt her husband. "You all right?"

"No! Everybody back home thinks you ran off with another guy. I've been worried sick about you...even suffered a heart attack."

All the anger she had evaporated in an instant. Her eyes welled

THE DOOR

up with tears and she reached out to him. "Oh, Ham! I'm so sorry!"

But he put up his arms as a sign of capitulation. "Hey, look if you're going to hit me again…"

She reached out to him and they hugged each other for a long time.

*   *   *

Back to the future…

The Hospital Chief of Staff had been out of town at a medical convention. His secretary informed him about the second incident in Room 19 and the disappearance of Ham Hamilton just prior to the flight home. When he arrived at the hospital the next morning he found Detective Dewey Mitchell standing inside Room 19.

"What's going on here, Dewey?"

"It happened again," said Mitchell, gesturing to the missing bathroom wall and door.

"The door is gone!"

"Our friends from the federal government took it…and all the bugs they planted in this room."

"Can you tell me what happened?"

"All I can say is, Ham Hamilton entered this room, early yesterday morning, following a seven or eight year old girl, who was dressed in a Little Red Riding Hood outfit. I have witness statements from both a security guard and nurse, who said they entered this room just as Hamilton and the little girl were stepping through the bathroom doorway into…and I quote *'another world'*." He pointed to the place where the bathroom door and wall once stood.

The Chief of Staff gave the hospital room the once over. "No explosive damage like the last time?"

"None. How do I explain that? I love a good mystery, but this is getting ridiculous." He started to turn, then stopped and gazed back at the Chief of Staff. "Oh, by the way, the IRS served a search warrant at Hamilton's business this morning."

The Chief of Staff sighed. "On top of everything, Ham now has the IRS after him?"

Mitchell shook his head. "They weren't IRS."

THE DOOR

"And how do you know that?"

"Hamilton and the previous owners kept records of every sale. Some records were fifty, sixty years old. They took them all."

"What are they looking for?"

"That's a good question."

Lomax and Daphne rewound the recording of Hamilton and Allison passing through the portal, thanks to the wireless video camera installed by Diciembre's people.

"Grainy and poorly lit," said Daphne, commenting about the picture quality. "They could learn a thing or two about covert video production from you. Okay, what do we have here? Steam locomotives, soldiers in gray uniforms armed with Enfield Rifles. Looks like the Civil War to me."

It took a moment, but when the reality of what she was seeing set in, it startled Daphne. She turned to Lomax, wanting to say something, but couldn't find the words.

"I know," he said, noting the look on her face. "I can't believe it either. But there it is. What you're seeing happened a hundred and thirty or so years ago."

"But I thought Einstein said time travel was impossible."

Lomax thought he'd make a joke with his response. "Who's traveling? They're just walking through a doorway." He thought he would then dazzle Daphne with his intelligence. "Actually, Einstein's Special Theory of Relativity, published in 1905, stated that when an object traveled close to the speed of light, it would physically alter time and space. It also had an effect on gravity. He proposed that distance and time were not absolute. He believed that the gravity of any mass, such as our sun, could have an effect on warping the space and time around it."

"Well, I'm impressed."

"You watch enough Star Trek, you learn a few things."

He worked the controls and zoomed in on a still frame of the locomotive, with Hamilton and the Calvary Officer standing to one side. "See the markings on that train?"

"Not really. There's a lot of smoke."

"Well, then clean it up for me. Chop! Chop!"

"What for? We no longer have a client."

He gestured to the control room that was now fully operational.

THE DOOR

"You don't pay for all of this and just walk away at the first sign of trouble."

He got up and stretched. He had been working for two days straight putting everything together and was tired. "So get to work so that I can cross reference those numbers with the Smithsonian database and get its operational history. The South used every locomotive they had to transport their troops and supplies. Most survived the war."

"All right. All right. I'm on it. Just stop lecturing me, okay?" She started typing on the keypunch with one hand and wiggling the mouse wildly with the other. What she didn't pay any attention to at all in the frame was the double door that was being held up next to the locomotive by members of the home guard. It took several hours, but when she got done the picture was crystal clear, right down to the delivery address plastered to the door.

There was one thing about the door in the frame that did get Daphne's attention. There was an etching in the wood that was filled with dirt. It read: Hell.

*   *   *

Meanwhile, at the Sanders Farm…

Someone gave a shove to the only door to the Sanders log sided barn and it fell into Hamilton's waiting hands. With an old saw and hammer, Hamilton had assembled the crudest examples of carpenter horses he had ever made in his life for the doors to rest on. The barn door would now be used as an operating table.

"How am I doing, *ma'am?*" he asked his wife.

"Good. Trust me, after today we'll never look at a door the same again."

Hamilton turned away. "Now that's something I never thought of."

"You're the Civil War historian. How bad is it going to get today?"

"We'll be needing more doors." A thought flashed though his mind. "Hey, you should have seen the double door that came off the train this morning." He gestured in the direction of the Saltville train depot. "It was shipped all the way from Salem Village, Massachusetts."

She stopped what she was doing, turned and stared at her

THE DOOR

husband.

"And get this," he continued, "it was addressed to a Cornelius Pilgrim!"

"Pilgrim?"

"I wonder if he's related to Israel Pilgrim?"

She grabbed her husband by the arm and directed him out onto the south lawn, well out of earshot of the other women who were working in and around the barn. "Is there something wrong with you?"

"What do you mean?"

"I go into a hospital room to check on Mary Pilgrim and her baby and then I hear the bathroom door knock. I open the door and the next thing I know I'm in the 19th century! Now you tell me that you've seen a door that was shipped all the way from Salem Village, arriving at the train depot—which faces the old Stuart place and the door we came through—and it's addressed to a Pilgrim, and you don't think that all of that isn't somehow related?"

"You don't think it's just a coincidence?"

Maggy pulled out a hairpin. "Let me have your liqueur flask."

He became defensive. "I don't have a flask—."

"—Yes, you do." Maggy patted his coat until she discovered a hard spot. "Like I was saying."

"Oh, that." He opened his coat and fished out the metal flask and handed it to her.

Maggy laid the flask down flat on the makeshift-operating table. She then held out the hairpin about three inches from the flask and let go of it. The hairpin shot off and attached itself to the flask. She pulled the hairpin off the flask, with some effort, held it out even further away and let go. The hairpin once again shot off and attached itself to the flask.

"How is that possible?" he asked.

"The flask has been magnetized. So has anything else you have that is made of iron or steel."

"How did they become magnetized?"

"There's only one explanation. The door! It has to be a very powerful magnet. How else would we be able to go back in time?"

He gestured to the haversack and garbage bag of supplies he had brought with him. "Hope that stuff will come in handy?"

THE DOOR

"Are you kidding? Infections killed more soldiers in this war than any bullet or bomb. Just the soap alone that you brought will save a lot of lives."

"But if you save the life of someone who should have died—?"

She raised a hand. "Don't go there. We're here and there may be no tomorrow."

"What about Allison? Do you know anything about her?"

"She's lost just like us. But she can do the one thing we can't."

"And what's that?"

"Open those doors without getting blasted through a wind tunnel. I'm lucky I survived it!"

The conversation ended by the sound of cannon fire, thundering through the valley.

"Those are northern cannons," he said.

"How can you tell?"

He pointed due north. "Because they're firing from the north."

They held hands as they trotted up a hill overlooking a little brook called Cedar Creek. It would run between the base of Chestnut Hill and a flat pasture called Broady Bottom. To the north, thousands of Union Soldiers, clad in blue uniforms, marched in cadence towards Saltville. Maggy turned and studied the look on her husband's face. He was excited and fascinated by it all.

"Are we dreaming all this?" he asked.

"To you this is a dream come true. For me, it's a nightmare. One you and I may not wake up from. Remember that, when you are out soldiering." She released her hand and backed away.

"You're letting me go?"

"I don't want to. I'm afraid I might lose you. But for some unknown reason, we were brought here to do something. So, you go do whatever you're supposed to do. I'll be here when it's over."

He gestured to Cedar Creek. "You see that little brook? That's Cedar Creek. In a few hours, it will run red with blood."

"Just make sure none of yours is in it."

They embraced like it might be their last time and kissed hard and long.

Afterwards, they parted. She went back to the Sanders Farm and Hamilton headed for Cemetery Ridge, in the hope that he would be assigned to crew and possibly command a cannon battery. There was a smile on his face.

THE DOOR

*   *   *

Christmas without Ham Hamilton just wasn't the same at the factory. The mood was somber if not downright depressing. Israel tried to cheer up the crew by giving them a bigger bonus than usual and even threw in a turkey. His efforts were appreciated and the employees had a little more respect for their new CEO. *At least he was trying!*

The hardest thing Israel had to do was hire a probate lawyer to put the Hamilton's affairs in order. The Hamiltons had no kids to leave their estate to or even brothers or sisters. There was a will and it specifically stated that none of their estate would go to their cousins up north, who they "despised". But what really threw a hammer into the works was the silent partner Hamilton had. This unknown person had provided the initial capital investment to build the factory and move Ham and about half of the initial employees from Massachusetts to Southwest Virginia. The silent partner refused to identify him or herself and refused to appear before the judge. Instead, a young nice looking lawyer wearing a very expensive suit and a Rolex watch came to the court to represent the silent partner. He had a distinct New England accent and he proficiently insisted that it was the wishes of the silent partner that the business and Hamilton estate be placed in the temporary care of Israel Pilgrim, "until at which time evidence can be presented before the court that Mr. and Mrs. Hamilton are in fact deceased."

"Counselor," said the judge, who stopped for a moment, spreading out the paperwork in front of him, "and what is your name again, son?"

The lawyer, who looked like he just graduated from law school, grinned when he heard the word '*son*'. He was in fact much older than he looked. "John Danvers, Your Honor."

"Ah, yes. Mr. Danvers, I have been on the bench for a long time and I too would prefer to withhold any judgment in respect to the Hamilton Estate until such time a sufficient amount of tangible and unquestionable evidence is presented to this court confirming the demise of the parties in question. Trust me, there's nothing worse for a judge than to declare someone deceased and then have them show up in their court six months later. It should

THE DOOR

be noted that the police have listed the Hamiltons as 'missing' and are continuing their investigations into this matter. For the record, I would like to say that I am well acquainted with the Hamiltons and may even go so far as to call them friends. However, I am not surprised that your client would make a request that Mr. Israel Pilgrim be given sole supervisory control over the Hamilton's estate, including all business assets. This court and the community at large have noted Mr. Pilgrim's stellar reputation, both personal and business. But unless Mr. Pilgrim objects, I see no reason to refuse your client's request. What say you, Mr. Pilgrim?"

Israel was shocked. He had to clear his throat before he could reply. "I too am surprised, Judge. And like you, I'm also not convinced Ham and Maggy are…*uh*…*uh*…gone. So, what ever you decide, Your Honor, is okay with me."

"The Court will note that there is no objection from Mr. Pilgrim as to the request issued by this so-called silent partner. So be it then. Mr. Pilgrim, this court awards you temporary supervision of the Hamilton estate. Case dismissed." He struck the gavel. "Bailiff, call next case and make it snappy. It's almost time for lunch."

The silent partner's lawyer slipped out of the courtroom without saying a word to anyone.

Dewey Mitchell was sitting in the courtroom. He met with Israel in the hallway. "Looks like you're a rich man, Israel."

"Don't throw that ball to me, Dewey," Israel fired back in a stern tone. "I didn't ask for any of this and you know it."

Mitchell glanced at his wristwatch and made a notation on his notepad.

That night, Daphne went into labor and had a little baby girl. She was given the name, Dara. Daphne and Lomax had been married in secret, with another name. But it was very embarrassing for Daphne when the nurse asked her for the name of the father for the Birth Certificate.

"John Doe," she answered with a straight face.

The nurse cocked an eyelid. It was the answer lots of single mothers used. "Oh, him again."

"Yeah, he sure gets around, *huh?*"

The only change in the neighborhood besides Daphne having a

baby was the for sale sign coming down at the house directly across the street from the Pilgrims. A single man named Eddi Dane, who drove the Hot Diggity Dog Electrical Man van, was now occupying it. The homeowners on the street recognized him as the Spanish-talking electrician who rewired both houses in July. Since both houses never looked so good, he was quietly accepted into the neighborhood. Even when the CIA ran an identity check on him it was rock solid including seventeen years of Commonwealth of Virginia and federal income tax forms.

During the months of fall, and being first time mothers, Daphne became close friends with Mary Pilgrim and they would visit each other almost daily. Running two houses became costly without the client. To maintain their deep cover and help pay the bills, Daphne put out a sign on the front lawn that she was a website designer. Mary was her first client and *muralsbymary.com* attracted so much business that she hired Daphne to answer her phone and schedule all her meetings.

Lomax, on the other hand, laid low, confining himself to the basement. Only about half of the monitors and computers were up and running. It had been that way for months, ever since the Agency pounded the town and county with Predator flybys and satellite scans. They were looking for any electromagnetic emissions that were out of the ordinary and came up with nothing. They would operate in the area for about a week, then go away, then come back two to three weeks later and start scanning again. Lomax knew when they were scanning by the special receivers the client had given him.

But Lomax, just like his former friends at the CIA was asking the same two questions? *"Who took the doors"* and *"Where are they?"*

In November, he got wind of another door sighting in Ohio from a telephone call Dewey got at the PD. One lesson the CIA ingrained in all their field agents who were involved in deep cover cases *'Always tap the phones at the local PD and Sheriff's Office'*.

"I understand that you're working a strange missing person's case," the caller asked Dewey Mitchell.

"I'm working several. What do you have?"

"A business owner and his building—"

THE DOOR

"—Did you say, 'building'—?"

"—It's been there for a hundred years, maybe longer. Witnesses say there was a loud bang, but not like a cannon or gun going off. One minute the building was there and the next it was gone. Right down to the concrete floor. No debris. No burn marks. Never seen anything like it. The witnesses say a little girl wearing a red outfit, uh, kind of uh, kid's fairy tale costume like Little Red Riding Hood was running through the place, just before it happened. But that's not even the real weird part. There was only one thing left standing from the building—."

"—Let me take a wild guess here. A door."

"You too? Oh, God! Well, what do we do?"

"Nothing. The Feds will take over the case. I'm surprised they let you make this call—."

Suddenly, the connection was cut and all Dewey heard was a dial tone. He didn't bother calling back the investigator. The Feds were obviously on the scene and everything would be blacked out.

*　　*　　*

Lomax listened to the phone tap sometime later and remarked. "Just another day, another case, another door…."

During his self-imposed exile from the world, he spent his waking hours surfing online through one historical database after another. On a large clipboard behind him was a picture of Hamilton standing in front of a locomotive and a double door. Parts of the original photo had been blown up and they were pinned to the original. On one of the blowups were the engraved words: Pilgrim Doors.

Lomax spent many days learning everything he could about the family of immigrants who established the first sawmill in a little town on the coastal region of Massachusetts. The Pilgrims were a family of carpenters who left England with many other Puritans to avoid religious persecution and wound up getting involved in the most heinous case in American jurisprudence, the infamous *Salem Witch Trials*. The largest sawmill stood on a dusty street that was the borderline between Salem Village and the port town of Salem. The scope of the Pilgrim Family's involvement in the trial proceedings was limited by one man's testimony: Nathaniel

THE DOOR

Pilgrim. Damning as it was, there was no record in either the town or county archives as to who cut down the trees, milled the wood and built the church that became the site of the trials. Lomax would describe it to Daphne as: "One of the best record purges I've ever seen." One fact that was undeniable was that the Pilgrim's owned two of four sawmills in the area. To Lomax, there was a fifty-fifty chance the wood used for the church came from the Pilgrim mills. The more Lomax researched the Pilgrim Family history the more fascinated he became about them. *He was hooked!* They operated in the same mills for decades, milling wood, making furniture, windows and doors. And they were more than just carpenters. They were landowners and tree farmers. They planted all kinds of trees and managed a huge tract of land—and even in those days land was expensive—for the wood they would use in their business. They not only grew the trees that they milled and used to make all kinds of products, they were merchants too. They owned stores in nearly every port city of New England, shipping their furniture and doors far and wide. It was always a family owned business starting with Nathaniel Pilgrim and continuing for generations to come. One basic fact about this company that Lomax discovered was that for about one hundred and sixty-eight years after the Witch Trials, there was always a man named Nathaniel Pilgrim listed as its "owner" or Chairman of the Board and/or CEO. Known for their high craftsmanship, some of their furniture and doors could be found even today in some of the most prestigious government buildings and homes in the Washington D.C. area. When America was booming, the Pilgrim's business thrived. When times were tough, they sold off most of their land holdings, shut down mills and concentrated on producing the one product that seemed to weather all the financial storms: doors. It was the stock market crash of the 1860's that caused the Pilgrim Door Company to close its mills and stores and move out of New England. *(Only one feisty mill manager by the name of Rory Hamilton remained and survived and prospered in the boom period after the Civil War. For a yearly stipend, he was given permission to add his former employer's name to his new company calling it Hamilton-Pilgrim. Ham Hamilton was the great, great, great grandson of the man who would keep that last Pilgrim mill going. Lomax would discover that it too fell on hard times after the*

THE DOOR

Korean War and closed its doors for good.)

Lomax explained everything he uncovered to Daphne, except the most important point. "Nathaniel Pilgrim's name keeps popping all over the data base. Search me how come I never heard of him before. I can't tell you how many New England newspaper articles were written about this Nathaniel Pilgrim and that Nathaniel Pilgrim. One generation after another of them, until at one point, puff—they're all gone."

"Just like that—?"

"—Like they fell off the face of the Earth."

"Are you sure it's not the same guy?" asked Daphne.

"Oh, please! He'd be hundreds of years old!"

*　　*　　*

With no sword or even a pistol, Hamilton trotted downhill. He was soon joined by a small group of raggedy clothed retreating teenaged home guardsmen armed with muskets. There were six of them and they couldn't have been older than fourteen or fifteen. They were typical bare-footed farm boys who had hunted all their lives to help put food on the kitchen table. Now instead of game, they hunted and shot blue bellies. None had ever killed a man before today. When they were given their orders two days earlier and told to hide out in the forest and pick off any enemy soldier they spotted, they were excited. They had waited a long time for the war to come to Saltville and this was their big chance! They were sharpshooters and had been given the job of harassing the approaching Union Army and they did a good job. But they were only a few against thousands of well-trained, armed soldiers. When these teenagers ran out of powder and shot they had no choice but to high tail it back to the Rebel lines.

Several Home Guard officers rode by the retreating teenagers but one Lieutenant from a neighboring town stopped, turned and walked his horse up to Hamilton.

"Well done, Sergeant Major. You found my sharpshooters." He gestured to the boys.

"I did?" He then realized the Lieutenant meant the six boys.

"We thought we lost you boys," the Lieutenant said to the six teenagers.

THE DOOR

The Lieutenant turned to Hamilton and pointed to the cannon emplacements on top of Chestnut Ridge. "Sergeant Major, I am placing you in command of this rifle squad. I want you to take these boys to the top of that hill and protect the McClure Battery at all costs." The Lieutenant turned to the teenagers. "You boys know what to do! ***Rain hellfire down on them!*** You hear?"

To the surprise of Hamilton and the Lieutenant, the boys didn't respond. No arm pumping with their guns or hysterical yelps. Perhaps it was because they had been running and fighting for hours and it wasn't fun anymore. Or maybe they knew what to expect if they went to the top of that hill.

"That's Chestnut Ridge," said Hamilton.

"I don't care what *y'all* call it. Just get up ***thar***," he turned to the teenagers, "as fast as you can. The whole damn Union army is going to hit that ridge with everything they got. If they take it, they'll pour right through our lines and we won't be able to stop them! Now move!" He spurred his horse and rode off.

Hamilton had run a business most of his adult life and thought he could handle any situation. He was a people kind of manager. But when he saw the frazzled look those teenagers gave him, he almost didn't know what to do. "Well, you heard the man."

"*Whooo*…are you?" one boy asked with a high-pitched voice that sounded like an owl. He was known as "Hoot." He would prove to be the best tree climber and sharp-shooter of the bunch.

"What are you?" asked the freckled face boy. He was the shortest.

"Oh, I'm just a darn fool," Hamilton replied. That made some of the boys smile and two even chuckled. "That's right. Would you believe that I asked to be here?"

"But you got no gun!" said the freckled faced boy.

"Do you have any ammunition, soldier?"

Hamilton calling him a "soldier" made the freckled face boy stand a little straighter. "I *be* fresh out, Sergeant Major."

Likewise, Hamilton seemed to regain some of his confidence when the freckled faced boy called him "Sergeant Major."

"Well, boys, I have been told that God takes care of fools and brave soldiers. So, I'd say we're in mighty good company."

"Amen to that!" said the freckled soldier.

"Yes, son," said Hamilton with a warm smile. "Amen."

THE DOOR

Hamilton gestured to another boy, who was oldest at fifteen and the apparent leader. "What's your name?"

"Moon, sir."

"Why did they name you Moon?"

"*Cause* I *were* born during a full one."

"Okay," Hamilton replied with a grin. He gestured to another boy. "And yours?"

"Fetch…*cause* I fetch *thangs*."

The boy with the high-pitched voice spoke up. "I *be Hoooot*."

"He talks *ta* birds," uttered Moon.

Hamilton then gestured to the quiet boy, but the boy didn't reply, just lowered his head in shame.

Moon spoke up. "He don't talk none. We don't know what his name be."

"Smartest man I knew," said Hamilton, "talked only when necessary. He was my father-in-law." *Too bad his daughter didn't take after him*, he thought. "And his name was Matthew, who in the Bible was considered a gift from God." He turned to the boy. "Would you like to be called Matthew?"

The boy's head shot up and he nodded excitedly.

"All right then." Hamilton turned to the sixth boy, who had red hair.

"I *be* Red."

"Yes," said Hamilton, with a smile, "you certainly are."

With that, they started the steep climb up Chestnut Hill with Hamilton saying, "Hail Mary, full of grace…." The boys (except Matthew) joined in and they prayed aloud all the way to the top of the hill to a place called Chestnut Ridge.

The Union Army marches towards Saltville.

THE DOOR

Chapter Nine

LIVING THE DECEPTION

An estimated four thousand Union soldiers marched on both sides of the North Holston River to reach the northern outskirts of Saltville. Unlike their Confederate foe, they all wore blue uniforms and shoes and were armed with a lever action magazine-fed fifty-two caliber Spencer Repeating Rifle. Unlike the single shot muzzle loading Enfield Rifles the Confederates stationed at Saltville were armed with, the Spencer carried a seven round tube that was much easier to reload. The Spencer also used metal cartridges that were less susceptible to rain and wet conditions. For the Rebs, the old saying of "Keep the powder dry" was a fact of life because if the paper charge got wet, it didn't fire. The Spencer was also shorter and lighter than the muzzle-loaders. The Spencer became the preferred rifle for the U.S. Calvary, and to his credit General Burbridge managed to supply his whole infantry with the rifle. He wanted to lighten the load for his foot soldiers so that they could carry more ammuni-tion. Each soldier was allotted two hundred rounds. None of their Southern counterparts were given anywhere near that many paper charges. For them, every shot did count! Burbridge's main infantry marched smartly into Broady Bottom, staying to the northern part, just out of Confederate rifle range. They only made way for the horse driven artillery caissons that came charging in, kicking up a cloud of dust in their wake. Burbridge's forces were an impressive sight to the Reb defenders. There was no doubt that Burbridge's forces outnumbered and outgunned the defenders of Saltville in almost every category of manpower and firepower. As the Union soldiers formed ranks, there was an eerie hush from the Rebel trenches. ***The Battle of Saltville was about to start!***

As formidable as the Union Forces appeared to their enemy, the

Confederate defenders of Saltville had one ace up their sleeves. The North Holston River had a ninety-foot high cliff that went virtually straight up and bordered Broady Bottom. At the top of the cliff was a deep trench better known as a "breastworks" that was lined with heavy logs and rocks. The only exposed parts of the breastworks were the rifle and cannon slits. The trees and bushes that grew on the side and at the top of the cliff also provided some cover to the defenders. The only thing the Union soldiers saw was the muzzle and cannon flash. It was called *"Cemetery Ridge"* because directly behind it was a church cemetery.

When Burbridge ordered his infantry to move forward, the Reb defenders opened up with their muskets and cannons. Many historians would describe the fire that came down from Cemetery Ridge in one word: *murderous*. For all the things that General Burbridge did right in supplying his men with the best provisions, weapons, ammunition and uniforms, he foolishly followed the old European style of warfare. He lined up his infantry in long rows, shoulder-to-shoulder and marched towards the enemy.

To the Rebs on Cemetery Ridge their enemy appeared as long solid rows of blue. How could they miss?

Burbridge also gave the commander of the unit he assigned to take Cemetery Ridge an impossible task. Some Union troopers did make it across the field and reached the Holston River. But it was ten feet deep in some places. Fewer soldiers managed to wade across the river and climb up the hillside, but they didn't get far. Even though hundreds of troopers stood at the waters edge and fired relentlessly at the Rebs on the ridge, the losses started to mount and eventually they had to withdraw from the field entirely.

The assault on Cemetery Ridge was over. Now the entire Union Army set their sights on Chestnut Hill.

Just as Hamilton had told Maggy, the water at Cedar Creek did run red with blood as the Union troopers came under murderous fire from the riflemen on Chestnut Hill. Once Hoot and the other boys replenished their cartridge boxes, they made their way through the highest tier of the trench system, filling in the gaps and loading their rifles. Hamilton stayed right at their side, telling them to use the rifle slits Ole Mudwall Jackson had constructed. The breastworks shook and fell apart from all the fire the Union riflemen were hurling at it. Hamilton spent most of his time effecting repairs to the breastworks. A bullet ricocheted off a rock, bounced around the trench and tore into Hamilton's upper right sleeve. He moaned. The bullet had grazed him, releasing a little blood.

The first wave of soldiers who marched on either side of Sanders Hill took pot shots at the two-story farmhouse as they passed by. That foolishness would continue even after several Union officers rode to the farmhouse, seized it and hoisted a series of unit colors and the Stars and Stripes on the southwest lawn. Even though her husband was fighting on the other side, Maggy presented herself to the highest-ranking officer, identified herself as a "certified operating room nurse" and asked for his help in setting up a field hospital. It didn't hurt that she had a Massachusetts's accent and swore like a Boston whore on a Friday night. She had troopers remove all the tables from the Sanders house and take down every door and set them up as operating tables on the lawn. The twenty sets of carpenter horses Hamilton made earlier came in handy. She also had a trooper tie the Hospital Flag that was yellow with a green "H" in the middle to the top to a makeshift flagpole. This established the Sanders Farm as a non-combat area, where both Union and Confederate could go to receive medical treatment. No one objected or hesitated to her many requests because the wounded started coming in with increasing regularity and she immediately went to work.

*   *   *

Ironically, the only cover the Union troopers got as they crossed Cedar Creek and formed ranks on the open bluff came from the smoke from their own guns. They fired volley after volley at the reb defenses on Chestnut Hill, pounding the logs and rocks that made up the breastworks with hot lead. Many of the Reb defenders found themselves being pelted by wood splinters and pieces of rock—but hardly any bullets. Very few Rebs got shot directly on that trench line. It was mostly indirect fire or a bullet ricocheting that brought down a defender. Many historians would describe the fire that pounded Chestnut Hill in one word: *wasteful.* With the officers shouting to their men to "***keep firing!***" and the cloud of smoke that lay between the two combatants, the Union soldiers hardly took aim. The only reason they would stop shooting was because they ran out of ammunition and had to retire and re-supply. This went on for hours.

Hamilton would have liked to have been one of the artillerymen on the line at "Chestnut Ridge", but when he reported for duty at one of the four cannon emplacements at the top of Chestnut Hill the gunner took one look as his fancy clean dress uniform, made a face, spat on the ground and promptly informed him that his services weren't needed. Hamilton respectfully retired to the trench line where the six boys were stationed, which was to the left of McClugg's cannons. From there, he had a clear view of the Sanders farm. Just before descending into the trench, he took out his binoculars in the hope of catching a glimpse of Maggy.

Suddenly, a filthy and bearded Calvary Officer cut in front of Hamilton. The horse whinnied as he pulled hard on the reins. ***Wooooo!*** shouted the Calvary Officer. "Say, you a General...?"

Hamilton stared at one of the most famous figures in the American Civil War and replied, "No...just a sergeant." He crooked his head to one side. "You look familiar. Who are you, sir?"

"Captain Champus Fragg, at your service—."

"—Oh, my God! It's you! It's really you!"

"No, I am not Him, but I'm here to tell you that I've sent plenty of them blue bellies to Kingdom come!"

That made a number of Rebs in the trenches burst out laughing.

Fragg turned his attention back to Hamilton. "So, you've heard of me, then? Well, Sergeant Major, you best dirty up that fancy uniform of yours right quick like before one of them Yankee sharp shooters gets a bead on *ya*. They might think you're some high *falut'n* officer and pick *ya* off."

Hamilton looked down at his almost perfectly pressed and tailored uniform and then glanced over to the dirty, poorly clad Rebs in the trench. No doubt about it. He stood out. "I'll keep that in mind."

Fragg drew his sword and Hamilton stepped backwards, thinking that he was about to taste cold steel. "We're going to kill us some Yankees today, right boys?" The boys in the trenches cheered, pumped their rifles in the air and gave a throaty yell. "Give them hell boys!" With sword held high, Fragg rode off on his horse in a full gallop towards the rear area.

THE DOOR

"Where's he going?" remarked Hamilton, as he descended into the trench.

"As far away from the fighting as a man can get," replied a gray haired Corporal.

Hamilton had noticed that this Corporal didn't pump his rifle in the air or give a Rebel yell when Fragg gave his pep talk.

"We'll do the *fight'n* and *dy'n*," said the Corporal. "He'll do the other *thangs*."

Hamilton gave the Corporal an odd look. He truly didn't understand.

The Corporal put out his hand. "Sergeant Major, my name is Bland."

Hamilton shook it. "Ham Hamilton."

Confederate Colonel William L Jackson, came trotting down the trench, checking the conditions of the breastworks. "More logs and rocks are needed here," he said aloud. "But there's no time for it now." He stopped and did a double take at Hamilton and his fancy uniform.

"Lord have mercy!" said the Colonel. "You look good enough *ta* bury!"

That made some of the other Rebs laugh.

"I hope not, Colonel," said Hamilton.

"What were you thinking, wearing your Sunday best to battle?"

"Sorry, sir, it's all I have."

The old Colonel nodded. "I have been hearing that answer with increasing regularity. But usually the soldier is bare-footed, half naked and starving." The old Colonel tapped Hamilton's extended girth with the back of his hand. "And I dare say that it doesn't look like you've missed a meal either."

"Are you '*Mudwall*' Jackson—Stonewall's cousin?"

The Colonel's face turned blood red. He poked his dirty index finger into Hamilton's chest. "I'll have you know that the last son of a— (his words were overwhelmed by the roar of the nearest cannon going off) —who dared call me that is buried in one of my walls. Good day to you, sir!" He turned to the other men in the trenches and doffed his Kepi. "And may God bless all of you here today!"

The Jacksons were a very religious family.

"God bless you, Colonel!" the men in the trenches replied.

Jackson went off cursing with every step he took.

THE DOOR

Hamilton smiled. "***Wow!*** I just got chewed out and swore at by Mudwall Jackson!"

His glee was shortened by the sound of incoming cannonballs. They whistled as they approached Chestnut Ridge. He had never heard the sound before and momentarily forgot that this was not a reenactment. *This was the real thing!*

Corporal Bland yelled, "Take cover!" He stood up, grabbed Hamilton and pulled him down into the trench.

The cannonballs struck the hillside about fifty feet away, but the impact was so great that the walls of the trench and even the ground under his feet shook. In all the years he participated in reenactments, he had never been on the receiving end of the cannon fire. ***It terrified him!***

Both sides were now exchanging cannon and rifle fire. Soon the air was choking thick with cordite. Hamilton wanted to help the gun crews on Chestnut Ridge, but they kept waving him off.

Another Calvary officer arrived at the cannon emplacements, but he wasn't going to ride off like Fragg. It was Lieutenant Barrett.

After he gave his horse a hard slap on the rump and sent it running off, Lieutenant Barrett jumped into the trench where Hamilton was taking cover. He shook his head and smiled when he touched Hamilton's empty scabbard and holster. "You still going to war without a weapon, Sergeant Major?"

"I'm afraid so, Lieutenant."

"Here, take this," said Barrett, as he gave Hamilton his spare pistol. It was a Model 1858 Remington. A six-cylinder forty-four-caliber percussion capped handgun that was considered one of the finest revolvers of the Civil War. It was a single-action handgun that meant the soldier had to manually cock the hammer each time before pulling the trigger.

"This is a Remington," said Hamilton, "a Yankee pistol. *How'd* you come across one of these?"

"I have two and let's just say, the previous owner didn't need them anymore…" Barrett tapped the muzzle of the pistol with his finger. "Remember now, the bullet comes out of this end."

Hamilton nodded, then gestured to the closest cannon. "Do you think you can get me a spot on that gun crew?"

"Wait a little bit. I'm sure they'll be needing replacements."

He patted Hamilton on the shoulder before going off to check on his soldiers.

"That is a good officer," said Hamilton, thinking out loud.

Bland drew his Colt pistol and held it out to Hamilton. "You can load all sixth chambers with that Remington. I don't dare do that with my Colt."

"That seems to be a contentious subject between many of the reinactors I—"

"—The who?"

"*Uhhhhh*, the *fellas*...I fought with. They loaded all six chambers in their Colts." Hamilton left out the fact that the reinactors didn't use lead bullets.

Bland pointed to the patch on his pants, right over his groin. "So did I *till* the dern thing done went off. Almost shot off the best part of me."

Hamilton glanced at the patch, then placed his hand over his heart. "I'd rather die."

Bland nodded. "Yeah, buddy!"

*   *   *

Maggy heard the cannon and rifle fire and stepped out of the barn to catch a breath of fresh air. Since the farm was at such a high elevation, she had no idea that four thousand Union troopers were marching towards Chestnut Ridge on either side of Sanders Hill, following separate beaten paths that would end up at Cedar Creek. The hill was so high that only when the soldiers reached a certain vantage point was the Colonial-style farmhouse seen. The flags were not seen either. Some of the arriving troopers opened fire on the house, smashing windows and forcing the daughter of the owner and her children to take cover inside the stone fireplace. Bullets stuck the log sided barn Maggy had converted into a field hospital, but did not penetrate. Maggy told the female volunteers to take cover in the barn, but she stayed outside. It was predetermined in General Burbridge's battle plan to establish a command post and field hospital at the Sanders Farm, since its location would afford an excellent place for the General's Staff Officers to view the fighting and yet close enough to transport the wounded for medical attention. When the General's Staff Officers arrived on their horses, followed by a wagon train of medical personnel and provisions, they were amazed that a field hospital was already in place and wounded were already receiving medical care. When Maggy presented herself to General Burbridge and offered her medical services, she was warmly received.

"Is there anything we can do for you, ma'am?" asked Burbridge.

"Yes, General. You can have your men erect some Hospital Flags at the base of the hill so those stupid sons of bitches will stop shooting at us!"

The flags were promptly erected and the shooting stopped.

Meanwhile, on Chestnut Ridge…

The Rebel defenders watched and waited as a force of four thousand Union troopers passed on either side of the Sanders Hill and headed for the ford on the North Holston River. They were under orders to hold their fire until the Union soldiers started to cross the river.

The Union soldiers reformed ranks just before they reached the ford between the North Holston River and Chestnut Hill. Before them was a high treeless hill lined with a sophisticated system of interconnecting breastworks, filled with hundreds of Confederate regulars and home guardsmen. The Union soldier's main goal besides surviving the day was to reach the ridgeline at the top of the hill called Chestnut Ridge and take possession of the four 6-pound cannons operating there. When the Union soldiers gazed up at the high ridge, they saw the shiny barrels from four 6-pound cannons being aimed right at them. No order had to be given. The Union troopers crossed the ford and charged up the side of Chestnut Hill, forming into two long and impressive lines. The Union force was comprised of the 12th Ohio and the 11th Michigan. General Burbridge held the 5th Colored in reserve, behind the ford in the river during the initial assault on the hill. The 12th Ohio and 11th Michigan pounded the lower trenches with a hail of fire as they closed in. Captain Hugh McClugg's four 6-pound cannons in turn harassed them. The distance between Cedar Creek and the first trench was less than a hundred yards. There was a small patch of wild corn surrounded by briar and bushes. None of them would provide any cover for the Union soldiers. It would prove to be a killing field. Here again, they were out in the open and the only cover they would receive was from the dense and choking cloud of cordite they created by firing their rifles. Their huge numbers and close proximity made them easy targets for the members of Colonel Robertson's 8th Tennessee Brigade, who manned the lowest trenches and were protected by Mudwall's breastworks. They smartly used the rifle slits that were fashioned between the logs and rock, giving the enemy as small a target as possible. The only problem for the Rebs was that their Enfield Rifles were too long and they couldn't stick the muzzle out too far of the slit, otherwise they would be seen and fired upon. The Enfield Rifles had a thirty-nine inch long barrel, and using them in a trench made it difficult to sight in their targets through the narrow rifle slits. However, the one thing the boys from Tennessee had going for them was a lot of experience in trench warfare. The South couldn't afford to lose their soldiers, so they learned how to build breastworks or take positions behind rock walls or trees to keep themselves as unexposed as possible.

On the other hand, there were so many Union soldiers and they were so packed together that very little aiming was required. Just point the rifle in the right direction and shoot. Next the Reb would have to quickly pull down his rifle, duck and crawl to either his left or right because the spot he just fired from would be pelted with bullets.

The outgunned and outnumbered soldiers of the 8th Tennessee who manned the lower trenches were pounded by the relentless gunfire they took. It wasn't long before they realized that their position was hopeless and started to withdraw to the higher trenches.

Corporal Bland pointed to the base of the hill. "Our boys are pulling back," he said to Hamilton. "This battle is lost…"

"Wait," said Hamilton. "Burbridge is about to make his biggest blunder of the battle."

The Corporal made a face. "How do you know that?"

Hamilton pressed the lenses of pair of binoculars to his eyes, swept it left and right, then stopped and focused on one spot. He backhanded the old Corporal with his free hand then pointed to the base of the hill. He handed the binoculars to the Corporal. "See that new line of blue coming from the left?"

Corporal Bland gazed into the binoculars. "I see it. They look different somehow."

"They're colored soldiers."

The Corporal lowered the binoculars, and shot a glance at Hamilton. "That they *be* for *sho!*"

Even over the din of cannon and rifle fire, Hamilton and the corporal heard men shouting in anger. The shouting came from the 8th Tennessee, who manned the lower trenches.

The Corporal peered into the binoculars again and his body jerked with excitement. "Robertson's boys are high tailing it back to their trenches! They look mad as hornets! Look at them return fire!"

It was General Burbridge who personally gave the order to send in the 5th Colored. Just when Robertson's brigade was getting low on ammunition and starting to retreat to the trenches higher up on the hill, they spotted colored soldiers firing at them. It enraged the Tennesseans. They returned to their positions and engaged the enemy with a level of ferocity greater than anything seen to that point in battle. The fighting continued for another three hours before the ammunition ran out and Colonel Robertson finally withdrew his command to the next level of trenches. When the 12th Ohio noticed the Tennesseans withdrawing, they charged out of the smoke and filled the trenches Robertson's men had so gallantly fought for. After sustaining an enormous number of casualties fighting out in the open, the Union soldiers finally had good cover.

For the next three hours, the shooting never let up on Chestnut Hill. Suddenly, Robertson's Tennesseans withdrew to the highest trenches. The 12th Ohio charged in and once again filled the trenches Robertson's men had withdrawn from. The Union was now halfway up the hill.

The young sharpshooters Hamilton was given charge of really proved their worth by helping to keep the Union troops pinned down. At this point in the battle he still hadn't fired the pistol Lieutenant Barrett had given him. Instead, he helped bring ammunition and water to his boys. He quickly gained the respect of the young fighters in the trenches and it wasn't long before all the young men on this trench became his boys. When one of them got shot, he made sure they were promptly given aid or taken away on a stretcher. A couple of hours into the battle his shiny new dress gray uniform was covered with dirt, blood and blackened with soot.

The soldiers on McClung's cannon batteries were now taking casualties from the increased rifle fire they were getting from the 12th Ohio. At one point, McClung himself signaled Hamilton that he needed replacements on battery number four. Hamilton jumped at the chance to man the big gun. First, he was given the job of brushing and sponging the cannon bore. When the men on the ammo line were called up to replace other injured artillerymen, it was Hamilton who took the initiative.

"Freckles!" he shouted.

"Sir!" Freckle's head rose slightly out of the trench.

Hamilton pointed to the ammunition chest, kept about twenty-five feet behind the cannon. "Form an ammo line and start bringing it up to us! Corporal Bland!"

"Sir!" replied Bland.

"Take charge!"

Bland and the boys put down their rifles and formed an ammo brigade to keep the flow of powder bags and balls going to McClung's cannon battery. When the gunner—the sergeant in charge, of battery number four was shot, Hamilton didn't have to be told to take charge. The 10th Ohio pounded the battery with rifle fire and more rebs fell. Eventually the whole cannon crew of battery number four was made up of the six boys Hamilton brought to the top of Chestnut Hill. After the boys emptied the ammunition chest and found all the others spent, Corporal Bland led them back to the trenchline where they retrieved their rifles.

Suddenly, there was a lull in the shooting. The Union soldiers on the lower trench were almost out of ammunition. Conversely, the Rebs on the top trench had resorted to their pistols.

"We need more ammunition!" A Reb in the trench told Corporal Bland.

"I'm *plum out*!" reported another.

"Make do with what you got!" replied Corporal Bland.

"How do you make do when you're *plum* empty?" asked Fetch.

Bland checked his pistol and realized it was empty. "You don't."

Hamilton fired off the cannon's last round and reported, "That's the last of it." He made a quick head count and showed the relief he felt in his face when all six and old Corporal Bland were present and accounted for. "Who's got ammo?"

Only three hands were raised.

"I got one round," said Freckles, raising his Enfield.

"I'm all out," said Moon.

"One round," said Hoot.

"*Got's* me one," said Red.

The other two boys and Corporal Bland shook their heads. They were out. It was the same for most of the riflemen and artillerymen on the line.

"Well," Hamilton shouted down the line to the other Confederates, "that's it! We're done here. Stay low and fallback to that row of houses down there." He pointed to the row of several logs houses. "Corporal, you take point."

"Come on, boys!" shouted Corporal Bland as he waved his arm. "Let's go home!"

The exhausted defenders retreated smartly down the west side of Chestnut Hill. Corporal Bland led the way to a place that historians would call "Seven Row" with Hamilton taking up the rear.

Hamilton knew the history of this battle and knew what was coming. What he didn't know was that he would play a significant part of this history. Those who could were now running down the hillside. The Rebs were now in full retreat and the Union soldiers were hot on their heels.

Hamilton found a wounded Reb lying on the ground and pulled him to his feet. "Come on!" He put his arm around the Reb's shoulder and they moved as fast as they could. Half way down the hill, he heard the sound of a horse whinnying and pounding of hooves. He glanced over his shoulder and spotted a Union officer riding a horse, leading the 5th Colored and soldiers from the other units down the hillside. The Union officer slashed at the retreating Rebs with his sword. He gave no quarter. Hamilton knew the Union officer was getting closer because the screams from the men he struck were getting louder. At one point, Hamilton stopped, dropped the Reb he had been helping and turned around to face the approaching Calvary officer. Their eyes met and the Calvary officer spurred his horse and pointed his sword at Hamilton. Up to this point in the battle, he hadn't even drawn his pistol, but now he he had no choice. He drew the pistol, cocked the hammer, took aim and pulled the trigger. *Click!* **Misfire!** He pulled back on the hammer again, took aim and pulled the trigger. *Click!* The horse was closing in and everything seemed to go into slow motion. He depressed the trigger and held it in the firing position while he repeatedly cocked the hammer as fast as he could. *Click! Click! Click!* The Calvary officer grunted as he slashed downward with his sword—! ***Bam!*** The sixth and last round fired. The Union officer was struck and fell off his horse.

Hamilton was in a state of shock. The last thing in the world he ever wanted to do was kill a man. "Oh, no! I killed him."

A Reb from Tennessee grabbed the fallen officer's saber and handed it to Hamilton. "Nice *shoot'n*, Sarge! " Together, they picked up the wounded Reb, rushed down the hillside and safely made it across the dirt road and to a place where all of the other Rebs had gathered. This time, it was *they* who were standing in a row out in the open with the enemy bearing down on them.

"Quite a reversal of fortune!" Hamilton said to Corporal Bland. "Now we're on the receiving end."

Colonel Preston, Commander of Saltville, appeared at Seven Row and called out to his men. "Reload and make ready!"

"With what?" one soldier fired back at him.

"We're all out," another said, holding up his Enfield.

"They don't know that," said Hamilton. He made some hand gestures. "Those of you who have a round spread out amongst the ones who don't. The rest of you look like you're armed and ready."

If anything could be said about Confederate Army, even the Home Guard, it was that their soldiers were well disciplined. When an officer gave an order, it was obeyed. Colonel Preston was the ranking officer, but he didn't issue the order. Hamilton did. So the Rebs hesitated until Preston said, "You heard the Sergeant Major!"

Meanwhile at the base of Chestnut Hill, the Union soldiers formed a skirmish line and started marching towards the Rebels, Spencer rifles at the ready!

As the defenders let out a rebel yell, Hamilton drew the only weapon he had—the Union Calvary Officer's saber—and joined in.

Colonel Preston waited until the Union line was as close as he

would dare let get to his force before giving the order. ***"Fire!"***
About forty Rebel rifles and pistols reported, creating a cloud of
cordite. The Union soldiers followed suit by also firing a volley.
When the smoke cleared, the Union soldiers were seen high tailing
it up the side of Chestnut Hill.

"What happened?" asked Corporal Bland.

"They're out of ammo too," said Hamilton with a smile.

Freckles screamed. Blood was streaming from his shoulder.
"Lord have mercy! I've been hit!" He fell to the ground.

Hamilton rushed up to him, then ripped strips from his own shirt
to plug the hole. "Hang on, Freckles."

"That boy needs to get to a field hospital right quick," said
Bland.

"Fetch," said Hamilton, "fetch me a wagon!"

"Yes, sir!" He came back with one in a matter of minutes.

Hamilton picked up Freckles and placed him into the cargo bed.

"The hospital at Emory Henry is miles from here," said
Corporal Bland. "He'll never make it."

"The field hospital at the Sanders Farm is much closer," said
Hamilton.

The look of surprise flashed on the faces of the old Corporal
and the other five boys.

"But there *be* Yankees there!" said Corporal Bland.

"My wife is a nurse there. We'll be okay. Moon, find me a tall
stick," Hamilton started ripping more of his new white shirt.
Moon came along with one and Hamilton tied the white cloth to it
and made a flag of truce.

"Hoot," said Hamilton, "get in and apply pressure on Freckle's
wound, but don't press too hard, hear?"

"I *hear'd ya*." He climbed in and stayed with Freckles.

Hamilton told the other boys, "I'm taking Freckles to the
Sanders Farm. Now, *ya'll* can either come or go home. The battle
is over."

"We're *stay'n* with *y'all, Sarge*," said Moon. The others
nodded in agreement.

"Good. Now throw down your rifles and let's move out."

Hamilton turned to the old Corporal. "You go home."

Bland reached out his hand and Hamilton shook it. "I
will...thanks to you."

THE DOOR

Hamilton took that as a complement for his leadership abilities.

Rifles were all these boys had and they were expensive. Instead of just throwing them down so that anyone could take them, Moon told Matthew to take them to the house they were all living at and wait for them there. Moon showed some smarts and leadership in that move.

Hamilton told Fetch, "Rustle up a couple of stretchers and load them on the wagon." He then took off his gray coat and Kepi hat and put them in the wagon.

On the way up Chestnut Hill, Hamilton had the boys load the most seriously wounded Union soldiers they found into the wagon. He and the remaining three boys carried two injured Union soldiers by stretchers all the way to the Sanders Farm. He cleverly figured that they wouldn't be shot at if some wounded Union soldiers were riding in the wagon or being carried by stretcher. Along the way, they passed the dead Union officer Hamilton had shot. Hamilton stared at the fallen officer and felt numb all over his body. Was it grief or exhaustion or both?

Moon saw the look on Hamilton's face. He had witnessed the shooting. "It *were* either you or him. He *done* gave you no choice *at'll.*" He gestured to the dead Rebs the officer had killed with his saber. "He gave them none."

Hamilton realized Moon was right. It was self-defense. He was on the run. This man came after him. "Thank you for that."

They reached Sanders Farm about an hour later. Hamilton carried Freckles right up to Maggy, who had just completed surgery on a Union soldier. "Can you save my boy, *ma'am?*"

Maggy was horrified by the look of exhaustion on her husband's face. "Oh, my God! Look at you!" She gestured to a table that was being cleared off and washed with soapy water by an orderly. "Put him there." She quickly and expertly removed the bullet and some cloth, irrigated the wound with soapy water, then stitched it up.

Hamilton noticed that his wife made splints out of the wood poles the farm owner used to hang tobacco in his barn to dry.

She handed a bloody saw to Moon. "I want you to cut down as many tree branches you can." She turned to Fetch, Hoot and Red and handed them some knives. "And I want you boys to whittle them down so I can use them as splints. Can *y'all* do that?" She could turn her Southern accent on and off without even thinking about it.

"Yes, ma'am!" said Moon.

"What's a splint?" asked Red.

*　　*　　*

The day Lomax lied to Daphne that the client's severance pay had run out, he drove his Hot Diggity Dog Electric Man van out of his garage and filled it with tools and supplies. He had Daphne design and print a batch of business cards and flyers. For a couple of hundred bucks in postage, he canvassed most of the residential areas in Marion, Chilhowie and Atkins. It was January. Heating systems failed. He got calls right away and word of mouth got him almost more business than he could handle. He found himself working seven days a week.

He confined himself to doing residential electrical work, where he wouldn't be so noticed. That was because most of the work was inside of a house or in the backyard, where prying eyes would have a hard time watching. He also moved around a lot, working from house to house and town to town. He had mouths to feed, including a baby, bills to pay, two houses to maintain and there was plenty of work available.

The New Year came and went and Lomax began to think that the CIA wasn't looking for him or the missing doors anymore. It was a cold winter with lots of snow. Since the Hot Diggity Dog Electric Man had rewired Daphne's house during its renovation and now lived next door, no one gave it much thought to see him taking down Christmas lights from her house—especially since she was a hot looking single mom—except the Pilgrims.

Mary and Israel were gazing out the bay window of their living room and watching Lomax talking to Daphne, who was holding the baby.

"Those two an item?" he asked.

"Can't you tell? He sneaks over late at night and goes home just before sunrise."

"Lucky guy. What's his name?"

"Eddi Dane."

"A real dog of a name, isn't it?" He was trying to be funny.

Mary had a sparkle in her eyes. "He's no dog."

"I like Daphne," said Israel. "We've had a five percent increase in business since we hired her to build our web site."

"I told you she's good!"

"When it warms up, let's have a barbecue and invite them over."

Always vigilant for a car that would pass his van more than once or a wandering eye from someone who wasn't a local, Lomax noticed a lot of activity at a house on Lake Street. Cars driven by teenagers with community college parking stickers on the rear windows were frequenting this ranch house at all hours of the day and night. They would pull in, then a passenger would get out, ring the doorbell, go inside and return a few minutes later, rubber-necking as they double-timed to the car. They must have been on drugs because they were so obvious and stupid.

Detective Dewey Mitchell received an envelope in the mail with no return address. Inside the bubble padded envelope was a DVD and a typed note. "Nail this drug dealer, will *ya*. Signed, a friend." He showed the DVD to the Chief, who in turn authorized a sting operation with the help of several drug investigators from a neighboring town's police department. It was hoped that they wouldn't be recognized and generally they weren't. They made several buys, ran chemical analysis to determine their authenticity as illegal narcotics and then Dewey raided the house. As Dewey stepped out of the house, he scanned the power poles across the street with his binoculars and spotted the same black box with a camera lens that he found on a light pole in the PD's parking lot. "Lomax." He gave it a wave. Three days later, he drove by the house he raided and once again scanned the power pole for the black box. It was gone.

The big news of the year was the kidnapping of a little girl from a day care center just outside the town limits. The news media made it their big story and every law enforcement agency in the area got together to find the little girl.

It had been over thirty hours since the incident and there were no solid leads.

Dewey was in the squad room at the Sheriff's Office when the cell phone Diciembre had given him started to ring. He excused himself and went into the shift commander's office for some privacy. "Dewey Mitchell," he said into the phone.

"Well, good evening, Detective," said a voice he never heard before.

"Who is this?"

"Oh, I think you know?"

"Lomax?" He waited a few seconds, but got no reply. "This was supposed to be a secure cell...."

"If there is anything that I have learned in this life is that nothing in this world is secure."

"Look, this is not the time for us to talk. I'm in the middle of a major case—."

"—The little girl is okay. Go to 327 Greenbriar Street. I'd put the owner on the phone, but he's all tied up right now." *Click!* Lomax hung up.

Dewey came out of the office, speaking into his radio. "Delta Two to Central. Dispatch all units to 327 Greenbriar Street, Code 3!"

Both the Sheriff and MPD Chief were in the squad room coordinating operations. They were instantly pissed off that Dewey jumped the gun and dispatched units before they were consulted first.

Dewey held up the cell phone he got from Diciembre and that made the Chief and Sheriff hesitate. "You're not going to believe this. Lomax made the call. He found the missing girl."

When Dewey arrived with the parents of the missing girl, the press was already there, thanks to an anonymous caller. The little girl had been wrapped in a warm blanket and given an ice cream cone to eat, while she watched cartoons on the TV. The kidnapper was hand and leg cuffed to a wooden support beam, which was next to the breaker box. A bare wire was wrapped around his head and hanging loose in the air, the end of which was less than an inch from the exposed wire on the breaker box. Every time he moved the slightest or took a deep breath, a connection was made to a bare wire in the breaker box and he got a jolt. His hair was already singed. Both the Chief and Sheriff laughed when they saw the way the kidnapper was secured.

"Looks like we have a Good Samaritan out there," Chief Grayson said to Dewey.

"I think he's trying to make a friend," said the Sheriff. "Watch yourself."

THE DOOR

Dewey Mitchell's picture was on the front page of all the local newspapers as he handed the little girl to her mother.

The former Lead Agent from the Marion "farm" handed Deputy Director Blackburn a newspaper with Mitchell's picture on the cover.

"What do we have here—another example of Lomax's handiwork?" asked Blackburn.

"The creep they arrested was a wanted sex offender on the run. Lomax led the cops right to him. He probably saved the little girl's life. Should we resume our search of him?"

"No. Lomax is letting us know he's there in Marion and not causing us any trouble. Besides, he's no longer our prime target. The doors are. I think it's time we briefed Detective Mitchell about Project Door…."

*   *   *

Hamilton heard screams coming from the other side of Chestnut Hill. It would be the first of many he and the others at the Sanders Farm would hear for the next hour or so. He had washed his coat and hung it out to dry on a clothesline along with rags and torn clothing. He had just washed and disinfected his white shirt, or what was left of it and hung it on the clothesline to dry. It would be used as gauze. He now wore a new shirt. The daughter of the owner of the Sanders Farm was so grateful to Hamilton for suggesting that she and her children hide in the fireplace during the battle, that she rewarded him with one of her husband's shirts. He yawned as he rubbed his eyes and face. He was bone tired. The sun was going down on the most adventurous and horrifying day of his life. *Was it all a bad dream!* No, it was real and he had been a part of it. He had been given the job of keeping the fires going at the kettles. His attention was averted when he heard his wife yelling at someone. She could be heard clear across the farm, arguing with a Yankee surgeon. Hamilton decided to see what was going on. He filled up a washbasin with hot soapy water and brought it to the front yard where she had been working most of the day.

"Why are you putting those disgusting maggots on a wound?" the old chief surgeon surgeon asked Maggy.

"This soldier was shot four days ago and the butcher who

removed the bullet did a lousy job of closing the wound," she replied. "It's infected. Maggots are sterile and they only eat dead tissue. They clean out a wound better than anything you have here!"

"Preposterous! I've never heard of such a thing."

She moved to another operating table, where a young soldier was moaning in pain. He had been shot in the leg.

"Orderly," said the old surgeon, "hand me a saw."

The young soldier reached out to Maggy. "I've seen what you've done with the others. Please, don't take off my leg. Please!"

"Orderly," she said, "belay that order."

"Can't you see the bone is shattered?" asked the old surgeon. "The leg must be amputated. Now hand me that saw!"

It was then she spotted her husband walking towards her. "Ham, I'm going to need you to hold him down. I've run out of Chloroform."

"Now see here," said the old surgeon, "you're a nurse and I'm the chief surgeon—."

"—You either assist me or get lost. Which one is it going to be?"

The old surgeon shot a glance to Hamilton, who was holding the steamy washbasin. "Sir, if you continue to burn my hands with your scalding hot water—."

Hamilton put down the washbasin and inserted his hands into the soapy water. "—And baby bear said, not too hot, not too cold, just right."

The old doctor relented and washed his hands before assisting Maggy.

Hamilton then brought Maggy a second washbasin of saline water and placed it on the operating table. He then picked up the bottle of Iodine and found that it was empty. "Is this why you wanted salty water?"

"No choice. I've run out of Iodine and if there's one thing they got a lot of around here in Saltville is salt. It will sting like the dickens, but it will kill the germs."

When Maggy gave a nod in the patient's direction—indicating that she was ready, Hamilton slid his arms under the soldier's armpit and held him down while she went to work, first cutting a three-inch long incision in the flesh with a knife. Next she irrigated the wound with saline water. She then used her latex gloved hand—one of the last she had—and a pair of forceps (fortunately, she always kept a pair on her lab coat) to search for any foreign material such as paper wadding or pieces of clothing. She removed the bullet and gave it a look. "It's intact."

"Thank you, Lord!" said Hamilton.

Maggy once again flushed the wound with saline water to its total depth. She then went in with her fingers and forceps to push the shattered bone back together. The bullet had broken the bone, but fortunately the chips were still attached. In the future, surgeons would drill pins and even super glue bones together. But none of that was available. She was accustomed to using catgut, which was still used to close wounds in her time. But this time she wrapped it around the chipped bone and tied it up as tight as any modern surgeon could. Her years of experience in the operating room really paid off today. The old Yankee surgeon watched everything Maggy did and was speechless. He'd never seen a surgical procedure like this before. After once again irrigating the wound with saline, she closed it and tied very tight splints around the leg. The soldier screamed through most of the procedure, but once Maggy tied on the splints, the pain subsided. "That bone needs time to heal," she told the soldier. "These splints don't come off for two months, you hear me, soldier?"

The soldier passed out before he could answer.

"You expect the bone to mend?" asked the old surgeon.

"Yes, Doctor. It will if he stays off it, changes the dressing daily and keeps this splint on, it should heal up…in time."

"*Where'd* you learn to do this?" asked the Doctor.

"Oh, I married a carpenter." She winked at Hamilton.

The old doctor took a moment to survey the front yard. He couldn't count how many wounded soldiers had splints on their arms and legs. The other thing he noticed was that there were significantly fewer amputated limbs near Maggy's operating tables than where his surgeons did their work. He thought that some orderly had taken them away, but there was no tell-tale sign of bloodstain on the ground where the pile would have been or cloud of hovering flies. Also, Maggy's patients seemed to be more at ease than the others. Losing a limb was far more traumatic than the surgical procedure Maggy employed on her patients.

THE DOOR

"You performed a similar procedure with all these men?" he asked Maggy, gesturing to the patients lying on the ground nearby.

"Yes."

He angrily shook his finger at her. "If these men die, it will be all on your head. Not mine!" With that he retired to the farmhouse.

"You look tired," Hamilton said to Maggy.

"I am."

It was then they heard a man scream in the distance, towards Chestnut Ridge. Soon thereafter, another screamed. The screaming continued every few minutes for about an hour.

"What is causing that?" asked Maggy.

"I think I know," said Hamilton. "And I hope I'm wrong. Champus Fragg...."

"And you thought he was a hero. You and your yearning for chivalry.... In war, there's no such thing."

A column of Union soldiers marched towards the Hamiltons and stopped. General Burbridge's personal aide de camp presented himself to Maggy and doffed his kepi respectfully. "The General would like to have a word with you, ma'am."

Maggy gestured to Hamilton. "This is my husband. May he join us?"

"Yes, ma'am." The aide gestured to the sword in Hamilton's scabbard and the holstered pistol. "As soon as he hands over his sword and pistol." This was the first time someone asked for his weapons.

Hamilton handed the pistol first to the aide, then the sword. There was a lot of dried blood on the sword. "This belonged to a Union Calvary officer who tried to kill me."

They were taken to a row of tents that had flags with the company regiment and battalion colors. The aide poked his head into a tent that was lit up with lanterns and said something.

General Burbridge came out of his tent, buttoning his coat. "I wanted to thank you for all the medical care you provided to my men," he said to Maggy.

"You're welcome," replied Maggy.

He held out his hand and she shook it firmly. "Thank you." The General turned to Hamilton. "Thank you both."

"Our pleasure, General," said Hamilton.

THE DOOR

"Your accent, sir," said the General. "You're not from around here. More like Massachusetts."

"We live here," replied Maggy. "And we love it here, but we're not from here."

"When this terrible war is over," said the General, "I can imagine it being a beautiful place." He gave a nod and started to turn.

"General," said Hamilton, "may I have a word with you? In private?"

Burbridge walked off with Hamilton until they reached a quiet place in the yard, out of earshot from everyone else.

"General," said Hamilton, "when your force arrived here last night, you stopped at Broadford to give your men a rest." Hamilton pointed to the north in the general direction of a small community called Broadford, which was about seven miles away. "You shouldn't have."

"Oh? And why not?"

"There were only 400 Home Guard on duty in Saltville at the time, mostly old men and barefooted boys. You could have walked right in and taken the place probably without firing a shot. The delay gave your counterpart, General Breckenridge, time to bring in every man he had to fill those trenches."

"I…didn't know." Burbridge's face showed his regret.

"How many Rebs do you think there are in these parts, sir?"

Burbridge thought for a moment. "Twenty, thirty thousand…"

Hamilton shook his head. "Less than three."

Burbridge was shocked. "How is that possible? With the way your men engaged us today, there must have been at least five thousand—."

"No more than seven hundred, maybe eight. The North has more men and you march them on foot. Breckinridge doesn't. He uses the railroad to concentrate his forces. That's the secret to his success. Rapid transit and concentration of forces."

This was all news to Burbridge and it made a lot of sense.

"But none of that matters in the slightest, General."

"Oh? And what does?"

"Salt. Without salt the South is doomed. This is the last place they can get it. Destroy the saltworks and the North wins the war."

This was not the first time the General heard this, but coming from a man who earlier in the day was fighting on the other side, defending the very saltworks in question, heightened its importance. If the South didn't need Saltville and its saltworks they wouldn't have fought as viciously as they had today.

Burbridge may have lost a battle today, but he was smart enough to know when a man like Hamilton had something important to say. "Go on."

"It doesn't matter how many trains Breckenridge has. When your strategy is to concentrate all available forces to meet the enemy head on, you can only do that one place at a time. If you want to take Saltville without firing a shot, make Breckinridge's trains go somewhere else...."

Hamilton revealed more information than Burbridge would get from all the spies the Union had operating in Southwest Virginia and Northeast Tennessee. He turned and walked off, leaving the General standing there, lost in thought.

The General's personal aide swept past Hamilton in a big hurry. It made the old carpenter curious enough to turn around and listen.

"General, they just brought in General Schofield's aide!"

"The Major?"

"Yes, sir. He was shot."

"How? He was with me during the whole battle."

"After the battle, he went into the field to help remove the wounded and then a crazy Reb Calvary Captain shot him."

"Fool! He's an observer not a combatant!" Burbridge was furious. He and his aide rushed past Hamilton, who took off after them.

When Maggy opened the blood soaked coat of the Major, she wasn't surprised to see a bullet hole dead center of the man's heart. "There's nothing I can do for this officer," she said to the Chief Surgeon, who stood beside her.

"Send for the Chaplain," the Chief Surgeon said to an orderly.

When Hamilton came along side Maggy at the operating table he gazed into the face of the Major the look of surprise flashed across his face. "No! No! This can't be! Danvers?" He backed away, shaking his head.

"Ham, what's wrong?" asked Maggy.

Hamilton pointed to the Major. "It can't be him." He moved back to the table for a second look.

THE DOOR

"You know this man…?" A thought flashed through Maggy's mind. "From here…or…?"

He turned to her and gave a look that said it all. "Or…."

Maggy's eyes widened.

"Let me die," said the Major. "Please, I beg of you."

A Chaplain went up to the Major and said, "I'm here, my son."

"Father, I repent all my sins. I'm sorry for what I've done."

But when the Chaplain stepped into the light and the Major got a good look at him, he screamed louder than any man who had been brought to the Sanders Farm during and after the battle.

"Get away from me—you bastard!" shouted the Major.

"But my son, I am here to give you comfort," said the Chaplain.

"I reject your comfort! And I reject you and all your evil!" The Major leaned forward and started to climb off the table, which was the rear door of the Sanders Farmhouse. "Do you hear me? Be gone, Devil! Be gone I say!" At this point, the Major collapsed back onto the table. "God, please forgive me for what I've done and let me die in peace!"

Hamilton grabbed the Chaplain by the arm and pulled, but it was like grabbing a heavy bolder. The arm or the man didn't move. "What are you doing to him?"

The Chaplain turned and walked off without replying. Hamilton went after him. "Hey, wait!" But the Chaplain took off with great speed, almost inhuman. Hamilton could not keep up with him and stopped. The Chaplain also stopped, slowly turned around and stared at Hamilton. He had a smile on his face that sent chills throughout the old carpenter's body.

"Ham!" shouted Maggy. "I need you!"

Hamilton turned and rushed to the aid of his wife. He was shocked to see the Major sitting up on the operating table, with Maggy hovering over him, trying to make him lay down.

"No, you're not alright!" she shouted.

"Madam, I can assure you that I will live on," said the Major.

"How, when you've been shot clear through the heart?"

The Major pulled his hand away from his chest and held out a lead ball to Maggy. "Yes, I know. But I will mend." He dropped the lead ball into her hand. In another surprising move, he stood up, buttoned his coat and then stiffened to attention in front of a shocked Burbridge. "Request permission to return to my duties,

General."

It was too much for Maggy. She became light headed and collapsed into Hamilton's arms, but didn't faint.

"Granted." Burbridge didn't know what else to say.

The Major walked away with a spring to his step.

Hamilton turned to Burbridge. "General, who is that officer?"

"We can't tell you…you're a Reb!" said Burbridge's aide.

"His name is Nathaniel Pilgrim," said the General.

Hamilton and Maggy turned to each other and said in unison, "Pilgrim?"

There was a thick mist in the air the next morning. General Burbridge and his staff were all packed and ready to go. He gave a wave to Hamilton and Maggy as he rode by them on his horse.

"God be with you both," said Burbridge.

"And with you, General," said Hamilton.

The General's aide presented himself to the Hamiltons. He gestured to the horse and wagon on his left. "Complements of the General." The aide also handed Hamilton the sword they had confiscated. It was cleaned and sharpened. "I was also ordered to give you this." He also presented Hamilton with Barrett's pistol. It too was cleaned and loaded.

"Thank you," said Hamilton, as he holstered the gun.

"The General heard that you intend to go to the Reb hospital at the college."

"That's right," said Hamilton.

The aide faced Maggy. "A lot of our wounded will be going there too. The General had me round up what I could so that you can tend to them." The aide gestured to the Quarter Master and several privates standing by an assembly of crates and wood barrels. "The Quarter-Master will see to your provisions."

Maggy noticed that her husband wasn't wearing his dress gray coat. "Where's your coat?" she asked. "Your prized possession?"

"Oh, I don't think I want to wear that thing anymore."

"This is about to become Reb territory again and winter is coming. So, put it on, soldier."

"You're right, as always, ma'am." He went over the clothesline and pulled off his coat. But he didn't put it on.

Next, he went to the tent where the boys were sleeping and

awakened them. "Fetch?"

"Yes, sir?" rubbing his eyes.

"We need a bale of hay."

"One bale?"

"Two would be better," said Hamilton.

Two of the three bales of hay Fetch acquired were spread out on the floor of the cargo bed of the wagon. An Army blanket was spread out on top of it. An unconscious Freckles was laid onto the blanket. He would survive his wounds, but he had lost a lot of blood and was very pale and weak.

Maggy was now sleeping on the ground.

Hamilton gently awakened her. "Time to go, Maggy." He pick her up and carried her to the wagon.

"Where are we going?" asked Maggy, in a low voice that showed her exhaustion.

He helped her onto the wagon's cargo bed. Only then did the Hamiltons realize all that General Burbridge had provided them. Two folded A-Tents, a barrel of salted beef, a fifty pound sack of beans, two sacks of flour and cornmeal, four bushels of potatoes, a wooden box filled with tins of salt, pepper, tea, and a couple dozen candles, a large frying pan—the kind used by the US Infantry, a coffee pot with a box containing tins of Chase and Sandborn Coffee, a box of eating utensils and enough metal plates and cups for a dozen settings that came from the Officers Mess, a dozen pillows and blankets, two sacks of oats for the horse, and spare sets of horseshoes, pliers and nails. There was also a box filled with bottles of chloroform and a generous supply of bandages.

Maggy was shocked by it all. "There's more chloroform here than what I had to work with here at the farm. What did you tell the General?"

"*Ah,* nothing honey. Just how to put and end this damn war."

It was then, the wounded called out to her one last time.

"Good bye, ma'am!"

"God bless you, ma'am!"

"You saved my leg!"

Maggy was touched by the affection the wounded soldiers gave to her. One and all waved goodbye to her as Moon drove the wagon onto a dusty road that led back to Chestnut Ridge. She then realized something as the last of the mounted Union officers and headed north. "Ham, they're leaving the wounded behind!"

"Burbridge has no choice," said Hamilton. "They barely have enough ammo to load their guns. And they're going to have to ride hard and fast to reach to the Union lines." He nodded in the direction of the wounded. "The Rebs will bring the most seriously wounded to the field hospital at Emory and Henry College. You'll be seeing most of these boys again."

Once away from the Sanders Farm, she lay down on a blanket next to Freckles and fell fast asleep.

A few minutes later, Moon spotted a lone Union Officer standing in the middle of the dirt road, walking his horse.

"There *be* a Yankee up ahead," Moon said to Hamilton.

Hamilton, who was walking with Hoot, Fetch and Red along side the wagon, stopped when he recognized the Yankee officer Moon was referring to. It was the Major who had been shot in the heart.

"My God!" Hamilton said softly. "Him again!" He then told Moon to stop.

Major Pilgrim confronted Hamilton and handed a heavy haversack. "Here, take this. You'll be needing it."

Hamilton opened the haversack and noted some tin cans, a couple of pounds of jerky wrapped in paper and a Quartermaster's money bag. He removed the bag and opened it. To his surprise, there was a bundle of Union Currency and a lot of loose change.

"The boys took up a collection…in appreciation for the lady's services. And there's something from the General…and me."

"I know you…from the future. But how is that possible?"

"Sir, I have no idea what you're talking about." Pilgrim turned, went over to the horse and gave it a sharp slap on the hind quarter and yelped, ***"Yaaaaaaahhhhh!"***

The horse and wagon took off.

As soon as the wagon crossed the ford in the North Holston, Hamilton put on his coat. The corpses of 5th Colored Regiment covered the battlefield. The carnage was horrific. It left Hamilton and the boys speechless.

When they were rolling by "Seven Row", the place where the Confederates made their last stand against the Union Army, Moon spotted the old Corporal and rode over to him. Corporal Bland was drinking from a jug and was slightly drunk.

THE DOOR

"I thought I told you to go home," Hamilton said to Bland

Bland gestured to one of the seven log houses. "This is my home. Be glad you were elsewhere last night. It was terrible."

"What was?"

"Remember when I told you that the captain '*did other thanks*?" Hamilton nodded. "I remember."

"Well, he done shot every *darkie* soldier he found alive. Whites too."

"Fragg!" said Hamilton.

"That *be* his name."

The old Corporal spotted Maggy sleeping in the cargo bed. "I see you found your Mrs.."

"Yes, thank God!"

"Take care, Sergeant Major. It was a pleasure serving with *ya*."

"Same here, Corporal."

Hamilton gave a tap to the side of the wagon. "Let's go."

Moon drove the wagon to a shack where "silent" Matthew was anxiously waiting for them. He was so excited to see them he leapt into the air.

"What's this?" asked Hamilton.

"This *be* our home." replied Fetch.

"Are you brothers?" asked Hamilton.

"No," replied Red.

"But, where are your parents?"

"They *be* dead," replied Hoot.

"All of them?"

None of the boys replied as they started off towards the shack. The look of sadness was painted on their dirty faces. They liked the Hamiltons and did not want to part from them.

"Wait," said Hamilton, making a command decision. "No. No, we're not going to do this. *Y'all* staying with me...I mean...you're staying with us. So, get back over here."

The boys became excited and smiled as they ran back to the wagon. They then waved to Matthew and shouted, "*Come on!*"

Matthew brought out their Enfield muskets from the shack and loaded them onto the wagon. Hamilton rewarded Matthew with some jerky. The boy ate ravenously. He was very hungry.

Later on, as the wagon rolled by the Stuart House and the door by which both Maggy and Hamilton had come to this place and time, an eerie feeling ran through both their bodies. It was enough to awaken Maggy.

She got up on her knees and pointed to the front door of the Stuart house. "There it is! The door I came through."

"Me too."

She was surprised that Moon was driving away from the Stuart house. "We're not stopping?"

"Nope."

"Well, where are we going then?"

"To the field hospital at Emory and Henry College. That's where the other door is...or should be."

She gestured to the front door of the Stuart house. "But there's the door! It's our way out of here!"

"Yes, but we can't open it. Not without Allison. We need that little girl to take us home."

"How do you know we'll find her at Emory and Henry?"

"I don't. But I got a gut feeling that is where she went. You see...I recognized that other door they off-loaded from the train. It's from the old Puritan Church at Salem Village."

"But the church was demolished..."

"Not all of it. Honey, somehow, someway, that church door has something to do with you and I ending up here. I can't explain it. I just know it!" He then realized that she had fallen asleep. He climbed onto the wagon, sat down next to Maggy and put his arm around her shoulder. For the first time in three months, he slept with Maggy and it felt wonderful.

During the eleven mile trip to the college, Moon drove the wagon passed a burnt out wood frame house, where the only thing standing was a door. He was too tired and busy to notice the door open and a young girl wearing a red costume stepping out. When Allison recognized Ham and Maggy Hamilton riding in the back of a wagon, she smiled, spun on her heels and went back to where she came from and closed the door.

Chapter Ten

☆ THE HAMILTON WAY ☆

It was Richard's first birthday party

and several friends and neighbors were invited, including Daphne and her neighbor.

Israel had already fired up the gas grill and was burning steaks and ribs. Lomax was all smiles as he went through the house, trying hard not to look at the colorful curtains covering the doorways to the rooms. Eventually, he was led to the outside patio. "Howdy," he said to Israel.

Israel reached out and shook hands with Lomax. "Well, we finally get to meet our famous neighbor from across the street."

"The name is Eddi Dane."

"Israel Pilgrim. You drink beer?"

"Oh, yeah!"

"Help yourself then."

Lomax reached into a vat of iced beers for a cold one and popped the cap. "Nice place you have here."

"Been in the family for ages."

"Well, they don't make them like they used to."

"Would you like a tour of the place?"

Lomax smiled. "Yeah, sure. I'd love to."

Still smiling, Lomax exchanged a glance at Daphne and gave her a wink. The last thing he wanted to do was to be seen in public, but everyone who came knew him personally from all the houses he had worked on. That is, except one person.

"Dewey!" said Mary.

Lomax almost choked on his beer.

"You okay?" Israel asked him.

He raised his free hand. "Fine. I'm fine."

Mitchell came out onto the patio and Israel made the introductions.

THE DOOR

"Dewey Mitchell meet our neighbor Eddi Dane."

They shook hands.

Mary interrupted. "Honey, that's Sergeant Dewey Mitchell."

There was some "ohs" and "ahs" from the other guests. His promotion had not been made public.

"Oh," asked Lomax, "are you in the Army?"

"No, local police department."

"Come on Dewey," said Mary, "show us your gold badge."

"All right, all right." He pulled out his shiny new gold Detective Sergeant Badge and held it high for everyone to see. Pilgrims and their guests whooped and cheered. Mitchell was popular in Marion.

"Congratulations," one gray haired man said. "You deserve to get promoted after saving that little girl's life."

Lomax and Daphne exchanged a glance.

Mitchell raised his hand. "No, no, no. Don't go there. Now hear me out, people. I can't take the credit for the work done by someone else. Whoever called and told me where that little girl was…is the real hero. Not me."

Lomax was impressed with Mitchell's statement.

A short time later, the steaks and ribs were served and the beer flowed.

Hours passed and Lomax was actually laughing at Mitchell's cop jokes and Israel's corny carpenter stories. Everybody was having a good time. Some of the women were commenting how much Daphne's baby resembled "Eddi" and what a "cute couple you two make." Lomax wouldn't admit it to Daphne but Richard's birthday party was the most fun he had had in years…if ever. For the first time in his life he felt welcomed by people who were kind, hardworking and decent. It was then he realized that the world he had been living in was a truly lousy and lonely place to be.

And he and Israel had hit it off.

"How about that tour?" asked Lomax.

"Wait until you see the antiques in the basement," said Mitchell.

There was only one interior door in the Pilgrim House and it led to the basement. Mary insisted that a new metal door be installed there to prevent the baby from falling down the stairs. Israel flipped the switch to turn on the lights in the basement, then opened the door and led the way downstairs.

THE DOOR

It was the only floor Lomax did not bug or venture into. He didn't see the need, nor did his former client. He was shocked at what he found down there.

"My grandfather was a great carpenter, a sainted man and one heck of a good sculptor."

The upper floors had a number of Christian symbols on the walls, but nothing to the number that existed in the basement. Half the floor of the basement was covered with wooden religious sculptures of famous Christian figures, such as Jesus Christ. The tallest sculptures were covered with dusty white sheets.

"Your grandfather made all of these?" asked Lomax.

"Yes. When he retired, he spent most of his golden years down here, whittling away at wood."

"Very life-like," said Lomax.

It was Mitchell who noticed something right off about the statues. "Why are they all facing that wall?" He gestured to the west wall of the basement.

Israel was taken aback by that question. "I don't know. This is the first I've noticed it. My father also did some of the sculptures down here. But when he died, I just left the place alone. As a matter-of-fact, I haven't been down here in years."

Lomax became excited when he found all kinds of antique wood crafting tools and books. "This stuff must be hundreds of years old."

"Grandpa said that they were used to build this house…in 1864."

"During the war?" asked Mitchell.

"The Civil War?" asked Lomax.

"That's the one."

"Look at this!" exclaimed Lomax as he pointed to the long saw hanging from the ceiling. It was a two-man buck saw, with a twenty-foot blade that was used to split logs. "Now this is ancient!"

"It was used by my Puritan ancestors when they owned a saw mill in Massachusetts."

"Where in Massachusetts?" asked Mitchell.

"A little town called Salem Village. But they don't call it that anymore."

"What do they call it?" asked Lomax.

THE DOOR

"Danvers," answered Israel. He then made a face. "You know, I just realized that the lawyer representing Ham's silent partner was a man named Danvers...."

"Small world," said Lomax.

Mitchell made a face. "Is it just me, or is it hot in here?"

"It's always warm down here," said Israel. "We hardly have to put on the heat during the winter." He tapped the brick wall on west side of the basement—the one all the religious sculptures faced. "There must be an underground stream near this wall. It's always giving off heat."

Both Mitchell and Lomax touched the wall and exchanged a glance. They then turned around to face all the Christian figures that were so life-like and staring back at them.

A week later, Israel hired Eddi Dane to do some electrical work at the factory.

When Dewey returned to work from his two-week vacation the next month, he found a private security company ripping down drywall at the PD in search of surveillance cameras and microphones. "What's going on Chief?" he asked Chief Grayson.

"Our friends have pulled the plug on all of their covert ops in this area and I've decide to clean out all the bugs in this building once and for all." He held up a pinhole camera. "This one was in my private restroom."

Dewey would have loved to make the comment that since the Chief had a urinary problem and made a lot of cell phone calls from his private restroom. It was a logical place to put a microphone, but not a camera. That was low, even for the CIA.

"No more funding from our friends either," continued the Chief, "and no more Washington bull. Just plain *ole* police work."

"I'm for that, Chief."

"Besides, Lomax is long gone. I tried to tell them...."

Mitchell nodded. "He flew the coop a long time ago. But they wouldn't listen. I mean, we're just small town cops. What do we know?"

*   *   *

THE DOOR

When Moon drove the wagon through the entrance of the Emory and Henry College, he had to be careful not to collide with or run down any of the Confederate and Union Soldiers trying to make their way into the place. There were a lot more wounded soldiers here than at the Sanders Farm. Many of them had walked for miles to reach this hospital. Many succumbed on the way. Among them were prisoners of war from the 5th Colored Regiment.

"Sergeant," called out Moon. "Sergeant Major, we *be* arriving at Emory and Henry."

Both Hamilton and Maggy were awakened. They got up for a look.

"Looks like I'll be busy for a while," she said.

Moon pulled the wagon to a stop and Hamilton helped his wife off the wagon.

Hamilton turned to the boys and asked, "Any of those rifles loaded?"

Silent Matthew answered by shaking his head.

Hamilton drew his Remington pistol and handed it to Moon. "Here. You take this." He then buried the haversack in the hay to hide it. "Now you guard this wagon and especially that haversack with your life. *Hear?*" The boys said 'yes' and Hamilton went into the closest building, which was a dormitory. There, to his dismay, he found Lieutenant Barrett, lying on the floor. He had been shot in the upper right shoulder and had a bandage over his wound. "Lieutenant? You all right, sir?"

"I'll be fine, Sergeant Major." Barrett grinned as he gestured to Hamilton's soiled and torn dress gray uniform. "Well, you certainly look like the rest of us now."

Hamilton smiled. "Thank God for that, sir. I had grown tired of being called a General."

"I had aspired to be a General…one day."

"And you'll be a good one too, sir!"

Suddenly, a woman screamed and went running through the room.

Hamilton turned around to see Captain Champus Fragg standing in the doorway, pistol in his hand.

"Where *be* the *darkie* soldiers?" shouted Fragg. "Show me where they are!"

"You have no business here!" replied Barrett, as he struggled to

THE DOOR

get to his feet. "This is a hospital— "

When Fragg spotted a wounded colored soldier, he shot him dead. The shot was heard throughout the dormitory.

Maggy came running into the room and shouted, "Someone stop him!"

Fragg went charging through the room shooting every black Union soldier he came upon.

Barrett raised his hands. "Captain—for God's sake—stop!"

One colored soldier tried to get away and ran into Barrett.

Fragg shot the colored soldier in the back at point blank range. The bullet went right through the colored soldier and stuck Barrett in the chest. Both men fell to their deaths on a large operating table.

Fragg's pistol was now empty. He resorted to his sword.

Hamilton drew his sword and engaged Fragg.

"Get out of my way or I'll run you through!" shouted Fragg as he deflected one strike after another.

Hamilton had been fencing for years and demonstrated this talent to Fragg, forcing him to back off towards the doorway. "You're not so tough without a gun…are you?"

Everyone, Reb and Union soldier alike cheered when Fragg retreated out of the building. Some even called him a coward.

When Hamilton turned and went up to the operating table Barrett and the colored soldier were laying on, he realized that it was the church double door that was shipped from Massachusetts. Both the blood from the colored soldier and from Lieutenant Barrett mingled and flowed and filled the cracks and crevasses in the wood. There was one spot on the door where a word was carved into the wood. It was located on the lower left side of the door and just below the postal shipping slip—the one with Cornelius Pilgrim's name and address hand written on it. This carving only became visible when it filled with blood.

Maggy came alongside of her husband and stared at the two men lying dead on the makeshift operating room table. "Is this the church door…you talked about?"

Hamilton couldn't answer. He was shocked and heartbroken about the fact that a fine young man like Lieutenant Barrett had died right in front of him.

Both Maggy and Hamilton watched as the carving in the door

THE DOOR

filled with blood and spelled the word: "Hell". At that precise moment, someone rang a bell at a local church.

Maggy pointed to the blood filled carving and said, "I've heard that there are eight doors to Heaven, but one to Hell. I hope this isn't it."

"And what if it is?"

"Then we're doomed!"

The killing did not stop there.

A shot was fired. A horse whinnied. Moon and several other boys started yelling. Three ragged men stood in front of the wagon, one had his hands on the horse's bridle. The other two were armed with muskets, but it was obvious by the fact that they didn't pull the hammers back that the rifles were empty. However, the bayonets at the end of the rifle barrels still posed a threat to the boys.

Maggy looked out the window and saw what was going on. "Ham, the boys are in trouble!"

Moon rested the barrel of the pistol that Hamilton had given him on his left forearm and was taking deadly aim at the man who held the bridle. "I will shoot you, Mister."

Hamilton drew the pistol out of Lieutenant Barrett's holster and went outside. He cocked the hammer back as he approached his wagon. "What's going on here?"

"You stay out of this," the man in the center said. He was obviously the leader of the three. He and the third man took aim with their muskets at Hamilton, but didn't fire.

Four of the five boys were pointing their muskets at the three men, growling and yelling at them to, "Let go of our horse!"

"This here is a Yankee horse," declared the leader, "and I aim to take it."

"No you won't," said Moon.

"You either let me have it now," warned the leader, "or there will be another day—."

"—Oh, no there won't." Hamilton raised the pistol and shot and killed the two rebs who were aiming their muskets at him.

Moon shot the leader right between the eyes and blew off the back of his head.

"So much for chivalry," said Hamilton.

*   *   *

THE DOOR

Just as the killing wasn't over for Hamilton, the intrigue with the CIA wasn't over for Mitchell either. He was supposed to be on a stake out at a suspected meth lab operating just inside the town limits. It was the CIA who identified and reported the lab to Mitchell, just before they pulled out. The Chief rewarded Mitchell by authorizing him to form a team of investigators and supervising the surveillance of the drug lab.

The one thing the sworn personnel at the police department liked about Dewey Mitchell was that he was hands-on all the way. They were not surprised when he took a night shift to give his stakeout team a break. However, tonight a CIA agent would take his place while he met secretly with Diciembre. No one at MPD knew he was still communicating with the Agency.

Mitchell was surprised to see Diciembre driving a junkie old station wagon.

"Get in the back seat," said Diciembre. "We're going for a little drive."

Mitchell did and Diciembre drove off.

Diciembre passed him two manila folders. The one on top had **TOP SECRET: PROJECT DOOR** printed on the cover.

"Project Door?" asked Mitchell. "Now that's original!"

"Shut up and open it." Diciembre turned on the interior light.

The first thing Mitchell saw was a picture of Lomax. "Who's this?" he said calmly, acting as though he didn't recognize him.

"It's Lomax and you know it." Diciembre was staring at the rear view mirror, studying Mitchell's face, in an obvious attempt to read his body language.

Mitchell grinned slightly. "He looks like a jerk. This is the guy who has your people running around in circles?"

Diciembre suddenly and dramatically pulled the car over onto the highway's shoulder and shifted into park. He turned and faced Mitchell. "I just want you to know that I am sticking my neck out meeting you like this." This was no lie.

"Then why are you doing it?"

"Like you, I want to keep Marion a safe and quiet place to live."

"Okay, you've made your point."

"Good. Read on!" Diciembre floored the accelerator and drove back onto the highway.

Diciembre had provided a portable reading lamp for Mitchell to

THE DOOR

use and he read quickly, learning everything he could about this rogue agent. He would pause from time to time to reflect on what he had just read and glance at the CIA Agent. He wondered if the CIA knew about his chance meeting with Lomax at Israel's barbecue. When he reached the end of Lomax's bio, he came upon a page that had a piece of wire with bumps that was taped to the paper.

"What's this?"

"He named it: '*Haywire*'."

"He…as in Lomax?"

"He invented it. He felt he had the right to name it. The Director didn't agree, but everybody calls it Haywire. Hook it up to a live electrical wire and it will create an electromagnetic pulse that will wipe every hard drive and computer chip clean to within a hundred feet. It will also fry itself out and leave no trace of its existence."

"That's his *forte*, isn't it? Leave no trace behind. The man is a genius!"

"That's part of the problem….Okay, next file."

Mitchell closed the file and opened a second one with **TOP SECRET: TRAVELLER** printed on the cover. He flipped through the pages, but stopped and studied the old pictures. "These pictures are ancient."

"So is he?"

"Come again?"

"His name is John Danvers. His birth name was Nathaniel Pilgrim. We call him: '*The Traveller*'."

"Traveller is the name of the horse General Robert E. Lee rode." Mitchell smiled to himself. He wanted to show Diciembre that he knew something about Civil War history.

Diciembre took away Mitchell's smile when he said, "Who do you think sold the horse to Lee?" It wasn't a question.

A few hours later, they arrived at an unlit, old and rusty warehouse. The place appeared abandoned. Discarded tires, a burnt out car and other unsavory items were found strewn about the parking lot. Mitchell was surprised to see the gate standing wide open and half of the security fence bent over and touching the ground. There were no guards or cameras or any of the usual security apparatus associated with a government facility. Diciembre didn't stop. He

THE DOOR

drove right up to the front of the warehouse where a garage door opened. The Special Agent in Charge only braked as he passed through the doorway into a dark room, where he parked. The garage door closed behind them, casting them into total darkness. Diciembre activated a flashlight, opened the driver's door and said, "Come on."

Mitchell was led to a steel door, which had no doorknob. It was opened electronically. There was a brightly lit hallway with two cameras mounted on the ceiling following their every move. "Well, I now know where all my taxes go."

"Detective, you are about to enter what we consider the most dangerous place in the world."

But that didn't shake Mitchell at all. "Right...."

Diciembre gave Mitchell the grand tour. First, through the Control Room, which had a bank of monitors on a wall, very much like the one Lomax had in his basement, and an assortment of high tech equipment, scanners, communication consoles and computers. Only two techs were manning the consoles. He then showed him the Observation Lab where a door stood in the middle of a white room. Several white-coated techs were in the room, conducting experiments. All kinds of wires and sensors were hooked up to the door and there were an assortment of video cameras recording constantly.

"You found them?" asked Mitchell, excitedly. "You found Israel Pilgrim's doors?"

Mitchell's question was so genuine that Diciembre knew that the Detective Sergeant didn't know where the Pilgrim Doors were. "No. This is not one of Israel's doors. We still haven't found them. This one came from California."

"You mean there are other doors?" He was too excited to wait for Diciembre to answer the question. "How many are there?"

Diciembre directed Mitchell to a steel door that went into the darkened warehouse. "Lights," he called out.

When the overhead lights came on, Mitchell was shocked to see hundreds of doors, standing erect, in lines fifty abreast in long rows that ran all the way to the back of the warehouse—too many to count with his eyes. "Oh, my God!"

*　　*　　*

THE DOOR

For the next five days, Hamilton stayed and waited with the boys by the wagon either sleeping in it or standing guard by it. They didn't let anyone near it. While they waited, they whittled a lot of wood for the splints Maggy needed. And when it was time to let the horse graze the wagon went with it. All Hamilton and the boys had to defend themselves was a sword, four pistol rounds and the bayonets on their muskets. They were six against hundreds. Horses were hard to come by in this part of the South and many of the Rebs at the hospital were feasting their eyes on this one. Not only would having a horse be an easier and faster way to get home, they could use the animal on their farm to help plant a crop next spring. Many of the Rebs were armed with swords, but when the word got out that this Sergeant Major had dueled with Champus Fragg and *"licked'em good"* and *"sent him a running,"* no one dared challenge him.

It was during these five very long days that Hamilton came to appreciate the special talent Fetch had, which no doubt was the reason the other boys gave him that name. Fetch was a scrounger. He acquired shoes for all the boys. They came from the Union soldiers who had died of their wounds at the hospital at Emory and Henry College. Some of them came from the colored soldiers, but the boys didn't care. It was their first pair of shoes and they loved them. But it was the boy named Red, who was the real surprise. He could make a deal with anyone! Red concentrated his bartering with the home guardsmen who were stationed at the field hospital. Sparingly, he traded some of the items in the wagon, mostly a tin of coffee, a few pounds of potatoes and a half dozen cuts of salted beef for some twenty rifle rounds and enough ball and powder to refill both Remington pistols. They were hard to come by since both sides had used up all their ammunition during the Burbridge Raid. However, the hospital home guardsmen didn't participate in the fighting and still had their ammunition. Now fully armed, Hamilton and the boys could relax and wait for Maggy to finish what she was doing.

Maggy worked practically non-stop during those five days and evidence of her work was clearly visible by all the splints the soldiers had on their arms, legs and chest areas. The doctors and orderlies who worked at the field hospital also noted the smaller than usual piles of amputated limbs. And on the fourth day, a

THE DOOR

wagon train arrived at the college, ferrying the wounded Union soldiers she had taken care of at the Sanders Farm. Most were found to be in good health and when the doctors asked them who had done their surgeries and attached them with splints, one and all pointed to Maggy Hamilton. When she collapsed from exhaustion on the evening of the fifth night, she was taken to a bed and left alone. The next morning, Hamilton awakened her with a cup of fresh coffee, something she rarely had since coming to this time period.

Two orderlies carried Maggy outside on a stretcher, with Hamilton at her side. Once again, the wounded, both Yankee and Reb alike, called out to her.

"Thankee, *ma'am*!"

"May God bless *ya!*"

"God be with *ya*, Doctor!"

"*Ah*," said Hamilton, "there you see. Now you're a doctor."

A second wagon driven by a mule was parked next to their wagon. A Confederate cavalry officer doffed his hat. "*Ma'am*. Sergeant Major. I bring you complements from the grateful Commander of Saltville, Colonel Preston." He waved to the two Calvary soldiers standing by at the college's main entrance. "We're to escort *y'all*."

"We're much obliged," said Hamilton, who had expressed concern about their safety once they left the college to the Confederate chief surgeon. Unlike his Union counterpart, the Confederate chief surgeon was very appreciative of Maggy's abilities and assistance. He wrote a personal letter to his friend, Colonel Preston about the wonderful care his men were receiving from Maggy Hamilton and requested the armed escort.

"What do we need two wagons for?" asked Maggy. She sat up and stared off at what was in the cargo bed of the other wagon. It was the double door. "No! No, Ham! You can't! Leave it here!"

"Maggy, we *gotta* see this thing through, which means we must deliver that door to its rightful owner. Otherwise, other good men may die on it. Do you want that?"

She shook her head and laid down in the wagon, next to Freckles.

They rode for two days with their escort at a very slow pace. Moon, Hoot and Red took point, while Matthew and Fetch took up

THE DOOR

the rear with their rifles. Colonel Preston also arranged for them to receive about a hundred rounds of rifle shot, which was warmly received by all. Not only did they have enough ammunition to protect themselves, but they would also be able to go out and hunt deer and rabbits.

Right after they broke camp on the third morning, Moon came rushing up to the wagons with a report. He had been scouting the area since first light and had found the Pilgrim farm. "It *be* right up ahead. Ain't nothing *mo* than a lean-to."

Moon's description was lacking, because he didn't spend enough time scouting the farm. There was an A-tent behind a berry bush and a lean-to. Positioned behind the lean-to was a contraption that Hamilton had only seen paintings of, a two-man sawmill. A further investigation showed that there was some smoke rising from a kiln that was about thirty feet from the sawmill.

The Calvary officer turned to Hamilton. "Who did you say this farm belonged to?"

"Pilgrim. Cornelius Pilgrim."

The officer touched the tip of his hat as an expression of thanks. He walked the horse over to a stand of trees that overlooked the small field and called out to the farmers. "You there…on the farm. Pilgrim. Cornelius Pilgrim."

"That is my grandfather's name," replied a young man in his teens, but in a very mature voice.

"Sir, I am escorting a gentleman who would like to visit with you," he glanced over his shoulder at Maggy and the boys, "with his family."

"What is his name?"

"Hamilton," called out Hamilton.

"I don't know any Hamilton," said the teenager. "Look, we are not looking for any trouble…"

"And you won't get any from us," said Maggy as she walked past Hamilton, then the Calvary officer.

Hamilton took off his gun belt and scabbard and put them in the wagon. He then double-timed it to catch up with Maggy.

"That's a feisty lady you have there," said the officer.

"One of the reasons I married the old girl."

When the tall and very muscular teenaged boy, who sounded

THE DOOR

so manly from afar, spotted Maggy coming out into the open, he trained his rifle at her.

"Easy now," old Cornelius Pilgrim said to his grandson, from inside the A-tent.

The grandson pulled his finger away from the trigger, then slowly retracted the hammer so that the rifle wouldn't discharge.

Cornelius called out to the approaching couple from his bed in the A-tent. "Good morning to you both and please don't do anything foolish. My grandson is an excellent shot!"

"We won't," said Hamilton.

Hamilton and Maggy stopped just short of the wood platform that surrounded the A-tent. "This is my wife, Maggy. She's a nurse. I am Ham Hamilton."

"I don't know you people and would prefer that you leave," said Cornelius.

"We come from the same town," said Hamilton.

"Salem Village," added Maggy.

"Did you hear that, Grandpa?" asked the grandson.

The old man had a hard time climbing out of his bed and getting into his wheelchair. "I heard." He wheeled himself out onto a wooden platform that the A-tent rested on. "Would you happen to be related to a Rory Hamilton?"

"Oh, yes," replied Hamilton, recalling his family history. "Distantly..."

"Very distantly," uttered Maggy.

"Then state your business, sir," said Cornelius.

"We have something of yours. May I call my boys to bring it to you?"

"Please."

Hamilton turned around and let out aloud whistle.

Moon drove their wagon onto the farm and parked it across from the A-tent.

It was Fetch who drove the other wagon.

When the old man spotted the door he let out a scream that surprised and shocked everyone who heard it.

Hamilton and Maggy turned to each other.

The Calvary officer thought something was wrong and drew his pistol. He spurred his horse and made it charge towards the wagons. "What's wrong?"

THE DOOR

The teenage boy spotted the Confederate Cavalrymen galloping their horse towards him and raised his rifle.

Hamilton raised both arms. "Nobody shoot!"

When the Calvary officer realized that it was an old man in a wheelchair screaming, he raised his hands to show the teenager that he did not intend to start a fight. He holstered his pistol and told his men to do the same.

When Cornelius fell out of the wheelchair, Maggy rushed over to him. She turned to her husband. "Ham, get my stethoscope, STAT!"

Hamilton rushed over to their wagon. "Give me that," he said to Matthew, pointing to the old style medical bag Maggy now used. It was a gift from a Confederate surgeon at Emory and Henry College. He took it and rushed to the platform.

"Why did he scream?" Hamilton asked the grandson.

Cornelius pointed to the door. "Don't you know? That's the Devil's…door!"

"We moved all the way from Massachusetts to get away from it," said the grandson, with anger in his tone. "Now you've brought it to us!"

"Did he say, Massachusetts?" asked the Calvary officer.

"They *be* Yankees," one of the other Calvary soldiers said aloud.

"Sergeant Major," said the officer, "my business here is done." With that he rode off with his men.

"How did it get here?" asked the grandson.

"It was shipped here," said Hamilton, "through the postal service."

"Destroy it!" said Cornelius as his body went limp.

"Cardiac arrest!" said Maggy.

"Grandpa!" shouted the teenager, sounding distressed. "Please don't die!"

"Ham," said Maggy, "I'll do heart compressions. You do the breathing."

It took a while, but they revived the old man via CPR, an unheard of medical procedure for the time.

Afterwards, Hamilton confronted his boys and gave an order. "Burn it."

The five boys gathered up all the kindling and dry wood they

THE DOOR

could carry and started a large fire in the middle of the cornfield. They waited until the fire was good and hot before placing the door onto it.

Nightfall…

When Cornelius regained consciousness, he realized that he was back in his bed and being taken care of by Maggy. "I don't know if I should thank you or curse you."

"Relax. They're burning the door now."

Maggy had placed her Bell Type Stethoscope on the bed next to Cornelius, while she organized her little medical bag. He picked it up and examined it.

His grandson came to the A-tent. "Thank God you are all right!" He knelt down next to the bed and reached out and touched his beloved grandfather.

"You're a good boy…just like your father. You look so much like him when he was your age. I miss him so…and your brother."

Cornelius turned to Maggy, who was attending Freckles in the other bed. "And how is your boy, *ma'am?*"

Maggy was uncomfortable with the question. She had not spent as much time with the six boys as her husband. She had wanted to be a mother in the natural sense, but not like this. And yet, she was quickly growing fond of the boys. "They are not my sons. They are orphans….But I am as proud of these boys as any mother could be."

That made Freckles, who was awake and listening, smile.

As Maggy stepped away from Freckles, she declared, "But they are a filthy lot." It was then she noticed Cornelius examining the stethoscope.

Hamilton came into the light of the campfire just outside of the A-tent when Cornelius pointed a finger at both of them and said, "If I didn't know better, I'd say you two came through one of the doors."

The grandson's mouth dropped. He stood up and turned to Maggy, then to Hamilton and nodded. "Yes, I see it now. Why are you here to—to torment my grandfather?"

Both of the Hamiltons said, "No!"

"The Pilgrim family has been friends of mine since I could

THE DOOR

remember," said Hamilton.

"Levi, my boy," said Cornelius, "calm down."

"Levi?" asked Hamilton excitedly. "You're Levi?" Levi was the founder of his company.

"That is my name," said the grandson.

"How did you know," asked Maggy, "about us…and the door?"

Cornelius held up her stethoscope and rubbed the plastic diaphragm with his thumb. "What ever this is, it's not wood or rubber. So what is it?"

"It's called plastic," replied Maggy, shooting a look to her husband.

"And it will be invented in 1907," added Hamilton.

Suddenly, the night sky turned red as the flames from the fire the boys had set in the field roared fifty feet into the air. It was enough to send the five boys who were tending the fire running flat out to the encampment.

A male voice, clear as day, echoed from the field. ***"Subiici mihi…!"*** Everyone heard it. Only one of them understood the words.

"That's Latin, isn't it?" asked Hamilton.

"Yes," said Maggy. "It's Latin."

"Well," insisted Hamilton, "What does it mean?"

"Submit to me."

"Like I said," said Cornelius. "It's the door to Hell."

Even after seeing Lieutenant Barrett and the colored soldier die on the door and hearing the shout coming out of the fire, Hamilton wasn't totally convinced that this door was what Cornelius said it was. "I don't know about that…."

"You have no idea of the unspeakable horror that accursed door has brought to my family," said Cornelius. He gestured to himself and Levi. "We are all that is left."

Hamilton turned and faced his wife. "Oh, we've had some very bad experiences with…a door."

"Not like this one," said Levi. "When the town finally dismantled the old Puritan Church and burned it, only the door remained. They tried to burn it several times but it would not burn. Then one day, it appeared at the front door of our mill."

"Appeared?" repeated Maggy. "You mean, someone moved it—."

THE DOOR

"No, it moved there by itself."

Hamilton made a face. He was finding this hard to believe. "That's impossible."

"No matter where we laid it," said Cornelius, "eventually we would find it at our doorstep."

"We found a deep track that went all the way to the church property—." said Levi.

"—So, someone pushed it!" said Maggy.

"If they did they must be able to walk on air because we found no footprints."

"Or wheel marks," said Cornelius.

"Well, no supernatural powers brought the door to your property this time. I…" Hamilton gestured to Maggy, "…we done it."

Maggy faced her husband with an angry expression. "Are you crazy? No supernatural powers? Ham, we were brought here through a time portal! You can't get any more supernatural than that!"

Hamilton turned away uttered something to himself.

"I hate it when you do that!" said Maggy. "If you have some-thing to say, then say it."

He turned to Maggy, then to the two Pilgrims. "What can you tell me about Nathaniel Pilgrim?"

Cornelius lowered his head in shame. "He is a doomed man. He is the cause of all of this horror and unfortunately, he's family."

"We saw him in Saltville," she said "after the battle. My husband thought he resembled someone he knew from...the future."

"That could very well be…" said Cornelius.

"He's told us about this little girl who had taken him to many strange places..." said Levi.

Both Hamiltons said, "Allison."

Cornelius nodded. "I regret now that I did not believe him. He left us before the war. I do not know where he is."

"He's a Union officer on the General's staff..." said Maggy.

"Always the power broker…" remarked Levi.

"…who was shot in the heart," said Maggy. "There was nothing I could do for him…"

"But he survived," asked Cornelius, "didn't he?"

THE DOOR

"Yes," said Hamilton, "and he climbed off the table like she removed a splinter from his thumb instead of a forty-four caliber lead ball."

"That is because of the pact he made with the Devil. He cannot die. You see, it was Nathaniel who made *that* door." Cornelius pointed to the field.

Suddenly, the fire roared high one more time then self extinguished itself, casting the field into complete darkness.

The next morning, Hamilton, the boys and Levi went out into the field to discover that all the logs they had placed on the fire were now ash. But the door was still there, undamaged.

Hamilton drew his pistol and shot a round at the door. The bullet bounced off without leaving a mark.

"What do we do now?" asked Levi.

"We dump it into a deep ravine…"

"I *know'd* one," said Fetch. "It *be* real deep. You can't see the bottom."

The door was loaded onto the wagon and Fetch brought it to the mountain where there was a rock formation that had a very deep crevasse. It took every ounce of strength for Hamilton, Levi and Fetch to drag the door to the edge of the crevasse and drop it in. The crevasse was so dark that they couldn't tell if it fell all the way to the bottom but it made a lot of scraping and crashing sounds on the way down.

For the next two weeks, there was peace at the Pilgrim Farm. Maggy took good care of Cornelius and he was now up and rolling about in his wheelchair. He and Hamilton became good friends because they had something in common. *They were carpenters!* Always the businessman, Hamilton made a business proposition Cornelius couldn't refuse. They were going to build a sawmill and teach the boys the trade they loved so much.

The two A-tents General Burbridge had provided the Hamiltons were set up directly across the one used by Cornelius. It wasn't long before everyone recognized the fact that nobody could cut down a tree faster than Levi. Hamilton used the bucksaw to cut the planks that extended the platform Cornelius had built for his tent so that it would now include all the tents. Hoot turned out to be the best hunter of the bunch, especially since he would climb a tree at night and wait there until a deer came by in the morning.

THE DOOR

"Some night owl we got there," he said to Maggy.

Fetch proved that he was a real scavenger by setting off for days on end and returning with items he found in the woods and abandoned homes. This was war and many civilians were killed and their homes, farms and businesses were pilfered. He was very good at finding wood stoves, which were a true prize now that it was getting colder. Before long, each of the A-tents had a small wood stove in them to heat them at night. Holes were cut into the fabric to allow the smoke stack to stick out. The bathtub was a real find and he got to use it—even though he didn't want to. None of the boys had bathed in many months, if years and they smelled it too.

All eight woodstoves Fetch found were fired up to heat the water. The first thing Maggy did was to give all the boys including Hamilton a haircut. Next, she grabbed a bar of soap with one hand and an ear from one of the boys with the other and directed them into the A-tent where the bathtub was set up. Finally, she personally did the honors of washing each of them. Oh, they screamed and hollered and splashed the water about. It created a lot of laughter from everyone involved.

"More hot water!" Maggy would shout and another water basin would be taken off a stove. Hamilton's job was to supervise this part of the operation making sure that some unheated water was mixed into the hot water so that no one got burned. He always put his hand into the water before saying, "Good to go!"

When she was done, the boys would emerge all angry, but clean. As a matter-of-fact, their skin was pink.

The last one to get a bath that day was Hamilton himself. But the boys had to knock down the A-tent to get him into the tub. He screamed and hollered worst than all of them, but it was all an act. He never laughed so hard in his life. *Ham Hamilton was a happy man!*

The next day, Hamilton, Maggy and the boys were getting ready to go to the dry goods store in Marion.

"You coming, Cornelius?" asked Hamilton.

"It's best that neither Levi or I go. They don't sell to Yankees."

But Hamilton was a man who never took no for an answer and insisted that Levi accompany them. Levi agreed on the condition that he would stay outside and guard the horse and wagon while

THE DOOR

the Hamiltons were shopping.

When Hamilton entered the dry goods store in Marion the proprietor announced, "I don't sell to Yankees!" He pointed to the Confederate Gray coat Hamilton wore. "And don't be *tell'n* me you ain't one just because you be wearing a gray coat...."

This is where Red showed his talent for business. He stood taller than the proprietor and grabbed the man by his coat collar. He pulled him to one side of the store and talked up a storm. Occasionally, he would point to Hamilton and Maggy. By the time he got done, the proprietor was no longer resistant.

"Well," he said to the Hamiltons, "what can I do for *y'all* today?" He even smiled.

All the boys from Saltville were fitted with new clothes and socks and a Sunday suit for church. The boys were excited because they never owned a suit before. Hamilton let Red negotiate prices with the proprietor and he only used the loose change they had gotten as a gift from the Union soldiers at the Sanders Farm.

Moon explained to Hamilton, "We *best* not let people *know'd* *y'all* got a cache of money otherwise we be raided upon by bushwhackers."

"What *be* your name boy?" the proprietor asked Freckles.

Freckles glanced over to the Hamiltons. "Why I *be* Freckles... Hamilton, sir."

The Hamiltons were stunned by what they just heard.

"I *be* Moon Hamilton."

"Red Hamilton."

"Hoot Hamilton."

"Fetch Hamilton is the name, sir."

Matthew raised his hand and spoke for the very first time. "*Maaathew Hammmilton.*"

That brought tears to both Hamilton's and Maggy's eyes.

The happy occasion was topped off when a traveling photographer arrived at the store for some provisions. Not too many locals could afford have their pictures taken so Red had an easy time negotiating a fair price. The photographer took the Hamilton family picture, with Levi Pilgrim, on the front steps of the dry good store.

The war seemed to stop in Southwest Virginia during the rest

THE DOOR

October and November. Life was slowly getting back to normal. People were now more concerned about baling hay, hunting deer and fowl and preparing their homes for the coming of winter than where the battle lines were.

For Cornelius and Hamilton and the boys, it was a time to teach, learn and build. While the boys cut down trees and sawed them into beams and planks, the scraps were used to fuel the kiln for the bricks they would use. There was a lot of red clay on the Pilgrim property. All they had to do was dig it up, mould it into a brick, let it dry, then fire it up in the kiln. Before long, there were three kilns working day and night. All three kilns were placed near the A-Tents because they produced a lot of heat. It was Hamilton who discovered the small gypsum deposit just outside the Pilgrim property. Actually, he didn't discover anything. He knew it was there all along. For fifty dollars, Union Currency, he purchased the property from a widow who wanted to move back to her family in North Carolina, but couldn't afford it. Now she could. The property also had one other advantage. It bordered a swift flowing stream. Hamilton drove Cornelius on the wagon out to the stream, where they planned and designed the watermill they would build together. They shook hands and were now partners in Hamilton-Pilgrim Mill. The logs that made up the widow's home were disassembled, then reassembled next to the stream. It would serve as the wood mill's wheelhouse.

"We'll wait until January to dam up the stream," Hamilton said to his boys, "when the water level is at its lowest."

With so many eager young hands, things got done fast.

Maggy did put her foot down on one thing. One day out of four, everyone stopped working and she and Hamilton became school teachers. When the boys objected, it was Hamilton, who put his foot down. "There's the wrong way and the Hamilton way! You boys are going to learn how to read and write." Ironically, it was "silent" Matthew, who could recite the alphabet the best and was the fastest learner.

The winter of 1864 was one of the coldest on record, so when it started to snow everyone moved into the wheelhouse, including the Pilgrims. A second room was erected from logs the boys cut. It was meant to be a workroom, but instead it became a field hospital. War was returning to Smyth County, Virginia.

THE DOOR

Maggy had the boys raise a flagpole for the Hospital Flag she sewed. The A-tents were erected in front of the wheelhouse, with smoke coming out of the smoke stacks.

The boys were busy cleaning out their Enfields and getting ready to join the fight. But Hamilton put a stop to all of that.

"It's not going to be like before. They will take Saltville without firing a shot. No more marching Union soldiers. They'll all be on horses ... riding hard and fast."

"Well, what do we do?" asked Moon.

"We stay here and protect our home. It will be over before you know it."

It was. The game trail that stood in front of where Cornelius had set up his A-tent got pounded into a roadway by all of the Union Calvary soldiers and wagons that went racing back and forth. When some of the members of the Union medical corps rode by the Hamilton property, they spotted the Hospital Flag and stopped in for a visit. They had heard tall stories by some of the medical corpsmen who served under General Burbridge about a civilian nurse named Maggy who refused to allow the chief surgeon to amputate. They could barely contain their excitement when they realized they had found her. She, in turn, convinced them to set up their tents at her field hospital. She had a reason for doing this. Her medical supplies were completely depleted and they had plenty. When General George Stoneman raided Southwest Virginia in December 1864, he brought herds of cattle to feed his troops. One of those herds ended up grazing at the Hamilton's.

Shots were heard in the distance along with an occasional cannon burst, but nothing in comparison to what Hamilton and the boys experienced on Chestnut Ridge. Injuries on both sides were slight and for a day or so the wagons ferried in the wounded, both Reb and Yankee to the Hamilton's. There were no violent incidents at the field hospital. Hamilton did not put on his dress gray uniform, but he did wear his gun belt. Hoot hid high up in a tree to get a birds eye view of the traffic and all the goings on in the area. Fetch and Moon scouted the wooded areas on either side of the property. Stoneman's Calvary soldiers attacked the town of Marion and "fired" a number of buildings such as the County Courthouse. But beyond that, Marion was spared. The saltworks at Saltville was destroyed, but after the Union had left the area, the

THE DOOR

slaves rebuilt the facility and got it up and running to full capacity within a month.

There was one Union Calvary Officer who stopped at the Pilgrim farm and studied the Hamilton's sawmill with his binoculars. He then rode into the field hospital and Maggy recognized him as the Major who got shot in the heart only a few months previously and walked away.

"You!" said Maggy.

"Hello," the Major said as he dismounted. "So, you remember me?"

Hamilton went to Maggy's side to comfort her. "How could we forget?" he said.

The Major didn't identify himself but Hamilton was absolutely certain that this was John Danvers, his silent partner in the future. The Major took off his hat. "I wanted to thank you for saving the lives of my soldiers."

"I don't know who you are or what you are," said Maggy, "but I want you to get off our land. Now!"

"You heard the lady," said Hamilton, in a low tone.

Cornelius rolled out of the house on his wheelchair and stared at his very long living ancestor. When Nathaniel spotted Cornelius, he gave the old man a respectful nod. "*Ah*, Cornelius! It does me good to see you up and about like this." He gestured to the Hamiltons. "You and the boy couldn't be in better hands. Fair *thee* well."

"And may God forgive you!" replied Cornelius.

Without further adieu, the Major remounted his horse. He turned to the Union surgeon who was standing behind the Hamiltons. "Doctor, make sure that you leave the good nurse here enough medical supplies so that she can carry on after we leave."

"I intended to," said the surgeon.

The Major gestured to the grazing cattle. "Leave them a dozen or so head of cattle too."

The Major then turned to Hamilton. "I suppose that you and I will be meeting again...under better circumstances."

Hamilton just didn't know how to respond to that.

The Major turned his horse and doffed his hat. "Good day to you *ma'am* and sir! And may God bless all here!" With that he rode off.

*　　*　　*

THE DOOR

On April 9, 1865, the Civil War ended.

"*Ah,* the ironies of war," Hamilton said to Maggy, as he held up a week old newspaper. "Wilmer McLean was a wholesale grocer in Manassas, Virginia. The Civil War started in his front yard with the first Battle of Bull Run and ended in his front parlor at his house in Appomattox Court, where Lee surrendered to Grant."

"Life truly does come full circle for some people," she replied. "But what about us?"

"I don't know about you, but I'm happy here."

"*Pa!*" called out Moon, from the roof of the wheelhouse. "We're ready!"

Hamilton turned to Cornelius, who gave a nod.

"Let her rip!" Hamilton told Moon.

A long wooden lever was pulled inside the wheelhouse, releasing the brake and the waterwheel started to turn. Everyone cheered. Inside the wheelhouse, metal gears started to turn and the band saw started to turn. Hamilton used the last of the money he got from Burbridge to purchase the band saw. It was old, rusted and in disrepair, but Hamilton got it to work.

"Boys," shouted Hamilton, "we're in business!"

*　　*　　*

Back in West Virginia…

Red warning lights were flashing in the control room as the shift supervisor called Diciembre on the telephone. "EMI readings are bouncing off the charts."

Diciembre turned on the light to a very small prefabricated cubicle that was his living quarters. His Spartan-like quarters were the same size as a prison cell. It had a bed with night table and a desk with an uncomfortable chair and a computer. He glanced at the only amenity he was allowed to affix to the vinyl wall. A clock. It read 0213 hours.

"Wake everybody up and follow mission procedures."

He dressed quickly, buttoning his white shirt as he hurried down a narrow corridor that was lined on one side with file cabinets marked "Pilgrim Doors." The file cabinets lining the hallway were the overflow for the room where he spent most of his time, pouring over the thousands of files found in cabinets that lined three walls

THE DOOR

and organizing strike teams to secure the doors. Giant wall maps lined the walls of the conference room and they were covered with red and blue pegs, designating the locations of those doors that were scheduled for retrieval (red) and those (blue) already taken. The large conference table was covered with opened files from Hamilton – Pilgrim and Pilgrim Doors companies. There were also Xerox copies of the files the government subpoenaed from the mill.

Diciembre went directly to the Armory. There were two US Army soldiers, a Sergeant and a private, in the Armory pulling rifles off the rack and checking them. Two additional soldiers entered the Armory through another hatchway. They were still dressing.

The Sergeant who commanded this elite Special Forces unit gave Diciembre a dirty look.

Diciembre raised his arms in defeat. "I know. I'm tired of it too."

"Five days in a row. You guys have us working double shifts with no relief and the food here is terrible!"

"A little adrenaline rush never hurt anybody. Besides, you all joined the service to see the world right—?"

"—That's the Navy."

"And this is West Virginia," one of the privates said.

"Please don't remind me," said Diciembre. "I'm stuck here just like you."

The Sergeant received a message over his headset and said to Diciembre. "Sharpshooter is in position."

"That was fast," said Diciembre.

"He's fast and deadly," said the Sergeant.

"Just make sure he doesn't cap me, okay?"

"No promises."

Diciembre reached for the handle to a door that went directly into the Control Room. "I'll try to get you guys back in your racks ASAP."

"That's sack, not rack," said the private. "Get it right, will *ya!*"

Diciembre grinned as he went into the Control Room and secured the door behind him. To him, he was having a little fun with the grunts.

The outspoken private backhanded his Sergeant. "What the

heck are we doing here…guarding a bunch of damn doors? And now we have to play this Red Alert crap every night."

"Can it, soldier. Check your weapons and stand ready."

Diciembre stared at the bank of wall monitors that projected a number of doors, both close up shots and wide angle.

Additional techs reported for duty through another door and they were just as angry as the soldiers.

"Every damn night," one remarked.

"I don't want to hear it," said Diciembre. "And will somebody turn off that blasted alarm!"

Both the alarm and flashing red lights were turned off.

"All cameras and sensors are on recording mode," one tech reported.

Diciembre glanced up at the wall clock and realized that ten minutes had passed. He then received a message from the Communications Desk.

"Langley on line two, sir."

Diciembre lifted a telephone receiver and pressed the flashing extension light. "Diciembre." The agent on the other end of the phone reported that they had noted another alarm. "Yes, but I think it's another false one." He listened to the caller, then nodded. "Yes, I will order a full diagnostic of the system." He then hung up the phone.

The shift supervisor made his way over to Diciembre, who by the expression on his face was frazzled. "Now the computers are saying that there were no increased EMI readings."

"There's got to be a glitch in the software. Find it."

"Sure wish we had Lomax here." He winced after saying it, not knowing how Diciembre would react. "Sorry, sir."

"Don't be. I wish the son of a bitch was here too…so that I could blame somebody…besides you."

A red light flashed, followed by several others, but no klaxon. Several cameras zoomed in on a juvenile girl wearing a Little Red Riding Hood costume who was running through the warehouse. It was Allison and she wasn't alone.

"Contact," said the sharp shooter over his headset microphone, "we have a contact! Row eight, aisle fifteen. And make that two contacts."

Diciembre sat down at one of the consoles and worked the

THE DOOR

controls to focus the cameras on the contact and the opened door.

"Where did she come from?" asked the shift supervisor.

"From that opened door on row nine," replied the sharpshooter. "Didn't the sensors pick it up?"

"Negative," replied Diciembre. He rewound the tape, then hit PLAY to see the door open and Allison cautiously stepping into the warehouse. She was not alone. Behind her was a man wearing clothes that were indicative of a bygone Colonial era.

"Who's he?" asked the shift supervisor, now working the controls next to Diciembre.

"That's Nathaniel Pilgrim a.k.a Special Agent John Danvers," said Diciembre. For months he had waited for this moment. He became emotional and struck his fist hard on the flat surface of the console. "Finally!"

"*The Traveller*?" asked the shift supervisor.

Nathaniel Pilgrim stepped through the doorway and surveyed the warehouse. He even looked directly at the camera that was being lowered from the ceiling and focusing on him, with great curiosity and fear. From the look on his face, it was as though he had never seen a camera before.

The shift supervisor radioed the soldiers. "Combat Team, lock and load." He glanced over to Diciembre, who gave his permission with a nod. "Sergeant, commence stealth deployment."

"There are two subjects: a little girl and white male adult," added Diciembre. "Keep your distance, don't spook them and for God's sakes no shooting unless I authorize it. Got that, Sergeant?"

"Roger that," replied the Sergeant.

Diciembre picked three of his best techs and went onto the main floor of the warehouse. Unlike the soldiers who stealthily moved about the floor, Diciembre headed straight for the door the little girl and Pilgrim passed through. It was still open. Unlike all the soldiers, who were fitted with a helmet camera, Diciembre carried a portable one in his right hand. He focused the lens on the opened door and the incredible view inside the doorway. He was seeing a vision of Colonial America, with wooden ships anchored in the harbor, dirt roads, people on horses and driving wagons. It looked so real. He reached forward and crossed the threshold with his hand. "It's not a projection," he said, knowing that the camera's microphone would record anything he said. His mind was racing.

THE DOOR

If he went through the door, would he be able to come back? Why would he want to? He looked down his right foot as it stepped across the threshold and pressed down on solid ground. A voice in his head yelled at him to: *"Go! This is your chance to find peace and happiness!"*

Knock! Knock!

It echoed throughout the warehouse.

Allison screamed.

It brought Diciembre back to reality. He turned away from the door. "What happened?"

Both the tech and combat teams rushed to the knocking door and surrounded it, rifles and hand sensors at the ready.

One tech went up to the door and reached out his hand.

Allison appeared. "Don't open that door!"

"Wait!" shouted Diciembre.

The outspoken private shoved Pilgrim towards the door. "Look who I found!"

"What is this place?" replied Pilgrim. "Your manner of dress, your language are all strange to *thee*? Who *art thou?*"

"What's with the '*thee*' and '*thou*' talk, Danvers?" asked the private.

"Danvers?" He made a face. "*Thy* name is Pilgrim. Nathaniel Pilgrim."

"Don't give me that," said the private. "You're John Danvers!"

Many years later, when Nathaniel needed to change his name he would remember his encounter with the angry soldier from the future and change his name to John Danvers.

"Is this Perdition?" asked Pilgrim.

"Per—what?" asked the outspoken private. He turned to Diciembre, who had been listening. "What is he saying?"

"Perdition," said Diciembre, in a calm but authoritative tone. "It means Hell."

Diciembre called out to the Sergeant of the Guard. "Sergeant, please have your men stand down and give me and my people some room in which to work."

The Sergeant replied with a nod, then confronted his men. "Back off, men."

They did and the private grunted as he released Pilgrim.

Diciembre went up to Allison and got down on one knee. "Easy

THE DOOR

now. We are not going to hurt you."

"You—I am not afraid of," she said with such feeling that Diciembre and the techs and soldiers were taken aback. She turned and pointed to the closest door. "Just him!"

Suddenly the doorknob on the very door Allison pointed started to rattle violently. It startled everyone. It was followed by a long moment where it seemed that someone was pounding their fists on the door from the other side. All weapons and cameras were instantly trained on the door. It seemed longer, but the event only lasted for a few terrifying seconds, then the door fell silent.

Everyone started to breathe again.

"What's your name?" asked Diciembre.

"Allison."

The little girl had some of the features of a Native American and she wore a Little Red Riding Hood outfit.

"Okay, Allison. Why shouldn't we open that door?"

"Because a terrible thing will happen if you do."

As she stepped away, Diciembre grabbed her arm.

"What will happen?" he asked. "Please be specific."

"Everything here and all of you will be pulled inside."

"And go where?"

"Different places. Some people live through it. Most don't."

Knock! Knock!

"Don't you hear him?" she shouted. "He's back and he wants me!"

Diciembre spoke into his headset mike. "Are we getting all of this?"

"Allison, who is doing the knocking?" asked the Sergeant.

"Please let me go," she pleaded as she tried to pull herself free from Diciembre's firm grasp.

Suddenly, the pounding resumed again on the same door but this time with such veracity that everyone in the warehouse thought it would break apart. Everyone backed up a step.

"Safety's off!" shouted the Sergeant to his team.

"Allison," asked Diciembre, "who's back?"

Pilgrim answered the question in a somber tone. "He is the Evil One. He, who was cast out by God Himself."

"How do you know this?" asked Diciembre.

"*Thy hast* seen him and he would *cometh* here and devour all of *thee* if *thee* opens that door. For we are all sinners...."

The intensity by which the door was being pounded upon grew even greater.

"It's going to come apart!" said the Sergeant.

"There's no locks on the door," said another tech.

"Why doesn't he just open it and come in?" asked a third.

"Because he has to be invited in," said Diciembre.

"I get it," said the Sergeant, "just like Dracula in the vampire books?"

"No—you idiot," said Diciembre, "Satan in the Bible."

"I'm out of here!" said one of the techs, as he ran off.

"If *thee* allows him to enter this world he will destroy it," said Pilgrim.

"All right," said Diciembre, "what do we do?"

"Let us return from *whence* we came."

Diciembre didn't have to think that one over. "Okay—go!"

As soon as Allison and Pilgrim stepped across the threshold of the door that opened to Salem Village in the past, the pounding stopped. The door to Salem Village slammed shut and all the power in the warehouse and all the lights winked out.

*   *   *

Lomax was having lunch at a fast food hamburger place when Detective Sergeant Dewey Mitchell strolled in. He ordered a hamburger and a soft drink then sat at Lomax's table.

"Well," said Mitchell, "if it isn't the Hot Diggity Dog man himself. How's business, Eddi?"

"***Rrrroouuuugggghhhhhh!*** " barked Lomax.

"I think these are yours," said Mitchell as he pushed a square foot cardboard box marked "Junk" he had been carrying across the table to Lomax.

Lomax opened the box and glanced at the pinhole cameras, wireless transmitters, motion sensors and microphones. "Some are, but not all."

"Well, they are expensive and we don't want them in our little police department anymore."

"When did you figure it out?"

"Oh, I had my suspicions at the barbecue...but they were

THE DOOR

confirmed when one of your friends from the CIA showed me your picture."

"I hope they showed you my best side." He turned his head and pretended to pose.

"Actually, it was Diciembre who showed it to me and he was acting in an unofficial capacity."

Lomax grinned. "No….Impossible!" He stared into Mitchell's face to read his body language. "You're lying."

"No."

Lomax surmised that Mitchell was telling the truth. "And to think he once said that I couldn't obey orders. How is my old friend doing these days?"

"Not good. They got him pinned up in a warehouse in some God awful place in West Virginia."

"*Tisk-a-tsk!* One should never refer to God's Country in such a manner."

"Do you know what they have in that warehouse?"

One of Eddi Dane's customers entered the restaurant and called out to him. He smiled back at them and gave a wave. "No, but I *gotta* feeling you're going to tell me."

"Doors. Hundreds of them."

Lomax's smile vanished. "Damn fools. They don't know what those doors are capable of."

"And you do?"

Lomax put down the hamburger he was eating and stared at Mitchell. "You fishing for something, Detective Sergeant?"

"Oh, no. I've already caught my limit for the day."

"Look. I'm done with that life. I'm just Eddi Dane now, your friendly neighborhood Hot Diggity Dog Electrical Man. I've got a wife and a kid and I couldn't care less if the whole world blew itself up. I'm not in the game anymore."

"What happens to Daphne and Dara if the world blows up?"

"You're a good cop and you care. There was a time when I was a good agent and I cared. No more. As for Dara, unlike my father…who I never met and whose name I don't even know, I'll be there for her right to the end."

Mitchell got up. "Fair enough." He started to leave.

"Wait! Are Israel's doors in that warehouse?"

"Your friend Diciembre said no."

THE DOOR

"Well, I don't have them. Trust me on that." Lomax's tone was sincere.

"I will. But it also means that until they are found and removed from this area, we're all in danger."

In a move that completely shocked Mitchell, Lomax put out his hand.

Mitchell hesitated, then shook it. "Nice seeing you again, Eddi."

"Like wise, Dewey!"

Lomax noticed that other people in the restaurant had been watching them. He gave the onlookers a winning smile and jerked a thumb at Mitchell. "What a guy, *huh!*"

THE DOOR

PART THREE

War of the Angels

Six years later...

"Eye of God" photo courtesy of NASA

Chapter Eleven

THE DIRTY WORK

They say that time heals all wounds.

But the passing of six years for Lomax aka Eddi Dane was slow, boring and barely profitable. How Lomax longed for the cash laden envelopes he got from the client (*some of which went to the "escape stash" in a safe deposit box he never told Daphne about. All good spies keep at least one just for emergencies*). Worse yet, now he had to pay income taxes! Nothing supernatural happened at the Pilgrim house or in the town itself. The twelve missing doors were for the most part forgotten. Occasionally a Predator Drone would do a flyby and scan the area for the unique electro-magnetic signature the doors gave off and sometimes Lomax's aging sensors in the attic would pick them up as they did a pass. That was about the extent of excitement he would have as the years rolled by. Maintaining two houses, a rusting utility van and raising a daughter had become a financial burden, so when Israel Pilgrim offered him a full time job with benefits, he took it. Lomax would explain that he did it for the money and the benefits, but he couldn't fool Daphne. Lomax and Israel had become very close friends and if they weren't off trout fishing, deer hunting, or building something together, they were working down at the mill.

Lomax had become Eddi Dane and rarely thought of his former name. Even Daphne called him Eddi and she was now Mrs. Dane. Living in the "*Deep South*", as it was, it was suggested that the locals might not appreciate the fact that they were living together in sin. So to fully secure their new identities Lomax and Daphne got married in a church—with Israel and Mary standing in as their best man and maid of honor.

The automated machinery Hamilton had installed when he and his silent partner bought out the Pilgrims was now old and all used up. Unfortunately, the company couldn't afford to replace every-thing all at once. So it was Eddi's job to try to fix, Gerry rig and maintain the machines that could still do the job and keep them working proficiently. No easy task. If he wasn't repairing old machinery, he was installing the new ones. Everything was now digital and laser guided. Pilgrim placed Lomax in charge of the upgrading and he showed the young and old timers his many talents, especially in organization. He was also their computer tech and if the manufacturer's software didn't meet their demands, Lomax tweaked it. The new laser systems would scan the logs and tell the computer what and where to cut automatically. It was a more efficient process, produced less waste and increased profits. It took a lot of time and effort for Lomax to upgrade everything but in the end the company became a state-of-the art manufacturer, producing a diverse product line. Profits soared and everyone received a nice bonus check. Lomax made a lot of friends at Hamilton – Pilgrim. But always the loner, he convinced Israel to let him work the midnight shift, when it was nice and quiet and he had the place all to himself.

"Eddi…!" Israel called out as he entered the mill.

Old habits die hard, even for CEOs. Israel was still the first employee to report for work in the morning. But it was different now. Lomax was there waiting for him with a cup of fresh hot coffee. "Here you go, boss." Lomax would report what he had done during the night shift and then the conversation would shift towards their kids, just like typical fathers.

Daphne became a stay at home mother, but still designed and managed several local corporate web sites. It gave her plenty of time to raise Dara and watch over Richard Pilgrim, who she baby-sat a couple of days a week. They were now six and seven years old and quite a handful. At first, Lomax liked the idea that Daphne would watch over Little Richard, thus giving both of them access to the Pilgrim's house to upgrade and maintain the surveillance equipment he installed. But as the years went by and nothing happened, the need to maintain constant surveillance waned considerably. In short, Lomax didn't have the money or a reason to spy on the Pilgrims anymore.

The past six years had been good ones for Mary Pilgrim. If she wasn't painting murals, she was taking classes at Emory and Henry College and studying business and marketing.

The Pilgrims still didn't have interior doors in their house, but

THE DOOR

who cared.

In all, life for the Pilgrims and the Danes had become humdrum and that's the way they liked it.

All the surveillance systems in the Lomax's basement were either switched off or put on motion detection mode. The recorders only came on if there was some kind of movement in the Pilgrim's house and not just when someone walked into the room either. It had to be on the level of an earthquake to activate the recorders.

At the same time Lomax turned his used four-door sedan into the driveway of his house, Mary was dropping off Richard at Daphne's. Having two houses did have its advantages. Since Eddi worked nights, he could sack out at his house and sleep all day while the kids screamed and hollered at Daphne's. *It was a perfect arrangement!*

Today, though, July 31, 2004, seven years and two days after the birth of Richard Pilgrim, everything was about to change.

Lomax was in his kitchen, raiding the refrigerator and drinking milk right out of the carton—something Daphne would kill him for doing if she caught him—when a visitor came calling.

Knock! Knock! went the backdoor of his house.

Lomax froze as he stared at the door. Suddenly, the door handle started to rattle violently. He went for a 9MM pistol he hid in one of the cupboards and chambered a round.

"Will you open the bloody door!" said a voice from the past. "Lomax!"

Lomax went over to the door, gun at the ready. "Who are you?"

"I'm your client...or used to be." The man's face appeared in one of the little windows.

Lomax reached over and unlocked the door. He then took two steps back and leveled his gun at the visitor.

"May I enter?" asked the visitor.

"Slowly and don't do anything stupid."

"With a gun pointed at me? Not likely." The well-dressed young man stepped into the kitchen. Lomax estimated that the man was between thirty and thirty-five years old. The suit he wore was custom-made and must have cost thousands of dollars. Even the leather suitcase and briefcase he carried were high dollar items. "Hello Lomax...or should I say, Eddi?"

"Been out and about, have we?"

THE DOOR

"Let's just say, I've been…traveling. These are heavy,"
referring to his suit cases. "May I put them down?"

Lomax answered by frisking the visitor for weapons with his
free hand. When he was done, he backed off to a safe distance.

The former client put down both cases and took the liberty of
sitting at the kitchen table. He gave the kitchen the once over.
"This is very nice. You do good work. That's why I hired
you...amongst other things."

Lomax closed the kitchen door and glanced out one of the
windows at the house directly behind his. "I'm sure they've seen
you."

"Count on it!"

"I don't know why you're here," said Lomax, "but you've come
to the wrong place. Haven't you heard? I'm out of the game. You
need to find someone else to do your dirty work."

"I can't and like it or not, you're involved."

Lomax shook his head. "No."

"You don't seem to understand the danger you, your family and
the Pilgrims are in."

"What danger? It's over."

"*Ah*, yes. Six years of quiet everyday life in the country.
Hmmm! You couldn't be more wrong. There's a war brewing the
likes of which you cannot imagine. And for the first time ever
humanity itself is at stake."

Lomax rolled his eyes skyward. He then pointed to the
doorway. "Look, nothing you will say can make me change my
mind. So just get up, turn around and leave."

"Allison is missing."

"Who?" Lomax tried to be coy.

"You know damn well who she is. The girl dressed in the Little
Red Riding Hood outfit." He reached for his brief case, then
hesitated. "May I open this?" Lomax raised the pistol and gave a
nod. The former client carefully opened his brief case and
removed a five by eight black and white still photograph. It was of
Allison and him standing in front of Wilbur & Orville Wright and
their airplane at Kitty Hawk, North Carolina. "I take a nice
picture, don't I? *Ah*, man flying without wings. I've heard from a
very credible source that not even the Angels can do that."

"You're saying that's you and that little girl is Allison and those

THE DOOR

two men are the Wright Brothers?"

"Yes. They promised to take her up the next time they flew, but the closest door to that time period was taken…"

"Taken? Taken by whom?"

"Your friend, Diciembre. He's in charge of a facility in West Virginia where there are hundreds and maybe a thousand of these Pilgrim Doors."

"I know. That's why they basically left us alone."

"Yes, they've been busy chasing me and Allison and gathering up every door they can find. But now she's gone and I am concerned for her well being."

"What happened?"

"Right after I released you, we went searching for a particular type of door that we never found."

"And what type is that?"

"A Wanderer…like Richard's bathroom door. They are very, very rare. All the rest are single destination portals. Something spooked her and she ran off and I just couldn't catch up with her. She can run like a deer. Well, I had no choice but to go back to the last door we came through and I ended up here. Just to give you an idea of what I am talking about, last week for me was when you came to my house."

"Last week? That was six years ago."

"So, that makes this 2004?" He turned away and shook his head. "Poor Allison. She must be found."

"And you want me to find her?"

"Not you. Richard. He's a Traveller, just like Allison. Only they can open those accursed doors."

Lomax became angry. He cared for the Pilgrims. They were his best friends. "No! No way! We are going to keep Israel's boy out of this!"

"I know that you and Israel are like brothers, but…."

Lomax pointed his gun at his former client. "You know nothing! But if I kill you now, I think this nightmare will be over!"

The former client was totally unafraid and showed it. "I will bleed and suffer with great pain, but I will not die. I cannot die. He won't let me."

"Who won't let you die?"

"The one who knocks on those doors."

THE DOOR

"Who, the Devil? I've been told that you are the Devil."

"When you see him in his true form then you will know exactly who he is. And you will know pain and agony the likes of which you have never experienced in your life. He is real, Lomax and he is coming here to get what he wants. And he will stop at nothing. He will destroy all that you love and hold dear...."

"If he's so powerful, how can I stop him?"

"You can't. But Allison and Richard can. Unfortunately, Allison is gone. I fear that he has her. He'll come for Richard now. We must protect him at all costs. That is the reason I came here."

"Why should I trust you? I don't even know your name."

"Like you, I'm known by several names."

"For instance?"

"I was christened Nathaniel Pilgrim. But you can call me John...John Danvers."

Lomax recalled the portraits of Nathaniel Pilgrim he found in the national archives and realized he was talking to a man who lived during the time of the Puritans—four hundred years ago! He suddenly felt light headed and sank into a chair. He felt trapped and powerless....

*   *   *

Beyond the backyard of Lomax's house, there was a paved alleyway that people used for jogging and walking. Some of Lomax's neighbors had their garage doors facing the alley, so that they could drive right in. But there was a banged up Mercury Cougar parked on the grass in a backyard that faced Lomax's house. The backyard did have a high wooden fence surrounding it, but no trees or outside structures to impede the view of the rear side of Lomax's house and his backyard. An old couple lived at the house along with several sons and daughters. But the only thing these people had in common was the Federal agency they worked for. They manned a surveillance center in the basement of the house just like Lomax did in his house.

The stakeout's Lead Agent, code name *"Father"* called Langley on a secure line. "Sir, we have a confirmed sighting of John Danvers."

THE DOOR

"Finally!" replied Deputy Director Blackburn. "Now what about the young female Traveller?"

"Negative. He arrived alone and is with Lomax now."

"Good work. Keep me informed."

*　　*　　*

After all the horror Israel and his wife had to endure after the birth of their son, the past six years had been nothing short of wonderful for the Pilgrims. Richard was a happy growing boy and Mary was as lovely as the day Israel met her. The business was making a good profit and it had been a long time since he heard someone say, "*Wish Ham was back*." His employees had by now accepted the fact that the Chairman of the Board wasn't coming back and that he was now totally in charge.

But something had been nagging Israel for quite some time. So, he decided to do something he hadn't done for a couple of years. He went to the private storage compartments, which were just off the highway and within sight of the mill, "To check on something." The company rented about ten units to store equipment they used occasionally, along with paint and other materials. Ham Hamilton liked his floor to be cleared of non-essentials, which meant if something wasn't being used, put it into storage.

Israel stepped up to the compartment with the number 19 painted on it. He hesitated. He found it odd how he never noticed that before. The same lock was still there. The key opened it and he raised the door.

This storage compartment was for Hamilton's personal effects, mostly Civil War "junk" like bags of lead shot he once sold to collectors and piles of lead pipes. Israel even recalled the day he loaded all these discarded lead pipes into this compartment when he was a little kid.

"Why are you collecting all this junk?" the eight-year old Israel asked a younger Ham Hamilton.

"It's not junk. It's lead. It's what they made bullets out of during the Revolutionary and Civil Wars."

When Israel pulled the string to activate the light bulb hanging down from the ceiling, his eyes widened. There was an open space between the the two high piles of lead bricks and pipes. He

THE DOOR

brought his hands up to his face and started to sob.

*   *   *

"You did a very foolish thing," Lomax said to Danvers, as he opened the steel door to the basement's stairway. He wouldn't say anything else until he closed the steel door behind them. "Coming here like this." He gestured in the direction of the house directly across the alleyway. "They now know you're here." He led the way down the stairway.

"So, you know that they've been watching you?"

"Of course."

"Why didn't you just up and leave?"

"We made a life here. Besides, nothing has been going on at the Pilgrim's house."

There were two steel doors at the bottom of the stairs. One led to the left side of the basement and the other to the right—which had no doorknob.

"Jesus Christ," said Lomax and the door on the left opened electronically.

"So, you use the Lord's name to open doors?"

"An old Irish grandmother once told me that the Devil can't say Jesus Christ…without difficulty."

"My grandmother said he would explode into flames."

"Well, I would consider that a form of difficulty."

Lomax pushed the door open and stepped back. "I need to show you something."

When Danvers entered the room it was dark. When the overhead lights came on, he stood in awe at twelve doors standing erect in a glass enclosure. Each door had heavy chains wrapped around them so that they wouldn't open. A number of cameras were focused on them and sensors were attached to them. A small control desk was placed near the door to the enclosure. A monitor displayed the sensor readings. All were zero.

"You crazy son-of-a-bitch!" said Danvers. "When? How?"

"About a year ago…. Israel had hidden them in a storage compartment that had a lot of lead in it. The lead acted as a shield against the EMI scanners."

"*Ah!* No wonder your former employer couldn't find them."

THE DOOR

Danvers reached out and touched the steel lined walls of the basement. "Hope this is lead lined too."

"Eighth of an inch thick."

Danvers touched one of a dozen steel beams that Lomax installed in this side of the basement to support the enclosure. "A lot of steel beams down here. Expensive."

"It pays to be a good scavenger and work at a factory."

Danvers suddenly became emotional. "Good God! You've got the doors closed! You said it yourself that they can go active when they are closed!"

"Relax, will *ya*. Notice all the chains around them? Trust me, they won't open. Also note all of the sensors they have on them."

"You're studying the doors? Have you gone mad?" He didn't give Lomax a chance to answer his questions. "Does Daphne know what you're doing here?"

"No, I think she would leave me if she knew."

Danvers turned and pointed to the CIA house. "What about them?"

"They don't know either."

"Are you sure?"

"I'm certain that if they knew the doors were here they would have come for them already. Besides, my neighbors are busy little beavers. They've tapped into the original line I had to the Pilgrims house, so they see what I used to see. More importantly, what I want them to see and no more. I've upgraded to a secondary line that they haven't tapped into."

"How do you know that?"

"I would know. Trust me on that."

Danvers shook his head in disbelief. "You want them to see what's going on over there?"

"Oh, yes! If they raid **either** house, they stand a good chance of exposing the existence of the doors. That's the last thing the government wants. The public would go nuts. Up to now, they've been lucky. So, as long as they are tuned into the Pilgrim's, they will continue watching, keep their distance and maintain their cover." Lomax hesitated for a moment. Revealing secrets wasn't something he liked doing. "What they don't know is, I've tapped into them. So, I know exactly what they're doing."

"You play a dangerous game, Lomax."

THE DOOR

Meanwhile across town…

"You wanted to see me, Chief?" asked Dewey Mitchell as he stood in the doorway to the office of the new police chief.

"*Ah*, Lieutenant. Yes, come on in and close the door."

Lieutenant Dewey Mitchell stepped into the Chief's office and closed the door as instructed.

"Sit down, Dewey."

Mitchell sat down.

"I know you got along better with my predecessor, who found it politically expedient to chase after all these meth labs. I don't. And to tell the truth, I was surprised when he got elected Sheriff that you didn't go with him to run his drug unit."

"This town is my home."

"Mine too. But as you are well aware this is an election year and we're probably going to get a new Mayor. Ironically, it may turn out to be someone I fired several years ago, when I was Police Chief in another town. Rumor has it that you may be taking my job come January 1st."

"Would it surprise you if I said that I don't want it?"

"Good, because I don't think you got what it takes to be Chief. As a matter-of-fact, I don't think you're doing a good job running CID. The only reason you got those lieutenant bars is because Hanson retired and you were next in line."

"If you feel that way, why don't you demote me?" Mitchell stood up and headed for the door.

"I want to, but I can't. Your friends on the coast want you right where you are. And nothing sticks in my craw more than when somebody tells me how to run my police department."

"They're not my friends and the Chief ordered me to work with them."

The new Chief stood up. "He no longer signs your paycheck. I do. If you want to play spy, go join the damn CIA. But if you want to keep working here, you better do as I say. Not them. You got it?"

"Loud and clear…."

Mary Pilgrim came to Daphne's house with Richard. She knocked on the front door like she had never knocked on a door in her life, hard and rapid.

THE DOOR

Daphne answered the door. "Mary? What's wrong?"

Mary was crying. "It's Israel!"

A few minutes later, Daphne opened the side door to Lomax's house and came face to face with John Danvers.

"Hello Daphne," he said.

"How do you know my name?"

"I should. I gave it to you."

Her eyes widened. ***The client!*** She turned around to see Mary and Richard and Dara standing in the driveway. She called out to them. "Mary, I need a few minutes. Why don't you wait in my house."

Mary brought the kids into the other house.

Danvers was watching them through a window. "So, that's Richard. A good looking lad."

"Okay you gave me my name, what's yours?"

"Danvers. John Danvers." As he put out his hand she spat at it. "Now, where's Eddi?" she demanded. "I mean, Lomax?"

"Sleeping. The poor man is exhausted."

"Well, life is a bitch and so am *I...!*"

She went to the master bedroom and woke him up. "Get up. Something has happened to Israel!"

Mitchell got up out of his swivel chair to stretch. When he glanced out his office window he spotted Lomax standing across the street in the parking lot of the public library, staring back at him. He told the dispatcher that he was going to "Look up something at the library" and left the PD.

They met in the Reference Section, and then went into a conference room.

"You won't mind if I check you out, first?" asked Lomax.

"Go ahead." Mitchell knew that Lomax was a suspicious man and had to be, so he opened his arms, knowing that the former CIA Agent wouldn't be interested in his service revolver. This was confirmed when Lomax scanned him with a small handheld device that almost looked homemade.

Lomax gave a sigh of relief when he realized Mitchell wasn't wired. "Thanks," said Lomax. "I don't need our friends and your candy ass Chief listening in on us. Israel is missing."

"What?"

THE DOOR

"His secretary said that he went out to check on something and when he came back to the office he was acting crazy, screaming and hollering and making no sense at all. When he left the mill, he tore out of the parking lot at about a hundred miles an hour and headed north."

Mitchell looked away. "I'd say he went to an old watering hole we frequented in our youth in Wytheville. I'll go get him."

As Lomax started to leave, Mitchell grabbed him by the arm. "There's something you're not telling me."

"Oh?"

"You didn't tell me the reason a man who is so stable would go off on the deep end like this."

"Maybe because I don't know?" Lomax tried to lie, but he wasn't convincing.

"Yes, you do. Now come clean or you and me are through."

Lomax raised both hands in defeat. "Okay. He checked a company storage compartment and realized that something of his was missing. "

"And what was missing?"

"The doors."

It was like getting hit with a bolt of lightning. "You mean…?" He stopped, looked left and right to see if anyone was eavesdropping on them. "He had the doors? His doors?"

"You're surprised?"

"Yeah!" He turned away, brought a hand up to his head and sighed. "Then again, if it were me, I'd probably do the same thing. Poor guy."

A thought flashed thorough his mind. "Hey! Wait-a-minute! If Israel didn't say anything about the doors being missing to his secretary, then how did *you* find out about them?"

Lomax was almost glad that Mitchell figured it out. He tilted his head to one side and nodded. "You're good. Only two people knew those doors were missing. Israel and the one who took them."

"You got the doors?"

"And…John Danvers…at my house."

"Jesus Christ!"

"Well," said Lomax with a smile, "now I know you're not the Devil."

THE DOOR

Mitchell didn't get the joke. Quietly and unofficially, he went to Wytheville and brought Israel home. He also arranged for Israel's pickup to be towed home.

*   *   *

Lomax ducked just in time otherwise the frying pan Daphne threw at him might have killed him. It smashed the antique plates that hung on the wall in a display. "I can explain everything!"

"You said it was over!" she roared.

"Honey, calm down now."

"Don't you honey me!"

She picked up a plastic trash can and hurled it at him. She continued yelling and swinging another frying pan as they went into the living room.

Danvers was sweeping the living room with the handheld scanner. When he was done and satisfied, he turned it off.

Lomax and Daphne went into the living room and continued the argument until Danvers closed the kitchen door.

"The rest of the first floor is clean," said Danvers. "They only bugged your kitchen."

"You must be important to them," Daphne said to Danvers.

"Yeah," said Lomax. "I swept the house yesterday and it was clean. They must have just planted those bugs." He smiled. "We'll let them think that they pulled one over on us."

Daphne agreed with a nod.

Danvers was confused and asked Lomax, "You're just going to leave them?"

"Being bugged has its advantages. It's all part of the game and how you play it."

"Well," asked Daphne, with a smile on her face, "how was I?"

"Great," replied Lomax. "Now who's going to clean up that mess?"

"You," she said. "You know, I forgot how much I loved the intrigue."

Lomax exchanged a glance with Danvers.

"I saw that," she said. "What are you *not* telling me?"

Lomax looked to the floor and turned away.

Danvers took possession of the frying pan Daphne was holding. "You better let me have that."

THE DOOR

"Honey," said Lomax, "there's something I've got to show you."

It had been over a year since Daphne went down to the basement. "When did you do all of this? I couldn't get you to tile the floor in the bathroom, but you had time to do all of this!"

Lomax said the Lord's name and the steel door opened.

Daphne's eyes widened and her mouth dropped when she spotted the doors. She fell to her knees. ***"Oh, dear God!"***

As it turned out, Danvers was equally surprised by what he saw, even though he had only been in the room earlier in the morning. "Lomax? Why are they glowing like that?"

Three of the doors glowed with bright white and green lights that occasionally swirled around them.

"I don't know. They've never glowed *down here* before." He went up to the console to make sure the event was being recorded.

"*Down here*," repeated Danvers. "Are you saying they've glowed somewhere else?"

"They glowed in the Bonham's house," answered Daphne, "before the place blew up!"

"Yes, I remember," said Danvers as he stepped closer to the glass enclosure. "Isn't it uncanny how these lights resemble the Aurora Borealis!"

A wild idea ran through Lomax's mind. But after giving it some thought, he shook his head. "No…"

"What is it?" asked Danvers.

"I know they are made out of wood," said Lomax, "but those doors are acting like batteries…you know…by the way they store and release energy."

"The basic component of a carbon battery is charcoal…which comes from decayed trees. Without knowing it, Lomax, you may have hit on something here. Ergo, the means by which these doors exploit energy."

Daphne turned to Lomax and stared at him with angry eyes. "How could you? Our daughter plays in this house. Have you forgotten what these doors did to the Bonham's place?"

"I know why they are glowing," said Danvers. "Richard is nearby."

"But why only three doors?" asked Lomax. "Why not the rest?"

"Because only three were knocked on…and therefore

THE DOOR

activated," said Danvers.

"What have we got ourselves into?" asked Daphne, as she got to her feet.

The house telephone rang. There was an extension line in the basement. Lomax glanced at the Caller ID box before picking up the receiver. "It's from across the street."

"Hello?" said Lomax.

"Eddi," said Mitchell.

Lomax was surprised to hear Mitchell's voice. "Hey, Dewey! What's up?"

"I'm at your boss's house. I need for you to come right over."

Lomax knew that the line was tapped and every word he said was being recorded, so he had to watch his words. "Is something wrong with Israel?"

"Yeah, he got in a big spat with Mary and he's drunk."

"I'll be right over."

Lomax met Mitchell by the front door of the Pilgrim house. They went immediately to the master bedroom. Mary was sitting on the bed, directly across from Israel, trying to console him.

"They're gone!" shouted Israel. "Don't you understand…?"

"Mary," said Lomax as he held up his cell phone, "Daphne wants to talk to you." She reluctantly left the room with the cell phone.

"Boss," said Lomax, "what gives? You go off on a bender and don't invite me along. I feel deprived." He chuckled.

"Watch what you say," Lomax whispered to Mitchell as he brushed up against him.

Mitchell scanned the room with his eyes, in a futile search for the bugs that no doubt existed and were probably planted by Lomax.

Israel shook his head. "The doors...I...*uh*...I...wanted to protect...*uh*…why is this happening to me?"

The client wanted Lomax to place the original spycams in the direction of all the interior doors of the Pilgrim House, which he did. It was an invasion of the Pilgrim's privacy, however, he went to great lengths not to focus the camera on the king size bed. Neither he nor the client was interested in producing porn. True the Pilgrims were videoed nude, this was after all a bedroom and that kind of thing was inevitable. All that footage was deleted after

Daphne got tired of looking at them.

"How do we get him to shut up?" whispered Mitchell.

Lomax answered by giving Mitchell a gentle shove and directing him around to the foot of the bed, where he stood in the both spy cam's way. All the lens could focus on was Mitchell's huge shoulders and head. Lomax went back in the direction he came from and gave Israel a hard punch to the forehead, knocking him out cold. The punch was not seen on camera.

When Mary returned, Lomax was spreading a blanket over her seemingly slumbering husband.

Lomax gestured for everyone to leave the room. They regrouped in the front foyer.

"He's all right," said Lomax, whispering. "Just let him sleep it off."

Mary thanked both of them as they left the house.

"Can your neighbors hear us?" uttered Mitchell.

Lomax was not surprised that Mitchell knew about the stakeout house. "No. The one good thing about them tapping into my bugs is, they can't hear anything when Daphne controls the microphones." He turned around so that the cameras would only see him from behind. "But they can read our lips."

Mitchell brought his hand up to his mouth and coughed. "One heck of a right cross you got there."

"It was a temporary solution to a big problem. We can't let them have the doors." Lomax started to laugh and raised his arm and cupped his fingers as though they were holding a bottle of booze. He turned around. "Boy, when Israel ties one on he goes all the way!"

Mitchell laughed, but in reality he was furious with Lomax. "How did you find them?" He backhanded Lomax. "Sure, I'll go fishing with you anytime!" He then uttered, "So I can drown you."

"He hid them in a storage compartment. I found them by accident a year ago." Lomax started walking towards Mitchell's unmarked sedan. "They're going to put two and two together and figure out I have them, then raid my house. We can't let that happen."

"I agree, but how do we prevent that?"

Lomax smiled and opened his arms wide. "We get Israel to put them back into his house."

THE DOOR

Mitchell's eyes widened. "That's crazy…"

"They have a warehouse with a thousand doors they watch twenty-four seven and they're as dead as the trees they were made from. These are the only active doors that I know about. As long as I am watching the Pilgrims and they are tapped in, they'll sit and watch." Lomax didn't wait for a reply. He just nonchalantly waved good-bye as he walked across the street.

Meanwhile, at the stakeout house, Father groaned as he turned away from the monitor showing a video of Lomax crossing the street to his house and said, "Get me Diciembre. He knows how to deal with this clown."

*   *   *

Lomax was right. All the Pilgrim doors standing erect in the warehouse in West Virginia had been powerless and quiet since their retrieval. Project Door had become an administrative disaster and a financial bottomless pit. It became the operational program where those CIA Agents and techs who received bad evaluations were sent to serve a penance for their sins. Stationing Special Forces there was a thing of the past. They were badly needed in Iraq and Afghanistan. Only those soldiers who received below average fitness reports, in other words screw-ups and/or were in the process of separating from the service, were stationed at the warehouse. Diciembre's personnel were for all intense purposes a motley crew.

So, when Diciembre was ordered to go to Marion and assist the stakeout's Lead Agent—and get away from all these losers for even a little while, he packed his things and was gone in fifteen minutes.

Diciembre arrived at the stakeout house three hours later. He placed a **TOP SECRET** file on the console in front of Father and opened it. "Per the Deputy Director, you are now authorized to see this file." He pulled out a still photograph of Danvers at the White House standing next to the President of the United States. "This photo of John Danvers was taken in '61 . His real name is Nathaniel Pilgrim."

An image of Danvers standing at Lomax's backdoor was being

THE DOOR

projected on one of the monitors. Father jerked a thumb at the monitor. "You're saying that guy is Danvers—the rogue the whole Agency has been looking for...for...damn near forever?"

"That's him." Diciembre pulled out a copy of the birth certificate with John Danver's name and date of birth on it. "According to this birth certificate, John Danvers was born in 1918 in Massachusetts. It's one of the few bogus documents in this file. However, these are authentic." He removed several other documents including college report cards and copies of diplomas. "We do know that he attended Princeton, earned a law degree then went to work for the Secret Service. He was a good agent. He served on the White House Detail for three years, then suddenly disappeared right after the Cuban Missile Crisis. There were rumors that he was involved in the assassination, but from all the accounts that I've read he truly worshiped the President."

"I'm telling you Diciembre, this can't be the same guy. That picture was taken forty-one years ago. He hasn't aged a day!"

"You need to learn something about what you're dealing with here. Time, space and the doors are all relevant. You and your people live next to the second most dangerous place in the world and maybe the universe." He pointed to the monitor showing the rear side of Lomax's house and garage.

*   *   *

Next morning...

It was the hardest thing Lomax ever had to do because he really liked Israel as an employer, a family man and especially as a friend. In some ways, he tried to emulate Israel, particularly in regards to parenting. Lomax hoped that he was half as good a father with Dara as Israel was with Richard. But now he had to do something to protect not only Daphne and Dara but the Pilgrims too. He knocked on the kitchen door and Mary opened it.

"Good morning, Mary. Is he up yet?"

Israel stumbled into the kitchen with a hand on his forehead. "Oh, man! What a hangover. Feels like I got hit with a baseball bat."

Lomax grinned slightly. "That must hurt."

Israel bade him to come into the kitchen where they had coffee. For the next few minutes, Lomax just sat there staring down at

THE DOOR

his cup of coffee.

Israel studied his neighbor's facial expression and said, "I don't know who's in more pain, you or me? But I have a good reason for the way I feel."

Lomax raised his head and stared Israel dead in the eyes. "I've got something to tell you…and you're not going to like it."

"Go on."

"I took them."

"*Huh?*"

"I found them by accident and I took them. I've got your doors."

Israel was instantly in a state of shock. His body and mind became numb. "How…how…could you…why, why, why…?"

"I wanted to protect you and your family."

Israel suddenly became enraged. He jumped to his feet and overturned the kitchen table, sending the coffee pot and a host of plates and cups crashing onto the floor. "Where are they?"

"In a safe place."

"No, no, no. Don't give me that! Where are they?"

"In my garage."

Father slapped his hand on the console. "That's it!" He jumped out of his chair and called out to two techs in the basement. "Wake up the family! I want everyone in fully battle gear and armed and ready to go in three-zero minutes. We're going to raid that garage."

"No, you're not," said Diciembre.

"Hey, I got orders to seize those doors the moment I locate them—."

"—You need to call this one in before you do anything. Make the wrong move now and it could be a career killer. Trust me on that."

He did and made the call to Langley.

Lomax opened the garage and stepped aside.

When Israel saw the doors all the anger and rage he held deep inside came bursting out like an erupting volcano. Lomax had conveniently left an axe on the floor, near the doors. Israel picked up the axe and started to pound the doors with all his might and

THE DOOR

fury. Sparks spewed forth with every blow as though the axe was striking metal instead of wood.

Lomax let him whale away at the doors with the axe and didn't intervene until after five solid hits were made. No damage was seen on any of the doors that were struck. "Now if only the doors we made at the mill could take a hit like that. Must be the wood or something, *huh* boss?" He then noticed the axe's blade was bent.

Israel turned to Lomax and raised the axe in preparation to strike his rather outspoken employee. But instead he growled at him, then hurled the axe on the front lawn. "This isn't funny, Eddi!" He pointed to the empty track of land where the Bonham House once stood. "Two people died in that house because of these doors." He pointed to his house. "A telephone repairman disappeared in my house…in my kid's bedroom!"

"These doors are the source of all of that horror," Lomax said in a relaxed tone. "And you were only trying to protect your family by hiding them. But now you *gotta* do the right thing again— "

"—And what's that?"

"By putting them back into your house."

Israel was stunned. He brought both hands up to his face. "After everything that has happened, how can you suggest that I do that?"

Lomax reached out his arms and rested them on Israel's shoulder. "You know that this problem is not going to go away. You have to face it head on."

"Oh, that's easy for you to say!"

"This time it will be different. We know about the danger and this time I'm going to be there with you all the way. I promise you that."

Israel stared into Lomax's face for a long time.

Together, they carried the doors back to Israel's house and spent all day installing them.

Israel used an old rag to plug the bored out rectangular shaped cavity—known as the mortise—so that the doorknob latch couldn't be inserted when the door was closed. He did this to all twelve of the interior doors so that they wouldn't close either. He noticed the odd look on Lomax's face as he did it. "I know this may sound crazy, but as long as these doors don't close, nothing bad will happen."

THE DOOR

*   *   *

"Can you believe Lomax talked him into doing it!" Father said to Diciembre. "I mean, would you put those doors back in your house?"

"No."

"You sure trained him well, Diciembre!"

Diciembre cocked an eyelid. "Yeah, well he was always full of surprises...."

*   *   *

23:23 HOURS, MARION, VIRGINIA

For the first week since they were installed, nothing unusual happened with the doors at the Pilgrim House. Unknowingly, the rag that filled the mortise in Richard's bathroom door had fallen out. So, when Richard went to relieve himself during the middle of the night he gave a little shove to the bathroom door and it closed. Both Father and Diciembre were on duty in the basement at the stakeout house when the sound of the latch scraping across the strike plate came over the speakers loud and clear.

"Did you hear that?" asked Diciembre.

"The door latch!" said Father.

"Here we go..." said Diciembre. He glanced at his wristwatch and noted the time for his report.

There was another who was glad to hear the latch engage. "Finally!" said Danvers, watching a monitor in Lomax's basement.

Suddenly, just before the door closed with a distinctive 'CLICK' as the latch engaged, a flash of bright light was emitted from inside the bathroom. Its intensity was such that the whole bedroom was lit up, but Richard was oblivious to it. He was rubbing his eyes as he climbed into bed. However, Father, Diciembre and Danvers saw it and could only wonder what it meant. Seconds later, the center of the bathroom door started to bend forward, like it was a piece of rubber and not wood, from the enormous amount of pressure that was being applied to it from behind. The door then opened on its own, giving Danvers, Diciembre and Father a view of a beachfront and an ocean with icebergs in the distance.

*   *   *

23:24 HOURS, REVELATION FIORD, ELLESMERE ISLAND,

CANADA....

There was one man who wished he hadn't opened the bathroom door in Richard's bedroom. He was the handsome, blonde twenty-five year old telephone repairman named "Sparky".

Even though it was late in the evening, being this close to the Arctic Circle during the summer meant that it barely got dark for a few hours. And yet, the Northern Lights were on fire that evening and so low some of the locals would later say they touched the ground.

When Sparky regained consciousness, he found himself lying on the muddy ground. *"Ohhhhhh*, I hate mud." It probably saved his life by cushioning the fall he took. If the ground had been covered with ice, like it was eight months out of the year, the fall would have shattered every bone in his body. He tried to get up, but couldn't. It was then he heard a dog panting, or what he thought was a dog. His vision was blurry, so when the face of the panting animal got up real close to his face, it looked like a white dog. But it wasn't and as his vision improved he realized the dog was in fact a wolf. The wolf licked him on the cheek. "Nice doggie or whatever you are." The wolf ran off, grabbed Richard's baby blanket and tore it to shreds. It was not something Sparky enjoyed watching. *He could be next!*

As he leaned forward, he noticed all of the bedroom furniture and baby toys lying around him. He turned around and spotted the opened door standing in the ruins of what was once a log house. He got a glimpse of a twirling vortex before it faded out. He then saw the interior of Richard's bedroom. It was then he began to remember. He was violently pulled through a doorway. ***The door!*** His eyes were slowly clearing up but he would swear that there was a glow around the door. As a matter-of-fact, what little of the house's foundation was left seemed to be glowing too! It was too much for him and he passed out. His head landed on one of Richard's plush toys. It emitted a squeaky shrill.

When a wolf howled, Sparky was jolted back to consciousness. Now he was surrounded by a pack of wolves. A couple of them growled and showed their teeth to him. "Oh, this just can't get any better!"

Someone whistled in the distance and all the wolves backed off.

Sparky managed to stumble to his feet and survey his

THE DOOR

surroundings. There was the tarmac of a small airport in front of him and the waters of a green arctic ocean beyond that. He spun on his heel to turn around. In all of the other directions he saw beautiful towering mountains with glaciers. "Is this some kind of joke?" He started to laugh hysterically. He cupped his hands and called out, "Hello? Can anybody hear me?" No answer. He touched his chest and felt his heart pounding. "What am I, dead? My heart is still ticking. Can't be dead. I'm still breathing!" His shouts echoed back at him. "This ain't right. I go to work, I'm doing a job, I open a door and the next thing I know I'm in Antarctica!"

"*...I'm in Antarctica...Antarctica!*" echoed off the mountains.

He stumbled up to the opened log cabin door and touched the framing. It was real. "Knock! Knock!" he said. "Who's there?" he answered. He gazed into the doorway and saw something that could not be. It was a dark swirling vortex. ***"Knooockkkkk! Knoooockkkkk! Whooooo'sss thereeeeeeee?"*** His voice echoed through the hills and mountains and came back to him.

"Trust me, you don't want to know," a voice cried out, but it didn't echo.

"What?" asked Sparky as he turned to the gray haired Indian who walked towards him. But what got Sparky's attention was all the growling wolves that surrounded the old Indian, protecting him. Sparky started to get dizzy and his legs felt like rubber. As he stumbled a few steps towards the old Indian the wolves mistook his movements as an act of aggression. They let out a growl as they pounced on Sparky, driving him backwards. One wolf leapt out of the doorway and struck Sparky from behind the knees, driving him backwards. The last thing he remembered before passing out again was glancing over his shoulder, watching the door slam shut and hitting his head on it with a ***bam!*** The impact echoed off the mountains and was heard by everyone in the town, whether they were indoors or not.

*   *   *

Back in West Virginia…

The head tech of the facility was staring at the window that faced the interior of the warehouse. Hundreds of doors were glowing with white and green colors. He raised the telephone

THE DOOR

receiver to his face. "Sir, we don't know why, but scores of doors, maybe a hundred, just started to glow. And we did not hear them knock. Repeat. They did not knock."

"How long ago—?" asked Diciembre.

"—Thirty seconds."

"Did any of them open?"

"Negative."

"A similar phenomenon occurred here when the kid closed his bathroom door. Be advised that the door opened on its own and it did not knock."

"Roger that. Now what are your orders?"

"Go on full alert. Lock down the facility. I'll get you backup ASAP."

Diciembre closed his cell phone and turned to the wall monitor that displayed the video of the opened bathroom door in Richard Pilgrim's room. There was no bathroom, no view of the arctic and for some unknown reason the door's threshold turned as black as pitch.

Father pointed to the fluctuating indicators on the audio monitor. "We're picking up sounds." He put on a headset and worked the controls to increase the gain. "I hear a voice."

Oddly enough, Richard was oblivious to everything. As soon as he returned to bed, he fell fast asleep and even started to snore. The other two active doors in the Pilgrim house remained dormant.

Suddenly, a set of glowing eyes appeared in the doorway.

The female agent screamed when she spotted them.

It took a few seconds for more light to appear in the doorway and everyone was able to make out the face of a wolf as it stared into the bedroom. It sniffed the air before stepping across the threshold.

"What is that," asked the female agent, "a dog?"

"No," replied Diciembre, "that's a wolf. An Arctic Wolf."

The female agent became even more terrified. "Oh, my God, he's heading for the boy! What do we do?"

Everyone, including Danvers, held their breath as the wolf walked up to the bed, sniffing some of the toys that lay on the floor, then sniffing one of Richard's exposed feet. He even licked it. The speaker emitted the sounds of a man whistling, then

THE DOOR

another man talking in a very distressed manner and several other wolves growling. The wolf turned around and leapt through the doorway. Now more of the Arctic scene was made visible by the increasing amount of light that was coming through. Danvers and the CIA Agents got a glimpse of a pack of wolves leaping on a man—including the one who entered the bedroom—and driving him back towards the opened door. Much to the surprise of everyone who was watching the event, Richard's bathroom door gently closed on its own.

The cell phone rang and Diciembre answered it. "Go ahead."

"They've stopped," reported the head tech from the warehouse. "They've all stopped glowing—all at once. Just like someone opened and closed a door."

"Same thing here," said Diciembre as he once again glanced at his wristwatch. "Cancel the alert. I'll be there in three hours. Just sit tight." He closed the cell phone.

"So," said Father with a smile, "now we have proof that these doors are portals."

"First time we recorded a destination," said the female agent, as she removed the DVD from the DVD drive and held it out to Diciembre.

"Yeah," said Diciembre, "a real nice place if you don't mind the wolves."

Diciembre turned to the female agent. "Burn me a DVD."
She replied with a nod.

"First time a door opened on its own and without knocking," said Father.

"This must be the day for firsts," said Diciembre.

"What do you think it all means?" asked Father.

"I don't know," replied Diciembre, "but I think the slumber party is over, people. We're about to earn our pay. Let's just hope we live to spend it." He turned and dashed up the stairs to get his things.

*　　*　　*

Nothing supernatural happened for the rest of that night.

All the personnel stationed at the West Virginia facility were

THE DOOR

immediately transferred. The losers were replaced with the best and brightest and twice as many of them. In a twist of fate, Deputy Director Blackburn actually asked Diciembre if he would mind staying on for a little while longer. It was a request, not an order. Always the team player, Diciembre accepted and gained some points in doing so.

And for the next two days, Diciembre and the new techs in West Virginia went over every frame of video they had on the glowing doors, from both their facility and the Pilgrim house. However, in the end, they had more questions than answers.

THE DOOR

Chapter Twelve

THE WANDERING

Midnight... **Knock! Knock!**

It wasn't as loud or as harsh as with all previous door knockings. It was more like a tapping. But it was loud enough to awaken the seven-year old Richard Pilgrim from a dead sleep. The pulsating glow from the bathroom door lit up his room. He leaned forward in his bed, yawned and rubbed his eyes. When the glowing stopped, he fell back asleep as soon as his head hit the pillow.

Danvers once again had the midnight shift and was manning the consoles alone in the basement of Lomax's house. A smile grew on his face as the monitor showed the door in Richard's room glowing. "Praise be to God...it's starting!"

He pressed a button that activated the buzzer on Lomax's and Daphne's bedroom. Lomax had taken a leave of absence from the mill and was sleeping with Daphne in the other house. Three minutes later, both came racing down the stairs to the basement.

"Something terrible is going to happen to Richard if he answers that door!" said Daphne. There was fear in her tone.

"Relax," said Danvers. "Richard, like Allison, can now go through his door at will, whether it knocks or not."

"At will? What...what does that mean '*at will*'?"

"Travellers don't always need for an active door to knock before they can venture from one realm to another. There are some doors that they can knock on themselves and open without the fear of being blasted to wherever." He pointed to the monitor. "This just happens to be one of them."

"Can you open any of these doors?" Lomax asked Danvers. "I mean, you're their maker...for the most part." There was a cynical grin on Lomax's face.

THE DOOR

Danver's eyes narrowed. He was not amused. "They won't open for me."

"That's why you need the kids?" asked Lomax.

Danvers leaned towards Lomax and gazed at him with his piercing eyes. "I'm not the only one...."

Lomax made a face. "You mean, the Devil?"

"Richard activated two doors and Allison activated one other in Bonham's house," said Daphne. "That leaves nine more doors that are not active." She faced Danvers. "You said that each door goes to one location, right?"

Danvers hesitated. He didn't know if this was the right time to tell everything he knew about the doors. He was worried that once Lomax learned everything and didn't need him anymore that he'd be thrown out the backdoor. On the other hand, what choice did he have? *None!* "Like I said, most doors can only go to one location. But there are a precious few that can wander. We call them: 'Wanderers'. Therein lies the true danger for Richard. If his bathroom door is a Wanderer, some of the destinations are very hostile."

"Oh, boy," said Lomax as he winced and turned his back on Daphne. This was something his wife did not need to hear. "Please shut up."

"You mentioned "we", said Daphne. "Who is 'we'?"

Danvers gave a chuckle. "If I told you, you wouldn't believe me."

"Try me," said Daphne, with more than a hint of anger in her tone.

"We as in Einstein and I?"

"You mean Albert Einstein?" Daphne shot a dirty look at Lomax. "You're right, I don't believe you."

"I minored in Physics at Princeton just so that I could enroll in his classes. He is...or was a truly brilliant man."

"You were a student of Albert Einstein?" said Lomax.

"Yes and as luck would have it, there's a door that goes to Princeton in 1939. Allison took me to visit my old professor."

"Now that's one door I'd like to go through," said Lomax with a glint in his eyes. "Wouldn't that be cool, Daphne? Think about it! To really meet Albert Einstein!" He tapped himself on the chest. "I bet we'd hit it off!"

THE DOOR

Danvers became annoyed with Lomax and let out a sigh. "I was hoping that you would understand the reason the government wants control of these doors. But, as usual, Lomax, you've missed the point to all of this."

"Which is?" asked Daphne.

"A door is a physical barrier between two environments. Certain doors, and I'm not just talking about the ones I made, have become time and space portals. Under certain conditions, they can take someone to different places and different times. Once these doors are activated they become impervious to fire and anything you can shoot or throw at them."

"We know," said Lomax, thinking about the Bonham House fire.

"But how is that possible?" asked Daphne. "Those doors are made out of matter. All matter can in one way or another be broken down into their basic chemical components."

"Bravo!" said Danvers. "I couldn't have said it better myself."

Daphne glanced over to Lomax, who was smiling at her. "High school Chemistry." She shrugged. "I got an 'A'."

"To answer your question, those doors are not really here…in this reality. They're half here and half somewhere else."

"They're out of phase?" asked Lomax.

"Exactly," said Danvers. "Very good, Lomax!"

"Yeah, well, I still don't understand what all the big fuss is about."

"My dear, Lomax," said Danvers. "There are certain things that man should not have access to. These doors are one of them. For he who controls the doors can control the destiny of humanity and beyond. Imagine being able to go back in time, not to watch and experience history, but to change it. Radically." He pointed to Daphne. "Let's say that I accidentally or purposely caused the death of your great, great, grandfather. Your existence would be negated…so would Dara's."

She didn't like the sound of that. "Accidentally or purposely, this scares the bejesus out of me!"

"Nazi Germany was close to developing the bomb when it surrendered in forty-five," said Danvers, "but what if someone gave them the plans in forty-one…?"

"Kaboom!" uttered Lomax.

THE DOOR

"*Ja vol, Mein Herr!* We'd all be speaking German now or we'd all be dead."

Daphne made a face. "There are people like myself who believe that the Devil is hiding behind every tree. If the doors can do all the things you say they can do, what is stopping him?"

"God."

"How's that?"

"Only God, His Angels and the Travellers can open the door portals."

"And Allison and Richard are Travellers?" asked Daphne.

Danvers nodded.

"How can they open these doors," asked Lomax "and no one else?"

"I don't know all the particulars," said Danvers, "but I do know that they were born on the same night." Both Lomax and Daphne were jolted by the memory of the Pilgrims being involved in a car crash during a storm and how they came to the rescue. "Richard was born during a hurricane. Allison was born during a massive Northern Lights event."

"But they're just lights in the night sky," said Daphne. "What can they do?"

"In 1998, the City of Quebec had a blackout because of a Northern Lights event. They are powered by the sun and their energy potential is enormous."

"And where was Allison born?" asked Lomax.

"A little Native American community on Ellesmere Island called Revelation Fiord," said Danvers.

"Revelation," said Daphne. "I wondered when we'd get to the spiritual part of all of this."

"And there is a spiritual part, Daphne. Only the purist may open and pass through these doorways. It's one of God's Laws."

"Then how is it you can pass through?" asked Daphne. "You sir, are anything but pure."

"Yes, I am a sinner and bad one. To answer your question, some of the safeguards have been broken."

"How do you know it's one of Gods Laws?"

Danvers looked away. "My source in this matter is... impeccable...even if he is not."

"You mean, the Devil?" Daphne shook her head. "Sorry, I'm

still not convinced. You're a great storyteller and you got me half scared to death. But you haven't provided us with one shred of evidence to back up any of your claims."

Lomax sided with Daphne. "She has a point there."

"*Hmmm!* But how do I provide you with proof?" He took a moment to think it over. ***"Ah!"*** He raised an index finger into the air. "I know. Daphne, how old do you think I am?"

Daphne gave him a quick once over. "Thirty-five…give or take a year."

Danvers smiled and touched his face as though he was complemented. "Oh, thank you, my dear, but I am well over four hundred years old."

"Oh, please," said Daphne, "Lomax, I've heard enough." She started for the stairway.

"I was born in the Town of Salem Village. My grandparents came over from England to build a true Puritan community." Danvers sat down in front of a computer, went online and typed out a name on Google. A file opened with a picture of a Puritan who lived in the 1690s. "And my real name is Nathaniel Pilgrim." He kicked the floor with the heels of his shoes to move away from the console and let Lomax and Daphne view his picture on the monitor.

Daphne's eyes widened. She had seen a painting of the Pilgrim Family patriarch and the man who called himself John Danvers was a spitting image of Nathaniel. She might have said something in reply, but a red light started to flash over one of the monitors on the wall.

"What's that?" asked Danvers, pointing to the flashing red light.

"Motion detector," replied Lomax, "in Richard's bedroom."

Daphne went to the second console and worked the controls. "Nothing is going on. Why did it activate?"

All eyes were now focused on the monitor marked "Richard's Bedroom". All was quiet.

The room was dimly lit with the nightlight Mary had installed. Richard climbed out of bed and walked over to the bathroom door, then stopped.

"It's the kid," said Lomax. "Why did he stop?"

"He's waiting for it," said Danvers. "He has the gift!"

"Waiting for what?" asked Lomax.

THE DOOR

Knock! Knock!

Daphne let out a yelp.

"Quiet!" shouted Danvers. "He's going to answer the door!"

Lomax was surprised. He started to think out loud, something he rarely did. "Wait a minute. He wakes up from a sound sleep, gets out of bed, takes two steps towards the bathroom door, then and stops and stares at it."

"Oh, my God, he knew it was going to knock!" said Daphne.

Lomax thought back to the moment before the Bonham House exploded, when Allison stopped by the front door, turned and gazed up in the direction of the door she came out of. "Just like Allison did…."

As Richard went up to the door and grabbed the doorknob, Lomax yelled, "No, kid. Don't do it. ***Don't!***" Lomax's forehead was covered with sweat.

"Lomax," pleaded Daphne, "you have to stop him! He's Israel's boy!"

Both Lomax and Daphne stood up and hugged each other as they watched the monitors.

Richard started to turn the doorknob, but then stopped and did something strange. He let it go.

Knock! Knock! went the door, but much more softly than ever before. It was an obvious attempt to come across as non-threatening as possible.

"What's going on?" asked Daphne.

"He's luring him in," said Danvers.

The tapping startled the young boy. However, he composed himself quickly. He had no reason to fear. His parents had said nothing to him about the door. To him it was all a game, so he did a playful thing by replying with double knocks of his own on the door before grabbing the doorknob and pulling hard.

There was no explosion. But there were voices. Richard peered into the doorway at a scene straight out of American history, one Danvers would recognize immediately. There were people milling out a public square wearing long dark clothing, even though it was clearly summer.

Lomax released Daphne and went back to the console, working the controls that panned the camera.

THE DOOR

"Who are those people?" asked Daphne. She looked to Danvers, who had the most distressed expression on his face. It appeared to her that he was having trouble even looking at the monitor.

"They look like Puritans," said Lomax.

Richard stepped through the doorway and mixed into the crowd of spectators.

"Oh, no!" cried out Daphne. "Richard crossed the threshold!"

When the Puritans spotted the little boy with odd night clothing, they stepped away, giving Lomax and the others a chance to see what was going on.

A woman, with no shirt on, was tied to a post. A man with a whip cracked the whip dangerously close to the woman's back. He seemed to be enjoying himself.

"That's Salem Village," said Danvers.

"Where you were born?" asked Daphne.

"Confess *thy* sins!" the man with the whip shouted.

 The woman was crying. "Please!"

"What are we looking at?" asked Daphne.

"Something that happened over four centuries ago," said Danvers.

The man with the whip lashed out at the woman, causing her to scream in pain. Some of the spectators screamed and some cheered. Richard went up to the woman and touched her, probably to see if she was real. "Step aside, lad!" shouted the man with the whip.

"Why are you hurting this lady?" asked Richard.

"Whose child is this?" the man asked the crowd, as he recoiled his whip. "Move him out of the way or by all that is holy, I shall thrash him as well."

Richard picked up the shawl that lay on the ground and covered the woman's back with it.

"Someone move this damn boy out of my way!"

An elderly man stepped forward and took a position behind Richard. "You have no cause to blaspheme this young lad. He's an innocent. Which is more than *thou* can say about all of *ye!*"

"She's a witch, I tell *ya!*" shouted the man. "She is bedeviled!"

"I thought witches were mean and had evil powers?" Richard asked aloud.

THE DOOR

"They do," one spectator cried out.

"Then why isn't she shooting lightning bolts or fire at *y'all?* And she don't look mean and evil to me." Richard pointed to the man with the whip. "You're the evil one here!"

"Well said, lad," the elderly man said to Richard.

All of a sudden, the crowd changed their attitude and turned on the man with the whip. While several men scuffled with the man with the whip, the woman was freed from her bounds.

"Bless *ye*, child," she said to Richard as several women took her away.

Richard yawned as he watched the man with the whip being bound to the pole and stripped of his shirt. He was getting tired. He only stayed long enough to see the man getting a taste of his own whip. He then stepped across the threshold of the bathroom door and re-entered his bedroom. With a slight push of his arm he closed the bathroom door and he went straight to bed.

"We were worried about him?" said Lomax.

"Son of a gun!" said Daphne. She turned to his left, then his right in search of Danvers. But he was gone. "Hey, where'd he go?"

Lomax was using the mouse with one hand and typing out commands with the other. A close-up of the man with the whip was brought up on the largest screen, at the center of the wall. He made some modifications to the face of the man, removing his beard and moustache. It was Danvers.

"Guess who?" asked Lomax.

"It's him! No wonder he walked away…the cruel bastard!"

"You wanted proof," he said, gesturing to the monitor. "Well, there it is."

Lomax got up and stretched as he headed for the door.

Danvers went out the front door of Lomax's house and stood in the shadow, staring at the Pilgrim house and Richard's bedroom window. He reached up and touched the place on his shoulder that was scared by his own whip on that memorable day, some four centuries earlier. How unsettling it was for him to see it unfold before his very eyes again.

Lomax was looking out the front living room window at Danvers, wondering if he made a dangerous mistake by allying with him. He too glanced across the street at his friend's house

THE DOOR

and the bedroom of their son. He went back to the control room and said to Daphne, "Pack up. You're leaving with the kid."

In a move that completely shocked Lomax she replied, "No, I'm not."

"But what if I'm wrong…about him?" He jerked his head in the direction of the stairway.

"Then you're going to need me…now more than ever." She got up and went face to face with him. "Learn one thing, Lomax. The greatest weapon against evil is love." She kissed him. "And I'm in a fighting mood right now."

"Love and war," he said, with a smirk. "Sounds like my marriage."

*   *   *

"Oh, that's so sensual," he said. "How about going a little lower?"

Sparky opened his eyes and realized that a wolf was licking him in the face. It startled him. For a moment, he froze with fright. "What? You again?" He turned his head slightly to the left, then the right to survey his surroundings. He was in the cargo bed of a moving pickup truck with the whole pack of wolves. He heard the brakes being applied and felt the pickup coming to a stop. The Indian Elder got out of the cab and pulled down the tailgate.

Sparky passed out again as he was placed onto a gurney and brought into the town's community center.

When he awakened again, the most beautiful native woman he had ever seen was staring down at him and smiling. A bright glowing light surrounded that gorgeous smiling face. "Am I dead? Is this Heaven? Are you an Angel…or a wolf?"

"No, no, **Hell no** and *huh?*" she replied. "To some of us, this is the end of the world." She moved slightly and Sparky realized that what he thought was a heavenly glow was in fact an overhead ceiling light. "Welcome to Revelation Fiord."

"Revel—what?" Not wanting to appear infirm, he tried his best to lean forward, but only got about half way up. The dizziness was overwhelming and he lowered his head back down onto the gurney. "*Ohhhhhh!*"

"That will teach you not to do that again. You have a concussion."

THE DOOR

His vision was slowly improving. He gave her and his surroundings a once over. "Who are you and what is this place?"

"My name is Kudluk."

"Good luck? That's what all the girls say to me."

"No, Kud…luk. It means Thunder." She pointed to the sign on the wall and repeated what it said, "And this is the community center in '*the place that never thaws.*' But lucky for you it did otherwise you would be in Heaven…*oh*, right about now."

He brought his hand up to his head. It was beginning to come back to him now. "No, no, no. This is all wrong. I was in Marion, Virginia…"

"The States? My, my! Well, we certainly are a long way from home, *huh,* sailor?"

"I'm not a sailor. I'm a cable TV repair guy."

She gestured to the TV what was very snowy. "Good. Maybe after I patch you up you can do something with our satellite dish."

The Indian Elder who brought Sparky to the community center entered the room and presented Thunder with a wallet. It was Sparky's. She opened it and studied his Virginia Drivers License. The photo matched her patient. She handed it back to the Elder. "Mayor, you better call Seacrest about this." The Elder went into his office to make the call.

"That guy is your Mayor?"

"Yes, why?"

"He's got wolves."

"Don't all Mayors?"

Sparky thought it over and cocked an eyelid. "True."

"He's also our Shaman…that's a holy man to you Yankees."

"*Whooo!* I'm a Southern boy. Don't be calling me that."

The community center was built to accommodate most government functions under one roof. There was a Post Office, Offices of the Mayor and Town Councilmen, a public meeting hall and the Town Clinic. There was a window in the clinic that afforded Sparky a sensational view of the ocean.

"Where is this place?"

"You're on island in northern Canada that is directly across from Greenland."

"Did you say '*Canada'*? How did I get up here?"

He was in no shape to talk, but she had a personal reason to

THE DOOR

keep pressing him for answers. "Did you walk through a door?"

"Walk? More like being sucked through a garden hose."

She made a notation on her report. "We've had others. You're the first to survive." When she looked up from her report, she found him asleep.

She left the clinic and went out the front door to stare at the old village and the door.

The Mayor came outside to speak with her. "I faxed Seacrest a copy of your patient's driver's license."

"And?"

"He said there's no need for him to come here."

Thunder cursed in her native tongue. The Mayor let her vent because she had a good reason to be angry at the Royal Canadian Mounted Police Inspector, who just happened to be a former lover and the father of her daughter. Once they were very close, then tragedy struck and it drove them apart.

When she finally stopped cursing, the Mayor said, "Kudluk, he too has suffered a great loss. But he is not a believer, like you."

After Thunder's daughter went missing, she became as cold as a glacier to everyone. But today, all those self-imposed emotional barriers were lifted. As she wiped the tears from her eyes, she replied, "I know I'm right. Polar bears did not take my daughter away from me." She pointed to the old village. "That door did!"

*　　*　　*

As soon as Israel came home from work, he went across the street and rang the doorbell to Lomax's house. Daphne answered it. "Good evening, Daphne."

"Hello, Israel," she said, "and I know why you're here." She bade him to enter Lomax's house and directed him to the master bedroom.

"You do?"

"And feel free to kick him in the butt…the big baby. Mommy I got a sore tummy."

They found Lomax in bed, sneezing. "Hi boss!"

"Oh, so you are sick."

"Me, *na!* Got a little cold is all." He waved her hand at Daphne. "She's *gotta* make a big deal out of everything."

THE DOOR

Israel held up a letter. "Well, then what's this? You've accrued plenty of sick days. If you need some time off you don't need to take a Leave of Absence."

"Actually, I do. I got some things that I need to take care of. Personal."

Israel nodded. "Okay. You go ahead and do what you have to do. The job will be waiting for you when you're done."

"Thanks, Israel." He then changed the subject. "Everything okay?"

"No problems."

As soon as Israel walked out the front door, Lomax pulled off the blanket and got out of bed. He was fully clothed in black combat fatigues and army boots. "I hated to lie to him like that, but I need to be ready on a moment's notice," he said to Daphne.

"I agree."

Lomax was genuinely surprised by her response. "Well, that's a first."

"And probably the last time I will agree with you. Now get downstairs and relieve Danvers. I don't like him being down there…alone."

He saluted Daphne. "Yes, *ma'am!*"

Across town, Mitchell was about to call it a day when the dispatcher informed him that there was a policeman from Canada on the phone. He took the call.

"This is Lieutenant Mitchell."

"Hello Lieutenant. My name is Seacrest. I'm an Inspector with the RCMP from the town of Resolute in northern Canada."

"Wow! Where's that?" He got up and referred to a map of North America he had on the wall.

"We're the second most northern township in Canada."

Mitchell shifted his focus on the map to the most northern landmass in Canada, a place called Ellesmere Island. "That would put you somewhere on Ellesmere Island? Correct?" The town wasn't listed on the map.

"Right, you are. I'm calling you in reference to a missing person's report you filed seven years ago." There was some static in the background.

"Oh?" Mitchell sat down on his swivel chair. "Which one?"

"A young man name of Sparky Powers."

Mitchell's body went instantly numb. "Sparky?"

"Yes, that was the name they saw on his work shirt."

"You found his remains, then?"

The connection was momentarily cut off by static.

"Remains? No, he's alive. He's a little banged up, but he's okay."

"Oh, my God!" Mitchell had given up all hope that he was still alive.

"You all right?" asked Seacrest, hearing the distress in Mitchell's tone.

"I knew his mother. She was so distraught by his disappearance that she suffered a heart attack and died."

The static on Seacrest's end was so bad all he heard was "mother…died."

"Did you say his mother died?" he asked the American.

"Yes." More static.

"I'm sorry to hear that."

"Is he with you now?"

"No, he's in a town north of here called Revelation Fiord. It's an Indian community. It's very remote."

"Sounds like it. How'd he get all the way up there?"

Seacrest was silent for a long moment. "I was hoping you could answer that question."

Mitchell went online and Googled: RCMP Seacrest. Seacrest's picture was displayed on a Canadian newspaper article entitled: "INVESTIGATION STILL OPEN but RCMP Inspector Seacrest, victim's father, has little hope they will find her alive." As he read the article and scrolled down another picture appeared. It was of a seven-year old girl wearing a Little Red Riding Hood costume. Suddenly, it all made sense to him.

"Sorry. I have no idea." Mitchell was lying. "Inspector, could I call you back later?"

"I'll be here."

Mitchell hung up. He had to break off the communication with Seacrest because he figured the line was tapped. There was only one secure telephone line in the town. He waited until dark before leaving the PD and parking his unmarked car in a commercial parking lot. He then he walked to Lomax's house. He stayed in the shadows at the front of Lomax's house, because he knew that all the cameras were focused on either the rear of Lomax's house or the front of the Pilgrim's house. He rang the doorbell to Lomax's house and Daphne answered it.

"Lieutenant Mitchell?"

"May I use your phone?" he asked.

"Sure. Come on in." She let him in and directed him to the telephone in the living room.

"No," said Mitchell. "I need to use your other phone?"

"What other phone?" she said with a nervous smile.

"The secure one…in your basement."

Daphne's smile vanished. For a long moment, she didn't move or say anything. She was shocked that he knew about the basement. She knew that he had been the CIA's confidential informant in the town, but didn't know how much information they would reveal to the Detective Lieutenant from the Marion PD.

The sound of footsteps was heard arising from the basement's stairway. The steel door swung open and out came Lomax, wearing his black combat fatigues.

"You going to a war?" asked Mitchell.

"I'm already in one and whether you know it or not, so are you." He shot a wink to Daphne, then gave a wave to Mitchell and said, "Come on."

Lomax led the way down the stairs and through the open door to the Control Room. Daphne followed Dewey downstairs.

Mitchell took one look at the bank of monitors filling the wall and let out a whistle. "*Gees!* Is there any house or building you don't have eyes on in Marion?"

Lomax pointed to a telephone receiver. "May I ask who you are going to call? Deputy Director Blackburn perhaps?"

"No. His name is Seacrest. He's an Inspector with the Royal Canadian Mounted Police. He called me a little while ago about a missing person's BOLO (Be On the Lookout) I put out seven years ago."

"For who?" asked Lomax.

"Sparky Powers."

Both Lomax and Daphne immediately recognized the name, but tried not to show it.

"For seven years," said Mitchell, after noting their reactions,

"I've tried to figure out how a cable repairman can go into a house in my town and just disappear. Of course I left out the fact that almost everything in the room he was in went with him. Now I learn that he's alive and well in northern Canada." He shrugged. "How do I explain that?" He raised a hand. "But wait. It gets better. Apparently, the Inspector has been working another missing person's case, someone who just happens to be his seven-year-old daughter. The last time he saw her she was wearing a Little Red Riding Hood costume."

"Allison?" uttered Daphne, in a knee jerk reaction. She looked away and chided herself for speaking her mind, something Lomax trained her not to do.

Mitchell heard the utterance and noted her reaction. "Why am I *not* surprised that you know her name?"

"Just another piece to the puzzle," said Lomax. He turned to Daphne and they stared at each other for a moment. It was almost like they were communicating telepathically.

"Show him," she said with a determined tone.

Lomax typed out a command on the keypunch and made several clicks with the mouse. "So, you want to know what happened to the cable guy. I have a feeling Diciembre didn't show you this." When he pressed ENTER, the center monitor showed a video of the bathroom door knocking, Sparky answering it and being violently pulled into the unknown. The clip was only ten seconds long, but it spoke volumes to the Detective Lieutenant. It shook him up. Now, not only did he know what happened to Sparky, but to Maggy Hamilton and the Bonhams as well.

When the clip ended and monitor went dark, Lomax lifted the telephone receiver and handed it to Mitchell. "Make the call."

"Put it on a speaker so we can all hear," said Mitchell. His voice was slightly shaky.

Lomax did.

Mitchell punched out the telephone number and waited for Seacrest to answer it.

"Hello, this is Inspector Seacrest." The static was even worse now.

"Inspector, this is Mitchell from Virginia."

"*Ah*, I was wondering if you would call me back."

"I had to find a secure phone…one that doesn't have extra

THE DOOR

ears."

That made Seacrest very suspicious. He then noticed that there was no phone numbers printed on his Caller ID. "Oh? Why all the hush-hush for a cold missing person's case?"

"It's been reopened and it's a very serious case…one with National Security implications." Mitchell changed the subject slightly. "I understand that you're also working on a missing person's case."

Seacrest exhaled. "My daughter. Actually, the RCMP has just closed the case."

"May I ask why?"

"Revelation Fiord is a very hostile place to live. We fear that polar bears may have taken her."

"Did you say, Revelation Fiord?"

"I did."

"The same place Sparky Powers was discovered?"

"Yes, but what does that got to do with—?"

"—And your daughter's name is Allison?"

"Yes," he replied at almost a whisper.

"I only have one more question for you, Inspector. Is there a door in Revelation Fiord…?"

*   *   *

It was Christmas Eve, 1865 and Fetch's present to his new family was the discovery of a cache of stolen items he found in a cave. The first thing Hamilton did was to inform the county sheriff. The sheriff arranged for a dozen wagons to be driven by his deputies and some volunteers through the woods to the cave where Fetch made his discovery. Even though the war was over, iron was virtually impossible to acquire and worth its weight in gold. Cast iron stoves were a premium at this time of the year and the cave had a number of them. There was also furniture and bags of clothing and dry goods.

"Must have been bushwhackers," the Sheriff said to Hamilton. "They couldn't take it with them, so they hid it here with the idea of coming back for it. They're probably all dead." He waved his hand at the iron stoves that were being loaded onto the wagons. "It's going to be another cold winter."

THE DOOR

"I'd say," said Hamilton.

The Sheriff reached out his right hand to Hamilton, who shook it. "Them stoves will warm up a lot of needy homes. You and your boys have done a good thing here, Hamilton."

It was a proud day for Hamilton. He was all smiles during the return trip home until Fetch spotted something odd.

"Look at that track," said Fetch, pointing to the deep furrow-like groove in the ground. It looked like someone ran a plow through the forest.

"You never seen a wagon track before?" asked Freckles.

"Wagons have four wheels…and they make two tracks. Not one."

Hamilton dismounted, went up to the track and inserted his hand in it. The track reached all the way to his wrist. "About five inches deep."

"No wagon done that," said Fetch.

"And it's been here for a while," said Hoot, the hunter of the family. He could tell by the way the sharp edges were rounded by erosion.

"Hoot," said Hamilton. "Track this thing and see where it goes."

Hoot spurred his horse and galloped off, following the track.

Fetch turned his horse around and galloped off in the opposite direction. "I *be look'n* to see where it came from."

"Good idea," said Hamilton. He watched Fetch disappear into the forest. "Wait a minute. I know this place." And then he recognized the game trail they had been following. ***"Oh, no! God no!"*** He climbed back onto the buckboard and raced off after Hoot.

"*Pa*," asked Red, "what is it?"

Moon raised himself out of his saddle, turning left and right. "This *be* the trail we done took last year—***remember!***" Moon spurred his horse.

It took a moment, but when Red recognized some of the land-marks and the trail they once used, it all came back to them. Red drove the horse on his wagon as fast as it could go and gave chase after Hamilton.

*   *   *

THE DOOR

Cornelius Pilgrim was a happy man, even though he was back to living in a tent. He and his grandson had become very close to Ham, Maggy and the boys. They had become family. They just celebrated Christmas and it was a joyous event. Now they were building his house and it was going to be beautiful. The elder Pilgrim may have been a cripple, but he wanted to be there to supervise the construction. So Levy once again erected their tent and brought over their furniture to make his grandfather as comfortable as possible. Ole Cornelius was a house builder by trade and really knew how to teach young men like his grandson and the Hamilton boys his craft. So when the boys dug out the basement and started putting in the foundation his advice and experience was invaluable to them.

The Pilgrims and Hamiltons did everything together and more importantly they protected each other. But this was one morning where Hamilton and his boys weren't there for Ole Cornelius. They were off with the Sheriff, leaving Cornelius by himself. He woke up later than usual and as he rolled his wheelchair out of the tent, he beheld a sight that sent him to his grave.

The door was standing erect, next to the wood platform, facing his tent.

When Cornelius saw it, he suffered a heart attack and fell out of his wheelchair.

*   *   *

Hoot was first to arrive. When he spotted Cornelius lying on the platform he started shouting, "*Ma!*"

Cornelius' grandson Levi was with Maggy at the wood mill when Hoot rode up to them. "*Ma*, come quick like! It's Cornelius! He in a bad way."

Maggy went into the wheelhouse for her medical bag. Levi went and got the buckboard. He drove it up to the front door of the house and braked to a halt just as she was coming out. She climbed aboard and was whisked away. Unfortunately, by the time they arrived at the construction site, Cornelius had been dead for far too long for her to resuscitate.

Everyone else stood in awe at the door standing on the platform.

Fetch was the last to arrive.

Levi was crying as he held his dead grandfather in his arms.

THE DOOR

Fetch went up to Hamilton and Hoot and pulled them aside. "I followed the track all the way *ta* where we done put the door in that ravine."

"As deep as that ravine was," said Hamilton, "how did it get out?"

Fetch shook his head. "I don't know. It would have taken more hands than what we got right here to lift that door out. You saw it. That ravine was right deep."

"Okay, but then how did it get here?" asked Hamilton in an angry tone. A friend of his lay dead a few feet away and he wanted answers. "Can someone answer that for me?"

"Somebody done pushed it," said Hoot.

"Or dragged it," said Freckles.

"No," said Fetch. "There ain't a foot print, a wagon track or a hoof mark anywhere to be found—."

"—Well," said Hoot, "it just didn't up and come here on its own."

Hamilton put a hand on Hoot's shoulder and said calmly, "No, Hoot, you're wrong. That's exactly what it did."

Hamilton went over to the door. It was covered with dirt and leaves, especially on the lower right side, where the door jam came in contact with the ground as it traveled through the forest to reach the Pilgrim farm. Even though it had covered some five miles there was no sign of wear and tear on the wood. Clear as day, he could see the blood stained carving in the door, stained with the blood of Lieutenant Barrett and the Union Soldier from the 5th Colored Regiment. It read: Hell. He knew then he was dealing with an evil force that was more powerful than anything he knew.

*   *   *

Revelation Fiord was in total darkness. The Northern Lights had struck again and shorted out all the power. The only lights that were seen in the town came from candles and flashlights.

Sparky spent hours climbing up and down power poles, replacing power lines and splicing power cables throughout the town. In the end, it all came down to the flipping of one main breaker. The power grid was reenergized and the town's power was restored. He heard cheers coming from many of the houses

THE DOOR

and the community center. When he re-entered to the community center, he was rewarded with pats on the back and a bottle of Canadian beer.

"Don't drink that," Thunder said to Sparky. "You have a slight concussion."

The television at the community center came back on and everyone seemed to gather around it. It was the only one hooked up to a satellite.

"Just in time, *eh!*" said the Mayor as he took his chair. "The soccer game is starting!"

Everyone grabbed a folding chair and pushed and shoved their way for the closest spot to the TV.

"Your people sure love soccer," said Sparky.

"We call it *'Football'*," she replied. "And this is nothing. You should see all the fist fights we have here during the Curling Tournaments."

"Is that the game where you Canadians use granite bowling balls without pins?"

"To us, Canadians, Curling is a national passion."

"Well, I guess this is my day to learn things. And by the way, thanks Doc, for taking care of me. I was under the impression that you were a nurse and not a doctor."

"I am a Registered Nurse and a Doctor..."

Sparky made an odd face, as though he was confused.

She smiled and finished her sentence, "...of Climatology."

"*Ah*, global warming! What a farce!"

"Lucky for you it does exists. If that ground hadn't thawed, the way you came out that door, you'd be dead right now."

"And they say global warming is such a bad thing." It was then the silliness turned to seriousness. "Door? You said that I came out that door."

She turned her back on him. She was fishing for answers.

"You think I came out of that door?"

"How else did you get here? You didn't come here by boat or plane and you certainly didn't walk all the way here. We just happen to be on an arctic island."

Sparky started to blink and sway on his feet.

Thunder grabbed his bottle of beer he was holding and put it on a table. She then grabbed his arm.

THE DOOR

"*Woooo!*" he said. "I feel ***woozie!***"

She helped him back into the clinic and onto the gurney. "Back you go, Mister *Cableman.*"

A short time later, when he got his wits about him, he gestured to the window at all the motioning lights in the sky. "I've heard about them," he said to Thunder, who was sitting on a stool. "Never seen them before. The Aurora Borealis I mean."

"They have a number of names. My people call it the "*Dance of the Spirits*". Aurora is the name of the Roman goddess of dawn and Boreas is the Greek name for the god of wind. We call them the *Northern Lights*." She got up, went to the window and gestured to the swirling lights. "They are the emissions of billions of protons into the Earth's upper atmosphere. You're looking at ionized nitrogen atoms regaining an electron and oxygen and nitrogen atoms returning from an excited state to a ground state."

Sparky held up his hand. "Lady, you're talking my language. It all has something to do with the sun and the release of radioactive particles from the solar winds. When these ionized particles strike Earth's magnetic field they collide with each other and give off a photon of light. *Bla, bla, bla.*"

Thunder clapped three times. "Not bad for a Southern boy."

He gazed out the window and smiled. "They are quite spectacular."

"And active. No other place in Canada is experiencing Northern Lights to the extent that we are. This is one of the reasons I am here."

Sparky started to feel better and slid off the gurney. "I want a better look at those Northern Lights. Give me a hand, okay?"

She took his arm and brought him out the front door.

Together they watched the Northern Lights swirl in the night sky.

Suddenly, the Northern Lights seemed to reach down and touch the ground near the old village.

"Did you see that?" asked Sparky.

All the lights and power in the town winked out, then came back on three or four seconds later. It took a little longer for the TV to come back on and show the soccer game. Cheers once again came from inside the community center.

"I want you to be straight with me," he said. "What's going on

THE DOOR

here?"

All of a sudden, the Northern Lights waned and the sky turned black.

"Is that normal?" he asked.

"Nothing is normal here and it all has to do with that door."

"You keep talking about that door."

"The Elders say its evil."

"Okay, then get rid of it."

"We can't. We've tried. Its very existence violates all the laws of Physics. We've tried to burn it, use it as target practice and even run over it with a pickup truck. All that did was wreck a good pickup."

Sparky was silent for a long moment. "Can you do me a favor?"

"Maybe."

"The next time I ask you to be straight with me, don't!"

*   *   *

"Isn't that Adolf Hitler?" asked Daphne as she worked the controls in front of her.

Lomax didn't answer. He just stared at the big monitor showing Richard walking into Der Furher's private office in Berlin. There was music playing over the speakers.

"What is that music?" asked Daphne.

"Wagner's *The Ride of the Valkyrie*."

Richard stood there and watched the German leader put down his pen, raise his arms and move them about as though he was conducting the symphony. When Hitler turned and spotted the unknown seven-year old boy, he stopped and appeared surprised. Richard gave him a wave and Hitler returned the gesture.

Richard then spun on his heels, walked back into his bedroom and with a sweep of his hand he closed the bathroom door.

"Well," said Daphne, "let's hope that's the most evil figure he meets."

"Don't count on it," said Lomax.

*   *   *

THE DOOR

Meanwhile, at CIA Headquarters in Langley, Virginia...

Deputy Director Blackburn was seated at his desk when a middle-aged agent presented him with a thin file. Blackburn opened it, skimmed over the content of the report, then focused on the cable company employee photograph of Sparky.

"His name is Sparky Powers," the agent reported.

"Where have I heard that awful name before?" asked Blackburn.

"He disappeared seven years ago in Marion, Virginia."

"Oh, crap! Not the Pilgrims again?"

"Yes, sir."

Blackburn flipped through the pages and found nothing of interest. He closed the file. "Okay, what of it?"

"He's re-appeared."

"What? Where?"

"You are not going to believe this."

"Try me and cut the melodramatics."

"Revelation Fiord."

Blackburn's eyes widened. "You mean—!"

"—Yes, sir."

Blackburn became furious. He pounded his fist on his desk. "Why haven't we picked up that door yet?"

"It's been inactive and the Canadian Government has not been very cooperative with our door removal policy. And this door just happens to be on a registered Native American historical site—."

"—Screw the Canadians and their damn Indians. Get a Black Ops unit up there on the double and get that door!"

*   *   *

It was a very sad funeral. Only the Hamiltons and Levi attended it. Even though the war had been over for almost a year, the funeral home owner couldn't find anyone to dig Cornelius's grave because he was a Yankee from Massachusetts. So the Hamilton boys had to do it.

Levi was heartbroken at the loss of his grandfather. "I'm all alone now."

"No, you're not," said Maggy. She hugged Levi.

While driving one of the wagons back to their house, Hamilton decided to clear the air with his wife. "The band saw is cracked and we don't have the money to replace it."

"How do we run a sawmill without a band saw?"

"We don't."

"What are we going to do?"

Hamilton shrugged. "All I know is… I make a lousy farmer."

"We still have that door to deal with."

Hamilton nodded. "I don't know what to do with that either."

"This is not the first time we've run into rough waters."

"Levi told me that a year before he and his grandfather left Massachusetts, his father paid the captain of a schooner a lot of money to take the door far out to sea and dispose of it there."

"I guess the captain refused."

"Oh, no, he was happy to do it. Said it would be the easiest money he would ever make. But none of the crew would go. So Levi's father and older brother went with the captain….The schooner never returned."

Maggy rested her head against his arm. "Oh, Ham…."

*　　　*　　　*

The next Saturday, Israel Pilgrim took the company pickup out on a little ride in the country with his son. He felt that his son was old enough for them to go off and have some quality time together and talk man to man. They had a good time. They went out and had hamburgers and ice cream. Israel enjoyed breathing the fresh air. He smiled and laughed the whole time until his son said, "I think she likes me!"

Israel's voice trembled slightly. "*Uh…uh*, a girl?"

"She's in my first grade class."

"How do you know she likes you?"

"Oh, she licks my face a lot."

Israel's smile evaporated. *Mary doesn't even do that and we're married!* he thought.

"She also kisses me before we go to class."

"Kisses you too…?" Israel brought a hand up to his face. "Here we go," he uttered to himself.

"Daddy, how old were you when a girl kissed you for the first time?"

THE DOOR

Israel was so numb he couldn't even remember that far back. He didn't know if he should be macho and slap the kid on the shoulder and say, "*Atta boy!* Chip off the *ole* block!" or "You're too young to be kissing girls!" Israel had to decide quickly if he was to encourage or discourage such activity. "I think I was twelve…no eleven…wait, maybe thirteen?"

"*Gee.* So you were pretty old by the time you started dating girls?"

"In comparison to you, I was ancient."

"I think I want to marry her."

Israel slammed the brakes and brought the pickup to a halt next to the barn at Don Beech's farm. He turned off the motor, turned to his son and said with a stern tone, "Do you know what zits are?"

"Yuck! Who doesn't?"

"How do you think you get them?"

"By kissing—?"

"—Licking too! Oh, yes, *kiddo!*"

Richard got up on his knees and looked squarely in the rearview mirror at his face. "Do I have any zits?"

"No, but if you keep playing with fire, you're going to get burned!"

Israel got out of the pickup and said, "Richard, wait here until I call you."

Don Beech was a former US Marine who served two tours in Vietnam and won all kinds of medals for courage, honor and bravery under fire. After retiring from military life and getting divorced, he took over his family farm, located just outside of Marion. At sixty-five years old, he was more fit and trim than most guys half his age and certainly more profane.

"Son-of-a-bitch-who-sold-me-this-damn-door-should-burn-in-Hell!" He was pulling on the door to the tack room with all his might and it wouldn't budge.

Israel went into the barn. "Howdy, Don! That door still *stick'n?* "

"Like-a-politician's-hand-on-a-woman's-thigh."

"Don," asked Israel, "can I bring my son into your barn?"

Beech waved his arm. "It's-all-right. All the critters are out grazing."

Israel turned towards the pickup. "Richard, come on in."

THE DOOR

Richard eagerly got out of the pickup and rushed to his father's side. He was immediately intimidated by Don Beech's size, anger and profanity.

"Mighty-fine-looking-boy-you-have-there-Israel. He'd-make-a-fine-Marine. To-me-there-is-nothing-finer-than-a-young man-serving-his country-and-kicking-some-commie-ass!"

"Okay, okay," said Israel, "Let me have a look at that door." Israel gave it a pull and couldn't open it. He tried oiling the hinges and that didn't work.

Don cursed constantly as Israel tried every trick in the book to open that door, but nothing worked.

"It must be the humidity," said Israel. "It swelled the wood."

"No, it's-damn-poor-workmanship-by-those-sons-of-bitches-who-work-for-you-at-that-mill."

Israel smiled to himself. He made this particular door, knowing how hard it was to please Don Beech. "I'll have another installed for you…free of charge."

"You're-damn-*toot'n*-it-will-be-free-of-charge!" He grabbed a sledgehammer. "Now-if-you-gentlemen-will-excuse-me-I-*gotta*-to get-into-my-tack room-so-I-can-do-an-honest-day's work!" Beech pointed the business end of the sledgehammer at Israel. "Some-thing-that-lazy-no-good-bastard-who-made-this-here-door--doesn't-know-anything-about!" Beech started pounding the door with the sledgehammer, making little if any damage but a lot of noise.

Israel chuckled as he led Richard out of the barn.

Knock! Knock!

Only Beech heard it.

Israel opened the driver door to the pickup and Richard hopped into the cab.

"That man sure curses a lot," said Richard.

"Is-this-some-kind-of-a-joke? Now-who-the-hell-is-in-my tack room? I-said-who-the-hell-is-in-there?" He waited. "Fine! Be-that-way." He threw aside the sledgehammer and reached out to the doorknob. "You just-wait-till-I-get-my-hands-on-you—."

He pulled open the door and was blinded by the light.

Israel was totally oblivious to what happened next as he drove the pickup out onto the paved road bordering the Beech Farm.

Richard was gazing out the rear window and watched in

silence as the whole barn was pulled through the doorway to the tack room. The event happened in a mere three seconds without creating a sound.

By the time someone noticed that the barn at the Beech Farm was gone, it was almost nighttime.

The farm was located outside the town limits, so Mitchell didn't know about it until the Sheriff called and told him about it.

"Gees!" he said aloud, gazing at the door standing alone where a barn used to be. "It's happened again!" he said to the Sheriff and his new Chief.

Noon, next Saturday…

It was a beautiful day in Kabash, Iowa. The sun was out, the flowers were blooming and there was the sound of laughter in the air.

The wedding of Ben and Nina Daniels was taking place in the garden at the family farm. This was Ben's third marriage and Nina's fourth. All twenty of their children and grandchildren were in attendance. When the Daniels were young, they embraced the "hippie generation" and never gave it up. Even though Ben was almost totally bald, what hair he had was long and shaggy.

What made this joyous event even more special was the fact that everyone in attendance was nude. The only article of clothing the Reverend wore was his white collar.

"…And now, if any dude out there has any reason why these two very cool people shouldn't be joined in holy matrimony, speak now or forever hold your peace."

The elderly father of the bride had to go and relieve himself. He didn't want to miss anything, so as soon as he flushed the toilet, he ran out of the bathroom and slammed the door behind him. He had to navigate through the living room where guests hung their clothes on genuine store clothing racks. He just made it out the front door when—**BAM!**

The bathroom door seemed to bend forward—like a piece of rubber— as an enormous amount of gravitational forces was applied to it from the inside. The door flung open and Don Beech was hurled out. He went headlong into the rack of clothes and continued on through the living room window and half way across the front yard, landing on a bail of hay that was covered with all sorts

THE DOOR

of pretty flowers. He was covered with clothes, which cushioned the fall and most likely saved his life.

The guests at the wedding were shocked and horrified at the sight of the long wood beams shooting out the living room window and landing in the field beyond the front yard. They all stood there, with their mouths wide open and watched as the old farmhouse was destroyed.

The whole event took place in no longer than three seconds.

The silence was broken, when the long haired best man said, "Far out!"

*   *   *

Two days after arriving in Revelation Fiord, Sparky found himself being unceremoniously released from the town's only medical center by Nurse Thunder, who told him to: "Go home, you damn American!" He spent the next three days going from house to house repairing phone lines and hooking up satellite systems. It seemed that every house in town had a satellite on a pole, but none of them worked properly. They lived too far north for the satellite companies to send repairmen. Well, they had one now and he earned his room and board by doing what he knew best. Being a good-looking young man made him instantly popular with the young girls and singles and not so single mothers.

Sparky was so naive that when he saw the young smiling Indian girls rubbing their noses with their fingers, clearly making a suggestive romantic gesture that was used by the Inuits, he thought they all had colds.

However, the one person he was hoping to have a relationship with was as cold to him as an iceberg. When they passed to within a yard of each other in the community center and he said, "Hi," she acted like he wasn't even there.

"I don't get it," Sparky said to the Mayor. "Did I do something wrong?"

"Thunder is madly in love with you," said the Mayor. "I can tell."

Sparky made a face. "How can you tell?"

"Has she spit in your eyes?"

Sparky shook his head.

THE DOOR

"Beat you with a stick?"

"No, thank goodness."

"Has she kicked you in the balls?"

"Good God, she would do that…?"

The Mayor waved his hand. "*Ah,* there you see. She's crazy about you." He patted Sparky on the shoulder. "***Ohhh!*** You poor man."

But Thunder had other things on her mind, specifically with Inspector Seacrest of the RCMP. The nine-passenger twin-engine commercial airplane was about to land on the short strip at Revelation. She charged out of her office and waved to Sparky.

"Come on!" she told him as she went outside.

They got into a red colored pickup truck and Thunder drove down to the airport terminal at a high rate of speed.

Seacrest was wearing his dress red uniform that the Mounties were known for and carrying a laptop case and overnight bag. He gave Sparky the once over. "Is this the long lost American from Virginia?"

"That's him," she replied.

"Am I going home on that plane?" asked Sparky.

"I'm afraid you will have to wait another day. The next flight out is booked solid."

After off-loading a mailbag and a number of cardboard boxes, the flight crew closed the hatch and taxied down to the runway without boarding a single passenger. Such activity made Sparky very suspicious.

"Besides," said Seacrest, "I need a day to fill out the necessary paperwork. You do understand, *eh?*"

"Yeah, sure."

They boarded Thunder's pickup and she drove straight to the old village. She skidded to a halt some thirty feet away from the door.

"Kudluk," said Seacrest, "I would have preferred that we had conducted my investigation at the community center."

Thunder turned off the motor. "I can't imagine why. You want privacy. Here it is." She took the keys and got out of the truck.

Sparky turned to Seacrest. "Strong minded woman, *eh?*"

"You have no idea."

They got out of the truck.

THE DOOR

"Kudluk, I need to ask this man some questions."

"Who's stopping you?" she asked.

"This is as good a place as any," said Sparky. "And this is where the Mayor found me."

"Here?" asked Seacrest.

Sparky pointed to the exact spot. Some of Richard's toys and personal items were still strewn about the ground.

"How is that possible?" asked Seacrest.

"Well, I certainly didn't walk here. Heck, I don't even know where here is! All I know is that one minute I was getting ready to put in a phone line in a house in Marion, Virginia and the next thing I knew I was laying on the ground right here."

"You want to know how he got here?" She pointed to the door. "Through that bloody door!"

Seacrest made a face. "Do we have to go through this again?"

"Yes and until you get it through that thick *Mountie* skull of yours that there is something very weird going on with that door, I am not going to give up!"

A loud argument ensued between Thunder and Seacrest. She marched right up to the door and Seacrest followed her, screaming and shouting at each other along the way.

"She's gone," shouted Seacrest, "and nothing is going to bring her back!"

"The problem is you've stopped looking!" shouted Thunder.

Sparky sensed something. He pulled back the sleeves on his shirt and noticed that the hairs on his arms were sticking up. "I knew it." He walked towards the arguing couple. "Don't you feel it too?"

By this time Seacrest and Thunder were out of breath and stopped to take in some air.

"I mean," said Sparky, "I can feel it!"

"Feel what?" she asked.

"It's hard for me to explain it, but I can feel electrical discharges in the air. And it's real strong here. I mean super strong!"

Thunder pointed to the door and said to Sparky. "How about you move closer to the door?"

"Right," said Seacrest, "good idea!" He rolled his eyes skyward.

THE DOOR

Sparky took a few steps towards the door and stopped suddenly. *"Whew!"* He backed off a step. "Talk about intense!"

Suddenly, he was lifted off his feet and held there in midair for perhaps three seconds, then flung backwards for about ten feet. Once again, he landed on a puddle of mud and was knocked out cold.

Thunder and Seacrest rushed to his side.

"Please tell me you saw that?" Thunder asked Seacrest.

"Yes…yes, I did."

While Thunder checked Sparky for broken bones, Seacrest stared at the door. There was a serious expression on his face. When he turned around and his eyes met with Thunder, the look on his face said it all. What he had just witnessed started him thinking…the unthinkable.

They brought Sparky back to the clinic, removed his muddy clothing and laid him out on a gurney. He woke up about an hour later. He was alone. He was stiff as a board, but managed to slide off the gurney and put on a robe. He went into the main hall of the community center and found no one there either. He decided to check out the only room he hadn't explored: Thunder's private office. He sat down on her expensive swivel chair and spotted the picture of her and a young girl wearing a red costume. He reached over, groaned slightly and picked up the picture to bring it closer.

When Sparky put the picture back down on the desk, he noticed Seacrest standing in the doorway. "Who's the little girl?"

"That was my daughter," said Seacrest. "Her name was Allison."

"You speak of her in the past tense."

"That's because she's missing and presumed…" He couldn't say the word: dead. His eyes started to well up.

"I'm sorry," said Sparky. "I didn't mean to pry."

"I still have several questions for you," said Seacrest.

"Sure."

"Have you seen any calendars since you arrived at Revelation Fiord?"

"No, I haven't," said Sparky. "I wondered why there weren't any."

"I hid them from you," Thunder revealed as she came from behind Seacrest.

THE DOOR

"Why?" asked Sparky.

"Do you know what year it is?" asked Seacrest.

"What kind of question is that?" Sparky took it as an insult. "I'm not stupid, you know."

"Okay, what year is it?"

"1997."

Thunder went to one of her filing cabinets, pulled out a calendar and laid it on the desk before Sparky.

He read the year at the top of the page. "No! That's impossible! How can this be 2004?"

"It is," she said.

Sparky was stunned. "That's five, six—seven years! I've lost seven years? How is that possible?"

"Tell the Inspector here the last thing you remember before coming here."

"I can do that. The last thing I remember, I was in a kid's bedroom, I think his name was Richard, and I was installing a phone extension. Then the bathroom door started to knock. I answered it…and ended up here…seven years later." A thought came to his mind. "My mother! I forgot about my mother. She'll be worried sick about me. I've got to call her!" He reached for the nearest phone and got no dial tone.

Sparky started to weep. "Mom!"

Thunder went around her desk to console the American. But not before giving Seacrest an angry look. "Still convinced there's nothing going on with that door?"

*   *   *

Just when everything seemed to be going bad for the Hamiltons and Levi Pilgrim, a small miracle came to Marion, Virginia….

A boy on a mule came riding up to the mill. "Excuse me, sir."

Levi stepped outside. "Yes?"

"I have a message here for a Mister Pilgrim."

"That's me." The boy handed a piece of paper to Levi and he read it.

"Ham!"

Hamilton came out of the mill, followed by Moon and Red. "What is it?"

THE DOOR

"It's from the depot manager in Saltville. He's got a delivery for me. He wants me to bring every wagon I've got down to the depot."

Levi led all four wagons he and the Hamiltons had to the train depot in Saltville.

As Hamilton drove by the Stuart House, he gazed at the front door that was his passageway to this place and time. He wondered if he would ever go back to 1997.

"Are you Cornelius Pilgrim?" asked the depot manager.

"No, sir. I'm his grandson."

The depot manager then spotted Hamilton and a smile flashed on his face. He even took off his hat and slapped it on his thigh. "Well, bless my soul! Sergeant Major Hamilton! How are you and your little army *gett'n* on?"

Hamilton recognized the depot manager as Corporal Bland who fought along side him and the boys on Chestnut Hill. He got down from the wagon and shook the man's hand. "Pretty fair. I didn't know you were the manager here."

"Well, I was a lineman for twenty years. I'm too old to do that anymore so when this job came open, they offered it to me." After the pleasantries, the new depot manager took Levi and Hamilton to the new warehouse next to his office. Both were under construction. Both buildings had to be replaced because the originals were destroyed by General Stoneman's forces during the last Union raid on Saltville. There were about twenty very big and heavy wood crates in the middle of the warehouse marked with the words CONFISCATED by order of the US GOVERNMENT. There were also the words PILGRIM DOORS painted on the crates along with the shipping information.

Levi recognized the boxes and got excited. "My grandfather shipped these just before we left Massachusetts, two—no, three years ago."

"Seized as contraband," said Bland, "by the Union army." He raised up a pile of papers for everyone to see. "Some blue-belly General sent them to Illinois…for safe keeping."

"Yeah, right!" said Hamilton, with a smirk.

Everyone within earshot shook their heads. They knew better. Bland held up a letter that was part of the pile of papers. "This is from the widow of that General, who refused to pay the shipping charges and had the whole thing shipped back to Washington, where someone else paid for the shipping and sent it here." He ruffled through the paperwork. "But it doesn't say who."

"What *be* in them boxes?" asked Moon.

Levi went up to one square box that was about four feet high, but only a foot wide and tapped it with his gloved hand. "There's a brand new band saw in here!" He pointed to the biggest crate. "And in that crate is a steam engine. The rest of the crates contain all kinds of tools and spare parts from our mill in Salem Village."

"In other words," said Hamilton, "everything we need to get the mill up and running again!" He slapped his hands together. "God bless you, Cornelius! Boys, we're back in business!"

The boys whooped and cheered.

Hamilton took a little walk with his former corporal. "I hear tell that them folks up in New England are begging for fresh cut lumber."

"You heard right, but the telegraph dispatches I've been getting all say them Yankees need plaster more than anything else."

"Plaster, you say." For Hamilton, it was just another way of saying gypsum. "*Hmmm!* Now you got me thinking."

"Well, if you wouldn't mind taking a little advice from your former corporal," said Bland, "use the wood you would have shipped north to make barrels and fill them with plaster. Then ship *them* north."

Hamilton was impressed with his former corporal. "Not a bad idea. This county is loaded with plaster. But the problem is that depot manager in Chilhowie doesn't like the way I talk and refuses to do any business with me."

"What's he *fuss'n* about? The closest he ever got to real *fight'n* was when he was *retreat'n*. Someone needs to tell that old fool the war is over. You bring me your goods and I'll see to it personally they get shipped without further adieu. You hear?"

"Loud and clear. Much obliged." They doffed their hats.

And as Hamilton turned and walked away, he looked up at the sky and said aloud, "And thank you, Lord!"

After the boys loaded up the wagons and drove off, the front door of the Stuart house opened and out stepped Nathaniel Pilgrim wearing expensive civilian clothes. The train's engineer followed him out of the house and onto the front porch, counting the money he had just been given.

"I told you that I would deliver them crates safe and sound," the engineer said as he stuffed the wad of currency into one of the pockets in his overalls. "You didn't have to come all the way from Washington City to see them off."

Pilgrim smiled. "Oh, yes, I did." Through his connections in the War Department in Washington, he located the confiscated machinery and made all of the arrangements to have them shipped to Saltville.

*   *   *

It was 3:30 PM on a Wednesday, when Daphne arrived home with both Richard and Dara from school. Richard was in the first grade and Dara was in Kindergarten. She would watch the kids at the Pilgrim house while Mary was off to paint a mural at a day care center in Abingdon. Before the doors were reinstalled into the house, Richard would play with Dara or watch cartoons with her in the living room. But now he had other interests. He preferred traveling!

Daphne allowed this activity on one condition, that she was able to monitor "the event" and keep an eye on him—without him knowing about it. Danvers bought her a laptop that she could plug in to the better of the two cameras in Richard's bedroom. This camera also afforded her the ability to communicate with Lomax via a landline that the stakeout house wasn't tapped into.

"Mrs. Dane," said Richard, "I'm going up to my room."

"Okay, sweetheart" replied Daphne.

She opened up her laptop, turned it on, plugged into the telephone extension that never worked for the Pilgrims and put on her headset. "Traveller is en route." The laptop monitor came on and she saw and heard everything Lomax did.

"Copy that," said Lomax.

Lomax glanced over to Danvers, who was seated about a yard away, gazing intensely at the bank of monitors. He typed out a command on the keypunch to override the signal coming from the camera in Richard's bedroom he had installed seven years before and started broadcasting a very dull recorded event. Lomax had wisely built up an archive of recorded dull events for him to utilize at times like this. "What color shirt is Richard wearing?" he asked

THE DOOR

Daphne.

"The Redskins jersey."

Lomax just so happened to have a video clip of Richard wearing his prized football jersey and played it. "Got it." One of the monitors on the far left side of the wall displayed the recorded event.

Seconds later, it was being played on the center monitor in the surveillance room at the stakeout house. The bored and sleepy techs in the basement observed Richard enter his bedroom, climb into bed and take a nap. They would be totally oblivious to what was about to happen.

Lomax and the others watched as Richard threw his book bag on the bed, then turned and faced the bathroom door. It was ajar. The rag had been put back into the mortise. Richard removed the rag.

"Traveller has removed the rag," Lomax reported to Daphne.

"I hate this part," she said. "The not knowing where he will be going." She reached for her handbag, removed the 9MM pistol she kept there and chambered a round. That was the other condition she made to Lomax in exchange for allowing Richard to face such unknown danger. No matter what, she would have the means to protect him and Dara if the need presented itself. She had never fired a gun in anger, but she was certain that if either child was threatened that she would do whatever was necessary.

Richard pushed open the bathroom door and went inside to relieve himself. Daphne heard the toilet flush. However, she did not hear him close the door. He understood that his parents were terrified of the doors and he was smart enough even at this tender age to know that they would never approve of what he was doing. But he was enjoying it too much to tell them. So he learned how to close the door quietly and re-insert the rag into the mortise after he went traveling. But this time he quietly closed the door.

"Did he close the door?" she asked.

"Affirmative," said Lomax. "Relax, Daphne."

"I can't."

Richard looked over his shoulder to see if Daphne was anywhere near his bedroom, tapped the door twice, then opened it. He had no idea his every move was being observed and recorded.

A very intense bright light came through the doorway. Everyone who saw it, including Richard, turned away from it because of its harsh brightness. There was also a thick, dense fog.

"I can see the light from down here," said Daphne, who started to get up. "I hope our neighbors didn't see it…."

Lomax's fingers raced across one keyboard, then went to another one. "Relax darling. They are only seeing and hearing what I feed them."

Richard's bedroom started to fill with fog.

"What is that," asked Danvers, "coming out the doorway?

"Is it smoke—?" asked Lomax.

Daphne sniffed the air and thought she heard something. "—No, its fog. Now shut up both of you!"

A voice emanated from the doorway. It was crisp and clear. "Centurion!"

"Don't move kid," said Lomax.

"No," said Danvers. "This is it! This is the one!"

"What is he talking about?" asked Daphne.

It was as though someone was shining a very bright light at the other side of the door. When the light faded away, Richard and the others could now see after all the spots in their eyes went away. Richard would rub his eyes for about another minute. His temporary blindness caused him to lose his balance and he fell forward across the threshold of the doorway.

Daphne let out a yelp, but was not heard by Richard.

To his and the others' surprise, he did not fall onto anything. He merely floated in the air. This made him smile. ***"Wow!"*** But the smile went away when the fog dispersed and he realized that he was only inches away from the sharp end of a hundred spears. There were all packed together so tightly that nothing else could be seen.

"Hello," he said. He even reached out to touch the end of one spear. He quickly retracted his hand.

"Make way for the Commander!" someone shouted beyond the wall of spear points.

"What is this place?" Lomax asked as he turned to Danvers.

To the rogue CIA agent's surprise, Danver's face had streaks of tears running down it. "A place I thought I would never see!"

The wall of spears seemed to part towards the middle and the next thing Richard and the others saw was a magnificent Angel with wings. This Angel was pointing a glistening broadsword in Richard's direction. He wore a thin gold crown with white stars that Lomax would later say designated rank. This Angel, as with all the others, wore a Romanesque uniform, but white and not red. He also wore a shinny silver breastplate.

"Who are you?" the Angel asked. "Speak!" His voice boomed like thunder.

"I-I am Richard. Richard Pilgrim, sir."

The Commander turned to another Angel with a similar crown, but a few less white stars. The look of surprise was written all over his face.

"Pilgrim," repeated the second Angel. "I thought we were finally rid of that scurrilous lot!"

Lomax glanced over to Danvers, who appeared distressed.

"Apparently not, my Lord," said a third Angel, a blonde female named Joan. She too wore a white crown that had one gold star at the center.

The soldier Angels started to speak to one another, creating a loud commotion. Richard and the others noticed that the ranks were made up of both men and women warriors.

"Praetorians," the Angel with the broadsword said in an authoritative but calm voice. "Be silent and stand down!"

The Praetorian Guardsmen responded by raising their long spears in an act of unison and backing off in silence, gliding through the air.

"You're Angels!" said Richard. He was very excited.

The three crowned Angels turned to each other. The Commander then faced Richard. He was about to answer the boy when the other male Angel touched his arm.

"My Prince, you cannot answer him. The Rules of Engagement clearly state…"

"He's already seen us...and he's crossed the threshold of the door. Uriel, that in itself is significant. He's not evil."

"He called him Uriel," said Lomax.

"That name is familiar," said Daphne.

She heard Lomax moan over the headset.

"I have read the Bible," she said. "Unlike somebody I know."

"Note the crowns they wear," said Danvers. "They're Archangels!"

THE DOOR

"He's right," said Daphne. "Uriel is an Archangel!"

"But who's the other one?" asked Lomax. "The leader?" No one answered.

While the Commander sheathed his broadsword, Uriel, his second in command, reluctantly glided over to Richard and extended his hand. "Boy, take my hand." Richard took it and was brought before the Commander.

When Richard looked down, he realized he was very high off the ground. He became fearful and grabbed onto Uriel with both hands.

"Relax. You will not fall."

Now that the Praetorian Guards had backed off and returned to their posts, Richard and the others got a glimpse of a mighty city in the distance with towering spires. It was Heaven.

When Richard was presented to the Commander, he let go of Uriel and smiled at the thought that he was hovering in midair. "This is fun!"

"So," said the Commander, "your name is Richard."

"Yes, sir. Are you God?"

That brought laughter from some of the Praetorian Guards.

"Be silent," said Uriel to the guards in what many felt was an offensive tone. "Maintain your bearing."

"No, I am not…God." He shot a glance to his second, who was shaking his head. "I am an Archangel."

Richard's eyelids shot upward. "A real Archangel? *Wow!*"

"You know of us then?"

"A little….Are you…Gabriel?" Richard asked with heightened enthusiasm.

"No."

Richard's shoulders sank, as did his enthusiasm. "Oh. Well, then who are you?"

"I am Michael."

Richard's enthusiasm perked up somewhat. "Archangel Michael?"

"You've heard of me then?"

"A little, but I've heard a lot about Gabriel!"

Michael found that amusing and smiled. He glanced over to Uriel, who by the expression on his face was not so amused.

Richard also looked over to Uriel and asked, "Then are you

Gabriel?"

"No!" His tone was stern. "And you don't need to know my name."

Richard rocked his shoulders. He was young, smart and had good ears. "But I think I already do. You're Uriel."

Uriel frowned as he released Richard and floated off.

That made Michael chuckle. He then said to Uriel. "Be gentle with the child. He's just being inquisitive."

"But my Lord, he has seen what man was not meant to see."

Michael waved his free hand. "He's not the first…and I pray he will not be the last."

"Are you an Archangel too?" asked Richard, as he gestured to Uriel.

"*Ah!*" said Michael with a sparkle in his eyes. "You are a bright boy!"

"My Lord, I beg of you. Attend *thee*."

Michael turned to the female Angel and jerked his head towards Richard. "Joan, if you please."

She flew over to Richard, who was now upside down and reached out her hand. Richard took it and was able to float upright.

Uriel flew off to a distance well out of earshot of Richard and the Guards. Michael floated over to him and a slightly less than heated argument ensued for about a minute.

Richard was too excited and too inquisitive about his surroundings to pay any attention to the dispute between Michael and his second in command. He was more interested in this place the Angels called: "The Junction." He even heard one of the guards refer to it as "The Junction." But he was about to see something that would truly amaze him.

"Do you know what they are talking about?" Lomax asked Danvers.

"I have no idea."

"I thought Angels didn't suffer from the sin of vanity," said Daphne.

"The Devil's favorite sin," said Danvers. "Remember, he was once an Archangel too."

"Any idea who the angry Angel is?" asked Daphne.

"Archangel Uriel," said Danvers. "He's the Fire of God and the Light of God."

THE DOOR

"That sounds important," said Lomax, but he rolled his eyes skyward. "I think."

A horn sounded in the distance and both Angels stopped arguing, turned towards Heaven, hovered there in silence for a long moment, then both gave a respectful nod.

"What was all that about?" asked Lomax.

Daphne answered that question. "Oh, I got a feeling they just got a message from God."

"Yeah," said Lomax, "stop acting like mortals and get back to work! The old man knows how to crack the whip."

"Lomax!" said Daphne. "You're talking about the Almighty."

Lomax raised a hand. "Okay, okay. I was just being stupid."

"Yes, something you're very good at."

Uriel gave a respectful salute to Michael, then glided off.

Michael returned to Richard and took him by the arm. "Well, my young adventurer. It seems we have a task to attend to."

"*Huh?*"

"But first, I want you to see something." Michael turned Richard around and showed him The Junction. It was a towering mountain filled with doors. There were thousands of them, standing erect and each one had a squad of nine or more Praetorians standing guard, spears at the ready. A vast army of armed Angels guarded the junction of doors.

Richard's eyes widened. "Holy cow!"

"What are they looking at?" asked Danvers.

Lomax was busy working the controls to the new camera.

"There's so many," said Richard.

"So many what?" asked Lomax. "Doors?"

"Yes and this is one of the reasons we are here."

"To protect Heaven? From who?"

"I think you are smart enough to know."

Richard's body jerked. "Oh? Him! The Reverend says he's evil."

"Yes, he's very evil. He is also very smart and he's after you."

The way Michael said it, sent shock waves through Richard and the others listening in. "Me? Why me?"

"Because you have the gift. You can open the doors. There is another. We do not know where she is."

"But I thought Angels knew everything."

THE DOOR

Michael pointed to Heaven. "Only HE is all knowing. But…"

"But?"

Michael hesitated, searching for the right words. He was the warrior and great protector of Heaven. Gabriel was the one who did all the talking. And giving history lessons wasn't something he did everyday. "When God created Angels, he gave us the means to do his will."

"You mean superhuman powers, like Superman?"

A puzzled expression flashed across Michael's face. He had only heard of Superman in passing. He glanced over to Joan, who referred to a transparent tablet she was holding. In an instant the table received a library of information and images about the famous comic book character. "Oh, him! Yes, a man who can fly…without wings. *Hmmm!* Well, that wouldn't work here."

"My Prince!" said Joan who appeared all stressed out by Michael's statement.

"Oh," said Michael, who dismissed her with a flick of his hand. "I shouldn't have said that." Fortunately, Richard did not grasp the significance of that statement, but the adults watching this drama unfold would, but not immediately.

Richard gestured to The Junction. "What is this place?"

"We call it, '*The Junction*'. When you go out at night and look up, what do you see?"

"Stars."

"Correct. You do know what the universe is?"

"It is a place made up of stars and galaxies."

"Correct again. The Universe is big, right?"

"Very big."

Michael held out both hands, about a foot apart. "Let's just say that everything in the universe is in between my hands."

Richard looked at the hands, thought about it, then nodded.

Michael opened his hands as wide as he could go. "Now this is the distance between Heaven and Earth."

"*Gees!* That's far. No wonder you have wings."

"Flying would take too long…and like you mortals, time is a luxury we sometimes don't have."

"Then how do you Angels get to Earth?"

Michael pointed to the bathroom door. "Through doors like these."

THE DOOR

"Ohhhhh!"

"But not all doors." A perplexed expression flashed on the Archangel's face. "It has something to do with the warping of space, but I never studied or liked science. When the Lord God says that this thing does this or does that…I…like the good old soldier I am… just accept it." He studied Richard's face. "Did that make any sense to you?"

"Kinda." The kid gave a shrug. *Maybe not!*

"There is another reason we are here and will remain here until our task is completed." He then called out to his soldiers. "Praetorians! Why-are-we-here?"

In a thunderous roar they replied, "**FOR THE NINETEEN!**" They then struck the shafts of their spears against their shield, creating a loud and echoing metallic sound.

"For the what?" asked Lomax. When he looked over to Danvers and saw the look on the man's face, he realized that his client was well aware of the reason Michael and God's Army were stationed there. "Do you have any idea what all of that was about?"

Danvers did not reply, *but he knew!*

Michael drew his sword and pointed it at the doorway of Richard's bedroom. He carried Richard into the room and lowered him gently to the floor.

Daphne was standing in the first floor hallway with one eye on the laptop monitor and the other on Richard's bedroom. Her eyes widened when she saw the bedroom fill with brilliant white light. She made the sign of the Cross.

Michael also gently stepped onto the floor. He then did something that completely surprised Lomax and Danvers. He gave a sigh and said. "Oh, that feels good!" He sheathed the sword and walked around the bedroom. He even took some time to examine some of Richard's toys and personal effects.

"How long has it been since you walked?"

Without thinking, Michael replied, "Centuries."

Richard was surprised—he wasn't the only one. "Really?"

Michael drew closer to Richard. "All right, boy. Now I have something to tell you."

"Okay."

"As I have said, you are not the only child who can open doors. Her name is Allison. Like you, she can come and go through the doors. She has been through many doors and has left her mark with something called…crayons." Richard nodded. He knew what crayons were. "Can you read?"

"A little."

"Learn fast because if you open the wrong door you will end up in the same place as Allison."

"You mean the place where there is a lot of fire?"

Michael hesitated for a moment, then gave a nod.

"Can you go get her?"

"No. But you can. Just not right now. The day will come when someone you truly trust will ask you to open…another door…in this house."

Richard backed off. "I don't want to go there!" He shook his head and became fearful.

"I'm with you on that…."

It was then Michael noticed something as he lifted off the floor and gently floated up towards the ceiling and stared right at Lomax's two cameras. "*Hmmmm!* Let me tell you people something. He who deals with Lucifer gets scorched…*ad infinitum*."

Michael's wings unfurled as he backed away from the wall. He glided across the room, reached down and grabbed hold of Richard and guided him to the bathroom door. He landed on one knee to be at eye level with the boy.

"Sir?" asked Richard. "Why me?"

"You were chosen to do a great thing. It is God's will and one does not question such things…except when you're a little boy in a lot of danger. Know this, my courageous little friend. I will be there when you need me." Michael held up a fisted hand. "And these are five things you need to know." He shot a glance at the cameras and snapped his fingers. Instantly, the concealed microphone was shattered, along with the other gizmos Lomax attached to the coaxial line that ran to both his and the stakeout house and the whole neighborhood experienced a short power outage. "The Devil cannot kill you or anyone. Fear is his only weapon." He raised a second finger. "He cannot go back in time." Third finger, which covered his lips and made it difficult for Lomax and the others to see them move and read. "Tapping the Wandering Doors twice will make them change their end point. Tapping them three times will send you home. But I think you already know that."

THE DOOR

Richard's eyes narrowed. "I *kinda* knew that but I don't know how."

Michael raised his fourth finger, which completely blocked the view of his lips. Now nobody could read his lips.

"What is he saying?" asked Danvers.

"You got me," said Lomax.

When Michael raised his thumb, he cupped his hand and placed it over Richard's ear so that no one would be able to see or hear what he was about to say.

When Michael was finished, he patted Richard on the head. He then opened his wings slightly to rise off the floor. As he whirled around, he got a glimpse of Daphne staring at him from the second floor hallway. Their eyes met for a second as he glided backwards through the bathroom doorway. Suddenly, the bathroom door slammed shut.

*   *   *

The Pilgrim sawmill was up and running with the brand new band saw and a steam powered engine. It was producing lumber more efficiently than ever before. Levi was the family lumberjack. It was now spring and the first thing he did was to hire a crew of men to clear off the trees on his property.

The telegraph came into its own during the Civil War as the fastest mode of communication. It was the Internet of the 1860's. It took a while for Corporal Bland and his telegraph operator to befriend some northern train depot managers and convince them that he had a good supplier of plaster. After the war, northern builders became desperate for lumber, bricks and plaster and they relied heavily on their local railroad telegraph operators to find the best deals. So when Bland got the word out that he had a reliable supplier of plaster at a reasonable price, they requested samples. Hamilton, the consummate businessman, complied and used all of his marketing skills to win these potential clients over. Orders started coming in and word of mouth did the rest. It wasn't long before Hamilton and Levi's mill started to make money again. With some of the profits, Hamilton bought more forested land for Levi to cut and the boys to farm. He also bought a huge tract of land where he knew there was a gypsum deposit. He hired many former slaves who had escaped from the saltworks after the war

THE DOOR

was over and were far from home. Many of them were starving and had no money or a place to live. Hamilton hired as many of them as he could afford to dig out the gypsum and pound the chunks into powder. One bonus Hamilton didn't expect was that some of the former slaves were experienced barrel-makers. He put them right to work. A tent city was erected near the mill so that the Hamiltons could provide them with food, shelter, medical care and some measure of security. The former slaves may have been set free, but they weren't exactly safe in the hard times that followed. The Confederacy had lost the war and left most of the south a shambles. The people of southwest Virginia after the Civil War had lost a lot of men—most of whom were farmers. Food was now hard to come by. Losing their slaves meant that the farmers had to do the work themselves and they didn't like it.

Maggy taught Matthew how to take care of the company's books and finances. Red was the salesman. When he heard of a family moving into the area he rushed out to them with a sample of his lumber, bricks and plaster and got orders. When Fetch wasn't sawing wood, he was out scrounging the countryside for every scrap of metal he would lay his hands on. Moon and Freckles were the farmers of the family. They had a knack for taking care of the livestock and before long everyone in the family had a horse. Maggy now rode around in a new buggy and younger horse. She was a very busy midwife. She didn't charge much for her services—if at all, but she saved a lot of lives and made a lot of friends. Hoot remained the hunter of the family. Still the crack shot that he was during the Burbridge Raid, he not only provided for the Hamiltons but for the hungry neighbors as well, many who were widows with children. He also provided security for his farm and family. The kid preferred sleeping high up in the trees than on a bed. All he needed was a horse blanket to lay on and another to cover himself and a little rope to tie himself to the tree branch, so that he didn't fall. From high up in the trees, he could see and even hear everything that was going on and no one ever suspected he was up there, except when he was snoring.

Hamilton spent a lot of time laying the foundation for Levi's basement. He had promised his late friend Cornelius to help Levi build a house. Concrete was very expensive in those days and it took time to save up for what it would cost. Instead of cash, he traded plaster for the concrete, which had to be shipped from afar. Fetch scrounged around the burnt out homes for all the discarded mattress springs, broken cast iron stoves, barb wire and anything metallic he could take. Hamilton spread them out on the layer of gravel rock that covered the floor. He gave the boys a long lecture about *'tinsel strength'*. "Concrete is nothing but chalk. What gives concrete its strength is when you add anything metallic to the mixture. Put a piece of metal, and the rustier the better, into the mix and it will make the concrete form stronger and last for darn near forever." But whatever he said fell on deaf ears. They were country boys and country people built their houses out of wood. For the next two days, everyone helped mix up the concrete, pour the floor and level it off. It was a big basement and took a lot of work. Every once in a while, Hamilton and the boys would stop and gaze at the old double door that remained exactly where they found it the day Cornelius died. None of them liked being so close to that door. When the concrete floor had had enough time to cure, Hamilton and Levi erected the forms and spent a whole day pouring the walls of the basement. They came home well after dark with the happy news that the forms held and the concrete was hardening nicely. All they had to do now was lay the brick.

The next morning, the six boys went to see Hamilton's and Levi's handiwork. But there was something that put a damper on this joyous event. "The door!" shouted Moon. "It *be* gone!" It was true. The old church door was gone!

Hoot went around the old campsite, searching the ground. "There's a track that leads off to the north." They followed the deep rut in the ground for about five hundred feet until it ended at a big granite boulder. They circumvented the boulder and found no other tracks. "The track ends at this boulder and goes no further."

"Where'd it go then?" asked Red.

"Maybe it done flew off like a bird?" said Hoot.

"You see any other tracks?" asked Red.

"Just the one," said Hoot, the best tracker in the family. "But there be a lot of leaves and broken branches covering the ground."

"You *think'n* someone done took it?" asked Freckles.

"Who would be crazy enough to do that?" asked Moon. "This

THE DOOR

door is cursed!"

"It's a killer," said Matthew. "Look what it done to ole Cornelius!"

"Well," said Hoot, "whoever they *be* they done went *plow'n* through here in one heck of a hurry!"

"I for one am glad it's gone," said Fetch. "Maybe now we can have some peace around here."

"Let's head back," said Moon.

Hamilton was all smiles as he drove both Maggy and Levi in the buggy to the house. But as he got off the buggy, he noticed the strange looks on the boys' faces.

"Boys," asked Hamilton, "what's wrong?"

"Ham!" said Maggy. "The door is gone!"

"What?" Hamilton became very emotional. "Oh, no!" He clutched his chest. "Not again! Please God, no!" He fell to his knees and Maggy got down right next to him.

"Ham!" she said. "Lay down and relax. Freckles, get my medical bag!"

"Yes, *ma'am!*"

She checked his heart with her stethoscope. "Regulate your breathing, Sailor."

"What," he replied, "no snap to?" He started to breath easier.

"Your heart rate is still high," she said.

Hamilton was feeling a lot better. "*Uh,* could it have anything to do with the fact that a hot harbor chick like yourself is laying on top of me with your clothes on?" He then grinned and gave her a suggestive wink.

She did not expect that response. "You are insatiable!"

The boys turned away. Some made faces or rolled their eyes skyward as they mounted their horses and rode off. They had grown accustomed to the romancing Hamiltons.

Freckles said to Matthew. "How can they *not* have any *youngn's* when they *be* going at it all the time?"

"What about the door?" asked Fetch.

"What about it?" replied Moon. "It's gone and I say to hell with it!"

But Hoot wasn't satisfied. He searched the surrounding woods and pastures but never found the door.

THE DOOR

Chapter Thirteen

GROUND ZERO

Sparky opened his eyes and leaned

forward in the bed. He heard the shower running in the bathroom. He touched his head and winced. "Boy, what do these Canadians put in their beer?" He was hung over and almost didn't remember how he got here. But when Thunder came out of the bathroom wearing a robe and drying her hair, it all came back to him.

"Did I wake you?" she asked.

"No, my hangover did. You know, back in the States they say bad things about your socialized medicine."

"Oh?"

He grinned. "Personally, I don't think it's so bad."

She put down the hairdryer and leapt into bed, where they embraced and rubbed noses. "And I've got some other good news about our healthcare system."

"What's that?"

"It's free!"

"*Ooooooh*, Canada!"

They then kissed passionately until a large helicopter buzzed the village so low that it shook the walls and windows of Thunder's house.

"That was low," he said.

"Too damn low! Are they crazy?" She got out of bed, went over to the window and pulled open the drapes. He followed her. The sun was low and evening was fast approaching, but there was enough light for them to see the giant black HH53 Super Golly Green Giant Helicopter landing on the runway, directly facing the old village. It was followed by a black C-130 Hercules transport plane that also flew low and shook the houses of the town as it passed overhead. As soon as the giant plane landed at the airport

THE DOOR

and pulled to a halt, the rear ramp door was lowered and out came several military type vehicles.

"Who are they?" he asked.

"They're Americans!" she answered.

"Oh, no—not them." He was trying to be funny, but when he saw the dirty look she gave him, he knew it was a mistake. "Sorry. You think they flew all this way from the States?"

"No, I'd say they came from the airbase in Thule, Greenland."

"I hope they didn't do all of this for me?"

"Not for you, you silly fool."

Thunder went into a closet and removed a pair of binoculars. She then opened the front door of her house, stepped out onto the front porch and watched as at least thirty men deplaned from the helicopter. They were dressed in black combat fatigues and carrying automatic weapons. "Those are Black Ops." She spotted the Mayor's pickup truck parking near the helicopter and Seacrest getting out to meet them. "Seacrest, you bloody idiot! This is no time to play hero." The Americans drew down on him and he responded by raising his arms. They removed his pistol and made him turn around so that he could be checked for other weapons. As he turned, he stared in the direction of Thunder's house. Their eyes met. He shook his head. It was the only way he could signal her that all was not good.

Thunder backed off into the house and closed the door. "Get dressed fast! We got trouble!"

She opened a closet that had men's clothing in it. "Help yourself. Just make sure it's camouflaged and warm."

After they dressed, she unlocked her rifle vault. "Do you know how to use a gun?"

"Are you kidding? I'm from Virginia."

She handed him a 30-30 Marlin hunting rifle. She grabbed an AK 47, with a forty-five round banana magazine.

"Where'd you get that?"

"From a Russian weatherman," she flashed a smile.

"Why do I get the feeling he liked the free health care too?" said Sparky.

She opened the back door and led the way outside and into the barren wilderness.

THE DOOR

*   *   *

Lomax knew that it would be extremely difficult for Daphne to remain calm after what she had witnessed. So when Mary and Israel arrived home at the same time they found Eddi Dane playing catch with Richard and Dara in the front yard.

"Hi boss," said Lomax. He gave a wave to Israel.

"Eddi," said Israel, "what are you doing here? I thought you were sick?"

"Oh, I'm better now."

"Where's Daphne?" asked Mary.

"She had to go to the house and powder her nose or something."

"Is she all right?" asked Mary, detecting that something was amiss. "Do you want me to go and check on her?"

"*Na!* She's fine! I've played catch with the kids here before. It's no big deal."

"Richard," said Mary, "let's get cleaned up for dinner."

"Okay, mommy." He followed his mother into the house.

Israel pulled out a big frozen pizza out of the car trunk. "We're having pizza tonight. Would you like to join us?"

"No, no, no thanks. Some other time, boss. Let's head on home, Dara."

Danvers was waiting in Daphne's house for Lomax and Dara. He had cooked a spaghetti and meatballs dinner for everyone. He was in a jubilant mood, while Lomax was anything but. However, Daphne went to her master bedroom and did not join them for the meal.

After dinner, Lomax asked his daughter, "Dara, why don't you go watch cartoons while Daddy has a talk with Uncle John?"

"Okay, Daddy!" She went into the living room and turned on the TV.

He waited until his daughter was out of earshot before asking, "Where's Daphne?"

"She took a sedative and is resting right now."

"Why are you so happy?"

The question surprised Danvers. He turned and stared into Lomax's eyes. "And you're not? My boy, we just witnessed something incredible…something that probably no other human being has ever seen and lived to tell about it."

THE DOOR

"Who can we tell? Diciembre?" He turned towards the Pilgrim's house. "Can we tell Israel we're spying on them and *oh* by the way, your kid met an Archangel today?"

Danvers shrugged. "Well, I'm sure the phones are ringing off the wall at CIA headquarters."

"No they're not. All they saw and heard today was a recording I made of one of Daphne's babysitting visits. I've been very selective in what they see. If they knew we had this—."

"—They'd raid your house in a heartbeat. I said it before, you're playing a very dangerous game…."

"Learn one thing, Danvers or Pilgrim or whatever you call yourself. I don't play by their rules anymore."

Daphne entered the kitchen. "I'm up."

"Good, because I got work to do." Lomax left and went to his house.

Danvers served Daphne a plate of spaghetti. "I was like him once, head strong and full of anger. It caused me to do terrible things."

"What will become of us?" she asked.

"Oh, my dear Daphne. You have looked into the blinding light of hope and peace and yet you do not see. We have been chosen by God to do *His* will."

"How do you know that?"

"Michael looked right into the camera. He knew we were watching."

"I'm so afraid." She was shaking all over. She reached out to him.

He put his arms around her. "Me too…." But, he wasn't.

Meanwhile, at the stakeout house…

Father called Diciembre on a secure line and said, "*Ola, amigo.*"

But Diciembre could hear the distress in the stakeout supervisor's breathing. "You okay?"

"No. None of us are. We just witnessed a major event here. I may lose half my people because of it. We're all pretty shook up by it. It looks like Lomax found out that we had tapped into his coaxial line—."

"—And you're surprised?"

THE DOOR

"There was a power surge. We think it came from the Pilgrims. It caused all of our systems to shut down, then come back on again. Like someone flipped a switch on and off. We lost audio but when the cameras came on we saw an Angel in Richard's bedroom."

Diciembre could tell by Father's nervous tone that he was being truthful. "And what was this…Angel doing?"

"Talking to the kid. He then lifted off and flew right through the doorway. Wait until you see it. I'm sending one of my people to you with a DVD."

"Why don't you just E-mail it to me—."

"No, no, no, no, no, no. This is too hot for that." He hung up.

A thunderstorm was brewing. Dusk was another hour away, but the sky was already black with pillowing and towering thunder-clouds.

Lieutenant Dewey Mitchell looked up at the sky and said to his three-man team of detectives, "We'd better go in now before it starts to rain." He put on his breathing mask and gave the signal to his sergeant, who opened the van door and led the charge to the house. The detective with the battering ram struck the front door once and gained entry into the house.

"Police! Don't move!"

With pistols drawn, all four cops raided the house, checking every room. The meth lab was in full operation in the living room, giving off a toxic cloud of chemicals.

"The house is clear, Lieutenant," said the Detective Sergeant.

Mitchell gestured to the dining room table that had hot plates of food and iced drinks on it. "We missed them by a minute."

"Somebody tipped them off," said the Sergeant.

"Okay," said Mitchell, "get everybody out."

As Mitchell went outside, it started to rain. As he pulled off his mask, several flash cameras fired off and video cameras were focused on his face. A reporter thrust a microphone into his face. In a matter of minutes, the street went from being empty to completely full of satellite vans, reporters and spectators.

"Did you apprehend any suspects, Lieutenant?"

"Does it look like it?" Mitchell could tell by the tone of the reporter that he was no longer the darling of the news media.

"This is the second time you've come up short with these meth

THE DOOR

labs, isn't it, Lieutenant Mitchell?" another TV reported asked.

"You keeping score?" said Mitchell. "And how did you guys learn about this raid so quickly?"

The reporter didn't answer.

Daphne was starting to enjoy Danver's spaghetti dinner when Lomax came rushing into the dining room and announced, "We've been compromised!"

*   *   *

A column of three Humvees drove to the old village and formed a line behind the remnants of the buildings. The armed occupants got out and formed a perimeter.

Both the C-130's engines and the helicopter's engines were running. The noise was deafening.

The Mayor of Revelation Fiord led a group of villagers to where Seacrest was being held at gunpoint.

"Mayor," said Seacrest, "take your people home before someone gets hurt."

Men with jackhammers, a portable electric generator, shovels and picks were coming out of the cargo compartment of the C-130 and went marching towards the old village.

"We know what they want and they can't have it," said the Mayor. "It stands on sacred ground!"

The Special Agent in charge of the Removal Team went up to the Mayor and said, "Please get your people out of here."

"This is our land and our country…"

"Sir, this is a national security matter. I am going to ask you nicely to remove yourself and your people from the area. Just let me do my job and we'll be out of here in a matter of minutes."

No one noticed the Northern Lights stirring high overhead and descending towards the ground.

The jet engines on the C-130 and the giant helicopter started to sputter.

Everyone looked up at the swirling colors.

"What the…?" went the Special Agent in Charge.

"The Spirits are angry!" said the Mayor. "You will all die now!"

THE DOOR

Thunder and Sparky managed to crawl into the ruins of the old village without being discovered by the armed men that patrolled the perimeter. They were too busy gazing up at the Northern Lights.

"What do these people want?" asked Sparky.

She turned to him and gave him an angry look. "They want the door, dummy."

*   *   *

"When Michael snapped his fingers, he must have shorted out my line splitter and amplifiers," said Lomax as he led the way down the stairs to the basement of his house.

"All of them?" asked Daphne.

"Yeah. I'm sure our neighbors saw everything after that. Although, the signal will be greatly degraded without the amplifiers—."

"—Oh, God!" said Daphne. "We're all going to go to jail!"

"I don't see the problem," said Danvers. "It's high time the government realized what they have here."

Lomax opened the door to his surveillance center and went in. "Trust me, the less they know…" He worked the controls, and rolled by the tape to the interior camera of the stakeout house.

"I'm sending you because you know the way to the warehouse," said Father as he presented the agent with an envelope. "Guard this with your life and hand it to Diciembre. No one else! You got that?"

When the agent left the stakeout house the time code on the recording read 20:34 hours.

"I know how they think," said Lomax, "and this not a good thing." He glanced at the clock on the wall. It read 20:45. "He has an eleven minute head start."

"Let him go, Lomax," said Danvers.

"No!" Lomax then heard something on the police radio frequency. He raised his hand. "Quiet!"

"What is it?" asked Daphne.

Dewey Mitchell was talking on the radio. "Central, there's two-car accident at the intersection of Main and Curran, send FD code 3."

"That's Dewey."

THE DOOR

"Yellow pickup truck, Virginia tag: Two One Foxtrot Delta Tango," said Mitchell. "And a black four door Ford, Virginia tag: Alpha, Alpha three three Delta Delta."

Lomax rushed over to a desk and opened a note pad. One of the things he did was write down all the car tags that frequented the stakeout house. "That's an Agency car!" Lomax grabbed a blank DVD and a few other things from the other side of the basement before dashing upstairs.

Danvers pointed to the monitor displaying an agent leaving the stakeout house and getting into a car. "That one?"

Lomax drove to the accident scene at breakneck speed and met up with Mitchell. It was raining hard. It was a terrible crash. The two vehicles were all mangled together and on fire. The pickup had t-boned the Ford, which had its hood standing straight up and flames shooting out. Debris was scattered all over the roadway. He could hear the sirens of the approaching fire engine and EMT ambulance, but they were some distance away.

It was Mitchell and a traffic officer who courageously pulled the unconscious driver out of the burning Ford. They carried him to where Mitchell had parked his car.

"Where's the driver of the pickup?" asked Mitchell.

"He's not in his truck."

"He can't have gone far. Find him!"

The traffic officer went off in search of the pickup's driver, but never would find him.

When Mitchell turned and saw Lomax walking towards him he bemoaned, "Oh, no, not you!"

Lomax pointed at the burning pickup. "Dewey, that's the yellow pickup that did the hit and run on Israel's car the night Richard was born."

Mitchell was surprised. "Are you sure?"

"I'm positive. I saw it happen."

"You never told me that! Then again, the only time you tell me anything is when everything is about to hit the fan." Lomax's presence made Mitchell nervous. He started looking over his shoulders.

"Who are you looking for, your Chief? Relax. He's no-where near here."

"How do you know that?" He then raised his hand. "Wait. I

THE DOOR

don't want to know. Now why are you here?"

Lomax gestured to the burning Ford. "Do you know who owns that car?"

Mitchell looked down at the unconscious driver and recognized him from one of the meetings he had had with the CIA. "Your favorite neighbor?"

"Yeah, and this one has something of mine." Lomax took the liberty to pat down and search the clothing of the unconscious agent and came up with nothing. "It's a DVD. It must be in the car. I want you to get it for me." Lomax noticed the change in Mitchell's facial expression. He should have not been so demanding. "I mean, I'm asking you to get it….Please."

Mitchell glared at Lomax angrily, then said, "Wait here."

But Lomax followed him to the car.

Mitchell went into the car and conducted a search. When he found the sealed envelope on the floor on the passenger side, he took it and backed away from the car—colliding into Lomax.

Lomax tossed a blank DVD onto the front seat, then a small plastic container filled with magnesium shavings onto the burning backseat and said, "Run!" They did.

Seconds later, the whole passenger compartment erupted into flames.

"What was that?"

"Magnesium. It burns at 5,000 degrees and leaves no trace behind." He knew the powder residue would be washed away by the fire hoses.

"Just like you."

Lomax grinned. "You read my file."

Mitchell handed the folder with the DVD to Lomax. "Don't thank me. Just get out of here."

Lomax slipped away just as Father arrived in a SUV with the remaining members of his team.

Daphne called Lomax on a secured cell phone. "Get back here quick! Richard just closed his bathroom door!"

*   *   *

Back at Revelation Fiord…

They turned on the portable electric generators to power up the

THE DOOR

jackhammers. They thought it would only take a minute to pry the door loose from the floor of the abandoned house. The agent pounded the concrete foundation with the jackhammer with no effect. Another one was brought in. Nothing! Suddenly the electric generators sputtered, then shut down completely. The rotors on the giant helicopter stopped turning and the jet engines whined down. The C-130 also experienced engine and power failure. All the lights winked out, even the flashlights, casting the entire community into darkness. The only lighting came from the Northern Lights. For a long moment, all was quiet. Even the pilots from both aircraft left their flight decks and went outside for a look.

"It is a sign from the Great Creator," said the Mayor. His people agreed.

Thunder pointed to the sky. "The energy from the Northern Lights is shorting out everything!" She gave away their position and was surrounded by men with automatic rifles in a matter of seconds.

"Freeze!"

The servicemen relieved Thunder and Sparky of their rifles and escorted them to where the Mayor and townspeople had gathered.

A piercing light emanated from the door as Richard opened it and stepped out onto muddy ground. It happened so fast that the gunmen didn't have a chance to form a skirmish line.

"Hi," Richard said to one of the men holding a jackhammer.

"Grab the kid!" someone shouted.

The two agents threw down their jackhammers and lunged towards Richard, but he managed to elude them and run towards the townspeople.

Sparky moved to a place where he could get a better view of the door. He pointed to the door. "That's it! That's the bedroom I was working in!"

Thunder rushed over to Sparky's side and peered at the open doorway to see the interior of a bedroom. It confirmed everything she ever felt about the door.

Seacrest joined her and took a look.

"Now what do you have to say, Inspector?" she asked.

Seacrest was speechless.

A team of three armed agents approached the door. One did a quick peek to see if it was safe to venture in. He then called out to his team leader. "All clear!"

"Go in," said the team leader.

But before the agent could make a move the door slammed shut.

Richard was terrified and started to cry. "I want my mommy!"

Thunder went over to him and reached out her arms. "It's okay."

Richard saw the men in black moving closer to him and figured the beautiful woman presented less of a danger to him. So, he went to her.

The villagers surrounded Thunder and the boy.

Seacrest came along side Thunder and got down on one knee in front of Richard. "I'm a policeman. You're safe with us."

"I want to go home!" said Richard.

"Okay," said Seacrest, "but first, what's your name, son?"

"Richard."

Seacrest shot a look to Sparky, who cocked an eyelid.

"Now do you believe me?" said Sparky.

It seemed that all of the agents had surrounded the villagers.

"We want the kid," said the team leader.

"No!" said the Mayor.

Knock! Knock! went the door in the old village.

With the jet engines and portable generator off, everyone on that tarmac heard it. Its echo bounced off the mountains.

"Oh, my God!" said Sparky. "It's happening again!"

The team leader had his men and several servicemen form a skirmish line. He then went up to the door and reached for the door handle.

"Whatever you do—don't open that door!" shouted Sparky.

The team leader stopped, turned to Sparky and said, "Shut up!"

Thunder called out something in her native language and all the villagers responded by walking briskly towards the airport tarmac, putting as much distance between them and the door as possible.

When the team leader opened the door, a very bright flash blinded him. A very powerful vacuum lifted him off the ground and pulled him and the three agents who were closest to him into the doorway. The vacuum was so powerful that it lifted all the villagers off their feet and caused them to fall on their rear ends. They, like most of the servicemen guarding the outer perimeter, were the lucky ones. Acting on pure instincts alone, they reached out and either grabbed each other or something affixed to the ground and hung on until it was over. What probably saved the remaining black ops agents was the giant helicopter being pulled through the door, compressing as it was driven inside. The flight crew was fortunate in that they had already left the aircraft when it happened.

The one aspect of the event that everyone would report was the eerie silence. Nothing was heard, not even the crumpling of metal.

In three seconds, it was all over.

When the door slammed shut, the helicopter, one portable generator, all the tools, most of the weapons and four members of the CIA Door Retrieval Team were gone.

One by one, the survivors of the event got to their feet and stared in silence at the closed door. Everyone was in a state of shock. None of them had ever experienced anything like this.

The howling of the Mayor's wolves broke the silence.

*   *   *

Lomax opened the door to his surveillance center and held up the DVD. "I got it!"

"We got more problems—," said Daphne.

"—Richard went traveling again," said Danvers.

"—And the door closed!" said Daphne.

Lomax's shoulders drooped. "How are we going to get him back?"

"We can't," said Danvers.

"We've got to tell Israel and Mary—," said Daphne.

"—Tell them what?" said Lomax. "They won't believe us!"

"Then what do we do?" she boomed.

Lomax looked to Danvers for guidance, but the former client gave a shrug.

*   *   *

The commanding officer of the military unit assigned to this mission at Revelation Fiord was a US Air Force Major. He had to be helped to his feet by one of his men. He had a nasty gash on his

THE DOOR

forehead that was bleeding. He had been dragged to within ten feet of the door when the door closed and the vacuum stopped. He patted himself down and realized that his automatic rifle, pistol, ammunition belt, knife, radio and satellite phone were gone. He went staggering towards the hole that was dug out of the ground by the giant helicopter as it was dragged towards the ruins of the old village and sucked into the doorway. He helped several of his men to their feet. They too had lost their weapons and most of their gear. Some of them also sustained minor injuries.

One of his staff sergeants reported to him, "Major, our people are all present and accounted for."

"Oh, thank God!"

"But four agents are gone, including the team leader."

"Four? Great! How am I going to explain this?"

The Mayor, Seacrest, Thunder, Richard, Sparky and the rest of the villagers started to walk to the town proper.

The Major called out to them and said in a very authoritative tone, "Stop right there!" The villagers did. "Nobody goes anywhere until I get witness statements from all of you."

"Why we'd be more than happy to write witness statements for you," said Seacrest. He turned to the crowd and asked, "Wouldn't we, *eh?*" No one replied. "And allow me to tell what we're going to say. We're going to say that you buzzed over this town at a very low altitude, shooting your automatic weapons at our houses and then you crashed your helicopter into the ocean, where it sank."

This time the villagers voiced their affirmation with the RCMP Inspector.

"Furthermore," continued Seacrest, "the Mayor here will have the town attorney file a civil lawsuit against the United States Government for all the environmental damage the escaping jet fuel from your helicopter will cause to the wildlife here. Should fetch several millions of dollars…."

The villagers cheered. They liked the sound of that.

"Not to mention all the bad press your *flipping* Air Force will get from all of this," said Seacrest.

"Kiss goodbye to your career," said Thunder.

The Major's body went numb.

"Or," said Seacrest, and he raised his hand to quiet the crowd, "in the spirit of cooperation between our two great countries, you

THE DOOR

could take your injured to the clinic in our community center to have their wounds looked after." He turned to the other Americans. "The rest of you can be our guests and have a nice seal steak dinner, drink a couple of Canadian beers and wait for the bloody phones to work again."

The Major was surprised and perplexed by the Inspector's offer. "Well, with an offer like that, how can I refuse?"

"You can't. But let's be clear about one thing. The door stays, or we will call a news conference and tell the world what we saw tonight." Seacrest walked to within a few feet of the Major. He pointed to the bleeding gash. "You need to have that looked at straightaway."

The Major agreed, then told his men to pick up their gear and head towards the town.

"Why are you letting them off so easily?" Sparky asked Seacrest.

"We have business to conduct here," replied Seacrest, "with this door. And maybe there is a chance that Allison is alive and somewhere on the other side."

That brought a smile to Thunder's face. She reached out and gave him a hug. "Thank you!"

Sparky looked down at Richard and asked. "Do you think you can open that door without getting hurt?"

Richard nodded confidently.

Sparky gestured to the door. "Will this door take you back home?"

"Archangel Michael said that all I had to do was tap the door three times to take me home."

Seacrest and Thunder glanced at each other. *Was it a kid's tale or did an Archangel really tell him how many times to tap on the door?*

*   *   *

"ALERT!" the computer said repeatedly over the public address system.

The four field agents came flying out of a glowing door towards the middle of the warehouse's main floor. They flew through the air and collided into the lineup of glowing doors, sustaining

THE DOOR

serious and life-threatening injuries. The mangled and compacted helicopter followed them out of the same door a second later like sausage coming through a tube, with jet fuel spewing forth. Sparks, created by all the friction of passing through such a confined space caused the jet fuel to ignite and explode. The compacted helicopter flew through the air like a meteorite, trailing fire and smoke, and then it plowed into several lines of glowing doors, lifting them off their floor mounts and launching them high into the air. The impact was such that some of the doors hit the warehouse's ceiling. The helicopter crashed through and came to a rest inside the control center, setting it ablaze.

"FIRE!" the PA system repeated as the Halon fire suppression system activated.

Diciembre was struck down by flying debris, but not injured. As he slowly got to his feet, he surveyed the interior of the warehouse that at first resembled a scene out of Hell. Seconds later, the interior was enveloped with clouds of Halon. He bravely went through the huge opening in the front wall of the burning control center to locate survivors. He carried one of his female techs through the opened hatch of the Armory. A Special Forces corporal rolled out a gurney for Diciembre and he placed the moaning tech onto it.

"We need to call 911," said the corporal.

"Negative! The fire suppression system will contain the fire. Now get her to the infirmary."

"We only got one medic and he can't handle these kinds of injuries."

"I know!"

Diciembre pulled out a portable fire extinguisher, opened the hatch to the warehouse and went inside. Within twenty seconds of fighting the fire that he came in contact with, his CO_2 extinguisher was all used up. He put down the extinguisher and pressed on, keeping to the Halon cloud. When he came out the other side of the cloud, he was stunned by what he saw: four black ops field agents lying on the floor near a thirty-foot long rectangular metallic object that burned with white-hot fire. When the fiery object came out of one of the doors, it plowed down about fifty doors before crashing into the control room, bashing down the front wall. Three soldiers were fighting the fire with water hoses.

"Be careful—that's jet fuel!" Diciembre said to the sergeant, who was spraying water on the fire.

More gurneys arrived and the wounded agents were taken away.

The fire finally subsided and the sergeant turned off the fire hose. "Do you know what that is? That's a helicopter! One of the heavies."

Diciembre stared at the smoking mass of metal.

His new second in command, a female agent, came rushing up to him and made a report. "I recognized one of the four agents. He's a member of the door retrieval team stationed at Thule."

"I know." Diciembre also recognized the four agents.

"Their injuries are serious. They need immediate EVAC."

"Yes, I know." Diciembre raised a hand to silence his second in command. He needed a moment to think of his next move. "See to it that all seriously injured are wheeled out on gurneys to the dirt road. I'll arrange for their transport." The second in command started to turn, but Diciembre grabbed her arm. "Containment, Special Agent. We must maintain containment at all costs. Do you read me?

"Yes, I read you!" She pulled herself free and ran into the Halon.

Diciembre called the county Fire Chief's personal cell phone number and arranged for a half dozen EMT ambulances to be dispatched by landline to the dirt road in front of the warehouse. It took more time to accomplish by phone, but by doing it this way neither the news media nor any local law enforcement agencies who monitored the fire department's frequencies got wind of so many ambulances being dispatched to one location. Containment was maintained, he would write in his incident report at the top of the page.

Fortunately, one of the members from the retrieval team was conscious long enough to give Diciembre a short report on what happened in Canada.

Diciembre had all of the injured field operatives stripped of their combat fatigues and anything that would link them to the Agency. The techs and soldiers who wheeled the gurneys out of the infirmary had to stop and put on FBI coats and caps.

"We will say that they were on a training exercise," said Diciembre, as he helped wheel one of the injured off the warehouse

THE DOOR

property. "Their SUV was involved in a hit and run. There will be no reports filed. This facility cannot be compromised. This is ground zero, people, and we are in a war that we cannot lose. The lives of your wives, husbands and kids weigh in the balance. Questions?"

There were none. This was one of those times when their duty to the service and to the country outweighed everything else.

Diciembre personally closed the front gate and secured it with a chain and heavy lock to maintain the appearance that the old warehouse was abandoned and unoccupied. Several agents came out with brooms and covered up all of the gurneys' wheel marks and any footprints that led to the warehouse. One of the facilities' SUVs was purposely crashed into an oak tree near the warehouse entrance to give credence to the cover story. The injured techs were lifted off their gurneys and laid out on the softest ground their fellow workers could find near the wrecked vehicle. Their gurneys were hidden in the woods. A few minutes after the techs and soldiers wheeled out the injured onto the unlit dirt road, the ambulances arrived without sirens or flashing emergency lights. The arriving EMTs quickly lifted the injured onto their gurneys and immediately started to provide medical care. Once the gurneys were loaded, the ambulances sped off to the closest hospital. A second SUV loaded with agents would accompany them to the hospital to do all the paperwork and create a cover story. The EMTs were told to drive at least three miles before turning on their emergency lights and sirens. A half hour after the ambulances had left the scene a tow truck came to remove the damaged SUV. A deputy sheriff was there, sweeping his side spotlight all around in search of the wrecked vehicle. He shined the beam on an oak tree that had some obvious signs of damage to its bark.

"I was told that a SUV wrecked up here," said the tow truck driver.

"Well, it ain't here now."

They drove off.

They were in panic mode. Lomax and Daphne paced the floor in the surveillance room, while Danvers buried his head in his hands.

"It's all over," said Danvers.

THE DOOR

"No, it's not," said Lomax.

"Mister confidence here," said Daphne.

"Just be patient," said Lomax. "Something will turn up."

One of his cell phones rang. Lomax checked the caller ID.

"Who is it?" asked Daphne.

Lomax shook his head. "I'm not sure. But I think I should know this number." He had been under a lot of stress and he just couldn't remember the phone number. The phone rang three times before he answered it. "Hello?"

"Lomax?" asked Diciembre.

"Diciembre!" Lomax winced. At this critical moment, the last person in the world he wanted to talk to was his nemesis. "What a pleasant surprise! Now, what *can't* I do for you?"

After what had happened at the warehouse, Diciembre was in a state of shock. Most of the computers and communication systems were fried. But when he did manage to get through to Langley and make a situation report, he was shocked by the indifference of the agent he was reporting to. Even though Deputy Director Black-burn had given him a supervisory role in Project Door it became quite obvious that someone at CIA Headquarters didn't want him to be informed about the retrieval mission at Revelation Fiord. Nor was he informed that the field office in Thule and the communications center at Langley had lost contact with the retrieval team and both aircraft. He learned about that through another source in the agency. That person would not even confirm or deny that the four injured agents were members of the Door Retrieval Team. For whatever reason, the powers that be at the CIA had decided to take him out of the loop in respect to this mission and possibly others. His life and the lives of his people were on the line and someone far from the action was deciding what information he should and should not be told. In short, he was being sandbagged and he didn't like it one damn bit! It was then he made one of the biggest decisions of his life. He decided to call Lomax. "We've just had an incident here."

"You mean at your banged-up old warehouse out in the middle of no-where?" Lomax had no idea of what just happened at the warehouse.

Diciembre closed his eyes shook his head. *The most top-secret facility in the CIA and Lomax knew all about it!* "Yes, and it

THE DOOR

involves a door in northern Canada.”

Lomax sat down and wrote, “*Door in northern Canada*” on a piece of paper. He then held it up for Daphne and Danvers to see. “Why are you telling me this?” He put the cell phone on “Speaker Phone” so that all three of them could hear Diciembre.

“I was hoping that we could work together.”

“Oh, I don’t know about that. We never could before and to be honest with you, I don’t think I can trust you.”

“I’m going out on a limb here, Lomax. Way out. I’m breaking a lot of Agency rules and regs by doing this.”

Lomax grinned. “Sounds like something I was accused of doing…by you. *Uh*, hey look. I’ve had a rough day, so I think I’ll say *buenas noches* —.”

“—You lose the kid?”

Lomax froze and didn’t answer.

“Thought so,” said Diciembre. “I know where Richard is. You interested…or should I say good night—?”

“—No, no don’t hang up!” shouted Daphne.

Lomax gave her an angry look, then said, “Where is he?”

“He’s in a little town called Revelation Fiord. You know of it?”

“No, but it does have a nice biblical ring to it—.” Lomax frowned, then made a fist with his free hand and hit himself on the chest. It was stupid for him to try to lie to his former superior from the CIA, especially since Diciembre was obviously reaching out to him.

“—I said, do you know of it?”

“Yes, I do. It has a door.”

Daphne went online and typed **Revelation Fiord**. A map of Ellesmere Island and the town’s location were displayed on the main wall monitor.

Lomax glanced at the map and thanked Daphne with a nod.

“All hell just broke loose up there,” said Diciembre. “The damn door sucked in four agents and a heavy lift helicopter and dumped them here in my warehouse. That door is the most powerful one we’ve come across so far. The readings we got were off the chart.”

“*Ah,* come on Diciembre! How can a helicopter go through a doorway?”

“You should see it. It looks like it was passed through a trash compactor."

Lomax shook his head. The defiant side of Lomax was coming to the surface. "No, you still haven't explained to me why I should trust you."

"Like it or not, we're on the same side now and before this facility was wrecked, it was Ground Zero. Now your street in Marion is. If you and I don't work together, this world is doomed! This facility is out of service. From this point on, you're the only one with eyes on the target."

"What about the other set of eyes? You know, the ones looking at my house?"

"You need to shut them down ASAP and permanently."

"If I do that it may force Blackburn to shut me down."

"I'll hold him back as long as I can. Now get off the phone. You got work to do." Diciembre closed his cell phone.

*   *   *

Meanwhile, back at Revelation Fiord...

It had been three hours since the incident with the door and Seacrest had remained with Richard, Sparky and Thunder in the airport terminal. Richard felt so comfortable with these three adults that he told them everything.

The Major stood on the front porch of the community center, staring off into the distance. A large bandage covered the stitches that closed the gash on his forehead. The Air Force medics assigned to the team gave the injured the medical care they required and released them. One of the uninjured retrieval team members came out of the center, leaped off the porch and vomited on the ground. Some of his teammates laughed.

"What kind of barbecue was that?"

"Didn't you hear the Inspector?" asked the serviceman who followed him outside. "It was seal...!"

"Oh, God!" said the one who had vomited.

The Major jerked his head to the right, due east. He thought he heard something. He did.

Three CH91 Helicopters were flying over the water, with no lights on, on a heading that would take them to Revelation Fiord.

"Finally!" The Major turned to the serviceman. "Assemble the

THE DOOR

team. We're moving out!"

Richard looked out a window at the door and stared at it intensely.

Thunder noticed the odd look on Richard's face. "Richard, what's wrong?"

Sparky let out a groan.

"What's the matter with you?" Seacrest asked him.

"I can feel it."

"Feel what?"

"The door is coming alive with energy."

Thunder went over to Richard and got down on one knee to be at eye level with him. "You okay?"

"It's calling to me."

It was Seacrest who spotted the three blimps on the radar screen. "Radar contact. We got company."

"Who are they?" asked Sparky.

"Reinforcements," said Seacrest. "Probably more choppers from Thule."

"What does that mean?" asked Richard.

"It means we've got to go," said Thunder. "We need for you to open the door and let us in."

"I can go home now?"

"Yes," said Thunder, "and we're coming with you. Is that all right?"

Richard smiled and gave a nod. "Okay."

There was a rifle vault in the terminal and Seacrest knew the combination. He removed the double barreled shotgun the airport personnel used to protect themselves from the polar bears.

Thunder confronted Seacrest as he loaded the shotgun. They had a short and stormy relationship, but since Allison's birth, they had treated each other with civility for the sake of their child.

"I'll stay and hold them off for as long as I can," he said to her.

"Don't get your bloody head blown off. When I bring Allison home, she's going to be looking for her daddy."

He made a fist and gave her a little tap on the cheek. "Right. Off you go now!"

The three USAF helicopters came roaring over the town and broke formation, dropping flares on the runway and abandoned village. The surviving members of the door retrieval team had commandeered what vehicles they could start up and were driving towards the abandoned village, honking their horns.

"This is the United States Air Force!" someone ordered over a speaker mounted on one of the helicopters. "Stand away from the door!" A powerful spot light was shined on the two adults and young boy as they ran towards the old village. "Don't move or you will be fired upon!"

Two of the helicopters landed and the strike team disembarked, weapons at the ready. Someone on the strike team opened fire.

Bullets bounced around Thunder and Sparky as they escorted Richard to the door. Richard tapped the door three times and opened it. On the other side of the threshold was his bedroom.

Seacrest fired off both barrels of the shotgun into the air to get the Americans' attention. One of the strike teams confronted him and he dropped the shotgun and surrendered to them without further incident. His actions bought his friends the time they needed to escape.

Richard led the way through the door and Thunder and Sparky followed.

The leader of the second strike team got to within twenty feet of the door and even got a good look inside before the door slammed shut.

THE DOOR

Chapter Fourteen

HAYWIRE

Michael was wearing the black suit of a
Catholic priest as he presented himself to Uriel. "How do I look?"

Uriel, who was floating near a massive hologram that displayed Earth and the locations of all the door portals, gave him a once over. "Mortal and vulnerable."

"Good enough, then."

"Are you sure you don't want a Praetorian to accompany you?" Michael didn't answer. Uriel waved his hand in the direction of the hologram. "You do realize that once you are off the grid we won't be able track you?"

"Yes and yes, I know my dear brother."

"Do I need to remind you that the last time you went to earth—and the time before that, you assumed the personality of a Catholic priest? You're developing a pattern."

Michael cocked an eyelid. "Exactly the reason I am doing it."

Uriel noticed that other Angels were watching and listening to them. "Michael, I am not one to question your decisions, but it has been decades since you've been earthbound. It has changed considerably. I ... need a Praetorian to escort me when I go there." Admitting any personal limitations openly wasn't easy for this Archangel, especially when his competition had been Lucifer, Gabriel and Michael and in that order.

"How do the mortals say *'good bye'*?" Michael searched his mind. "Oh, yes! See you later, crocodile."

Uriel shook his head. "No, it's: see you later, alligator."

"That's it! Makes no sense at all, but that's it."

"Gabriel was floating in that same spot when he said good bye to me. That was four hundred years ago…and no one has seen or or tracked him since."

THE DOOR

"I know and I will find him and the missing girl. Until my return, the Army is yours to command."

"I relieve you," said Uriel, in a low tone. "Reluctantly."

"I stand relieved...unreluctantly."

They exchanged a salute.

When Michael spun round and gazed up at the thousands of Praetorians stationed in the Junction, he received the same salute from his soldiers. He humbly returned the gesture. He could see the worried expressions on their faces. His soldiers loved him and they did not want to see him go. And there was a rumor that Lucifer was more powerful and dangerous than ever. They respected Uriel, but it was clear that Michael was their favorite commander. Gabriel was always hard charging and ready to attack. Uriel was too distant, too restrained. Michael was calm, consistent and more warmhearted towards his soldiers. They knew where he stood at all times and they would follow him to the gates of Perdition without hesitation. "You have been unwavering in your support to me and this mission. Much has been asked of each and every one of you and you have not faltered in your dedication. The good news is that closure is at hand. Take heart, all of *ye* who have served me so well, for we do this not for fame nor glory nor wealth." He then shouted: "Praetorians, why are we here?"

"FOR THE NINETEEN!" they roared, then slapped their spear shafts against their shinning shields, creating a loud clang!

Michael had to have his long curly locks of hair trimmed off as part of the disguise. He put on a black fedora and smiled. Many of the Praetorians laughed. Wearing this hat gave the Archangel a curious sensation. He too found it amusing. He thought to himself that it would be a long time before he would ever be amused again, so he took a moment to relish the feeling. He then floated to an open door and crossed the threshold. A Praetorian closed the door behind him.

Uriel turned to Joan and said, "Request a private audience at *His* convenience." There was a sense of urgency in his tone and the female saint recognized it.

"Right away, my Lord Prince...."

*   *   *

THE DOOR

Danvers was almost the same height and build as Lomax, so he raided the rogue agent's closet for a set of black combat fatigues. Lomax had about a half dozen sets along with a host of other suits and clothes he used to disguise himself. He then joined up with Lomax in his lab, the side of the basement where Israel's doors were once kept. The custom made glass and steel walled containment enclosure that Lomax had built for the doors had been taken down and replaced by a large wooden worktable. He recognized the bundle of wires with bumps in them. *"Ah,* so this is the infamous Haywire?"

"Uh, ha." Lomax removed the connection wires to the other device and carefully placed the device into a black carrying bag.

He gave Danvers the once over and asked, "You up for this?" He knew that Danvers looked young, but was in fact very old.

"You just lead the way and tell me what to do."

Lomax lifted a cardboard shaped bomb off the worktable. It resembled the gravity bombs dropped by B-17s during World War II. But it was made of cardboard and paper and there was a short fuse hanging between its fins. "You will carry this and ignite it. Bring a lighter."

"I thought you said we were going to shut them down, not blow them up?"

"Relax. It's not an explosive, per say. It's made of the same stuff they make ping-pong balls and sparklers with. And for good luck, I added a few of my… special firecrackers, to give it a little **'boom!'**."

"Sounds like the Fourth of July."

"Well, let's just say, it will have a liberating effect on our friends on the other side of the alley."

As Lomax led the way up the stairway and stopped in front of the back door, Daphne called him on the headset. "I just did another infrared sweep on the house."

"Good. Anybody home?"

"That's a negative They must still be at the hospital."   .

"Okay, input Lomax One."

Daphne then hacked into the local power company's mainframe and activated a program Lomax had written that changed the cooling cycle for the streetlights. All street lamps need to shutdown every few hours for a couple of minutes to allow their lighting elements to cool. They did it automatically. But this program made all the streetlights for a four-block radius shut down at the same time. It made the area a little darker, especially in the alley behind Lomax's house.

"We got ninety seconds," Lomax told Danvers.

Lomax and Danvers put on their night vision goggles and went out the backdoor. The darkness would cover their movements from the cameras that scanned the rear sides of both Lomax's and Daphne's houses. Lomax also didn't want any of the other neighbors to see what they were about to do either. They didn't use the gate that led to the alley because Father's people had put a seismic motion sensor on it, to alert them anytime someone opened the gate. The first thing Lomax learned in spy school was that one never opened a gate because it was probably booby-trapped or wired with a trip sensor. Lomax had three sturdy wood crates stacked next to the fence earlier in the day. They would act like steps. Lomax bolted up the two makeshift steps and vaulted over the fence. Danvers was right behind him. They didn't even grunt when they landed.

"Not bad for a 435 year old man," whispered Lomax.

"*Ah*, shut up and press on!" whispered Danvers.

The stakeout house also had a wooden fence with a trip sensor on its gate. Lomax and Danvers had to vault over this fence the hard way, but they did it without making too much noise. Once they crossed the backyard, they split up. Lomax went to the west side of the house and uncovered the outside breaker box. He removed the haywire device from a canvas bag and inserted the point into the paper sided breaker. It wasn't long before the bundle of wire started to glow with an orange color.

Danvers opened the glass door to the rear porch and placed the bomb in the middle of the floor, on its fins so that the device pointed straight up. He then lit the fuse and leisurely walked off.

They opened the gate to the front yard and walked across the street. Seconds later, the Haywire erupted with a colorful arc of magnetic energy that traveled though the stakeout house's power lines and fried every hard drive and electrical system in the house and basement, but nowhere else. It used the house's electrical wiring to carry its damaging effect. It was a perfect example of a highly effective surgical strike. When the cardboard bomb went off, it appeared from all the sparkling, smoke and noise being emitted as though the house was on fire. A neighbor called the fire department and fire trucks arrived at the scene within five minutes. No trace of either device was left, especially after the way the firefighters hosed down the house and rear porch.

"And that ends that," said Lomax.

Danvers gestured to the street sign, which read: '**The Hamilton Way**'. "How appropriate."

Lieutenant Dewey Mitchell was wearing his pajamas and getting ready to go to bed when the telephone rang. He answered it. "Hello..."

"Lieutenant," the dispatcher from the PD reported, "there's a house fire on Moon Street."

"What address?"

"1864. I figured you'd want to know."

The stakeout house!

"I'm on my way!"

Mitchell dressed quickly and raced to the intersection of Moon Street and The Hamilton Way. He parked his unmarked car, got out and stepped over to where Lomax and Danvers were watching, along with about fifty other spectators. Lomax and Danvers had already stripped off their combat fatigues so that they could blend in with the crowd.

"Well, well, well," said Lomax. "Lieutenant Dewey Mitchell. Come to see the fireworks show?"

All civilian, fire and police personnel were ordered by the Fire Chief to evacuate the area because of the loud booms being heard inside the stakeout house. It sounded to him like ammunition firing off. He was correct. All of the ordinance stored in the basement ignited, adding to the fireworks show. Lomax's timing was perfect. None of the CIA agents were at the stakeout house so there were no causalities from the fire he started. But the old wood framed house would be burned down to its foundation.

Mitchell stared at Danvers. "You're him, aren't you? John Danvers?"

"And what if I am?"

"You have more federal warrants on you than he does," he jerked a thumb at Lomax.

Danvers glanced over to Lomax. "I knew there was a reason

we get along so well."

Lomax rubbernecked for a moment. "Say, I wonder where your Police Chief is?" he asked Mitchell, as though he knew exactly where he was. "He's missing out on all the fun."

Finally the last of the special firecrackers and ordinance went off and about five minutes later the Fire Chief gave the all clear for the emergency personnel to return to their duties.

Lomax and Danvers stayed with Mitchell, who said, "You two are going to be the death of me yet."

"Headquarters to Lieutenant Mitchell," the radio dispatcher called out.

Mitchell heard the radio and went to his car to answer it. "Mitchell, go ahead."

"Suspicious incident at 1919 Cornelius Drive...."

"That's Israel's house!" said Lomax as he bolted to his house, with Danvers in tow.

"Headquarters," said Mitchell, "I am *en route*." He got into his car and raced to Israel's house.

"Ten-four. Be advised, they requested your presence. Shall I dispatch a patrol unit to back you up, sir?"

"Negative and I am 10:97." 10:97 was a police ten code that meant he had arrived at the scene.

"10:97 at 23:00 hours," said the dispatcher.

Lomax went charging down the stairway to his basement and immediately got it from Daphne.

"Took you long enough...!" she roared.

"What's going on?" asked Lomax.

"Richard is back and he brought a couple of friends."

"Friends—who?"

Lomax and Danvers arrived just in time at the surveillance center to watch the drama unfold.

"Containment," said Danvers. "We must contain this incident."

"Too late for that," said Daphne as she pressed the "Rewind" button to show Richard, then Thunder and Sparky coming out of Richard's bathroom door.

"That's the phone repair guy!" said Lomax.

"Who's the woman?" asked Daphne.

Danvers smiled. "Allison's mother!"

Israel appeared at the doorway to Richard's room. "Oh, no!" he

THE DOOR

said.

"Oh, hell!" said Lomax.

When Mary entered Richard's bedroom, she started to scream and weep. "It's happening again!" she said repeatedly.

By the time Mitchell arrived, Thunder had administered a sedative to Mary to calm her down and put her to sleep.

Mitchell was overjoyed to see Sparky. He even hugged the man. "So, glad to see you again! I thought for sure we'd lost you boy!"

"I guess my mother is very worried too," said Sparky. He spotted the telephone receiver. "Well, somebody installed the phone extension in this room." When he reached for the telephone, Mitchell placed his hand over the receiver.

"Sparky, I've got some bad news to tell you…." He turned to Israel and Richard, and politely asked if they could leave the room. Once alone, Mitchell informed Sparky that his mother had passed away seven years earlier.

The news of his mother's passing made Sparky distraught. He waved his hand in such a way as to indicate that he wanted to be left alone. He then turned off the bedroom lights and laid down on the floor.

While Sparky sobbed in Richard's bedroom, Mitchell went down the stairs and introduced himself to Thunder. "Lieutenant Mitchell, Marion Police Department. And you are?"

"Dr. Kudluk, which in your language means Thunder. I'm a Climatologist and part time nurse in a small Indian community in northern Canada—."

"—Yes, a quaint little place called Revelation Fiord?"

Thunder's eyelids shot up. "Not so quaint. How do you know where I came from?"

"I've spoken to Inspector Seacrest and I've read about your missing daughter."

"Everyone said that a polar bear got her, but I always knew her disappearance had some thing to do with that horrid door. I was right and she's alive! And I am here to find her!" Her tone was forceful.

Mitchell nodded in approval. "I'll help you in anyway I can."

Israel spent sometime with Richard in the living room. He then put on the TV and said he needed to speak to Lieutenant Mitchell.

THE DOOR

"Okay, daddy."

"You okay, Israel?" asked Mitchell, as Israel entered the foyer.

"Our nightmare is back." Israel went over to Thunder and shook her hand. "Thank you for helping my wife…and my son."

"My pleasure and there's something you need to know. Your son is a very brave and special young man. He may have saved all our lives."

"From who?" asked Mitchell.

"Your bloody government! They came at us with helicopters and soldiers with guns. They even shot at us."

"Why?" asked Israel, who became terrified at the thought that his son was involved in a shooting.

"They know your son has the gift."

"What gift?" He made a face. "There's no gift."

"I've seen it," she said. "How do you think we got here from thousands of kilometers away? He has the ability to open time/space portals." When she saw a confused look on Israel's face she cut to the chase. "To open doors!"

"Lady, you're not making any sense."

"Actually," said Mitchell, "she is. Go on. Tell him. He needs to know." He turned to Israel and pointed at him. "And you need to listen."

"There are certain doors in this world that you dare not answer if someone knocks on them," said Thunder. "Your son can answer those doors without disappearing…like Sparky did." She jerked her head in the direction of Richard's bedroom.

That statement took Israel aback. He pointed in the direction of Richard's bedroom. "Him?"

Mitchell nodded.

"Seven years ago he was working in Richard's bedroom when he heard a knock on the bathroom door," she continued. "He answered it and ended up coming out of a door in Revelation Fiord. He arrived a week ago."

Israel brought a hand up to his face. "Do you realize what you are saying? How can someone open a door in Virginia and end up in God knows where Canada seven years later?"

Mitchell interceded. "Israel, were you and Richard anywhere near Don Beech's farm yesterday?"

"Yeah, what of it? The door to his tack room wouldn't ...

THE DOOR

open."

"The FBI had us keep what I am about to tell you under wraps. Don is missing…and so is his barn. Only the door to his tack room remains."

It was then Israel and the others realized that Richard was standing by the doorway to the living room, listening. "Daddy?"

"Yes, Richard?"

"That farmer you know who curses a lot is on TV."

Mitchell did a double take. "Is he talking about Don?"

Everyone rushed into the living room to watch the news report.

"…Now folks," said the TV news reporter, "You're not going to believe what I am about to show you." He was standing in front of a large sign which read: **Bear Thy Soul and Everything else Wedding Chapel.** "I'm reporting to you from Wabash, at the only nudist wedding chapel in Iowa. This is where everyone, right down to the Reverend is buck-naked. That's right! Now they were just about to complete the nuptials when a wood beam came flying out of that farm house." He turned and pointed to the wrecked farmhouse with a long wood beam sticking out the front of it. "We got some homemade video on what happened."

The show's director cut to the shot showing a long wood beam crashing through the living room window. The director then cut to another home video of Don Beech who was lying in a pile of clothing, waving his arms and growling like a bear as he fought to get free. "Give-me-a-hand-here!"

A group of people appeared and pulled away the clothes until his body was visible. There was a mammoth-sized panty covering Beech. His head was sticking out of one of the leg openings.

"What-in-the-hell-is-this-a-boat-sail-or-a-whale's underwear?"

A naked fat woman confronted Don and smacked him across the face.

Suddenly the satellite feed was cut off and the TV displayed only snow. It did that for about five minutes.

"Well," said Mitchell, "we know that Don is okay."

"I'm surprised your government let it air that long," said Thunder.

"How did he get from here to there?" asked Israel.

"I think you know," said Thunder.

Israel shook his head. "No! I've heard enough of all these wild stories from you people."

"He's in denial," said Thunder.

"Hey, look lady! I don't know who you are or how you got here! All I know is that I want everyone to leave!"

Thunder went toe to toe with Israel and stared him straight in the eyes. She held a photograph in her hand and brought it right up to his face. "You see this picture? This is my daughter. Her name is Allison. I took it when she was getting ready to go to a costume party. But she never came back. Why? Because she kept hearing this door we have in our town knock. She even said that it called to her. Then she started telling me about all the strange places she went to. I thought it was a kid's tale. I didn't believe her. I didn't want to believe her. Now she's gone and I'm here to find her. Not you, not your government or anyone is going to stop me." Her eyes were full of tears. It was the first time she allowed herself to cry since her daughter's disappearance.

"Israel," said Mitchell, "there's more to this than you know."

"Oh, Dewey," said Israel, "don't tell me you believe this junk?"

Sparky heard the commotion downstairs as he lay on the floor in Richard's darkened bedroom, with his back to the bathroom door. Tears filled his eyes too and flowed down his cheeks. The mother he loved so much was gone. She was dead and buried for seven years! All because he answered a knocking door! He pulled out a small flashlight that he kept on his belt and flashed the beam on the colorful mural on the wall in front of him. He recalled the first mural was of a circus with clowns and a lot of colorful balloons. Now it was a mural of King Richard the Lion Hearted. Even in his grief, he was impressed with the artistic talent of the artist. But as he flashed the small beam of his flashlight from right to left, he noted a glint. He panned the light again and once again spotted the glint. He got up, turned on the lights and went right up to the wall to investigate.

"We're cooked!" said Daphne as she, Lomax and Danvers watched Sparky get right up close to the old pinhole camera.

Sparky exited the bedroom, leaned over the stairwell banister and called out, "Hey, did you guys know this house is bugged?"

When Israel turned to Mitchell, who couldn't look him in the face, he knew that something was up!

To prove his statement, Sparky used a knife to dig out the

pinhole camera—the original one Lomax had planted. He then led the way up to the attic to search for the coaxial wire that ran to Richard's bedroom. It wasn't long before he discovered all of the cables and all the gizmos attached to them. "Every room in your house is wired."

"Every room?" Israel was furious.

Sparky held up the coaxial wire that ran outside. "They're all connected to this line, which means whoever has been watching is close by."

"Follow it!" said Israel.

They did, from the roof to the power pole. Sparky walked down the driveway and went half way across the street, before stopping. He then pointed at Lomax's house. "It ends up at that house."

Israel was never so enraged. He went into his garage and grabbed a sledgehammer.

"Israel," said Mitchell, "don't do something you will regret."

Israel crossed the street and swung the sledgehammer at the front door of Lomax's house, punching a hole in it. "Knock! Knock! Anybody home?"

Mitchell had to wrestle his old high school football friend to pull the sledgehammer out of his hands. "Give me that before you kill somebody!"

Lomax opened the door and stepped back.

Israel entered the house and threw his fist at Lomax, connecting on the chin. They both fell on a coffee table, smashing it. Israel threw a lot of punches, but Lomax did not retaliate.

It took both Mitchell and Sparky to separate them.

"Why?" asked Israel. "Why did you do this? I let you into my house, my business! I thought we were friends!"

For once, Lomax was speechless.

"He is your best friend," said Daphne, in her husband's defense.

"You were part of this too!" said Israel.

Mitchell had all to do to restrain Israel, but he managed to push the man to the far wall. "Now you are going to listen to me!"

"Let me go, damn you!"

"No, damn you! Now you're going to listen and listen good." Mitchell jerked his head in Lomax's and Daphne's direction. "Yes, your precious privacy was violated. For seven years they've watched and protected you and your family. And they weren't the only ones watching. The house on Moon Street that the FD went to tonight...that was a CIA stakeout house. They've been there for six years. It was Lomax who took them out!"

"Lomax? Don't you mean, Eddi?"

"No, his real name is Lomax."

"Wait!" said Israel. "You mean the CIA was watching me?"

"And waiting for Richard to open the door," said Danvers, as he stepped into the light.

It started to sink in. Israel's body went limp.

Mitchell eased up and eventually released his hold on Israel.

Israel pointed to Lomax and Daphne and even Mitchell. "You're no friends of mine. I don't want anything to do with any of you ever again. You hear?"

With that, he stumbled out of the house and went home.

Lomax was equally devastated. He left everyone and went to Daphne's house.

"Everything has gone haywire," said Mitchell as he exited the house.

"*Hmmm!*" said Danvers. "How appropriate."

Two days later, while Israel was at work, Daphne and Thunder asked Mary to have tea with them at Lomax's house. They then gave her a tour of the basement and showed her several recordings. Mary was numbed by it all, especially the footage of Prince Michael.

"This isn't over, isn't it?" asked Mary.

"Not by a long shot," said Daphne.

Thunder pointed to Daphne and said to Mary, "They can't protect your boy unless they have both eyes and ears working twenty-four-seven."

"And right now we got no ears," said Daphne.

"What do you want from me?" asked Mary.

"I need for you to let Sparky go through your house and replace all of the microphones," said Daphne.

Mary turned her gaze from Daphne to Thunder, thought it over, then back to Daphne. "Do it."

THE DOOR

THE DOOR

Chapter Fifteen

JUDGEMENT CALL

It was almost 11AM when Sparky awakened. He and Thunder were invited by Daphne to stay in the guest room on the second floor at Lomax's house. When he reached out his hand, he realized he was alone in bed. "Thunder?"

He got dressed, went down stairs and found the door to the basement opened. He ventured on and found Daphne and Thunder in the surveillance center.

Thunder was all teary eyed. When she realized Sparky was in the room she pointed to the main screen that displayed a little girl running through the Bonham house. "Look! There's my baby!"

"That's Allison?"

"Yes, and she's alive!"

"But we don't know where she is," added Daphne. "This is the only recorded sighting we have of her."

Thunder reached out and hugged Daphne. "Thank you."

"I bet you can't wait to tell Seacrest," said Sparky.

"I'm not sure that would be wise," said Daphne. "Right now they don't know where you are. I think it would be best for all concerned if the CIA thought you were still at the Pilgrims. If they thought you were here with us, it might give them a reason to raid this place…and take you away."

"Boy, what did I get myself into here?" said Sparky.

"Tell me about it," said Daphne. "I've been living with this for seven years. As a matter-of-fact, that sighting of Allison was seven years ago."

"But how is that possible? asked Thunder. "I gave birth to her a short time after this sighting occurred."

That fact never crossed Daphne's mind, but Danvers already had the answer. He was standing by the doorway to the stairs, directly behind Sparky, watching and listening. "The answer is simple. She came from the future."

That statement took both Daphne and Thunder by surprise.

Thunder shook her head. "No! That would mean that even though this is the present for us, it could be the past for someone else?" asked Thunder.

"Like God?" said Sparky. "Maybe that's how *He* knows what's going to happen in our future. Did you ever think of that?"

Thunder made a face. "Now that's a stretch."

"How is that possible?" asked Daphne.

"This is just another example of the power of the doors and the laws of Relativity," said Danvers. "All I know is, everything is as it should be."

"What does that mean?" asked Thunder.

"It means that in three days," he replied, "I will be meeting Richard Pilgrim for the second time…in 1962. And he will give me this." He held up an old, yellowed newspaper with the date August the fifteenth, 2004. All three gazed wide-eyed at the newspaper that was destined to be printed three days into the future.

*   *   *

Wearing his beautiful dress white uniform and gold armor, which was covered with colorful decorations on his shiny breastplate, Archangel Uriel floated out of one of the foyers to the Great Hall with a very disappointed look on his face. Uriel was well known to wear his emotions on his sleeve. Being one of the first Angels to be created by God, and thus one of the oldest and most powerful, meant that he was rarely challenged or questioned by subordinate Angels. Of the three Archangels assigned to the security of Heaven, Uriel was the most modest and subservient to Gabriel and Michael. He preferred to remain in the background and out of the limelight. His rapport with the Holy Trinity was impeccable, warm and close. Uriel was a good and loyal soldier of God, who rarely asked for anything and was never refused a request, until today.

The Palace Lord Administrator, who was an Angel of considerable high standing was hovering by the giant doorway. "My Lord Prince," he said with a respectful bow.

THE DOOR

"I was granted a private audience…" replied Uriel as he glided towards the Lord Administrator.

"Ah, yes." The Administrator referred to a crystal clear tablet that lit up with colored text. "A scheduling conflict arose and we did not have the opportunity to advise *thee*."

"Scheduling conflict," repeated Uriel, with a hint of discontent in his tone.

"Lets just say, *He* was…detained."

"That, my Lord Administrator, is a word that I am beginning to hear to all of my queries as of late. I have never been denied a private audience. Ever!" He gazed up and gestured at the dimmed light in the foyer. "And why is it so dim in here?"

"My Lord, you are *"the Light of God."* You know better of these things than I."

Uriel drifted forward and the Lord Administrator accompanied him.

"Is there anything else I can do for you, My Lord Prince?"

Uriel entered a museum that contained all sorts of human memorabilia. First and foremost was a sixteenth century British Man-of-War wooden ship floating in the middle, with full sails and gun ports opened. A number of winged Angels, parents and their children, floated around and throughout the old ship and gazed upon it inquisitively like tourists at a theme park. No one walked anymore in Heaven and even the displayed memorabilia had to be chained down to prevent them from floating away. There were also Angelic memorabilia on a display. Uriel appeared impressed by it all.

"Do you approve of the way we have preserved our history and humanity's?"

"The word *"magnificent"* pales in its usage in describing what has been placed on display here. I wonder if I will end up on display here, like all these old things?"

The Administrator smiled. "But my Lord, *thee* is an Archangel."

"A title I rarely call myself, nor press my rank upon others…a practice I might need to amend." His tone was as sharp as a razor.

The Administrator stood his ground. "Your dissatisfaction is noted, but these are perilous times for us all. And, we've had a history of Archangels who forgot who they are and from *whence*

THE DOOR

they came."

Uriel went right up to the Administrator and pointed to his chest. "My love and loyalty to God is unquestionable."

The Administrator bowed and backed off. "I meant no disrespect. But we have seen so little of you or any of the Archangels."

"Michael and I have been at our posts. As for the others, I cannot say."

The Administrator rubbernecked to see if anyone was within earshot. "But what of Gabriel? No one has seen him for ages. There is talk that he has gone over...."

"Gabriel...is detained," replied Uriel, with a glint in his eyes.

The Administrator was not satisfied with that answer and showed it.

"So, you don't like that word either," said Uriel. "Well, I must confess, neither do I."

A sign got Uriel's attention. It read: **Michael's Spear.** The very one Michael used to drive Lucifer into the fiery lake so long ago. Uriel glided over to the display and gazed upon it.

"*Ah*, Michael's spear," said Uriel. But horror flashed across the Archangel's face when he looked into the case. "This is not Michael's spear!"

"Are you sure?"

Uriel pointed to the case. "That is a Praetorian Officer's lance!"

The Administrator appeared distressed. "Someone has taken Michael's spear! But who would do such a thing?"

Uriel shook his head in disbelief and floated away. He had no idea the Lord Administrator had recorded their meeting via the crystal tablet. The Palace Lord Administrator rewound the footage to check it.

*   *   *

Deputy Director Blackburn arrived in a convoy of black SUVs at the warehouse in West Virginia and he was furious. Diciembre was standing outside the front entrance, waiting for him. Ordinarily, he would have opened the door for the Deputy Director, but not today. He had not shaved or changed his clothes since the incident.

"I should fire you right now," said Blackburn.

THE DOOR

"You go right ahead, you dumb bastard!" It was said loud enough that all of Blackburn's entourage heard it. "When the President finds out how badly you've screwed things up with Project Door he'll probably have you shot!" That got the entourage exchanging glances with one another.

Blackburn noted the looks he got and decided to back off on his public criticisms of Diciembre. "You have something to show me?"

They went in and Diciembre gave a tour and a full situation report. He figured his days with the CIA were over, so he didn't hold any punches. He told it exactly the way things were without any sugar coating. The compacted helicopter remained exactly where it had landed in the command center and the floor of the warehouse was still covered with all kinds of debris and evidence of an intense fire. In the end, Blackburn and the entourage were stunned and speechless.

Blackburn pulled Diciembre aside. "I need a drink."

They went to Diciembre's private cubical. Diciembre removed the bottle of scotch he had in his desk and poured his boss a generous drink.

Diciembre held up his glass. "Cheers."

Blackburn gulped down some scotch and Diciembre noted the Deputy Director's hand shook slightly. The old man was definitely rattled by what he had just seen and what was reported to him. "I must apologize to you, Diciembre. The reports I received did not do justice to what has been happening here. It certainly is the most dangerous place in the world."

Diciembre shook his head. "Not anymore."

"What do you mean, *'Not anymore'?* Where then?"

"1919 Cornelius Street, Marion, Virginia."

"The Pilgrim's house?"

"Richard the Traveller is back."

"And what about that crazy Indian woman and cable repair-man...?"

"They're with him and that's exactly where they need to be. What we need to do right now is stay out of their way!"

Blackburn sighed. "I don't know about that. You know who lives across the street."

"Thank God for that!"

THE DOOR

"We're talking about Lomax, aren't we?"

"He's the best asset we could ever hope to have over there."

"Lomax has gone rogue and he's not with us."

"I believe he is…in his own way. I may have been wrong about him." That was hard for Diciembre to say.

Blackburn finished his drink and handed Diciembre the glass. "I can't believe my ears. You…wrong about Lomax? Now I know we're in trouble!"

"We are and it's only going to get worse if we continue on with the way we have been handling this situation. Sir, we have no business interfering with what is going on over there."

"What about national security?"

"This problem goes well beyond our borders."

"I'm going to have one hell of a time convincing the Director and the President to keep a hands off approach on that little street."

"If you don't, we're all dead. *Adios!*" Diciembre went closer to Blackburn. "Look, there is a higher power involved here. One we don't understand and should keep our distance from." He gestured to the main floor of the warehouse. "All we've done so far is cause more potential harm. I'm convinced that grouping all those doors in one place is the worst thing we could have done."

"I'm beginning to agree with you. But the White House will not share that point of view. As a matter-of-fact, it was they who ordered the Director to gather them up and bring them here. Now, I just can't go there and say to those desk-bound pencil-pushing know-it-alls that they were wrong. They'll have me fired!"

"Then buy me as much time as you can."

"I can't promise you anything…but I will try to give you some time. It won't be much…."

*   *   *

Richard was the first one up in the house. He went to the kitchen and made himself breakfast with a bowl of cereal and glass of orange juice. When he finished breakfast, a strange feeling ran through his body. He gazed up at the ceiling. He would describe the feeling as, "The door was calling me." He had felt this sensation before, probably all of his life, but not with such intensity. After putting the glass and dish into the sink he went

THE DOOR

back to the master bedroom, where he slept on a cot, and looked inside. His parents were still sleeping. He knew that they were very tired from all that had happened last night, so he tiptoed up the stairway and went into his bedroom. His father told him not to go up there, but he needed to change his clothes. He was old enough to pick out his own clothes and brush his teeth. When he was done brushing, he walked out of the bathroom and instinctively grabbed the doorknob and pulled on it. But Israel had hammered in a piece of wood into the mortise so the door wouldn't close. Unlike the rag, Richard was unable to pull out the piece of wood. But Israel only did this to Richard's bathroom door and not the others. Besides, the bathroom door wasn't the one calling to him.

Richard went to the guest bedroom, which was on the rear side of the second floor. There was a piece of cloth jammed in the mortise. He reached out and ran his hand across the surface of the door, then stopped at the doorknob. The energetic feeling was even greater now and it made him pull out the cloth and close the door.

He then tapped the door twice, grabbed the doorknob and turned it. When he pushed the door open, he was stunned by what he saw. *"Gosh!"*

There were hundreds of doors in front of him. Hesitantly, he stepped across the threshold and got his first glimpse of all the wreckage. He had never been to the warehouse and had no idea why it had so many doors. Many of them were calling to him, but one stood out three rows away. He took out a small piece of crayon he kept in a pocket and drew an "H" on the guest room door before closing it. He trotted over to the other door and noticed the smudged crayon writing on the lower left side of the door. It read: "Big House." This was the first time he had seen the crayon markings Prince Michael told him about and it would not be the last. He tapped the door twice, opened it and went in.

It was Sunday at the White House and it was customary for some of the office personnel who worked in the West Wing to bring their children with them, after attending church. It was rare for the President to be in the White House during weekends. But when he was he enjoyed seeing children at play in the West Wing and he often rewarded them with candy if they didn't make too much noise or break anything.

So Richard had an easy time of it going from the Roosevelt

THE DOOR

Room to the Oval Office. No one stopped him. Upon entering the Oval Office, he stopped and stared at the President, who was talking to his Secret Service agent. Richard did not recognize the Secret Service Agent as the man who was whipping a woman back at Salem Village some four hundred years earlier. It was Nathaniel Pilgrim a.k.a John Danvers.

Danvers was weeping. "She's such a good woman and I've done nothing but hurt her."

The President tried to console Danvers by putting a hand on his shoulder. "Lord knows I too am guilty of that."

"There's no excuse for my behavior. I should have been happy to hear about the baby, but no. I go and make a complete jerk out of myself."

"Okay. You know you've done something wrong. You want to make amends. Just tell her that and for now on you'll be there for her…no matter what."

Danvers nodded in agreement, then spotted Richard. The young Traveller may not have recognized Danvers, but he immediately recognized Richard. He wiped the tears from his eyes and said, "Excuse me, Mr. President, but duty calls."

He confronted Richard and said, "Come with me please." He gave a gentle shove to the boy and brought him out of the Oval Office. They didn't stop until they were standing in the hallway, next to the Roosevelt Room. "I remember you. But do you remember me?"

It took a moment. Richard peered into the man's face and his eyes and nose. "You were whipping that lady and calling her a witch."

Danvers rubbernecked to make sure no one was in earshot. He then rubbed his cleanly shaved chin. "So, you do recognize me without the beard?"

"Yup." Richard stepped away from Danvers.

"Are you from the future?" asked Danvers. But Richard didn't answer because he lacked the understanding of time travel. "What year is it for you?"

"2004."

Danvers was relieved. "Fifty-two years! Well, it's good to hear we're still around then. You've got to go back…through the door. Okay?"

THE DOOR

Richard's eyes narrowed as he studied Danvers. "You want to know where it is, don't you?"

Danvers grinned and shook his head. "What are you, a mind reader and Traveller? Yes, I want to know where the door is."

"Why should I trust you? You're not a nice man."

Danvers let out a sigh. "Well, I'm not the same man that I was when you first saw me. And there's no better way for me to prove that than to get you back to where you came from safe and sound."

Richard closed the door to the Roosevelt Room, then tapped it twice before giving a pull on the doorknob.

For a moment, Secret Service Agent John Danvers was given a vision of the future and the interior of a toy store in a shopping mall at night. He reached for the small flashlight he kept in his coat pocket. He clicked it on and handed it over to Richard. "Here, take this. You'll need it."

Richard took the flashlight. "Thank you."

"Wait," said Danvers. "What's your name?"

"Richard Pilgrim."

That revelation completely stunned Danvers.

Richard stepped across the threshold and waved goodbye. Suddenly, the door closed behind him. He didn't stay long in the toy store. He grabbed a small box of crayons and wrote "toy" on the door. For now on, he would mark each door he exited, just like Allison had done. He ventured through three more doors before entering a holy place. He knew it was holy because of all the Crucifixes and paintings of Jesus on the walls. He stepped lightly into a large private bedroom, where an old man in white robes was on his knees saying a rosary in a language he never heard before.

The old Pope looked up and spotted the wide-eyed little boy staring at him. Even though his vision wasn't what it used to be, he spotted the English wording on Richard's T-shirt. "Good morning, my child." He bade Richard to come closer. "Please, come in. It's okay." The old Pope got up and held out his hand. "I wondered when you would arrive."

Richard's mouth dropped. "How did you know I was going to come here when I didn't know?"

"Oh, I hear things…and I know a lot of things…just like you."

Richard stopped and pondered for a moment on what the Pope said, then looked around the room with great interest. "Is this the

THE DOOR

place where the big church is?"

"Yes, and we call it the Vatican."

"I knew that. Can I ask you a question?"

"By all means, my young adventurer."

Richard recalled that Prince Michael had called him a "*young adventurer,*" during their one meeting. "People say that God talks to you. Is it true? Did he tell you about me? And what about Prince Michael?"

The Pope raised a hand and said, "So many questions from someone so young. My son, God speaks to all of his children. I just listen better." The old Pope grinned. He liked that answer.

The Pope waved his hand at the two chairs that faced each other. "Now, please, sit down…Richard."

"How did you know my name?"

The Pope pointed to a place on Richard's T-shirt that bore his name.

"Oh!" said Richard.

"Now," said the Pope, "let me ask you a question. Do you know what a rule or law is?"

"Mommy said she wrote the house rules but it's daddy who lays down the law."

The Pope would have liked to sit back and laugh at that, but he had to be as serious as possible. "It was Jesus, son of God, and Joseph the carpenter who created the system by which Angels could use doors to travel from Heaven to Earth. God made it one of *His* laws that only Angels could use them. *Only the good may pass through.* But long ago in your country, something terrible happened and not only did the Devil enter a House of God he did it through…a door."

"But you said he can't go through a door?"

"The Devil may enter your house and your heart only if you let him in. Four hundred years ago, someone let him cross the threshold. But he needs both you and Allison to open the doors. He can't do it alone…not yet anyway."

Richard became nervous. He got up and paced about the floor. "Michael said that only I can find Allison." He stopped and faced the Pope. "I don't think I want to do this anymore. The doors aren't fun like they used to be."

"As you grow up, you will learn that the important things in life

THE DOOR

are rarely fun to do."

"My daddy said my bathroom door is dangerous. He doesn't want me to open it anymore."

"He is your father. He loves you and he cares for you."

"But it calls to me. They all do. I hear them...even in my sleep."

The Pope stood up. "I know."

"Sir, out of all the boys in the world, why was I given this gift?"

"God works in ways we do not understand. However, in this case, it is because your great, great, great grandfather gave false testimony in a trial—"

"—What does that mean?"

"He lied and nineteen innocent people were condemned to death and eternal damnation. He was a carpenter and it was with his hands and his tools the door was made."

"The one the Devil passed through?"

The Pope gave a nod "He even made the gallows the villagers used to hang most of those poor people. He profited from their deaths when the judges awarded him their property in payment for his services. Blood money. When it was all said and done he realized what he had done, instead of repenting and begging God for forgiveness, he blamed the church. He blamed everyone. But that was not the worst thing he did."

"He did more bad things?"

"During the trial, he recognized who the Devil was and promised to do his bidding. The Devil promised him a long life if he continued to make more doors. But the Devil deceived him. Only God has the power over life and death. Remember that." The Pope held out his hand. "Now come here and let me bless you." He made the sign of the cross and said a Latin prayer. He ended it by giving Richard his rosary. "This was the rosary from the two Popes who were here before me." The Pope put the rosary over Richard's head.

"Does it have any power?"

"Only if you believe it does."

The Pope went over to his desk and lifted a simple spear with a wood shaft. He handed it to Richard. "Hide this in your house in a place no one else will find it."

"You're giving me a spear?"

THE DOOR

"Not just any spear. It's Michael's spear. He wanted you to have it."

"Michael!"

A wide-eyed Richard took the spear and headed for the door. He stopped suddenly, touched the door with his free hand and turned to the Pope. "This door is a Wanderer!"

The Pope nodded.

Richard tapped the door three times to take him home. He opened the door and saw the interior of his house. He turned and waved goodbye as he crossed the threshold. Part of him didn't know what to believe until the Pope said one last thing.

"Remember the five things Michael told you, especially numbers four and five. May God be with you, my son."

The door closed by itself.

The Pope looked up at the ceiling. "Oh, Lord, what has become of us, using children to fight our wars...?"

*   *   *

When Richard arrived home, he immediately went to the basement and hid the spear just as the Pope told him to. Since Lomax didn't place any cameras in the basement of the Pilgrim house, the eyes across the street couldn't see where he put it. While he was in the basement, he heard a **THUMP!** It startled him. He stood in absolute silence, not even breathing. **THUMP!** It came from one of the walls in the basement. It frightened Richard so that he dashed up the stairs and slammed the door shut.

"Did you see what the kid had in his hands?" asked Danvers, as he pointed to the main screen in the basement.

"Looked like a spear," said Thunder.

"I have a feeling," said Sparky, "that that's not just any spear." He looked around the room. "Where's Lomax?"

"He's lost," said Daphne.

*   *   *

There was a lot of commotion amongst the ranks of Praetorian Guards at the Junction. Since Michael transferred command to Uriel there had been nothing but discord within the Guard and

THE DOOR

some fights had even broken out. It was becoming more and more frequent. Many had left their posts and even resigned from the service. They all blamed Uriel, but he really didn't do anything to warrant such discontent.

His only crime was that he wasn't Gabriel or Michael.

To make matters worse, the Palace Lord Administrator and several members of his staff, glided by The Junction just as a nasty scuffle took place between some twenty Praetorian Guardsmen and their officers. All of which was recorded on the staffers' tablets.

Archangels had one major advantage over all other Angels. They could cloak themselves and were untraceable. However, they had to de-cloak before entering a door portal. Uriel appeared in a translucent state for a second or two, just long enough for Joan to see him. She unfurled her wings and floated in front him and a door he had previously selected, effectively blocking the Praetorians' view of the Archangel. She opened the door and he slipped swiftly and silently across its threshold. She then backed up and closed the door.

Joan then shot a long look to the Palace Lord Administrator, who replied with a nod.

*   *   *

A guard opened the gate to allow a mid-sized U-Haul truck into the parking lot of the warehouse in West Virginia. The U-Haul only slowed down when it got dangerously close to an opened double-door that looked more like the old rusted out siding on the building than a garage door. As soon as it crossed the threshold the double door closed behind it. The interior of the building was a wreck but it was still a top-secret facility.

Diciembre was not informed of the delivery. He stepped out of the command center through the opening the helicopter made. The chopper was still there. "What is this?"

A group of men and women wearing white jackets and carrying laptops came into the warehouse through another entrance.

Someone lifted the rear door of the U-Haul and pulled out the loading ramp. A moment later, a four-foot high robot on a set of tractor wheels appeared and drove down the ramp to the warehouse floor, where it came to a halt. The mechanics of this robot

THE DOOR

were similar to the ones used by police bomb squads, but with extra attachments.

"You're looking at the latest in robotics," said the young, overly confident tech who appeared to be the dominant one in the group. "The next time we hear a door knock, we will have the robot open the door. No one need get hurt again."

"Just so that you know," said Diciembre, "the last cocky genius from MIT who designed and maintained the security systems here will be in traction for...*uh*...*oh*...six months or so. If he's lucky!"

The other techs didn't appreciate that and it showed on their faces.

The dominant tech pointed to the automatic shotgun mounted on the robot. "That's why we armed it with a shotgun called '*The Street Sweeper*'." He gave a tap to the round magazine. "This baby holds twenty-five shells and we could hold off an army."

"*We?*" asked Diciembre. "You keep saying '*we*'."

"My colleagues and I have been assigned to this facility." He gestured to the others.

"By whom, Blackburn?"

"No, unfortunately, Deputy Director Blackburn has suffered a heart attack. The Director has taken personal charge of all operations related to Project Door. I answer only to him." He handed Diciembre a manila folder. In the CIA, when someone hands you a manila folder, it's usually filled with bad news. This one was no exception. In short, Diciembre was in charge of the facility in name only.

"I thought the shotguns on armed robots were single shot," said Diciembre.

"That's the law enforcement version. This is DOD. They invented the word '*overkill*'. Or didn't you know that?"

The other techs laughed.

Diciembre wasn't amused.

"All right, people," said the head tech, "let's get to work."

Diciembre held up a hand. "Excuse me," he said to the head tech. "Do you believe in God?"

The young Ivy League graduate student smirked at the mentioning of the word "God." He replied, "When it suits me."

"Well, son you're in luck. Because this is the place where you will find religion...in one hell of a hurry." Diciembre turned, went

THE DOOR

back to his cubical and had a stiff drink.

*   *   *

It wasn't odd for Lomax to go jogging without telling Daphne. As a matter-of-fact, she would have been more suspicious of him if he did tell her where he was going. He left the house about two hours before sunrise and jogged on a nature trail that went through the mountains. He reached his destination just as the sun came over the horizon. He had spent a number of sunrises at this very spot during his seven-year stay in Marion. He had hoped that it would cheer him up and make him change his mind. But it didn't. Life had been hard on Lomax and he gave back as hard as he got it. But seeing the look on Israel's face the other night was more than he could stand. He never really had a close friend, someone who he could go fishing with or just hang around and watch a football game, until he met Israel. For the first time in his life there was a man who he could talk to about the little things in life: wives, kids and grilling hot dogs. Israel was the brother Lomax longed to have. Now their friendship was destroyed all because of him and he never felt so low. He couldn't sleep or eat or think about anything else except that it was because of him his friends and neighbors were in so much danger. He could have been up-front with Israel from the beginning and revealed everything. That might have ended this whole sordid affair. But no, there was a job to do and there was a lot of money involved.

He also knew that it was only a matter of time before the Agency raided his house and took him, Daphne and the kid into custody. Add two more names to Lomax's list of shattered lives. The Pilgrim's house would also be raided and they would be spirited away, all in the name of national security.

The hiking trail he jogged on had a spot where there was a sheer granite cliff that overlooked a river below. He estimated it was about a hundred-foot drop. He stepped over to the edge of the cliff, gazed up at the sun, opened his arms wide and said aloud: "I suppose someone with black wings will say to me, '*You should have prayed more*'. Truth is, I never prayed to *You* or anyone cause I didn't know how. Didn't read the Bible either. Never saw the benefit of any of it. But now…now that it's over, I can truthfully say to *You* up there that I wish I had. Maybe I wouldn't

THE DOOR

have turned out like I did. Maybe I would have found peace and happiness in my life. Or maybe I would have ended up standing on this cliff, looking up at the sky and wondering if anyone really cares what I do or say. I know that *You* exist and that *You* mean well for all of mankind. Heck, I've seen *Your* Angels. I have seen more than anyone alive on this planet. And yet, I have so many questions and so many doubts." He lowered his arms. "I've done so many terrible things to people, for which I am ashamed. I've hurt the very people I love and I can't live with that fact. And *You* know me…I'm not good at saying *'I'm sorry'*. But I am. Well, if it means anything to *You*, I'm not doing this because I am afraid to face the consequences for my actions. Where I'm going… I'm going to get it but good and we both know it. No, I'm doing this because I don't want to hurt the ones I love anymore. It has to stop here and now and it has to stop with me. There is no other way!" He sighed. "That's all I've got to say."

"God," he concluded, "it's time for me to pay for my sins…."

He closed his eyes and in his mind he could see Daphne with Dara laughing and having so much fun at a picnic they were having with the Pilgrims. Tears rolled down his cheeks. "I do this for them! For them!" He opened his eyes, gazed skyward, reached out his arms and took a deep breath. ***It would be the last breath Lomax would ever take—!***

A dog barked. A man whistled.

Lomax opened one eye and scanned around until he spotted an old man with a cane used by the blind walking towards him.

"Hello there," the old man said. "And don't be afraid of my dog. He's very friendly."

The dog came by and sniffed Lomax's leg, then trotted off to spray a scent mark on the side of a tree.

Lomax lowered his arms. The distrust he had for most of humanity came back to him in an instant. He even reached for his pistol, but forgot that he didn't carry a gun today. "What do you want?"

"Oh, nothing, I guess." The old man sniffed the air. "*Ah*, smell that air. You know, when you live in the city you lose your sense of smell. That's why I go hiking every summer."

Lomax stepped away from the cliff to give the old man a closer inspection.

THE DOOR

The old man wore a backpack that must have weighed a hundred pounds. He had all kinds of things hanging on pieces of rope like a frying pan and portable radio.

"If you don't mind me asking, how blind are you?"

"Oh, totally."

"And you go hiking, alone in wilderness like this?"

"Son, I'm never alone. God gave me the best friend I ever had in this rotten world." He slapped his hands and the Golden Retriever came running up to him. The old man patted the dog affectionately, then said, "Find me a rock to sit on, Moses." The dog did and scratched the surface until the old hiker sat on it.

"Your dog's name is Moses? Odd name for a dog."

"Oh, I don't know about that. Moses freed the Hebrew slaves from Pharaoh. And my Moses here freed me from an assisted care room where I laid in bed all day listening to soap operas and wishing I were dead. No, sir! Moses freed me from my own kind of bondage. Out here, I am a free man!"

"Don't you get mad…?"

"Every time I miss the urinal. But that's the nice thing about nature trails. There are plenty of bushes to do your business."

Lomax grinned.

The old man got up and whistled. "Moses, say goodbye to the nice young man."

The dog rubbed up against Lomax, who smiled and gave him an affectionate pat on the side. "Good boy."

"I'll be leaving you to your business now. Just remember one thing…"

"What's that?"

"When everything goes completely black, just ask someone to turn on the lights." The old man chuckled. "*Ah*, don't mind me. It's a blind man's joke."

"Old man, I think you can see more than people with sight."

"Well, son, I hope and pray I will be seeing you again. Let's go, Moses!"

Lomax watched the old man leave. He went back to the edge of the cliff and looked down at the swift flowing river below. It was a beautiful sight with the way the sun's rays showed through the trees. The birds were chirping and even a deer appeared to have a drink of water.

THE DOOR

Right there and then he made the decision to live and fight on, for himself, his family and his friends.

*   *   *

THUMP!

It awakened Israel and Mary from a sound sleep. It wasn't an ear shattering sound, but like all audio emissions it resonated from the basement and rose to the first and second floors of the house, loosing strength the further distance it traveled. They searched the bedroom with their eyes and waited for it to happen again. Seconds passed and all was quiet, so they closed their eyes.

THUMP!

Israel opened his eyes and leaned forward in his bed. He waited and listened. Was he imagining things? No, because Mary heard it too and was now wide awake and listening also. Nothing. He started to fall back down onto the bed when...

THUMP!

"What is that?" asked Mary.

"I don't know," he said as he climbed out of bed and put on a robe. "But I will find out."

Mary decided to join him and put on a robe.

They went out into the hallway and stopped and listened. Israel held up his wristwatch.

THUMP!

"Nineteen second interval," he said.

"There's that number again," she said. "Nineteen. Even the address of our house has it twice."

As it turned out, the Pilgrims weren't the only ones who heard the thump.

Across the street, Daphne and Thunder were in the basement and heard it over the speaker.

"That's something new," said Daphne.

"Where in the house is it coming from?" asked Thunder.

Daphne pointed to the monitor/speaker marked: Master Bedroom. "That's the closest mike to the sound's origin."

"I thought every room in the house was bugged?"

"Not every room. We didn't bug the basement."

THE DOOR

"Why?"

"No one ever goes down there…"

THUMP!

"What's down there?"

"Lomax said there's a lot of old stuff. Ancient carpentry tools and junk like that."

"Ancient tools, as in caveman ancient?

"No, Puritan."

Daphne heard some movement and turned around. Lomax was standing by the doorway, ringing wet from his morning jog. She stared at him with concern in her eyes. "You okay?"

He gave a nod and replied in almost a whisper, "I am now…." He then heard the thump for the first time. It startled him.

Every nineteen seconds a thump was heard.

Israel went down to the basement to find where the thumping sound emanated from. When he returned, he met both Mary and Richard at the top of the stairs.

THUMP!

"Under no circumstances does anyone go down there." Israel pointed to Richard. "That goes double for you, mister!"

"Yes, sir. But…"

Israel exchanged a glance with Mary then asked, "But what?"

"I hid something very important in the basement."

"Why would you hide anything in the basement?" asked Mary. "That's not like you."

"Because the Pope told me too."

Israel sighed. "Oh, please!"

But Mary wasn't so fast to wave it off as a childhood fantasy. "Richard, you wouldn't lie to your mother, would you?"

"No, *ma'am*."

"Did you really meet the Pope?"

"Yes, and he gave me this." He pulled out the crucifix from the rosary he wore over his neck.

Israel removed the rosary from around his son's neck for a closer inspection. He turned to Mary.

"Don't look at me," she said. "I never had anything like that."

"When did you meet the Pope?" Israel asked Richard.

"Last night."

THE DOOR

Both Israel and Mary closed their eyes and let out a sigh.

"Are you saying you went through the bathroom door?" said Mary.

"No."

For a moment, the Pilgrims were relieved.

"I went through another door."

Mary brought a hand up to his face and sighed. "You went through a door when we specifically told you not to."

"Yes, *ma'am*."

THUUMP!

Israel became angry. He reached out and grabbed Richard by the arm. "Didn't I tell you NOT to open any doors?"

"But they call to me."

"Let go of him!" said Mary.

Israel did. "What do you mean they call to you?"

"It's a strong feeling that I get. I can go into a building or a house and pick out which doors I can use to go places."

Israel felt his body go numb. He knew his son was telling the truth and the truth of the matter was horrifying. He looked over to Mary. "What are we going to do?"

She shrugged.

Nightfall….

THUUUUUUUUUUMP!

The sound came over the speaker in the basement and Lomax and Daphne listened to it.

"Sounds different," he said, as he typed out a command on his keypunch to record and study the audio frequencies of the sound.

"For one thing," said Daphne, "it's longer in duration." She typed out a command on her keypunch and replayed one of the first thumps that was recorded. "Its harmonics have changed."

Lomax noticed the difference. "Okay, but what is it?"

"You got me."

"Well, what ever this is, it can't be good."

THUUUUUUUUUUUMP!

"And it happens every nineteen seconds on the dot," she said.

"Lately, everywhere I go I hear or see that number," said Lomax, shaking his head. "What is its significance?"

* * *

THE DOOR

The Pilgrims bedded down in the guest room upstairs, where the thumping was muffled. But no one slept there or in the house across the street.

Cracks had developed in the mortar of the brick wall on the west side of the basement. By morning, several bricks had dislodged and fallen to the floor. Every nineteen seconds the thumping was heard and bit by bit the brick wall was coming apart. It wasn't until a section of the brick wall came down with a crash that Israel and Mary had had enough and they went below to investigate. With flashlight in hand, he discovered a haversack, the kind used by soldiers in the Civil War, lying with the fallen debris. It had been buried inside the wall. He opened the bag and found a tin picture of Maggy and Ham Hamilton and seven young boys. "Oh, my God!"

"That's Ham and Maggy!" said Mary.

"Yes, alive and well in 1865."

"Who are the boys?"

Hamilton opened a leather case that was in the haversack and found a two page handwritten letter. He held it under the light so that Mary could also read it.

THUUUUUUUUUUMP!

After reading the letter, they went upstairs to the first floor.

Israel then did something that shocked everyone across the street.

"Eddi....I mean, Lomax," in a calm and collected tone. "I know that you can hear me." He shot a glance at his wife, who told him that she had allowed Sparky to replace the shattered microphones. "I need for you to come over here right now. I have something to show you."

Lomax was out the front door of his house in thirty seconds.

He rang the doorbell at the Pilgrim house. Israel opened the door and held out the two-page letter to him. "Read!" He stepped back and bade Lomax to enter the house with a hand gesture.

Lomax read the letter quickly. "How do we know it's from Hamilton?"

"I know his handwriting." Israel then held out the tin picture.

"The son-of-gun found her!" A smile grew on Lomax's face. And here he thought he'd never smile again. He then read Hamilton's letter aloud for the benefit of all the others watching

THE DOOR

and listening in his house.

To Whom It May Concern:

My name is "Ham" Hamilton. I was born in 1954 but by means I still cannot explain, I was taken by a little girl named Allison through a hospital door and ended up in Saltville in the year 1864. My wife, Maggy, had gone through this same door three months earlier, but to her it had only been three days. We both participated in the Civil War battle known as the Burbridge Raid. Maggy tended the wounded at the Sanders Farm, while I fought on Chestnut Ridge with the Rebs. I was given command of a rifle squad of six orphaned local boys named: Freckles, Moon, Fetch, Red, Hoot and Silent Matthew. They are good boys and after the battle Maggy and I adopted them. Actually, they adopted us.

After the battle of Saltville, we all went to Emory and Henry College so that Maggy could provide medical care to the wounded who were brought there. It should be noted that General Burbridge provided us with a wagon, a good horse, plenty of provisions and Chloroform so that Maggy could help tend to the wounded, both Reb and Union.

Now I am going to tell you about the door. When I first arrived here, there was a double church door being off-loaded from a train at the depot in Saltville. It was addressed to Cornelius Pilgrim of Marion, Virginia. A Lieutenant named Barrett ordered that the door be broken up and used as firewood, but I convinced him to have it brought to Emory and Henry College to be used as an operating table. Shortly after we arrived at Emory and Henry College, I witnessed Captain Champus Fragg shoot a colored soldier. The bullet passed through the soldier's body and struck Lieutenant Barrett. They both died on that door. The boys and I brought the door to Cornelius, who became a dear friend along with his grandson Levi. I had no idea the horror this door possessed. Cornelius told me that he had made several attempts to burn and destroy the door to no avail. His son even commissioned a schooner captain to take it out into the ocean and dump it there. The schooner was lost at sea with all hands including Cornelius's son and oldest grandson. How it got on a train to Saltville, no one knows. I myself brought the door to a place in the forest some five miles from Marion and disposed of it in a deep ravine. Months later, it had returned. We found a deep rut in the ground all the

THE DOOR

way from the place where I had dumped the door. It was as though it pushed itself to return to the Pilgrim farm. When Cornelius saw the door, he suffered a heart attack and died. Cornelius was a good man and I feel responsible for his passing. So, Levi and I did the only thing we could do to rid ourselves of this accursed door. We buried it in the concrete foundation of this house.

You may be asking why this door has followed Cornelius and Levi to Marion, Virginia. The answer is that it was hand made by Nathaniel Pilgrim, a man who is no doubt in league with the Devil. Beware of the door. It is evil and cannot be destroyed.

In closing, I just want to say that Maggy and I are struggling to survive with so many mouths to feed. But we are happy here.

Signed,
Ham Hamilton
15 June, 1865

THUUUUUUUUUUUMP!

Several more bricks and a significant piece of concrete broke free from the wall, exposing the door that was entombed there.

Israel and Lomax were in the basement when Danvers came half way down the stairs and stopped. He gazed wide-eyed at the exposed part of the door. "Imagine. It has not seen the light of day for over a hundred and forty years."

"Who the Hell are you?" asked Israel.

Danvers continued down the stairs and went toe to toe with Israel. "My legal name is John Danvers."

"Danvers," said Israel. "That's the name they changed the town of Salem Village to."

"I know. I was one of those who suggested it."

Israel cocked an eye. "That was a long time ago."

"To me, it seems like only yesterday." He stepped away from Israel and went up close to the wall. "It was an attempt to erase the past."

"You mean from the Witch Trials?"

"Correct."

"You stare at it like you have a connection to it."

"I do, actually." He turned and faced Israel. "I made this door."

THUUUUUUUUUUUMP!

THE DOOR

They continued the conversation in Israel's office. Danvers spent some time looking at the old black and white family photos on the paneled wall.

"Recognize anyone?" asked Israel.

To Israel's surprise, Danvers rattled off the names of the people in several pictures and even spouted a tale or two about them. It was information that Israel's grandfather had told him many years before, so he knew what this strange man was saying wasn't far from the truth.

"And that's me!" said Danvers as he pointed to one photograph.

Israel removed the framed photograph from the wall for a closer examination.

"There is a resemblance," said Lomax.

THUUUUUUUUUUMP!

"How is this possible," said Israel. "This picture is turn of the century. You don't look thirty-five."

"I did a terrible thing many years ago and good people suffered and even died for it. To this day, I still don't know why I did it. I suppose that I was caught up in the moment. Mere words could never foretell how it was in those days in that village and during those trials. And I was in the middle of it all. Yes, Nathaniel Pilgrim held the power of life and death over people and I loved it. So, I lied. I gave false testimony and people were condemned to death because of it. Yes, the Devil did come to Salem Village. When he made his presence known to me, he showed me a vision of Hell and told me I was doomed to spend eternity there for what I've done. It terrified me. I was so full of fear that I made a pact with him to continue building doors in exchange for a long life. As long as I was alive, I wasn't in Hell. So, I built many doors and lived many life times, regretting what I had done-every-single-day."

"Did you know the reason he wanted you to build doors?" asked Lomax.

Danvers shook his head. "I had no idea. For me, what harm could they pose to the world? When I realized what was afoot, I stopped. I figured that I would immediately die and pay for my sins. I didn't. From that moment on, I tried to help people instead of hurting them. I volunteered to fight in many wars and have been seriously wounded. But I wouldn't die."

THE DOOR

"The Devil can't take a life," said Israel.

"But can he prolong one?" asked Lomax.

"That I don't know." Israel jerked his head in Danver's direction. "But, he's just like the doors he made. Ageless and indestructible."

"That's it!" said Lomax. "You're just like the doors. You're out of phase. Lucky you."

This was when Danvers became angry. "You fool! My life has been a living Hell. I've known only sadness and loneliness and so much regret for what I've done. I've spent the better part of four hundred years trying to make amends for my sins. I've asked God for forgiveness, but *He's* not given it."

It was then Lomax said something very profound. "How do you know?"

Danvers was taken aback. "I…I wouldn't be here if *He* had."

"Maybe yes," said Lomax, "and maybe no."

"Maybe there's something you need to do," said Israel.

"Some unfinished business," added Lomax. "Like a ghost."

Danvers shook his head. He couldn't imagine that there was anything he needed to do to right the wrongs of his past.

"Who are you then?" asked Israel. "Really?"

"I am Nathaniel Pilgrim. Your not so great, great, great, great, great, great, grandfather."

THUUUUUUUUUUUMP! THUUUUUUUUUUUMP!

"If you don't mind," said Israel, "I'll withhold judgment on that for the time being."

"No problem. I have all the time in the world."

Lomax had a question that he was dying to ask. "I've got to ask this. How were you able to afford buying two old wrecked houses, have them completely refurbished and then supply me with the most expensive and state-of-the-art surveillance equipment on and off the market?"

"Time travel has its perks. When I traveled with Allison, I made sure I grabbed a newspaper or financial magazine. When you know what the future holds and know how a certain stock will perform, many fortunes can be made." He turned to Israel. "It afforded me the opportunity to buy out your grandfather and form a partnership with Ham."

Both Lomax and Israel were shocked by that revelation.

THE DOOR

"You're the silent partner?" asked Israel.

Lomax slapped his face. "Now why didn't I see that coming?"

"Well," said Israel in a stern tone, "I've got one question for you and it better be the truth."

"I think I know what it is, but go ahead."

"Are you still working for the Devil?"

Danvers took a moment. "No."

THUUUUUUUUUUMP! THUUUUUUUUUUMP!

Lomax made a face. "*Duh!* That's like asking a liar if he's lying. How do you know?"

"I will submit to any test you require," said Danvers.

"I know," said Lomax. "We throw Holy Water at him."

Israel rolled his eyes skyward. "What are we now, Catholics? My family were Puritans. No religious symbols, no Holy Water." A thought came to Israel. "Wait! I got it." He faced Danvers. "Say: Jesus Christ."

Without hesitation, Danvers said the Lord's name without consequence.

"I already had him do that and he didn't burst into flames," said Lomax.

THUUUUUUUUUUMP! THUUUUUUUUUUMP!

It was then Daphne called Lomax over the headset. "Lomax?"

"Yes, my love?"

"Remember what Michael told Richard that no demon may cross the threshold of a door."

"Thanks for reminding me honey." For Lomax, there was one way to test and see whose side Danvers really was on. He quickly formulated a plan.

"And what did dear Daphne have to say?" asked Danvers. He wasn't wearing a headset.

"She said there's only one man who understands the science of what we are dealing with."

"Are you referring to Einstein?" said Danvers.

"The one and only. Daphne thinks we should go see him."

Danvers smiled and a gleam came to his eyes. "I think that's a wonderful idea! Well done, Daphne!" he said aloud, knowing Daphne was listening.

"Yeah," said Lomax, "she can be quite brilliant at times."

Across the street in the basement, Daphne turned to Thunder.

THE DOOR

"I never said anything about Einstein! First time I get a complement from that sonofabitch for suggesting something brilliant and I didn't say it." She was yelling in her headset mike. "Just for that, you get no sex for a month!"

Lomax only made the situation worse by turning into the direction of the pinhole camera he implanted into the wall and blew Daphne a kiss and topped it off with a wink.

*   *   *

It was decided that Daphne and Mary would stay behind with Dara in the basement at Lomax's house, where they would be safe, until the others returned. The wall was still thumping and more and more of the door was emerging from its concrete encasement.

Thunder insisted that she and Sparky accompany Richard and the others to their meeting the Great One. She too had questions only the professor could answer.

Danvers confronted Thunder and said something that sent chills throughout her body. "There's something I need to tell you. The first time I met and traveled with Allison was over four hundred years ago. She brought me to the future and to the warehouse in West Virginia. It was one of the reasons I stopped making doors for Lucifer. She showed me the future and it was not as bleak as he said it would be. She set me on the righteous path to my own redemption. For that I will always be thankful to her…and to you. When we parted, I didn't see her again until I was a student at Princeton in 1937."

Danver's words gave Thunder an indescribable feeling. Above all, she was proud of her brave little girl and more determined than ever to find her.

Lomax wanted to record the event, so he handed Sparky an 8-millimeter video camera. "Here. Make yourself useful."

Richard placed his hands on the bathroom door and repeated the words Danvers had told him. "Princeton College, Doctor Einstein's private office, noon, August the second, 1939." He stood up, knocked on the door twice and opened the door. Normally, Richard would be the first to cross over, but Israel stealthily grabbed his son's hand and held him back, allowing Danvers to be at the head of the line.

"Why?" asked Israel. "Why this date and time?"

THE DOOR

"Because I know he'll be there," said Danvers. Just before crossing the threshold, he glanced over his shoulder at Lomax and Israel. "I guess we'll find out whose side I'm on."

With that, he crossed over into the past without incident.

"Well," said Lomax, "that answered that question."

"No," said Thunder, "it only means that the doors' safeguards aren't working." She led the others through the doorway.

They were now in Professor Albert Einstein's private office and domain. Chalkboards lined the office and they were filled with all kinds of physics. The old professor was sitting at his desk, typing out a letter and occasionally puffing on his pipe. He looked up and spotted the visitors and the glowing portal.

"*Guten Morgen*," said the old professor. When Einstein recognized Danvers, he got all excited and pushed himself away from his desk. ***"Oh, mein Gott, du bist es! Herr Danvers!"***

Einstein stood up and shook hands with Danvers.

"It's so good to see you again, Professor."

Einstein gestured to the others. "*Und*, who are your friends?"

Danvers made the introductions and Einstein shook their hands.

Einstein, who was well known for his playfulness, stuck his tongue out at the video camera. He then shook Sparky's hand.

Sparky was overwhelmed. He whispered to Thunder. ***"Wow!*** I just shook hands with Albert Einstein!"

Thunder rolled her eyes skyward. "Like a little school boy."

"So," said Einstein, "what brings you to 1939, *eh?*"

Einstein's statement shocked Thunder, Lomax and Israel.

"He knows?" asked Thunder.

"He knows that we're time traveling?" asked Israel.

"*Jawohl!*"

Einstein went over to the door and looked inside at Richard's bedroom. "*Fantastisch!*" He shook his head, then turned to the others. "So, where is the little girl?"

"She's lost," said Thunder. "She's my daughter."

Einstein gave a respectful nod. "I did not know. I am deeply sorry."

He looked to the others. "Now, what I can do for you, *hmmm!*"

"Nobody understands the science of that," said Israel, pointing to the door, "better than you…sir."

"*Und,* you were hoping I could explain it to you, *ja?*"

THE DOOR

"Something like that."

"Well, *Mein Herr*, I could tell you about the Laws of Relativity…"

"E=MC²," said Sparky.

"Good. You've heard of it, then. But what I cannot tell you about the doors is where the science ends *und* God's will begins. For that, you must go to a priest or a rabbi." Einstein went over to one of his chalkboards and erased some of the formulas written on it. He drew a circle and had some lines coming out of it, which everyone accepted as a representation of the sun. He then drew three spherical shapes to represent the planets Mercury, Venus and the Earth. To add a little drama to this impromptu lecture, he drew a line from the sun and ran by the three planets and continued on to the end of the board, making the piece of chalk screech in the process. "The ultimate energy source of *das Universum* is the stars. *Und* energy travels from stars at the speed of light."

Einstein then drew a door-like rectangle about half way between the symbols of the sun and the earth. He then drew a line from the sun and made it wave the closer it got to the rectangle. "Time goes more slowly in higher gravitational fields. This is called gravitational time dilation. A day spent back in time may take a week, *und* a month or more to pass in the present. There's no set pattern. *But*, the further back in time you go the greater the time dilation." He turned and gestured to the door. "These doors are part of a gravity field that warps space-time."

"What kind of energy source would be needed to create this gravity field?" asked Thunder.

"*Der* sun," he answered so quickly that there was no thought involved.

"You sound rather certain of that," said Lomax.

"I am. ***You are not talking to some first year physics professor. I am Albert Einstein!***"

Lomax received a few angry stares from the others and quietly stepped to the rear of the little crowd. *So much for hitting if off with Einstein!*

"Professor," said Thunder, "I come from Ellesmere Island, where we are experiencing some of the most active Northern Lights events my people have ever seen. They touch the ground where a door is standing."

THE DOOR

Einstein's eyes narrowed and he made a grunt. *"Und,* why haven't you removed it?"

"We've tried! We've tried to burn it. We shot at it and even tried to blow it up with dynamite. Nothing worked. It is totally impervious."

"That is because it is trapped between two dimensions. It is here and not here." Einstein grabbed his pipe and lit it. He went over to a big globe he had near his desk and uttered something in German. After he nodded to himself, he turned his gaze back to Thunder. "The power of your Northern Lights is enormous. If we could harness the electromagnetic energy from one minute of its emissions we would be able to generate all electrical power needs for the entire world for a year, in my time *und* maybe even yours."

"Now, that's a lot of juice!" said Sparky.

Einstein turned to the globe and took a heavy drag on his pipe. "That door in Canada is significant. Does it glow...like that?" He gestured to the glowing door in his office.

"Yes!" Thunder and Sparky said in unison.

Einstein turned to Danvers. "It didn't glow the last time you came here with the little girl."

"A recent phenomena, Professor," said Danvers "and with only some of the doors."

"But," said Lomax, "when one of the active doors are used, all the active doors glow."

"Hmmm!" uttered the professor as he puffed on his pipe. "That is significant! They've become connected...and they are drawing their energy from a powerful source."

"I know where there is a thousand of these doors in a warehouse," said Lomax.

"Having so many doors in such close proximity is inherently dangerous and foolish," said Einstein. "It allows them to build up and store their energy."

"Sometimes," said Lomax, "the doors open on their own...releasing those things they have sucked in."

"A shark disgorges itself when it has eaten too much, *ja?"*

"That explains the Don Beech incident and the helicopter exploding into the warehouse," said Lomax..

Sparky became emotional. "But these are doors...made out of wood! How can they have such power?"

THE DOOR

"All living things generate and unleash energy," said Einstein. "But that door in Canada is the key. Its location to the Aurora Borealis is significant. I believe that door channels the energy of your northern lights to the other doors."

"That's what Diciembre said," Lomax whispered to Danvers.

Thunder exchanged a glance with Sparky. *It was an ah-ha moment!* "Now that makes a lot of sense!"

"Sure does," said Sparky. "We're talking about limitless, consistent power. But, on the other hand, solar flares and sunspots play havoc on our electrical and communication systems. I wonder what effect they would have on the doors."

"I would say the effect would render them powerless," said Einstein.

"What do you do then?" asked Sparky.

"If you are the Devil, you wait…" said Thunder.

"Wait for what?" said Lomax.

"A solar minimum," said Thunder. "The sun's output would be drastically less. We're in one now. That is, in 2004. No sunspots or solar flare activity."

"This whole business has taken how long?" asked Sparky.

"Four hundred years," said Danvers.

"There have been plenty of solar minimums during the past four centuries," said Sparky. "What makes this one so special?"

"A higher than usual solar activity," replied Thunder, "without sunspots. Quite frankly, this isn't suppose to happen."

"That's it, then," said Lomax.

Einstein gave a wink to Danvers. "They would make a lively class, *ja?*"

"A truer thing has never been said, Professor," said Danvers.

Richard spoke up. "The Pope said that it was Jesus who made the doors for Angels to travel from Heaven to Earth."

Einstein grinned and tapped the boy on the head. "*Und* who am I to doubt the works of Jesus! If God wants *His* Angels to travel from one place to another, then it must be so, yes? Why not through a door? Man has used doors since the Egyptians. So, why not *His* Angels, *eh?*"

"But in doing so," asked Danvers, "isn't God manipulating science and nature to do *His* bidding?"

THE DOOR

"*Ja!*" replied, Einstein. "*Und*, if you were God, wouldn't you?"

Almost everyone nodded in agreement.

Einstein went over to his desk and lifted a tennis ball high enough for all to see. He then released it. The ball fell to the floor and bounced a few times before coming to a rest near Richard. "Young man, what just happened to that ball?"

"You dropped it…and it hit the floor."

"Excellent observation! But why did it hit the floor?"

Richard shrugged.

Einstein smiled. "That is the best answer I ever got from any of my students in this school!"

The others chuckled. Israel patted his son on the head.

"Gravity," said Lomax, "pulled it to the floor."

"Are you sure?" asked the professor.

"No," said Sparky, "it was pushed to the floor."

"Pushed?" asked Thunder. "By what?"

"Gravitons," said Sparky.

Einstein made a face. "I do not know this word." *The word 'Graviton'. would be coined by another scientist in 1940.*

"They're unseen forces of gravity," said Sparky.

"Unseen," asked Einstein, "even in your time?"

Sparky nodded. "Totally invisible."

"*Und*, I wonder why it is unseen even in 2004?" He raised a hand to indicate he was still talking. "Answer, because, it is the power of God." That shook up all the other adults in the room.

"Gravity!" said Sparky, as he nodded in agreement. "Yes, professor! Think about it. Everything in this reality, this dimension is dependent on gravity. Everything!"

"Not to mention all of God's great miracles," said Danvers.

"The parting of the Red Sea," said Thunder. "The destruction of Sodom and Gomorrah…"

"The Mets winning the World Series in 69," said Lomax, trying to be funny. He got an elbow in the gut from Thunder.

"One last question, Professor," said Danvers.

Einstein was becoming tired and impatient. "*Ja, ja!* Get on with it. I have a letter to write."

Lomax placed a hand on Richard's shoulder. "When someone other than Richard and Allison opens a door that is knocking, everything in the room is sucked out in a flash."

THE DOOR

"*Hmmm!*" replied the old professor. "I suppose when energy is traveling faster than the speed of light then suddenly is forced to slow down, explosive decompression could occur in the time-space continuum. It is like an elevator on the Empire State Building going down. You must wait for it to stop before boarding it, or else you will fall all the way down the shaft. As for *der kinder*, they like the doors are in between worlds. *Und* the elevator waits for them. Why, I do not know. For that answer you must ask God."

That made sense to Sparky. "That's it!"

"What is?" asked Lomax.

"The reason the kids are Travellers. They're just like the doors. They're out of phase too."

It made sense to everyone.

"Oh, my poor Allison," said Thunder.

"Relax," Lomax said to Thunder as he walked by her. "It means she can't be hurt." He couldn't help himself. He had to take a look at the letter Einstein was typing. "Hey, I know this letter. It's addressed to FDR."

"Lomax!" said Danvers. "That's private."

Einstein was amused and raised his hand to quiet his former student. "I am afraid Herr Hitler is tampering with the atom."

"Oh, I know him!" said Richard. "He's the guy with the funny little moustache."

"You have met Hitler then?" asked Einstein.

"Yes. He has a door in his office."

"A door in Hitler's office," uttered Einstein, shaking his head. "*Mein Gott!* You better go so that I can finish my letter."

"Lets just hope that only Angels and curious little boys can go through that door," said Danvers.

"*Ja,*" said Einstein. He gave a wave. "Now, good bye!"

*　　*　　*

The first thing Lomax did upon returning home was to call Diciembre to tell him what Einstein said about the door at Revelation Fiord. He then put in a call for pizza and assembled a folding table and chairs in his backyard. It would be the first time all of the people involved would get together for a meal. But hardly any of the pizza was eaten.

Now that only a blackened skeleton of the CIA surveillance

THE DOOR

house remained, everyone felt secure that no one was watching or listening in on them. Also, they wouldn't have to listen to the thumping wall. The mood was understandably somber. It was truly the first time all of the people involved in this predicament actually got together and talked. The conversation was centered on Richard and Allison.

"July 29th, 1987?" said Thunder. "That's when my Allison was born!"

"Lomax," asked Daphne, "did you hear that? Allison was born on the same night as Richard!"

"I hope you had a better delivery than I did," Thunder said to Mary. "The Northern Lights were very active. My helicopter lost power and we crash landed."

"We had a hurricane," said Mary.

"And a car accident on the way to the hospital," said Israel. "Mary and I were knocked out cold."

"Who do you think pulled you out of the wreck and brought you to the hospital?" Daphne waved her thumb at herself and Lomax.

"You brought us in?" asked Mary.

Israel sat there for a moment, staring at Lomax and Daphne. "You two have been there for us right from the beginning. I guess I owe you both an apology."

Lomax and Daphne froze. They never thought they would hear that.

"Did the lights go out in your hospital?" asked Thunder.

"Not just the hospital," said Mary. "The whole county."

"Born the same night, during violent storms and both kids can open doors," said Danvers. "You wanted to know if there was a link. There you have it."

"That old man is a genius," said Israel. "Einstein, I mean."

"He was," said Sparky.

"There is no past tense when all you have to do is open a door," said Danvers.

"That's the problem," said Thunder. "History can be changed. If the wrong sort ever gains entry into those doors mankind is finished!"

"Well," said Sparky, "now we know the source of its power."

"Okay," said Lomax, "but now we got to figure out how to turn it off."

THE DOOR

"Not before we rescue my daughter," said Thunder.

"And Ham and Maggy," said Israel.

"The thing I don't understand is," said Lomax, "if the Pope says the system is broken and *you know who* can pass through, then what is he waiting for?"

Danvers stood up and cleared his throat. "The Devil may not have to do anything, because tomorrow World War III in 1962 begins. That is unless Richard and I can stop him...."

*   *   *

RCMP Inspector Seacrest was standing on the shoreline at Revelation Fiord, gazing at the Canadian Navy frigate that was steaming a few miles out at sea. He was speaking to Diciembre for the very first time. He was gazing at the door through a pair of binoculars as he spoke on the satellite phone. The door was glowing in a multitude of colors. "If any one but Thunder had told me what Albert Einstein had said about our Northern Lights channeling their power to the door we have here, I never would have believed them. But, from where I'm standing, I think Einstein is bloody right."

Standing outside the warehouse, Diciembre glanced into a side entrance to get a glimpse of the doors, many of which were glowing. "It must be destroyed at all costs."

The forward battery of the frigate opened fire and sent a shell whistling over Seacrest's head. It was an armor piercing round meant to punch holes into enemy ship's hulls.

"What was that?" asked Diciembre.

"One of our frigates just fired an armor piercing shell at the door....Direct hit!"

The round bounced off the door. A loud "Clang!" sound echoed off the mountains and it was loud enough that even Diciembre heard it.

"And?" asked Diciembre.

"No effect. Still here...."

The satellite connection was broken off and now only static was heard.

Archangel Uriel was standing on the top of an ice-covered mountain, watching the naval ship fire upon the door for a second

THE DOOR

and third time. He was not alone.

"Pathetic," said Lucifer, who was clad in a long flowing black robe and a hood that covered his face, "aren't they?"

"Yes, and totally unworthy. They've lost and don't have the intelligence to even know it."

"It pleases me so that you now see it my way."

Uriel turned to Lucifer. "I believe I always have. But I was never in a position to say or do anything about it."

"You were a good soldier. Well, time to be a good soldier again! But this time you are in command! Come brother! We have much to do…!"

They vanished.

THE DOOR

THE DOOR

Chapter Sixteen

BLACK SATURDAY

THUUUUUUUUUUUUUUUUUUUMP!

It was five o'clock in the morning when the last of the brick and piece mortar fell onto the basement floor. A powerful vacuum emerged from a hole in the wall that was so strong it pulled some of the religious statues a few inches closer to the west wall. But it didn't stop there. It went through the whole house, pulling out the rags and wooden pegs Israel had placed in all of the interior door's mortise. In an act of unison and evil defiance, all the interior doors in the house slammed shut. The noise awakened the Pilgrims.

Israel was now wearing a headset given to him by Lomax. He slept with it on. Israel insisted that he and his family go back to their house. Lomax relented on two conditions: one that he wear a headset and the other that he'd be allowed to setup a video camera in the basement.

"Israel," said Lomax over the headset, "wake up!"

But Israel, Mary and Richard were already awake.

"I'm up." Israel leaned forward in his bed. He wasn't use to communicating via headsets. "Lomax, is that you?"

"Who else? Now wake Mary up. We got a problem."

"She's up. What's wrong?"

"Listen."

Everyone remained silent for a time.

"No thump!" said Mary.

"The last of the encasement fell," said Lomax. "The door is free."

Israel turned on one of the lights and noticed something odd with the bedroom door. He could almost see right through it. "What the heck...?"

"All the doors in your house are going active," said Lomax.

THE DOOR

Richard, who was sleeping on a cot, got up and asked, "What's wrong, Daddy?"

Israel got out of bed and reached out to the bedroom door. His hand passed right through. He quickly retracted his hand. "My hand went right through!"

Suddenly, the guest room door became solid again.

"Israel?" said Lomax.

"Yes, Eddi...I mean Lomax."

"Please, don't do that again."

Israel turned to the pinhole camera in his room and gave a wave. "*Gotcha!*"

A few minutes later, Israel flung open the door to the basement, flipped the light switch on and went racing down the steps. By the time he reached the bottom of the stairway, Lomax was ringing the front door to the house. Mary opened the door for him.

"I told him to wait for me!" Lomax said to Mary as he charged down the basement stairway. "Israel!"

Mary followed him and when she spotted the fully exposed church door, she remarked, "Oh, great! Now we have another door to worry about."

When Richard, still in his pajamas, came down the stairs from the second floor he found Danvers waiting for him in the foyer.

Danvers was wearing a gray suit that was indicative of the 1960's. "Time to go, Richard."

Mary heard his voice and came charging up the stairs. She was tired, scared and angry and prepared to give both barrels to Danvers. "You're not going anywhere with my son!"

Danvers gestured to the interior doors as they faded in and out with increasing regularity. "Look at how all the doors are going in and out of phase. Soon it will include your house, then all the houses in this town, the county and then the whole world. This reality is being erased."

"How do you know this?"

"Because I was there in '62 when it happened. I saw Richard and myself enter the Oval Office at the most critical time in our world's history. We were within a hair's breath away from nuclear Armageddon." He pointed to Richard. "He helped me stop it then. Now we must do it again to close out the cycle."

"I'm not letting him go," Mary said sternly.

THE DOOR

Israel came up the stairs, noted the interior doors going in and out of phase and made a very difficult decision. "Richard, get dressed. Quickly!"

Mary grabbed her husband's arm. "NO!"

"If we don't let him go," said Israel, "he dies along with the rest of us." He then pointed to the interior wall that just went out of phase.

Mary started to sob and released her son.

The paperboy came riding by the Pilgrim house, just like he did every morning and tossed the Sunday paper onto the driveway. Richard went out the front door to retrieve it. Thunder and Sparky crossed the street and followed Richard into his house.

With his parents accompanying him to his bedroom, along with the others, they watched and waited for the bathroom to become solid.

It was Thunder who looked out a window and noticed that the front lawn was starting to fade in and out. "It's spreading!"

"What's happening?" asked Sparky.

"This reality is about to become no more," replied Danvers.

"And here I thought you wanted to die," Lomax said to Danvers.

"If I've learned one thing after living for 400 years, it's that nobody wants to die, including me."

Richard reached out to the door and his hand passed through. He retracted it.

"We may be too late," said Lomax.

"Wait for it, then do it as fast as you can!" Danvers said to Richard.

A few seconds later, the door became solid.

"Now!" shouted Danvers.

Richard pressed his hands on the wood panel and repeated what Danvers said, "October, 27, 1962, Roosevelt Room, White House, 10:30 PM." He then stood up, tapped the door twice and opened it.

Smoke jetted out of the bathroom and the sound of blaring sirens and people screaming followed. When the smoke cleared a view of a burning and wrecked office was seen. The West Wing's ceiling had been blown away and smoke and sparks filled the night sky.

"Oh, no, no, no!" shouted Israel, reaching out to Richard. "You can't go into that!"

Danvers pushed Israel's outstretched hand away and said, "We must!"

The room, the hallway and the whole Pilgrim house started to glow in a multitude of colors.

Mary reached out to her son. "Richard!"

Richard turned to his mother. "Mommy!"

Danvers picked up Richard and crossed the threshold.

Immediately after they reached the other side, they turned to see the reality that they once lived in go completely dark.

"I guess we can't go back?" asked Richard.

"That's right…and we cannot fail!" He lowered Richard to his feet. "Do you understand?"

In a surprising move, Richard grabbed Danver's hand and pulled. "Come on! I know where there's another door! *A wanderer!*"

They had to climb over a tall mound of debris. Richard gasped when he spotted a dead woman laying half buried in the debris. When he dropped the Sunday paper he brought with him from the future, Danvers picked it up and handed it back to him.

"Whatever you do," Danvers said to Richard, "don't lose this newspaper!"

They continued on and would see many dead bodies along the way and Richard would not gasp anymore. He led the way out into the lobby, which was on the opposite side of the Oval Office and turned onto the hallway that led to the Cabinet Room. But it was no longer there. The roof and walls were all blown away. The famous rose garden, where the President made some of his best speeches was burning. Bodies lay everywhere on the lawn and no one was moving.

"My God," said Danvers, "this is Black Saturday all right. But it didn't turn out as black as this."

"Are they all dead?"

"Most of them. Looks like D.C. took a near hit with a nuclear weapon. Do you understand what that means?"

"Yes, an H-bomb."

They took a moment to catch their breath and survey the city. What few buildings that were still standing after the nuclear attack were aflame. The Colonnade that was used by all of the modern

Presidents as a private walkway to the Oval Office was now the only cleared way to that famous room.

The walls, windows and exterior doors to the Oval Office were blown out, leaving a long gaping hole for Danvers and Richard to enter by. Danvers recognized the faces of the White House policemen, Secret Service agents he considered friends and some Marine guards who lay dead on the lawn and rose garden bordering the Colonnade. Richard heard Danvers saying their names as he passed by them.

"We've got incoming!" someone shouted over a PA. "Everyone to the bomb shelter."

"Medic!" another shouted from the lawn.

"What happened?" Richard asked Danvers.

"War….The one that wasn't supposed to happen. Come on." He led the way into the Oval Office through the large gaping hole in the wall.

A man, covered with dust, struggled to get to his feet. Danvers pulled on his arm and came face to face with himself.

"Are you real?" asked the 1962 Danvers.

"As real as you," replied 2004 Danvers. "Now, where's the President?"

"Over here," a heavily accented voice replied. The President was covered with debris. Both Danvers worked together to lift off the debris and free the President.

The President was stunned when he saw two Danvers staring at him asking the same question, seemingly in stereo.

"Are you all right, Mr. President?" asked both Danvers.

"Am I seeing double…or are there two of you?"

They helped him to his feet.

"There are two of you!" said the President. "I could barely handle one John Danvers."

"Mr. President, I am from another reality," said the 2004 Danvers. He gestured to Richard. "And so is he. This is Richard. He is a Traveller, who can open door portals to other places and time. We are from the future."

The President shook his head in disbelief. "This can't be real. I must be imagining all of this." He stumbled towards the hole in the wall and gazed out at his burning Capital. "Dear God in Heaven!"

THE DOOR

Richard went up to the door that was closed and unlike the other doors in the West Wing it stood untarnished by the nuclear attack. It led to the President's private study or "Little Office."

"This is it!" said Richard. "But to use it, we have to be on the other side."

"Why?" asked the 2004 Danvers.

"I don't know. I'm just the doorman."

2004 Danvers made a face. "Cute, kid. You've been hanging around Lomax too long."

The President confronted 1962 Danvers. "John, what went wrong? Why were we attacked? The negotiations with the Russians were reaching fruition. This should not have happened!"

"A U-2 was shot down over Cuba this morning," said the 2004 Danvers. "Your standing orders were to attack any anti-aircraft battery that shot down our reconnaissance jets."

"Yes, but I countermanded that order an hour and a half ago." He looked over to the 1962 Danvers. "John, you were there when I called the Pentagon and issued that order."

1962 Danvers gave a nod but his 2004 counterpart said, "Yes, sir. And earlier today you said, '*There's always one...*" he spotted Richard and decided to substitute the swear word, "...*blankity blank who never gets the word.*'" He gestured to the burning Capital City. "Well, sir, from the looks of it, your order never got through."

The President stared at 2004 Danvers and recalled that Danvers was at that meeting when he made that comment and even chuckled a little.

"That's because historically *you* personally aborted the air strike," continued 2004 Danvers.

"But," said the President, "I didn't do that."

"And that's the reason all of this happened," added 2004 Danvers. "One other thing. You were told that *some* of the Cuban missiles are operational. The truth is, nearly *all of them are.*"

Both the President's and 1962 Danver's eyes widened and their mouths dropped. They were shocked to hear that nearly all of the short and medium ranged nuclear tipped ballistic missiles the Russians had supplied the Cubans were armed and ready for launching. All of the intelligence the President had received on the on the status of the Cuban missiles led him to believe that they were several days from being fully operational. The President thought he still had the time to negotiate for a peaceful solution to this crisis. ***Both men realized then and there that time had run out!***

"So," said Danvers 1961, "when our fighter jets went to Cuba to take out the SAM site that shot down the U-2, the Cubans responded with a full nuclear retaliatory strike." He gestured to the burning Capital City. "Would you believe that all of this happened less than fifteen minutes ago?"

"I had no choice but to retaliate," said the President.

"The last FLASH message we got," said Danvers 1961, "said that the Russians were launching their ICBMs." He glanced at his wristwatch. "They should be hitting their targets in twenty minutes or so."

The President brought a hand up to his face. "I didn't want this. I did everything I could to prevent this. Now what am I going to do?"

"There's nothing you can do…here," said 2004 Danvers, "but what if I told you there was another option?"

"I…I don't understand?"

"Mr. President," asked 2004 Danvers, "how would you like to countermand that order again…and this time make it stick?"

The President straightened up. "Yes!"

The two John Danvers grabbed the President's arms and guided him into the Little Office. Richard then slammed the door and placed both palms onto it.

"Richard, same date, but change the place to the White House Little Office and make the time 6 PM," said 2004 Danvers.

Richard did and then got up, tapped the door twice and opened the door.

As Richard stepped aside the President got a view of the Oval Office four hours prior to the missile attack. The President was alone, pacing the floor in front of his desk. A buzzer went off.

"Mr. President, I have the Attorney General on line one, sir."

The President lifted the telephone receiver. "Robert, what did Khrushchev say in his letter?" The President must have liked what he heard because he jerked his arm down, like he was watching a football game and his team scored a goal. "I knew that he didn't sanction the shooting down of that U-2." There was a pause.

"Well, it's a step in the right direction. I think we've proved to him that we mean what we say by not retaliating. Now make my offer to remove our missiles from Turkey and let's put an end to this mess." He hung up the receiver.

2004 Danvers cleared his throat and called out, "Excuse me, Mr. President."

The President gave his winning smile as he turned around. "Danvers, I've got great…news." He spotted the soiled President standing next to a young boy and two John Danvers. "What is this?" He stepped closer to the doorway for a better look. "And who are you?" he asked the soiled President.

"As incredible as this will sound," said the soiled President, "you will be me if you don't take some drastic actions immediately."

As the President cautiously drew even closer to the doorway a pair of fighter jets came roaring over the other White House, startling him. "What am I looking at here?"

"About four hours into the future," said the soiled President.

The 1962 Danvers spoke up. "Remember our little talks about time travel and Einstein?"

"Yes, I recall them."

Danvers gestured to Richard. "This is Richard Pilgrim. He's a time traveler with a special gift." He then opened the Sunday newspaper Richard had brought with him from the future and presented it to the President. "You see this? This newspaper is from the year 2004." He pointed to Richard, then jerked a thumb over his shoulder at the devastated White House. "This boy can stop this from happening."

The President thumbed through the Sunday paper and noted all kinds of futuristic devices for sale in the advertisement pages. "Okay," said the President in a hesitant tone. "But first tell me what went wrong."

"This morning a U-2 got shot down over Cuba by a SAM," said the soiled President.

"Yes, I know," said the President. "And I gave the order countermanding any retaliatory air strikes."

"Unfortunately, your countermand was never received," said 2004 Danvers.

The President sighed. "There's always one SOB who never—"

THE DOOR

"—gets the word," said Richard, finishing the sentence.

The look of surprise flashed across the President's face.

"Touche, kid," said the soiled President.

"And there's something you don't know," said 2004 Danvers.

"And what would that be?" asked the President.

"Nearly all of Cuba's missiles are fully operational."

"All of them?" said the President. "But the CIA reported that only some of their missiles were operational."

"Won't be the first time they were wrong," said the soiled President. "When we bombed the SAM site that shot down the U-2 they retaliated with their ballistic missiles." He swept his hand towards the wreckage behind him. "And this is the result."

"Mr. President," said the 2004 Danvers, "you must make sure your order is implemented immediately."

The President took a moment to think it over. In a shocking move, he said, "No."

Both Danvers were jolted by the President's response. ***"But Mr. President...!"***

The President looked over to his soiled counterpart. "There isn't time for you to tell me everything, is there?"

The other President shook his head. "I'm afraid not."

The President turned to the two Danvers. "Can I switch with him?"

Both Danvers exchanged a look, nodded and said, "Yes," at the same time. If the world and the lives of all its entire population weren't weighing in the balance, it might have been a comical moment.

Both Danvers stepped out of the way and allowed the President to cross the threshold, while the soiled President stepped into the past. 2004 Danvers and Richard followed the soiled President into the Oval Office.

The President turned to the 1961 Danvers and asked, "Aren't you going with them?"

"No, sir. You're my President. I'm staying with you."

The soiled President immediately went to his red phone. "Get me Omaha!" SAC Headquarters was located in Omaha, Nebraska.

"Yes, Mr. President," the voice said over the speaker.

"This is the President. I am countermanding the order for any and all retaliatory air strikes into Cuba even if any additional recon aircraft are fired upon or shot down."

"But, sir, our fighters are preparing to sortie—."

"—Issue a stand down order immediately to all commands."

"But sir, the General—."

"I said, *no!*"

Twenty very long seconds would pass before the SAC officer reported, "The abort order has been issued. All aircraft are taxiing back to their flight lines."

Danvers and Richard smiled as they watched history being made. They glanced over to the door to the Little Office and watched that reality of the other President and Danvers fade away. "Let's go," Danvers said to Richard.

The President hung up the phone, placed the palms of both hands on his desk and gave a sigh in relief. "Danvers, it worked!" He spun round to discover that Danvers and Richard were gone. As a matter-of-fact, he would never see Danvers again.

The event had a profound effect on the President. He would never look at war the same way again. Hours later, an agreement would be reached with Russia that would end the Cuban Missile Crisis. Historically, the order countermanding his Generals was one of the least known but most important actions the President would ever make. In short, he averted a global nuclear war and saved the world.

Chapter Seventeen

The Arrival of Father Lucious

With the Pilgrim house fading in and out, everyone evacuated to Lomax's house where after dinner, he served stiff drinks in the living room to calm the nerves.

Knock! Knock!

Everyone nervously shifted their gaze to the front door.

"Oh no," said Mary. "Not here too?"

Lomax went over to the door and reached for the doorknob.

"I wouldn't do that if I were you," said Sparky, who headed for the hallway in anticipation of being vacuumed to some other exotic place.

Lomax opened the door.

A man in a black suit and fedora was standing on the front porch. He took off his hat. It was a Catholic Priest who was the spitting image of Archangel Michael. The only difference was his thick mop of gray hair. "*Ah*, what a fine day it is," he said in a thick Irish accent. "Father Lucious is the name."

"You're a priest," said Lomax, who recognized the face as the Angel who entered Richard's room.

"How observant of you. I've heard that about you. You must be Lomax."

"How do you know my name?"

"Oh, I know lots of things about you, my son. Especially, the danger you're in. That's why I'm here."

Thunder, Israel and Mary gathered behind Lomax.

Father Lucious sniffed the air. "*Ohhh*, would that be the sweet smell of Irish whiskey *I be a* smelling now?" He glanced at his wristwatch. "A bit early in the evening, mind you, but who's marking time?"

"What do you want?" asked Israel.

THE DOOR

"Yeah, we're not Catholics," said Lomax.

"And I won't hold it against you. The Holy Father sent me."

"The Pope?" asked Thunder.

"*Aye!* You know him, then?"

Thunder rolled her eyes skyward. "Oh, please!"

Lomax glanced over his shoulders at the others, who were backing off. He then stepped aside and bade the priest to enter.

"Thank you now." He stepped inside. "And may God bless all here."

He spotted the bottle of Irish whiskey and jerked his head in that direction. "Oh, would *ya* be so kind as to give a poor priest a bit of the old country now?"

Lomax made a face. "What did he say?"

"Give the man a drink, Lomax," said Daphne.

Lomax did and the priest was very appreciative, savoring every drop. He even moaned at one point.

"Must have been a long flight," said Lomax.

"*Ahhhh*, right you are," said the priest. "That it was."

"You say your name is Lucious?" asked Daphne.

"*Aye*, that it is! And a proper name for an old priest."

"You're not so old," said Daphne.

"Oh, bless you now for not noticing."

"And Lucious in Latin means 'light'."

The priest grinned. "That it does."

"Since when do you know Latin?" asked Lomax.

"Since high school. The Latin translation for Lucifer is '*The Giver of Light*."

The priest finished his drink, eyeing the others in the room as he emptied the glass. "If anything could be said about Satan it is that giving anything was not his forte." He took a moment to give the room the once over. "I've come a long way to help you people."

"Why," asked Israel, "should we trust someone we don't know?"

In a surprising move, the priest fired back a question of his own. "Has the lad returned from his latest journey?"

"No," said Mary, with an obvious hint of concern in her tone.

"Well, not to worry. I have it on good authority that he and Mr. Danvers will be right along…any time now."

"Oh, thank God!" said Mary. She reached out to her husband,

THE DOOR

who hugged her.

"You got something against Danvers?" asked Lomax.

"Who me? *Ack* no!" He held out the glass to Lomax for another drink. Lomax gave him another drink, finishing the bottle, pumping his forearm to get out every last drop. "*Ah* bless you, my son. And may your glass be ever full." He consumed about half of the drink in one gulp. "As for Danvers, well, he's managed to live for over four hundred years. The question is…whose side is he really on?"

"It's true then," said Mary to her husband. "He is your ancestor."

"So," asked Lomax, "the Pope sent you here to help us?"

"*Aye!*"

"Good. Now, tell us how to defeat the Devil."

The priest looked away for a moment. He then faced Lomax and said, "You can't. He's just like your bloody doors. He's indestructible."

That shook everyone up.

"He has the powers of an archangel and nothing you do can hurt him or scare him or defeat him," continued the priest. "He is all-powerful, very smart and totally devious. This little journey Richard and Danvers went on was a waste of time. A ploy. A setup. World War III in 1962 never happened. It was a deviation created by Lucifer to keep both of them and you busy and off balance. He has all the time in the world to think up these schemes and he's the bloody master of it."

"What are you saying?" asked Thunder.

"The real crisis was not in Washington or even here. It's in that warehouse in West Virginia…where all the doors are kept. Foolishly, I might add. All that power in one place." He shook his head. "They just played right into his hands."

Lomax left the room and went out into the backyard with his satellite phone.

"Diciembre?"

There was a lot of static.

"Lomax? Is that you?"

"Get out of the warehouse—now!"

"I can't talk to you….having…incident."

"Get your people out of there! DICIEMBRE!"

𝔗𝔥𝔢 𝔇𝔬𝔬𝔯

Just before the signal turned to total static, Lomax thought he heard a door knock.

*   *   *

10:30 PM. West Virginia.

The door flung open and both Richard and Danvers were hurled across the threshold. They flew a considerable distance before hitting the the concrete floor hard. It stunned them, but not as much as what was going on around them. Alarms were sounding. Red emergency lights were flashing throughout the interior. There was a windstorm inside the warehouse that made standing or walking difficult.

Knock! Knock!   Knock! Knock!

It started with one door then all of them were knocking, creating an ear aching din.

Diciembre came rushing over to Richard and pulled the boy to his feet, then Danvers. "Get out of here!"

"We shouldn't be here," said Richard. "We should be home now."

"The whole system is out of whack," said Danvers.

Diciembre escorted them to the nearest exit. "Hurry, hurry!"

All of the site's personnel were evacuating the warehouse and Diciembre and Richard and Danvers followed them outside. Some of the white-coated personnel stopped in the parking lot to type out commands on their laptops.

"This place is about to pop and you're text messaging!" said Diciembre. "Run for your lives!"

The dominant white-coated tech called out to Diciembre. "The EM wave is coming from one door."

"Which one?"

"Number 19."

"The hospital room door?"

"Yes!"

Diciembre made a snap decision. "All right. Send in the robot."

The young tech handed his laptop to Diciembre and said, "You do it!" He then bolted from the property with the others.

Diciembre typed out several commands and gazed into the

THE DOOR

laptop's monitor. Danvers and Richard gazed over his shoulder at the screen. "I thought I told you to go."

They watched as the robot's hand grabbed the doorknob and opened the door. Standing inside was Uriel.

Richard's eyes widened. He recognized the Archangel.

"Who's he?" asked Diciembre.

"Uriel…!" said Richard.

Uriel spread forth his hands and unleashed two streams of fire.

One second after the monitor went blank, a tremendous explosion occurred that blew up the warehouse and sent hundreds of doors and just about everything inside the warehouse high into the night sky. Then, for a few, silent, terrifying seconds everything stopped. It seemed as though time itself had stopped for everything within the warehouse and above it. Diciembre, Danvers and Richard stood in awe at all the debris as it just hung in the air.

What followed was the most powerful explosive decompression ever created by a door. There was no sound. The vacuum pulled in all the metal that made up the warehouse and all the doors and all the interior structures such as the command center, armory and living quarters and the compacted helicopter. They were all sucked into one door.

Diciembre gave Richard and Danvers a shove, knocking them to the ground before he himself was pulled into the vacuum. All of the trucks and cars and even the chain link fence that surrounded the facility were pulled out of the ground and drawn into the door. Danvers grabbed hold of a piece of rebar that was sticking out of the pavement with one hand and grabbed Richard with the other.

Three horrifying seconds later it was over.

When it was over, the only thing left standing was door 19.

As a sign of closure, door 19 slammed shut.

Richard got up and surveyed his surroundings. "Where's the man who pushed us?" He meant Diciembre.

"He's gone."

*   *   *

10:45 PM.

"Father?" asked Daphne, as she stared at the priest who seemed to have fallen asleep while standing up.

Father Lucious opened his eyes. "It is done," he said in a

THE DOOR

matter-a-fact tone.

"What's done?" asked Mary.

"Relax," said the priest, "your boy is back and safe and sound."

"And how do you know this?" asked Thunder.

"Actually, I don't really know….I just have faith. Be comforted. It has been my experience that good has a way of winning over the bad."

"Well, father," said Lomax, "my life experiences have told me that for good to win over evil, the good has *gotta* be really bad!"

The priest shook his head. "My, my. What a tragic soul you are, my son."

"You're the Angel who was guarding the door," said Daphne. "Richard called you Prince Michael."

"Did he now? Awfully nice of the lad to promote me to Cardinal, but he is sadly mistaken. I'm no Angel. I'm just a poor priest from an old parish in Ireland, sent here by the Vatican to help you colonists out of this bloody jam you've gotten yourselves into now."

"So," asked Mary, "what do we do?"

A perplexed expression flashed across the priest's face. "You're asking me? How should I know?" He reached out his arm. "Go ahead and touch it." Lomax did. "There! You see. I'm flesh and blood and just like you. I'm here to help you. The Holy Father thought you needed an Exorcist. I was told there was a little boy I might need to save. Now it looks like I will have to exorcize the lot of *ya*. The Holy Father said the Devil was in Virginia. If you ask me, he's everywhere. But that's not the issue here. I need to know more about what you chaps have been up against and," he turned to Lomax, "you're the one who can tell me."

"Why me?"

"Because you don't trust me. Do you?"

Lomax thought it over and gave a nod. He opened another bottle of whiskey. "Thirsty, Father?"

"*Oh*, like a sailor on the high seas!" He held out his empty glass. "I thought you'd never ask!"

The telephone rang. Lomax answered it. "Hello."

"This is Danvers. We were successful and we're back safe, but not at the Pilgrim house."

"Where are you?"

𝕋𝕳𝔼 𝔇𝕆𝕆ℝ

"West Virginia…where the warehouse used to be."

"Did you say, *'used to be'*?"

"It's gone. So is your friend, Diciembre."

"I want you to stay put. I'll send a friend to pick you up."

Lomax called Lieutenant Dewey Mitchell and got him out of bed to drive Mary and Israel to the warehouse site in West Virginia. He knew that the Pilgrims would be all shook up and this was no time for traffic accidents.

It would be 1:35 AM before Mitchell and the Pilgrims arrived at the warehouse. They were totally unaware of the event at the warehouse. When the car's high beams reached all the way across the property and shined on the one door standing alone, the police lieutenant became emotional. "Jesus!" He parked the car and got out with his flashlight. He swept the area and spotted Danvers and Richard walking towards them.

Mary and Israel ran out to meet their son.

Richard was exhausted and practically fell into his father's arms.

"You have a very brave little boy there, Israel," said Danvers. "He saved the day. You should be proud of him."

"I am. But how many times do I have to risk his life to fix your mistakes in life?"

"I pray this is the last."

Israel carried the boy to the car. "He's exhausted."

"There was a giant warehouse here," said Mitchell, "with over five hundred doors, maybe a thousand. Now only one remains."

Danvers rubbernecked. "Where's Lomax? I thought for sure he'd come."

"He's home entertaining a guest," said Israel.

"Guest? Who?"

"A priest from the Vatican, no less."

The blood ran from Danver's face. "Did anybody bother to check?" He flipped opened his cell phone, but no lights came on.

"What are you saying?" asked Mary.

"He may not be who he says he is," said Danvers.

"We know," said Israel. "He's Prince Michael. I saw him in the video recording when Richard met him and the Praetorian Guards."

"My cell phone is dead too," said Mitchell.

𝕿𝖍𝖊 𝕯𝖔𝖔𝖗

Danvers was not comforted by what Israel said. "He may be a prince, but not the one you're thinking about." He turned to Mitchell. "Lieutenant, how's the siren and emergency lights working on this car?"

"Perfectly."

"Bloody good!" He said in his old Puritan accent. "Now turn them on and get us back to Marion as fast as you can!"

They climbed into the car and Mitchell floored the accelerator. He went Code Three all the way back to Cornelius Street.

*　　*　　*

Earlier that night, Lomax sat at the kitchen table with the priest, who was grasping the empty liquor glass. Lomax had Daphne take Dara next door and go to bed. Both were worn out. Thunder and Sparky manned the surveillance center in the basement, keeping an eye on the Pilgrim house. It had stopped phasing.

For what seemed a long time the two men sat and stared at each other, without uttering a word. Each was sizing up the other via body language. Each was trying to read the other. To Lomax, the priest was like a slab of marble, cold and statuesque. As it turned out, both were masters of the art, so neither moved a muscle as to not give away their inner feelings. Lomax knew deep down inside that he wasn't dealing with a priest. He never went to a Catholic Church, but he knew enough about priests to make a distinction. When Lomax realized that there was nothing to read, he decided to take the direct approach and ***piss him off!***

"So, father…"

"Yes, my son?"

"What's it like being a priest?"

"It has its moments, both good and bad."

"Just like Angels, good and bad?"

"For me, it was a calling."

"Same here, father. Except you use a Bible and I use a phone." Lomax chuckled a little, but the priest didn't respond in any way. "That was a joke, father."

"Was it now?"

Lomax raised his hands in defeat. "I guess not. Sorry. I get carried away sometimes."

THE DOOR

"Lomax, your hatred for figures of authority and anything holy will be your undoing. One must worship something…"

"Oh, don't get me wrong, father. I believe in God. I mean I've seen Heaven…through the door. But the question is, have I ever seen you before?"

The priest showed no emotion.

"You know, Father," said Lomax, "I envy you." He pointed to the priest. "Yes, I do. You get to screw with the Devil! And it's legal!"

The priest's eyelids slowly rose up.

"Yeah, I mean it must be a trip to see that idiot fall flat on his ugly face. Am I wrong when I say he was God's favorite?"

"That he was."

"He was God's right hand man! Therefore, who would question him?"

"No one."

"No one would dare!"

The priest nodded. "Right you are."

"Think about it, Father. In the early times, when God was off creating everything, who do you think he left in charge? Who do you think called the shots? Lucifer was the power. He had the run of the place and he did one heck of a job!"

The priest swayed his shoulders slightly. "I suppose…."

"You suppose! Give me a break, Father! You don't become *numero uno* to God and be a slouch! No sir, he was **the man!** When he said jump, they all jumped. This guy had it all! All the power and all the prestige…"

"Yes."

"…and all the women!" Lomax smiled and backhanded the priest on the arm. "Now don't tell me the women up there aren't the most beautiful and hottest babes of them all!"

"All God's children are beautiful, my son."

"And I bet Lucifer had them all. They must have been lined up for miles!"

"Women still find Lucifer attractive."

"Yeah, but it's all fake! He is the master of illusion. When he was cast out, he…was…"

"Burned."

"More like barbecued. Now Father, that must not look good at

THE DOOR

all.”

"Not a pleasant sight *at'll*...I would imagine.”

"The poor guy went from being called Prince Lucifer to the Prince of Darkness. What does that say?”

Lomax leaned closer to the priest, reached out his right hand and extended his index finger and thumb, holding them about an inch apart. "Now, father, he was that close to having it all. And he blew it! But it didn't end there. Oh, no! Now, I'm not saying he didn't stir things up wherever he went, but in the end he always loses. I'm telling you, Father, he's a first class screw-up! Am I wrong here? If I am, please tell me. But can you tell me when he's ever come out the winner in anything he's done?”

The priest peered at Lomax with narrowing eyes. "Only with the millions of souls he's acquired.” His hand started to grasp the liquor glass more tightly.

"And they're all losers and screw-ups just like him. Misery does love company! And I'm with you on one thing, Father. God is smart. Not only did he get rid of his main competition, but he got an absolute moron to watch over the garbage dump for him.” He went face to face with the priest. "Honestly, Father, is the Devil not the biggest asshole in the universe?”

The priest stared at him. "Lomax, if you suddenly found yourself...face to face with the Devil, what would you say to him?”

Lomax brought up his hand, pressed his elbow to the table and rested his chin on his fist and thought about it. *"Hmmmm!* Well, in the spirit of the moment, I hope that it would be something... profound. Knowing me, I'd probably ask him a question.”

"Such as?”

Lomax backed off slightly. "Oh, no, I couldn't.”

"Please...”

Lomax gave a nervous smile and shook his head. "No, I couldn't. You being a man of the cloth and all—.”

"—No, I insist.”

Lomax took a moment, studying the priest's eyes. "Well, if you insist....”

"I do.”

"Okay.” He cleared his throat. "Well, *uh*, Lucifer, is it true that when God said to you *'payback is hell'*...you didn't believe him?”

THE DOOR

The liquor glass exploded in the priest's hand. "Mercy! What have I done?"

Lomax noticed blood seeping from the priest's hand and reached for a towel. "I hope it wasn't something I said?" He retrieved a first aid kit that was kept in the kitchen and provided the priest with some antiseptic and a bandage.

The priest smiled. "*Ack* no, my son. I love a spirited conversation."

*   *   *

When General George Stoneman attacked Southwest Virginia in December of 1864, his troops successfully overran the once impregnable defenses at Saltville without firing a shot. A far cry from General Burbridge's raid which took place only a few months earlier. It was Stoneman's one and only success during the Civil War. Prior to his raid on Saltville, he was dispatched to free the Union soldiers at the infamous Andersonville Prison. His forces were overtaken by a Confederate army half the size of his and sent to Andersonville Prison. The Rebs had such a low regard for Stoneman that they freed him, figuring he would do more harm to the Union than to the Confederacy. However, his raid on Southwest Virginia was a textbook example in the use of diversionary tactics and the leaking of false information to the enemy. Many military analysts attributed his success to the "*excellent intelligence*" he acquired prior to the raid from an unknown source. Stoneman's forces were mostly cavalry, so that they could move fast and hit hard. When his army came to within sight of the town of Bristol, he had them turn tale at the first sign of Reb resistance and make a hasty retreat. That night, he sent his cavalry back in on a saber charge and they took both Bristol and Kingsport Tennessee without firing a shot. It was the same for Saltville. Stoneman's troops destroyed the saltworks, burned all of the buildings and even plugged the water wells with cannonballs. The only error Stoneman made in his historic raid was not sending out his troops to locate and secure the 2,500 slaves that toiled day and night at the saltworks. Once the Union forces had withdrawn, the slaves were returned to Saltville where they rebuilt the saltworks and got it up and running to full capacity within a month.

THE DOOR

When the war was finally over, the slaves who were owned by local farmers simply left the saltworks and walked to the only home they've ever known. However, most of the slaves who worked at the saltworks were the property of slave owners from other southern states. Many of them saw an opportunity to escape. One of them was Joe, the slave who was being whipped by his white taskmaster at the saltworks until Hamilton intervened. It was during one of his business trips into Saltville when Joe approached Hamilton with several other former slaves and asked if he needed any workers. Hamilton wanted to exploit the rich deposit of gypsum he had on his land and needed a lot of hands to make it happen. So he hired Joe and his people immediately and told him to recruit all the former slaves he could find, including some from the local farmers. It would cause some friction between Hamilton and the white farmers of the county, many of whom considered him a Yankee.

It was now the middle of July 1865 and the Pilgrim house was near completion. The rooms on the second floor were being plastered with gypsum that was dug out from the deposit on Hamilton's land. Hamilton's business was booming and he could now afford to hire carpenters to finish the house. As it turned out, it was the need for gypsum that was driving up the business. Nearly all the wood he and the boys milled was being used to make barrels to store and ship the gypsum. It was backbreaking work for the newly freed and unemployed slaves who had to dig out the gypsum with pikes and shovels. All modern carpenters use drywall to make walls, but that technology was decades away. The people of this era had to plaster their walls by smearing pure gypsum over wood slates. It was more difficult to do and time consuming, but when it dried no one could tell the difference. Now that the war was over and the economy was slowly picking up, the homes and buildings that were destroyed by all the fighting had to be refurbished or rebuilt and that required a lot of gypsum. And Hamilton knew where all the deposits were. For the next one hundred and forty years, billions of dollars of gypsum would be dug out of Smyth County and used to build homes and buildings all across America.

Hamilton drove a wagon with ten barrels of gypsum to the Pilgrim house. He pulled up to the front of the house. The front

THE DOOR

door had not yet been installed. "Levi?"

Levi Pilgrim came out of the house. "Yes?"

"I got the gypsum…I mean plaster you need."

"When did people start calling it gypsum instead of plaster?"

Hamilton shrugged. "I have no idea."

"Maybe it was you who started it all?"

"I hope not. I've made too much history already." He turned to the front of the house. "Say, when are you going to put a front door on that house? After all, you are the owner of Pilgrim Doors. It looks bad for business if you don't have a front door on your house."

"I'm working on it."

A stagecoach drove up to the Pilgrim house. It got a lot of attention. At that time, a stagecoach in war torn Virginia was like seeing a Cadillac drive in. The side door opened and a man stepped out, wearing a fancy and expensive business suit and hat.

"Would either of you gentlemen be the mill owner?"

"We both are," said Hamilton, with a smile.

The man reached out his hand. "My name is Lucious." He had a warm and friendly smile, almost hypnotic. There was no way for Hamilton to know that a similar looking man would present himself as a priest to Levi's descendants and neighbors.

"My name is Hamilton. Friends call me *'Ham'*."

"Well, sir. I hope to be your friend, Ham."

Hamilton gestured to Levi. "That's my business partner, Levi Pilgrim."

"*Hmmm!* Are you a Puritan?"

"The ones in my family who came to America were."

"Any relation to a Cornelius Pilgrim of Salem Village?"

Levi was hesitant to answer. "Yes. He was my grandfather. He's passed on."

"Oh, I am terribly sorry. I've done business with your grand-father. I know him well. He was…a righteous man."

"That he was…"

Lucious turned his attention to the barrels of gypsum. "And where did you get all this fine plaster?"

"We have a deposit on my land," replied Hamilton. "We also make the barrels to transport the plaster."

"My, my. You certainly are the enterprising sort. I like that! It

THE DOOR

reminds me...of me!" He patted himself on the chest. "I think we're going to do a lot of business."

Normally, Hamilton would have said, "Great!" But something about this man made him hesitate. It was just a feeling he had inside.

They watched as several carpenters carried off the barrels of plaster to the side of the house, where several other men were mixing the chalk like gypsum with water in a trough to make it into a workable plaster.

"The reason I came here is because of your reputation with door making," said Lucious.

Hamilton gestured to Levi. "He's the company door maker."

Levi bade for Lucious to come into his house. Hamilton followed them in and down to the basement, which was now a fully equipped and operating woodshop. About thirty doors were lined up on the north wall.

Lucious was impressed with the doors. "They truly are finely crafted doors."

Levi gestured to Hamilton. "I had a good teacher."

Lucious nodded to Hamilton respectfully. "You taught him well. They are very sturdy and good looking doors." He reached into his coat and removed a billfold. "I am empowered to purchase all of these doors and order another hundred for one of my suppliers in Washington D.C.. Who knows, one or more of your doors may end up in the Executive Mansion!"

Being a student of history, Hamilton quickly recalled that it was Teddy Roosevelt who changed the name of the Executive Mansion to the White House during his Presidency.

All of the reservations Hamilton had about this man evaporated as soon as he laid eyes on that fat money-laden billfold.

A door that was lying on a worktable caught Lucious' eye. "And what do we have here?" He went to the south side of the basement to inspect the door, which had just been completed.

"Sorry," said Levi, "you can't have that one."

"And why not?" asked Lucious.

"It's my front door."

Lucious grinned and placed his hand on the door. "And may all who pass through your magnificent front door bring you nothing but good news, good cheer and lots of business!"

THE DOOR

"Here! Here!" said Hamilton. He reached for his pocket watch. "It's a little early, but that kind of talk calls for a drink."

"Oh," said Lucious, "please don't tempt me."

"You look like a man who likes to be tempted."

Lucious gave a big smile and chuckled. "Oh, if you only knew...."

When Hamilton started off towards the stairway, Lucious followed, then stopped, turned and stared at the west wall. It was the way he stared at the wall that made Hamilton and Levi take notice.

"Something wrong?" asked Levi.

"No, I was just admiring the fine brickwork on that wall."

"You're the first one," said Hamilton. "I'm a carpenter not a bricklayer. I wouldn't be surprised if the whole *gall darn* thing fell in on itself one day."

For the next hour, Hamilton haggled prices with his new client, then signed an order and was paid cash for the thirty doors in Levi's basement. The new client then paid a hefty deposit for the rest and for one thousand barrels of gypsum. It was the most profitable day for Hamilton in that century. The man calling himself Lucious boarded his stagecoach and bid everyone a good day.

Hamilton rushed home to show Maggy. No sooner had he arrived, than five buckboards loaded with angry white farmers pull up to the front door.

"Hamilton," one farmer called out, "we got a bone to pick with you!"

From high up in a tree, Hoot let out a long whistle and all the Hamilton boys came running with their rifles at the ready.

All the farmers were armed with pistols, but they kept them holstered. When the Hamilton boys approached the house, leveling their muskets at them, the farmers responded by reaching for their pistol handles. In a lot of ways, the rural parts of Virginia resembled the Wild West in respect to the way the men felt about their guns. The war may have been over, but for some of the former combatants who carried a rifle or wore a pistol belt wherever they went, it was a habit that was hard to break.

Maggy Hamilton came out the front door and calmed everyone down. "You boys start gun battling with my family, so help me

Christ, I won't lift a finger to patch you up." She confronted the farmer named Buchanan, who was the one who called out to Hamilton. She pointed to his arm, the one with a lot of scars, the one the surgeon at Emory and Henry College told her to amputate but didn't. "Like I done before with you! How's the arm, Buchanan?" She laid on her Southern accent good and thick to give her statement more credibility.

Buchanan released his hold on the pistol handle and doffed his hat in a respectful manner to Maggy. "It *be* fine, *ma'am*. Thanks to you." He glanced over his shoulder. "Boys, hands off the hog legs." The other farmers pulled their hands away from their pistols.

Hamilton came out the front door and let out a whistle. "Stand down, boys," he said to his adopted sons.

They did and formed a line behind Hamilton.

"What can I do for you today, Mister Buchanan?" asked Hamilton.

"You can start by returning our slaves to us."

"They're not your slaves anymore. They're free."

"Says who?" asked the farmer standing behind Buchanan.

"The ones who licked us," said Hamilton.

"*Thems fight'n* words, Mister," a third farmer said.

"And you're looking at... '*The Lucky Seven*' who fought on Chestnut Ridge," said Hamilton. He gestured to the six boys, who stood a little straighter with pride. "Where were you when Burbridge's army came up that hill? I'll tell you where we were—!"

"—right in front *of' em!*" said Freckles.

Buchanan turned and gave a stern look to the farmer who talked about fighting. The boastful farmer backed off. "We know."

"The war is over and Lincoln freed the slaves," said Hamilton.

"And how are we going to work the land without slaves?" asked Buchanan.

"Pay them."

Buchanan's shoulders along with several other farmers' sank. "With what? We got taxes we can't pay. We may lose everything."

Hamilton brought his hand up to his chin and went, *"Hmmm!"*

Maggy turned to Fetch and whispered, "He's thinking. We're in for it now."

THE DOOR

Hamilton took a stick and drew a square in the dirt and drew lines to designate the boundaries of Buchanan's farm and three others. "Your four farms connect at the river."

"That's right," said Buchanan.

"During hard economic times, smart businessmen need to cut back on their overhead, in your case—slaves, and sell off poor producing assets. In other words, land you don't need or can't afford to cultivate. Trust me, you'll make more with less. Your farms are too big for your families to manage. Before the war, thanks to the cotton gin, the South overproduced cotton and drove the price way down. Now demand for cotton is high, so a small efficient farm can make as much as a big plantation. I propose that you sell off the inner corners of each of your properties…"

"To who?" asked Buchanan.

"Joe and his people."

"They ain't got no money. How are they going to pay us?"

"Okay, I'll buy the property and I will buy all the corn and cotton you produce at a fair market price. You just bring it all to me. I'll pay Joe and his people to do all the work and I'll feed them and house them too." He reached into his pocket and pulled out the money he just got from Lucious. "And I'll start with this." He separated the money into four shares and handed them to each farmer. It had been a long time since any of them had held so much Union currency. All of them were about to lose their farms, now Hamilton offered them a way out. "Now, go pay your taxes."

Buchanan and the other farmers stepped away to talk over Hamilton's ideas and offer over.

When Buchanan came back to Hamilton he sealed the deal with a handshake. "You got a deal, Mister."

"My friends call me *'Ham'*."

Buchanan made a face. "I'm not your friend." As he climbed back onto his wagon, he once again doffed his hat to Maggy. "Good day, *ma'am*."

As the farmers rode off, Maggy asked her husband, "Where did you get the idea of buying all of their cotton and corn?"

"Good business sense…and…"

"And what?"

"Charlton Heston did it in *The Ten Commandments*. Worked for him."

THE DOOR

"You idiot!" she said as she went back into the house and slammed the front door.

Hamilton brought a hand up to his face. He was thinking again. *"The Lucky Seven."* He turned to the boys. "You know, we've been trying to figure out a name for the farm. What do you think, boys?"

*   *   *

Midnight. Lomax escorted the priest to the other guest bedroom on the second floor of his house, facing the alleyway. He went into the small bathroom, turned on the light and even pulled down the comforter. "I hope that this is agreeable to you, Father?

"Agreeable indeed, my son! I think I've died and gone to Heaven."

Lomax headed for the door. "Well, good night. But if you need anything, anything at all, please feel free to help yourself."

"I've never had it so good."

"Good night, Father."

Lomax closed the door behind him and went straight to the basement.

Thunder was manning the controls. Sparky was sitting next to her.

"Sparky, is that camera you installed in the guest room working?"

Sparky pointed to the big monitor. "Take a look for yourself."

All eyes were affixed in the main screen, which showed the priest standing next to the bed, staring right at the camera. There was no expression on his face and he didn't move a muscle.

Lomax gave a thumbs up to Sparky. "Good work."

"What's he doing?" asked Thunder.

Lomax shook his head. "He's looking right at the camera."

"I'll tell you what he's doing," said Sparky. "He's creeping me out!"

A warning light started flashing on Thunder's control panel. "Got something." She worked the controls and a view from camera # 27 came on one of the wall screens. "A motion sensor was just tripped...." She read aloud the location as the computer printed it out on the monitor in front of her. "LOCATION: 1255

THE DOOR

South Street, Marion Virginia.”

“That’s Dewey Mitchell’s residence,” revealed Sparky.

“How convenient,” said Lomax. “His wife is out of town and so is he.”

“You’re saying someone knew he *and his wife* would be out?”

Lomax typed out a command on a keypunch and a printed record of all the telephone calls made on Mitchell’s house phone for the past two days was projected on a monitor. He darkened the newest call and pressed PLAY. A recorded phone conversation that was made hours earlier was then heard.

“Marion P.D.,” said the recording, “please standby and someone will be with you shortly.”

“You tapped his house phone?”

“Of course!”

“I thought you were his friend?”

“I am. That’s why I tapped it.”

“Marion, PD,” said the dispatcher. “How can I help you?”

“This is Mitchell. I’ll be out of the area for about six hours. I can be reached on my cell….” Lomax stopped the recording.

One of the two cameras that were monitoring Mitchell’s property showed three individuals in dark clothing and wearing night goggles going in and out of Mitchell’s house via the kitchen door, carrying heavy cardboard boxes. They made about four trips each before closing the door and getting into a black SUV.

“These guys are bringing boxes into the house and coming out empty handed,” said Sparky.

“They’re either the dumbest burglars alive,” said Thunder, “or…”

“They’re not burglars,” said Sparky.

“We’re only going to get one shot at this,” said Lomax as he approached Thunder, clearly indicating that he wanted to take over her controls. She got up and let Lomax have her seat.

As soon as Lomax started working the controls, a view from camera # 55 came on next to camera # 12 on the wall. The black SUV pulled out of the driveway to Mitchell’s house and drove without its headlights on until it almost passed the light pole. Lomax freeze framed the racing SUV and said, “Got it!” He zoomed in on the front license plate. It was blurry, but distinguishable.

THE DOOR

"Can you run the plates?" asked Sparky.

"Don't have to," replied Lomax, as he worked the controls and zoomed in on the driver, who was pulling off the night goggles. "That's the Chief of Police." ***Dewey Mitchell's boss!***

*   *   *

Joe was standing outside Levi Pilgrim's house, talking to Hamilton.

"*...Thankie Massa.*"

"Stop calling me that. I'm not your master. Nobody is. You're a free man. You and your people will work for me and it will be hard work. But you will be paid."

"Oh, don't worry about that none."

"Yes, I will worry about that. This is what our country is all about. Working hard, getting a fair wage and taking care of our families."

"*Yes 'm!*" The concept of freedom was new to Joe. There was no way for him to grasp it all in such a short time. But he trusted Hamilton and knew that he and his people would be taken care of and live better lives.

"Now we're going to need a lot of lumber to build houses for *y'all...*"

"*Yes 'm!*"

"...and to make barrels. We're going to need lots of barrels, Joe." He held up a piece of dried gypsum. "See this gypsum. We're going to sell this by the ton. You and I are going to start something here that will continue on for a hundred or more years. Gypsum, barrels and salt. That's what this county is going to be known for."

Joe smiled. "***Yes 'm!***"

Hamilton reached out his hand and Joe looked at it. No white man had ever shaken his hand before. He took Hamilton's hand and pumped it.

"God bless *ya, Massa* Hamilton."

"Call me: *'Ham'.*"

Fetch and Levi carried a door from the basement.

"Well," said Hamilton, "it's about time you installed a front door in this place. God knows what riffraff you'll keep out."

𝔗ℌ𝔈 𝔇𝔒𝔒ℜ

It took a few minutes to install the front door and test it.

"Looks great!" said Hamilton as he reached for the doorknob. To his surprise, his hand passed through the doorknob and the door itself. He let out a yelp as he pulled back his hand. He tried it again and got the same results.

Levi saw it. "Oh, no…"

"Something wrong, *pa?*" asked Fetch.

Hamilton retracted his hand and looked at it. "Send everybody home."

"But it's not even noon," said Fetch. Hamilton gave him a look that said it all. He cupped his hands and shouted, "*Quit'n* time, *y'all.*"

"Levi," said Hamilton, "make sure everyone uses the back door, not the front."

Levi ran off to the backdoor of his house.

As the carpenters left the house through the back door and climbed onto their horses and wagons to leave, the front door phased out, giving Hamilton and Fetch a view of the foyer in Israel's house in 2004.

"What is happening here, *pa?*"

"I don't rightly know...son."

*　　*　　*

05:45 AM.

Lomax was standing on the driveway of his house, when Lieutenant Dewey Mitchell pulled in with his unmarked police car.

Mitchell got out of the car and noticed the expression on Lomax's face. "You look like you just went to a wake."

"Yeah, yours."

"*Huh?*"

With their house no longer safe, Israel carried his son out of the car and then he, Mary and Danvers went into Lomax's house and closed the door.

Once they were alone, Lomax said to Mitchell, "You're being framed as a meth dealer."

"By whom?"

"Your Chief. He went into your house tonight with some of his goons and left several cardboard boxes."

"And why would he do that?" There was a hint of anger in his

THE DOOR

tone.

"Because you're an honest cop, who can't be bought and you're getting close to the truth. It's only a matter of time before you uncovered what's really going on at your police department."

"Are you trying to say my Chief is dirty?"

"Oh, he stinks worse than a garbage dump and you know it!" He pointed at Mitchell. "What you don't know is, that you've been helping *them* in their drug enterprise."

"In what way?"

"By taking out their competition. Eighteen labs in six years. Not a bad record, if you ask me. But all of a sudden, things are not working out so well. Look at your last three raids. Somebody tipped them off with enough time for them to clear out with ... most of the product."

Mitchell shook his head. "I'm the only one who knew the location of the lab—."

"Are you sure?"

"YES!" Mitchell was getting angry.

"—What about your dispatchers? Did you tell any of them?"

"Of course! That's Standard Operating Procedure. If some-thing went wrong the dispatchers would know where to send backup."

Lomax stared at Mitchell and didn't make a move or a sound.

Lomax's silence made the lieutenant think and he didn't like what he was thinking about. Mitchell raised his hand and shook his head. "No! No, way! They're sworn personnel just like the rest of us."

"Did any of them come with the Chief when he was hired at MPD?" asked Lomax, but he already knew the answer. He checked and found out that two dispatchers had transferred to Marion PD with the Chief and both of them worked the night shift, when Mitchell did most of his raids. As a matter-of-fact, one of them was married to one of Dewey's detectives.

Mitchell started to say something, then froze. He closed his eyes and exhaled deeply. "Oh, man! How could I have been so stupid?" The police lieutenant became uncharacteristically emotional and started to think out loud. "I even told one of his dispatchers that my wife was going to be in North Carolina for a week." He pointed to Lomax. "And right after you called me, I

𝒯𝐻𝐸 𝒟𝑂𝑂𝑅

called dispatch and told them that I would be out of the area for six hours.”

“Well, there you have it!”

“But how did they get into my house?”

“He had a key.”

“How do you know that?”

“I got it all on video.”

“You planted a camera outside my house?”

Lomax responded by holding up two fingers for two cameras.

Thunder called Lomax on his headset. “Lomax?”

Lomax lowered his middle finger and pressed the index finger to his lips to silence Mitchell. He then spoke into his headset. “Go ahead, Thunder.”

“DEA is surrounding Mitchell’s house. They got a battering ram. They’re going in.”

“Ten-four.” Lomax turned to Mitchell. “The DEA is raiding your house….”

“Well, they didn’t waste time, did they?”

“You need to go right now to the Sheriff’s Office and turn yourself in.”

Mitchell shook his head. “No, I’ll go my PD.”

“*Don’t do that!* That’s what they want. That’s what they expect you to do. Dewey, don’t play into their hands. Go to the Sheriff. He will protect you. Let him read you your Miranda Rights. Then shut up.”

“If I say nothing, people will think I’m guilty.”

“*Let’em!* If you tip your hand now, your Chief will dig in his heels so deep and we’ll never get him or his buddies. There are a lot of cops involved in this and some of them are from other departments. No, he’s *gotta* feel that he’s pushed you out of the way so that he can continue what he’s doing. I want him to relax and think that he’s won.”

“You’re asking me to act like I was some kind of criminal….”

“It’s all part of the game.” Lomax smiled as he reached out his hands and grasped Mitchell by the arms. “Dewey, I’ve got your back. Trust me.”

Mitchell studied Lomax’s face and saw sincerity in those eyes. He knew Lomax and he knew what the rogue agent was capable of. *Besides, what choice did he have?* “Okay.”

THE DOOR

Mitchell drove to the Sheriff's Office and surrendered to his former boss.

A few minutes after Mitchell had left, Danvers and Israel came outside and joined Lomax on the front lawn. It was still dark out.

"You ready?" Israel asked Lomax

"I was born ready," replied Lomax.

"Let's go," said Danvers.

All three men then walked across the street to Israel's house. Israel unlocked the front door and went inside. Danvers was the last one in and closed the door behind him. Almost instantly, the front door went out of phase. The foyer was suddenly filled with sunlight coming from the doorway. When Danvers and the others turned around they could see Hamilton and Levi staring back at him.

"That's Ham!" said Israel.

The door was transparent to the people on both sides. They could see and hear through the doorway as though it wasn't there.

Hamilton heard him, pointed to him and called out. "Israel? Is that you?"

"Yes, it is! Are you and Maggy all right?"

"We're fine. Did you get my letter?"

Israel nodded. "Yes, and it helped explain things."

"What's wrong?" asked Thunder over the headset.

"Thunder," said Danvers over his headset, "the front door has become active."

"The front door?" she asked.

"But how?" asked Lomax. "Richard isn't here. Why is it suddenly becoming active now?"

"What about the old Puritan church door?" asked Hamilton.

"It broke free from the brick wall," replied Israel.

Hamilton made a face. "I figured it would…eventually. Be careful. It's a killer."

"Oh, it's more than that!" said a man standing behind Israel. He then stepped into view. "Hello, Ham."

Hamilton recognized him immediately. "So, we meet again, John Danvers. Or should I call you by your real name?"

Israel pointed to Danvers and said to Hamilton. "So, you do know this man?"

"I should," replied Hamilton. "He's my business partner. He's also a Union officer who was shot in the heart and just walked off like it was nothing."

"Let's just say," said Danvers, "I'm a little hard to kill—."

"—No," said Lomax, "more like impossible. Now let's focus on the front door. It just became active. Any idea why?"

Hamilton turned and bade Levi to approach him. "Allow me to introduce to you Levi Pilgrim, our door maker."

Levi stepped up to the doorway. The resemblance between him and Israel was remarkable. They were almost like twins, but Levi was a decade younger.

Israel presented himself at the doorway, but did not cross the threshold. "My name is Israel. I take it that I'm your great, great, great grandson?"

"Glad to meet you." Levi glanced over to Lomax. "And to answer your question, I just installed this door only a few minutes ago."

Lomax turned away. He was lost in thought. "Something or someone triggered it. Let me think for a minute." He turned his headset back on. "Sparky, you there?"

"Yes."

"Run back the tape for camera # 30 for the past fifteen minutes."

Sparky did and took notes.

Hamilton asked Israel. "What year is it for you?"

"2004."

Hamilton did the math. "So Maggy and I have been gone for seven years! But we've only lived here one year!"

"It's called time dilation," said Danvers. "The further back in time you go the slower time moves."

"Ham," said Israel, "it's time for you to come back to us."

Hamilton was moved by what Danvers and Israel said. He thought it over and shook his head. "No, no. I can't. Maggy and I have a life here now."

"Hamilton," said Lomax, "by this door becoming active it is a sign that you are needed back here."

"The situation here has gone from bad to worse," said Danvers.

"We need for you to come home now," said Israel.

Hamilton shook his head and turned away. "No, I won't."

Danvers took it upon himself to do something drastic. He

THE DOOR

stepped into the doorway and the door became whole again.

Seeing Danvers step through and the door going back into phase shocked Fetch, who fell backwards on the ground.

Hamilton grabbed Fetch's arm and pulled him to his feet.

"*Pa*, what does all this mean?"

"Fetch, my boy, I think all Hell is about to break loose."

Back in 2004, Lomax started shouting. "What just happened?"

"Danvers crossed the threshold!" said Israel.

"I saw that, but why did the door go back into phase?"

Sparky had the answer. "Lomax, the door went out of phase immediately after Danvers crossed the threshold going into the house."

"That makes Danvers the trigger," said Lomax. "Could it be that he is a Traveller, just like Richard and Allison?"

"No," said Sparky. "If he was, then he wouldn't have needed Richard to open all those doors to the White House…. Besides, the front door was already out of phase. He just walked through it."

Lomax thought over what Sparky just said. He was impressed. "I think you're right. Not bad for a Cable Man."

"What do we do now?" asked Israel.

"There's nothing we can do…until that door goes out of phase again," said Lomax.

"And if it don't," said Israel.

"Have a little faith, will *ya*," said Lomax, with a smirk.

"Any reason Mary, Richard and I can't spend the rest of the night in our house?" asked Israel.

"Why," asked Lomax, "you don't like my house?"

"No, just some of the company you keep." He meant the priest. Israel went and got Mary and Richard and brought them home.

*   *   *

All the local news channels made the raid on Mitchell's house and his surrender and subsequent arrest at the Sheriff's Office their main story for the 7 AM morning news.

Mitchell's police chief went to the Sheriff's office to make a statement to the press. "The reputation of our police department has been blemished today by the despicable actions of one of our own. As head of the Criminal Investigations Division, Lieutenant Dewey Mitchell had access and full knowledge to all law enforcement activities in the area, especially in the area of drug interdiction. This is a sad day for our department and our beloved town. But the good news that I want to tell our citizens is that Dewey Mitchell has surrendered to the Sheriff and is behind bars where he belongs. Justice has prevailed!"

Lomax was watching TV while having breakfast with Daphne and Dara in Daphne's kitchen. "That bastard set him up!"

"Lomax," said Daphne, "don't do that!"

"Don't do what? Swear? *Ah*, she don't care." He gestured to Dara. "Sweetheart, do you care if I swear?"

"Hell, no," replied Dara.

Lomax's eyes nearly popped out of his head.

"There you see," said Daphne. "Some father you are."

At the mentioning of the word *'father'*, Lomax gazed up at the ceiling. Suddenly, the power cut off in the house.

"Did you forget the pay the electric bill?" asked Daphne.

When the power came back on some ten seconds later, Lomax's headset crackled.

"Lomax," said Sparky, calling from the basement, "the good Father is not in his room!"

"Well, where is he then?"

Thunder looked out the window of the bedroom she had been sleeping in and spotted the priest crossing the street. "He's heading for the Pilgrim house!" she reported on her headset.

Lomax dashed for the side door.

Across the street, Richard was the first to wake up. He slid out of his bed, stretched and went to the bathroom. When he returned, the priest was standing in his bedroom, hat in hand.

"Hello, Richard. Remember me?"

"Michael?" He smiled broadly.

"Yes," the priest said with a wide smile.

But something wasn't right. Something about the man in his room frightened Richard. He backed away.

Lomax ran across the street and used a key he had to open the front door of Israel's house. "Father?" he called out.

Richard bolted by the priest, came out of his room and went dashing down the stairs. "Mommy!"

Israel and Mary came racing out of their bedroom.

"What is it?" asked Israel.

ᔕHE DOOR

"What's wrong?" asked Mary.

The priest came out of Richard's room and slowly made his way down the stairs. "Nothing is wrong. All is well. Everything is as it should be."

Thunder was buttoning her shirt as she entered the Pilgrim house.

"Father," asked Israel, "how did you get into my house?"

"The front door was unlocked. I just merely walked in." The Priest made a silent headcount. "Well, now. I see that we're all here. Excellent! And it is time...."

"Time for what?" asked Thunder.

"To rescue your daughter, doctor. This is the reason I am here. It's time to get Allison."

*   *   *

Hamilton went into his bedroom and pulled open the drawer to a dresser he had made with his own two hands. He removed the leather gun belt and put it on. He then drew his Remington pistol and checked to see if all the chambers were loaded. Lastly, he removed the Union officer's sword he had mounted over the fireplace in the main room of the house.

Maggy opened the front door and entered the house. "What are you doing?"

"Pack your things. We're going back."

She was shocked. "How? The door at the Stuart's house doesn't phase anymore."

"But Levi's front door does and it opens to his house in the future."

She thought it over. Her mind was going a million miles an hour and he wasn't surprised when she said, "I don't want to go back. We have a life here. And we have the boys to think about."

He went up to her and they embraced. "Baby, I don't want to go. I love it here! Back there, I was just a CEO of a company. *Whoopie!* But here, I feel that I can make a difference! And I don't want to leave my boys. But we got to!"

"Why do we have to go?"

"Israel is in trouble."

"Then let Israel handle it."

THE DOOR

"You know I can't do that." He pulled away from her and made a decision. "You stay and I'll go…and one way or another I'll find a way back to you. I promise."

She reached out to him and they embraced and kissed. They kissed so hard that Hamilton had to take a deep breath afterwards.

"You know," he said, "I hate it when you do that."

"That's why I do it."

They boarded the buggy and drove to the Pilgrim House, where Danvers was waiting for them at the front door.

The boys were there too, with their muskets.

When Maggy spotted Danvers she pointed to him. "You again!"

"Hello, Maggy."

She was not so pleased to see him.

It was Freckles who spoke for the others. "*Ma, pa*, we all decided and we're going with *ya*."

"No," said Hamilton. "You'll stay here and look after your mother."

Maggy shocked Hamilton by saying, "Forget that. Come Hell or high water, I'm standing by my man and don't you try to talk me out of it." She turned to the boys. "We'll be back as soon as we can."

The boys' shoulders sank as the reality of the two people who took them in when nobody else would and who loved them, were leaving.

Hamilton reached out and touched the front door. It was solid.

"It hasn't changed," said Levi.

Hamilton turned to Maggy. "We may have missed our chance."

Danvers was standing a few feet away, taking in the view of the countryside, thinking it would be his last. "Don't ask me how, but I think I can now open this door and *presumably* any door Levi made."

"Well," said Hamilton, "we're ready, when you are, partner."

Danvers gave a respectful nod to the Hamiltons. After which, he reached for the door and it phased out, giving everyone a view of Israel's front foyer. He pulled back his hand. "I'll follow you in," he said to the Hamiltons.

The Hamiltons turned to their boys. Maggy started to weep. So did all of the boys. "If we don't come back," he said "I want you

THE DOOR

all to work together and make us proud." He took Maggy by the hand and they raised their legs to cross the threshold when suddenly the door became solid again.

"What happened?" asked Maggy. "I thought you said you can open this door!"

Danvers placed his hands on the door, but this time nothing happened. "Someone must have opened the door on the other side. Both doors have to be closed for this to work."

*   *   *

Richard hadn't said a word or even looked the priest in the face from the moment he first laid eyes on him.

Lomax noticed the way Richard acted towards the priest. He recalled how excited the boy was when he met Prince Michael. Now he was totally different. "You okay, Richie?"

Richard did not reply, confirming Lomax's worst fear.

"Something isn't right here," Daphne said to Lomax over her headset. She was now with Sparky in the basement. The local news channel was being displayed on one of the monitors. "Channel 6 just reported that the County Magistrate just set bail for Lieutenant Mitchell for a hundred thousand dollars."

"Somebody doesn't want him out and about," said Lomax. "Daphne, I want you to get the key to the bank's safe deposit box and post a cash bond to bail out Dewey."

"You have a hundred thousand—?"

"—Daphne, go spring Dewey! And take Dara with you."

"I was going to drop her off at the day care center."

"No! Keep Dara with you at all times. You got that?"

"I got it. And boy are you going to get it when all of this is over! Crying poverty like you did when you had a hundred—!"

"Trouble in paradise?" the priest asked Lomax.

"Father, be glad you can't marry!" He went out the front door, faced his house and the camera that he installed, and used sign language to communicate with her. When he was finished, he spun on his heel and reentered the house, slamming the door behind him. But it didn't shut. A piece of white cloth was jammed in the mortise. Lomax and the others were too occupied to notice the front door wasn't closed.

THE DOOR

"Ready?" asked the priest, as he stepped lively towards the door to the basement's stairway.

"Shouldn't we wait for Danvers?" asked Lomax.

"We are better off without him," said the priest. "He's not to be trusted."

When Israel opened the metal door to his basement a whiff of smoke came out.

"I smell smoke!" said Lomax.

"And where's there's smoke…!" said Israel as he went down the stairs. He stopped about half way and pointed to the smoke arising from the sides of the church door. He coughed. Smoke is lighter than air so it didn't surprise him to see the spaces between the floor joists were filled. It gave the basement a scary other-worldliness appearance.

Lomax was next down the stairs. "Oh, this is just lovely. A foreshadowing of things to come…?"

Thunder followed Lomax. She covered his mouth with her hand.

Richard followed her, but stopped. "I don't want to go." When he turned around, the priest came down the stairs and blocked his route of escape.

"You have nothing to fear," said the priest.

The priest scared Richard more than the basement, so he turned and rushed down the remainder of the stairs.

It would be only the second time Lomax had been in the basement. He couldn't help but admire all the woodcarvings of religious figures. He pulled off the fabric covers of several statues for a better look.

Thunder watched Lomax and was amazed by the craftsmanship of the statues. "They look so life like! Who did all this?"

"My grandfather and father," replied Israel. "When they were very old."

One sculpture really got Lomax's attention. It was the tallest, standing 7 feet high. When Israel gave him and Mitchell the grand tour of the basement seven years earlier, the only one he didn't uncover and show his guests was this particular sculpture. When Lomax untied the rope and pulled up on the cloth cover, he was stunned by what he saw. His body went numb. It was a replica of the *Christ The Redeemer* statue that overlooked Rio de Janeiro,

THE DOOR

Brazil, but more life like. What struck Lomax the most was the way Christ held out his arms, just like he did at the cliff with the hundred-foot drop. There was one other item that was covered by this cloth. Resting against the sculpture was a wooden pole with a silver spearhead. It was so primitive looking that it never occurred to him that it was once welded by an Archangel.

Richard crossed the basement, occasionally glancing over his shoulder at the priest, and brushed up against Lomax. He gazed up at Lomax and their eyes met.

Surprisingly, the rogue CIA Agent didn't see any fear in the young Traveller's face. What he saw was determination.

Lomax gestured to the spear and whispered, "You looking for this?" After Richard gave a nod, Lomax released the cloth and allowed it to recover the statue.

*   *   *

Across the street, Sparky was working the controls and zoomed in on the front door of the Pilgrim house. "The door is open. Now why would they do that?"

He rolled back the tape to the exterior camera that focused on the front of the Pilgrim house and stopped when he spotted the priest stepping out the front door. He backed it up a little more, then pressed the PLAY button to watch Father Lucious remove his priestly collar and jam it into the mortise of the front door.

Sparky didn't say another word. He just ran up the stairs and crossed the street as fast as he feet could take him. Upon reaching the front doorway, he pushed open the door and looked inside, searching for the priest. When he didn't see the priest, he reached over and pulled out the wadded up priest's collar in the mortise. "Looks like somebody didn't want this door closed." He stepped into the house and stood there for a moment. He could feel the energy surging through the house. He looked at his forearm and saw the hair standing straight up. "Oh, man I can feel it!" He turned and closed the door. It immediately went out of phase. He spotted Hamilton and Maggy standing on the other side in the past and bade them to enter.

After Hamilton and Maggy crossed over, Danvers motioned towards the door, but was shoved out of the way by Fetch.

ᛏHE DOOR

"What are you doing?" asked Danvers.

Fetch crossed the threshold and was followed by the other boys, including Levi.

Knock! Knock!

It came from the old double church door.

"There's that God awful sound again," said Israel.

"It will be the last time you will ever hear it," said the priest. He went up to the door and caressed it with his hand, almost lovingly. For anyone who had to contend with the doors these past seven years or longer, to see someone show any reverence to them at all made them look suspicious. The priest turned around. "It is time. But first, let us pray." He faced the door once again, raised his arms and said a prayer in language that no one understood.

While the priest prayed, Lomax got down on one knee and whispered in Richard's ear, "What was number 4?"

The question surprised Richard. He was totally unaware that his bedroom was bugged or that his meeting with Archangel Michael was viewed and recorded by Lomax. But he was a smart boy and deep down inside he knew that Lomax was a friend of the family and was there to protect him and his parents. So, he cupped one hand, brought it up to Lomax's ear and whispered the answer.

The answer surprised Lomax. His eyelids shot up. A grin grew on his face. When Richard finished and moved away, the rogue agent said to him, "Then you know what to do."

It was all Lomax had to say. Richard went up to the priest as he finished his prayer. "Father, I am ready!" There was determination in his tone and in his eyes.

The priest noted it and shot a glance to the others in the basement. "Bless you my son. Now, let's go find Allison."

At that precise moment, Hamilton and Maggy entered the foyer. They exchanged a quick glance, then proceeded to the basement door.

"Israel!" called out Hamilton.

Israel heard his name. "That's Ham!"

The priest became impatient. "Now, boy! Open the door!"

Hamilton came halfway down the stairs then stopped. "What is this? Wait!" He pointed to the priest. "I know you!" It was the man from the stagecoach! ***The one who bought all their doors!***

Richard got down on one knee and placed his hands on the

THE DOOR

door. At first he pulled them away. *"Ouch! It's hot!"* But he persevered and placed his hands on the hot doors and even pressed on them.

"You think you know me," the priest said to Hamilton. "That has been man's biggest mistake."

Richard made a fist and pounded on the door four times.

The priest's eyes widened. *"Noooooooooo!"* He shouted as he turned his gaze from Hamilton to Richard.

Richard got to his feet, grabbed the door handles and pulled on them with all his might, jetting his head back so that the weight of his body would add to the motion. He released the handles and continued backwards until he ran into Lomax.

When the doors opened, everyone was shocked by what they saw. It was exactly as Einstein said, a matter stream created by a massive decompression of the time space continuum and it even looked like an elevator racing downward. What the old professor didn't mention was the earsplitting noise created by the descending energy stream, punctuated by the sounds of screaming people as they whisked past the doorway. The priest turned to the door. There was fear in his face.

Lomax handed the spear to Richard.

The young Pilgrim charged and struck the priest in the back and drove him across the threshold, where he came in contact with the energy stream and erupted into flames. Lomax came up from behind Richard, grabbed the end of the spear and pushed as hard as he could, driving the priest deeper into the energy stream. As the priestly clothing burned away, Lucifer's true form emerged with long horns, a tail, scalded skin and blazing red eyes. Coming into contact with the energy stream must have been very painful for the fallen Angel because he wailed in agony. *"STOP, I SAY!"* He turned and glared at Lomax just before there was a flash of energy and he was taken away.

The flash sent Lomax and Richard flying into the air in the opposite direction. Richard landed in his father's outstretched arms. Lomax wasn't as lucky. He hit the floor hard and slid on the floor until he struck the base of the stairway.

Danvers crossed over the threshold and the front door became solid again. He and the boys heard all the commotion coming from the basement and they scrambled for the opened doorway, with

Fetch leading the way.

"*Pa!*" shouted Fetch, as he went racing down the stairs.

Hamilton was shocked to see the boys and Levi. "I told you boys to stay…"

Lomax stumbled to his feet and closed the double door. "Richard…tap the door twice. Make it change its end point."

Israel went with Richard to the door and watched him tap it twice. The terrible noise abruptly ended.

Lomax turned to the six boys with muskets and Levi, who came unarmed. "Are those rifles loaded?"

"Primed and ready!" said Moon.

Lomax armed himself with the only weapon he could find in the basement: a sledgehammer. He then looked to Thunder and the others. "If we're going to go, now is the time."

Israel looked down at Richard, who gave his permission with a nod.

Richard handed the spear to his father, then got down on his knees and once again placed his hands on the door. He jerked his head around.

"What is it?" asked Israel.

"I can feel the presence…" said the boy.

That made Thunder excited. She brought her hands up to her face. "Oh, please, dear God let it be Allison."

"…no, someone else," said Richard. "A Spanish man."

"Diciembre?" asked Lomax.

*   *   *

It was all the screaming that awakened Diciembre. He found himself laying on a mound of debris from the warehouse in a place straight out of Dante's Inferno. His worst nightmare had come through. He was in Hell. "Oh, no! Dear God—no!" He slowly got up to survey his surroundings. A door was standing not too far from where he was lying. He realized that all the doors and all the debris from the warehouse had come through that one door, including what was left of the compressed helicopter. The door was now a shambles and aflame. Seconds later, it fell over. There wasn't as much fire as he thought it would be in Hell, just enough to illuminate the place. But it was a hot and foreboding place.

THE DOOR

Hundreds of dark minions were savaging through the debris piles, removing the doors and carrying them on a beaten path to a maze of corridors that reminded him of volcanic lava vents. Indeed, as he gazed up at the towering heights of where he was he couldn't help but think that he was in a dormant magma chamber. He was surprised that no one paid any attention to him, save for the dark minion who shoved him out of the way—sending him flying through the air—so that it could get what Diciembre was laying on. He hit the ground hard and scraped his arm. He pulled up on his shirt to see scratches and a small amount of blood. "I'm still alive!" He uttered to himself. For a while he stood and watched as the minions picked up what was left of the helicopter that crashed through his command center and carried all of it off to the most primitive looking smelter. Once the metals were melted, they were poured into sand molds and recast into spears and swords. He decided to follow the minions who carried off the recast weapons. The brightest light he saw came from the spotlight on the robot that was also being carried off with the doors. The robot was damaged, but still operating.

He entered another large chamber where there were other doors and even larger mounds of debris. The raggedly clad minions fought over the clothing, especially the military uniforms, they uncovered. One door stood wide open and water poured from it into a volcanic vent, extinguishing a fire and sending jets of steam high into the air. *They used the door to put out Hell's fires!*

Wisely, he stayed in the shadows, taking pathways that were covered with loose rocks and boulders and seldom used. He crossed a third cavern where thousands of blacksmiths were sharpening swords and spears they just forged. There was no wood seen or used here. It would decompose in all this heat. No, the weapons were all metal and totally offensive. No shields or chain mail. There was no electricity here or electrical systems so all the work was done by hand on grinding stones. Everything the minions had to work with came from the doors.

It all started to make sense to Diciembre. "So, he used the doors to provide all the materials they couldn't get here. Ingenious!"

In the next cavern, a huge army was being assembled and outfitted with clothing and weapons. But what struck Diciembre

In the next cavern, a huge army was being assembled and outfitted with clothing and weapons. But what struck Diciembre about this army was that it seemed to include everyone, big, tall and small, and even females.

Sometime later, he entered a fifth and the largest cavern of them all where hundreds of doors were being lined up on one side and a massive army of minions on the other. In the middle of it all stood the double church door and a single door. He felt his heart begin to race. The church door must have had some importance to it because the minions placed the robot close to it. *Was this his way out!* But that feeling evaporated the moment he heard a little girl scream. It echoed off the high walls of the massive chamber. He turned to see an Angel in a white uniform holding up a girl in a Little Red Riding Hood costume and threatening her.

"You will open this door!" said Uriel, pointing to the single door standing some 30 feet away from the double church door.

"No, no!" said Allison. "I won't. And you can't make me!" When she pointed her finger at Uriel, all of the gold and silver medals on his shinny breastplate lifted up just like piece of steel would to a powerful magnet. Normally, a magnet, no matter how powerful, wouldn't have an affect on gold or silver.

"Feisty little one, aren't you. Well, that will change in time—say a million years!"

Diciembre's luck had run out. Someone grabbed him, lifted him up and hurled him against a wall. He groaned in pain as he hit the ground. Other minions started kicking him and threatening with saying, "Fresh meat for the taking!"

"His clothes are mine!" another minion shouted.

When he got his wits about him, he grabbed a rock and smashed it into the face of the minion who had assaulted him. He then bolted to a place where there were hundreds of pillar-like boulders.

"Get him!" the minion who was smashed ordered.

But Diciembre managed to elude his pursuers, keeping to the shadows and remaining absolutely quiet. He almost gave a sigh of relief when he saw that the pursuers had turned and headed back in the direction they came. But his blood pressure soared when he realized that another group of minions had come to help in the search.

"Diciembre," one of them called out. "Don't you know you

𝔗𝔥𝔢 𝔇𝔬𝔬𝔯

can't hide from us?"

There were too many and they were closing in when a hand emerged from a rock formation and grabbed Diciembre. He was then pulled into the rock formation. The hand came from a Heavenly Angel, wearing a white uniform, who gave off a lot of light.

To Diciembre's surprise, the minions walked right passed him and what they thought was a rock formation.

"Who are you?" Diciembre asked the Angel who still had him by the arm.

The Angel released him and replied, "Gabriel."

Diciembre turned and noticed that there were others in this hidden place in the rocks. He counted 19 people, all clad in early colonial clothing. "And who are you people?"

"We are from Salem Village," one woman replied with a smile.

"You're Puritans!" He turned to Gabriel and asked, "Are they the ones who were condemned at the Witch Trials!"

"They are," said Gabriel, "the 19."

"I don't understand," said Diciembre. "They were all innocent. They don't belong down here."

"Neither do you," said one of the condemned men, "and you're here."

"The Devil did come to Massachusetts," another woman said, "and we were taken before we could be saved."

"But how?"

Gabriel pointed in the direction of the church door and a part of the shield that protected them dissolved slightly to show it. "Through that door."

Diciembre nodded. It was beginning to make sense now. He turned back to Gabriel. "So, you've been protecting these 19 souls for more than four hundred years." Gabriel made no reaction. "You really are the best of the best."

"I do what I do in the service of God."

Gabriel then placed his hand over Diciembre's eyes. "Behold."

Diciembre was shown the entire history of the Salem Village Witch Trials from beginning to end and all its horror. One Puritan stood out the most: Nathaniel Pilgrim. It was he who sealed the fate of all the nineteen of the condemned, giving false testimony and profiting from his lies. When the Devil confronted Danvers, he swore his allegiance to him.

When Gabriel pulled away his hand, the imagery ended.

"Danvers…I mean, Nathaniel Pilgrim," said Diciembre. "He's the guilty party here, not these people."

"We know," said one of the women, "but we have forgiven him."

Diciembre was stunned. "To be here, in this terrible place all these years and you still forgive the one who took your lives and had you condemned! Oh, you people are truly good."

"Why do you think I'm here?" said Gabriel.

Diciembre gestured to Uriel, who was now shouting louder at Allison. "What about him? He's one of yours, isn't it?"

KNOCK! KNOCK!

Unlike any previous knocking, these thundered and echoed throughout the cavern, sending many of the minions into a panic.

They were so loud, Diciembre had to cover his ears.

Gabriel pointed in the direction of the church door. "Your friends are coming to rescue Allison. But, it's a trap. If either Richard or Allison opens even one door—all of them will open and Heaven is doomed!"

"You're kidding me, right?"

"No." Gabriel grabbed Diciembre with both hands, lifted him over his head and hurled him across the cavern.

Diciembre was terrified and screamed all the way. He landed on both feet near the single door Uriel and Allison were facing.

"Welcome to Hell, Diciembre!" said Uriel. "With all your deceased brethren we have down here from the CIA and KGB, you should feel right at home!"

Diciembre drew closer to Allison. "Allison, don't listen to him. No matter what he says or does, don't open any doors!"

Uriel gave a kick to Diciembre, sending him crashing into a pillar of rock.

Uriel turned back to Allison. "You will open this door! Yes, you will!" He didn't expect what happened next.

Allison gave him a powerful kick to the stomach. He groaned as he doubled over. She then gave him a right cross on the chin, knocking him on his butt. "No, I won't! And you can't make me!"

Uriel turned to the church door. "Your mother is coming."

THE DOOR

"Mommy? Here? No!"

"She's coming to save you." He stumbled to his feet.

Allison turned to the door. "Mommy!"

He grabbed Allison. "Yes, mommy, come to Little Red Riding Hood."

Allison fought to free herself from Uriel's grasp, kicking him and even biting his hand.

"You truly are a spirited child. But you won't be when you see what I do to your mother."

That truly horrified Allison. "No, you leave my mother alone!"

"Oh," said Uriel, "I can't wait for her to come here!"

"Please don't hurt my mommy!"

"If you don't want me to hurt your mother, then open the door!"

Diciembre staggered to his feet. "Don't do it, Allison!"

Several minions attacked Diciembre and pounded him with their fists and kicked him with their feet.

*　　*　　*

"Allison?" said Richard. "I can feel her presence too…!"

That made Thunder excited. She brought her hands up to her face. "Oh, my God!"

"Is this door a Wanderer?" asked Lomax.

In what can only be described as totally eerie both Sparky and Richard said, "No," at the same time.

"It's a single destination door," added Richard.

Lomax then remembered an old 50's tune and sang it. "Well, then, *open the door, Richard.*"

Richard stood up and tapped the door twice. It BOOMED on the other side.

"I always thought I'd end up there," said Lomax. "But not like this." He turned to Israel. "Let's do it!"

Israel handed the spear to Thunder, then grabbed one door handle.

Lomax grabbed the other.

When they opened the door, Thunder screamed. Her scream was almost inaudible by all of the screams heard in Hell. The thought of her daughter being in such a horrible place got the best of her. Terrible smelling smoke and sulfur filled the air and burned the lungs of everyone who breathed it.

THE DOOR

Lomax, with sledgehammer in hand, led the way in. "Keep Richard inside!"

Thunder, armed with Michael's spear, bolted across the threshold. "Allison!"

Sparky followed her.

Hamilton turned to his boys. "Lucky Seven, form two ranks in front of the door!" The boys formed two ranks of three and pointed their muskets into the cavern. He gave Levi his pistol.

"How do we know these musket balls can hurt these devils?" asked Hoot.

"You hear all that screaming?" asked Fetch.

"They wouldn't be screaming if they couldn't feel pain," said Levi.

Hamilton drew his sword and gave an order to the boys. "No demon gets past us. Understood?"

"Understood," they replied.

Hoot spat on the floor. "Just like Chestnut Ridge."

*   *   *

Allison finally relented and opened the door. She was surprised to see the face of an Angelic Praetorian guard gazing back at her.

"We have a breech!" shouted the Praetorian.

Uriel shoved Allison out of the way and raised his arms in victory. "We're in…!"

The demon army let out a thundering yell. But when a foghorn was heard in the distance, all the yelling and screaming stopped. For a moment, there was silence.

"Our master comes!" shouted a minion. The army yelled even louder.

Diciembre staggered over to Allison, grabbed her hand and ran with her towards the church door. When he couldn't keep up, he let her go. "Keep running!"

Allison didn't stop until she ran into her mother's outstretched arms.

Diciembre fell and couldn't get up. He glanced over his shoulder at the phalanx of minions, armed with long metal spears and swords, closing in on him. When he turned round, he spotted Lomax running towards him. "No—leave me!"

Lomax stopped next to the robot and hit it twice with the

THE DOOR

sledgehammer, breaking the metal mountings to the automatic shotgun. He then tossed the sledgehammer to Sparky, jerked his head in direction of Allison and Thunder and said, "Get them out of here!"

Sparky bolted, grabbing Thunder by the arm and directing her and her daughter in the direction of the door.

The cavern was suddenly filled with a thunderous roar. It was so loud it made the walls shake and debris fall from the ceiling.

As Lomax freed the shotgun from its mounts, he called out, "Hi honey! I'm home!" He lunged towards Diciembre and pointed the shotgun at the approaching hoard of minions. He fired off three shots in rapid succession. Upon reaching Diciembre, he grabbed the man's arm and pulled him to his feet.

"You're a mad man," said Diciembre, "do you know that?"

Hundreds of minions charged towards them and Lomax opened fire with the Street Sweeper. He mowed down scores of minions as he and Diciembre retreated.

"First rank, fire!" shouted Hamilton as Thunder and Allison swept past him and into the basement. The three boys on the front rank let loose with a round, then got down on their knees to reload their muskets. "Second rank, fire!" The second rank discharged their muskets and quickly reloaded them. Levi fired off all six rounds with the pistol, then realized he couldn't reload. When both ranks were primed and ready, they let fly with a round that created a cloud of cordite.

A giant fiery form entered the cavern and swept aside the minions, sending them screaming through the air.

Hamilton didn't have to be told who the approaching fiery form was. "Oh, here comes trouble!" A thought and a feeling came to him. It was a strange and powerful feeling—the likes of which he had never felt before. Something compelled him to turn around and stare at the largest covered statue. He went over to it, pulled up the covering to get a look, then lowered it. The statue was so big and heavy that it had its own dolly. "Boys, put down your guns and give me a hand here!"

It was then Hamilton spotted a front gate sign that one might see as they were about to enter a western ranch. It read: *The Lucky Seven.* It was old, weather battered and even had a bullet hole in it. It made him think he, Maggy and the boys had a future

THE DOOR

in the past....

Hamilton and the boys pushed the covered statue across the threshold to the other side. It was so tall that it barely cleared the top of the doorway.

"*LOOOOOOMAX!*" the fiery form bellowed.

"I didn't know you're so popular," Diciembre to Lomax, as he struggled to run.

"Hey, what can I say? We're drinking pals!"

The fiery form condensed into a dark winged figure and he landed a short distance behind Lomax and Diciembre.

When Diciembre's legs gave out, Lomax had to toss the empty shotgun aside and drag the CIA Special Agent in Charge to the door.

"Come on!" shouted Lomax.

Lomax glanced over his shoulder and saw his face on the face of the dark winged figure. It did not give him a good feeling. But when he turned around and saw Hamilton and the boys pushing the seven foot tall covered statue out of the basement, a thought came to his mind. "I need help here!"

Hoot, Red and Freckles rushed out, grabbed hold of Diciembre and brought him into the basement.

Lomax stopped, spun on his heel and faced the dark figure. He would stand up to the Devil with no sign of any fear.

Once again, Lucifer's face resembled that of Prince Michael and Father Lucious.

Lomax raised a hand and the dark figure stopped in mid air. "Well, I've got to hand it to *ya*. *Ya* pulled this one off beautifully. I have to say, I'm impressed." He gestured to the door Allison opened. "You got the door open. But something tells me you wanted all of them open. Didn't work out like you planned, *huh?*"

The dark figure snapped his fingers and all the doors flung open.

Lomax's shoulders sank. "You know, I really hate it when that happens."

The dark figure started to laugh. With each passing second, he laughed even louder until it was ear shattering. He then moved forward, in pursuit of Lomax.

Lomax bolted, then skidded to a halt next to Hamilton. Together, they pulled off the cover from the Christ the Redeemer

𝕿𝕳𝕰 𝕯𝕺𝕺𝕽

statue. In that seminal moment, a miracle occurred. The face on the statue came alive. The eyes opened.

The sudden presence of Jesus not only shocked and stunned Lomax but it also terrified the dark figure. He stopped in midair and gasped!

Jesus looked down at Lomax and he said three words. "Close the door."

For someone who had a history of discontent for authority figures Lomax replied with a snappy, *"Yes, sir!"*

Lomax and Hamilton crossed the threshold and closed the double door just as a stream of fire was unleashed at them.

THE DOOR

Chapter Eighteen

ALL HELL BREAKS LOOSE

Daphne parked the car in her driveway

and got out with Dara and Dewey Mitchell. They turned to the Pilgrim house and heard all kinds of terrible sounds.

"What the…?" said Mitchell as he took off running across the street.

"Oh, no!" shouted Daphne as she and Dara followed him.

The front door was opened and they rushed in.

A man wearing a black suit and a Fedora, stepped out of Richard's bedroom and stopped at the top of the second floor stairway. Daphne recognized him as Father Lucious. When he saw Daphne heading for the basement door, he said, "Stop! Don't go down there!" But there was no Irish accent.

"Like Hell I will!" She scrambled down the stairs to the basement, with Dara and Mitchell right behind her. "LOMAX!"

When the priest came down the basement's stairway, he was met by screams from Allison, Mary, Maggy, Hamilton and even Richard.

"It's the Devil!" shouted Israel.

"Now what do we do?" shouted Thunder.

They all backed off to the part of the basement where all the religious sculptures were lined up, hoping they would protect them in some miraculous way.

Lomax relieved Thunder of Prince Michael's spear and pointed it at the priest. "Back for seconds?"

When the priest calmly stepped onto the basement floor, he stopped and gave the people and the room the once over. He then reached up, grabbed his priestly collar and pulled downward, pulling off the suit and exposing his dress white Commander's uniform and wings. He then removed the fedora.

THE DOOR

"It's Prince Michael!" said Richard, as he went up to him and even hugged the archangel.

Michael smiled and patted Richard on the head. "Well done my lion-hearted friend." He looked to the others. "And to you all."

"Well done?" said Lomax. "We just got our butts kicked back there."

"We done held them back," said Moon.

"Earth was not his intended destination," said Michael. "Lucifer can come and go here as he pleases here."

"Where does he want to go?" asked Sparky.

"Heaven."

"And we just opened the door for him," said Thunder, meaning her daughter.

"Yes, unfortunately…but not unexpectedly."

Thunder made a face. "What does that mean?" She didn't get an answer.

Lomax lowered the spear that he was pointing at Michael, then presented it to him. "I believe this is yours?"

Michael smiled as he inspected his old spear.

"Thank you for telling me secret number four," Richard said to Michael.

"How is it," Hamilton jerked his head towards the door, "the Devil looks just like you?"

"We were brothers…once," replied Michael.

"That's secret number five," said Richard. "He likes to look like Michael."

"Okay," said Israel, "what's secret number four?"

Michael noticed the curiosity in the faces of the people in the basement and when he exchanged a glance with Richard, he raised a hand. He would explain it. "We call it…*The Last Ride*, because it's the last one the damned will ever take. It was something similar to the one Lucifer and his treasonable followers took when they were cast out from Heaven."

Lomax glanced over his shoulder at the door. "It messed him up good."

"That's its sole purpose."

Diciembre got to his feet. "I saw Gabriel."

"As in Archangel Gabriel?" asked Daphne.

"Yes, and a small group of souls he was guarding. They were

THE DOOR

the ones you help get condemned!" He pointed to Danvers.

Danver's shoulders sank and he hung his head low. "I know."

"How many were there?" asked Hamilton.

"I counted 19."

Lomax shook his head. "There's that number again! The hospital room number, the number on this house. 19. 19. Everything is 19!"

Michael felt that it was time to reveal what was going on. "There were hundreds of Puritans who were accused of witchcraft and consorting with the Devil. They were all innocent, but 19 were condemned." He gestured to Danvers. "It was Nathaniel here who made this door and who welcomed the Devil into a House of God. In doing so, he disabled all of the safe guards we had placed in the door portal system to make it demon-free." Michael noted the nasty looks some of the people in the basement were giving to Danvers. "But you shouldn't place all of the blame on one man. The whole village took part in the hysteria. And, we didn't help things by installing deficient safeguards."

"Prince," said Lomax, with a grin, "safeguards are like rules. They're meant to be broken."

"Not in Heaven!"

Danvers spoke up. "Am I never to be forgiven for my sins? What must I do and say to show the remorse that I feel deep in my heart?"

"I can promise you this," said Michael, "that opportunity is forth-coming, but it will be costly."

The sound of blaring horns was heard coming through the double doors.

"What is that?" asked Thunder.

"He is forming his army," said Michael. "We haven't much time." He handed the spear back to Richard. "You hit him in the same place I did…long ago. An old wound." He then pointed to Richard and Allison, "Now I need for both of you to open a door for me." He then turned and floated up to the stairs. Both Richard and Allison dashed up the stairs after him.

Just before they reached the foyer, Israel dashed up the stairs and grabbed Michael by the arm. "Wait! You mean, it's not over?"

Michael jerked his head towards the door. "That was just a

THE DOOR

prelude of what is to come."

"But how do we beat this guy? Nothing hurts him! Nothing frightens him!"

"Oh, I wouldn't say that," said Lomax.

"Didn't you see the fear in his eyes," said Hamilton, "when he saw the statue?"

"From a statue?" asled Israel.

"That's because he saw more than a statue...." said Lomax.

"Oh?" At first Israel didn't understand, then he did. ***Oh,, Jesus!***"

"Exactly."

Israel released Michael and followed the archangel as he floated up the stairs.

Meanwhile, the army of darkness was forming ranks before a line of opened doors. Lucifer no longer resembled Michael. He would appear before the damned in his true darkened form. They greeted their master with cheers and rhythmic pounding on their long spears on the ground as he prepared to address them from a pulpit of stone. The roar of their cheering and growling was deafening. But when he raised a hand to silence them, they immediately stopped. Silence befell the giant cavern. What power this horned dark lord had over his minions! His long red cape unfurled and fluttered in the wind caused by the suction of the doors.

He opened his arms wide and high. "Brothers and sisters…such a joyous day! I have wonderful news for you. Today, we all go to Heaven!"

The cavern was once again filled with the roar of cheers and growls.

Uriel appeared and took his place on the dark lord's right and gave a respectful bow to his new master. The minions stopped cheering and growling.

Lucifer returned the gesture to Uriel. "It will be like before... but without," he rubbed his chin, "what are the words the stupid mortals use to protect children on the Internet?"

"Parental controls," said Uriel.

Some of the minions laughed.

"Trust me there won't be any of that!"

Lucifer raised his hand and instantly brought silence to the place.

"After waiting four hundred years for the power levels to build up," he continued, "we can now go where we could not before. And I have it on good authority," he gestured to Uriel, "that the oppressive gravity and bright light that prevented us previously from venturing to our eternal reward have been eliminated—all thanks to the doors!"

"Blessed be the doors!" the minions shouted.

He brought a hand up to his face and seemed to whimper. "The deprivations you have suffered…we have suffered…all these millennia have been unfair, uncalled for and in most cases the penalty did not fit the offense. No, my dear brothers and sisters, a great wrong has been committed and we will have our retribution!" The cavern shook from all of the shouting and pounding of feet and pikes. Pieces of the ceiling came crashing down on the minions. "And when you've had your fill of manna and wine and every form of debauchery, then we will rebuild! Palaces for all and our oppressors as our slaves! I ask you, is that Heaven or what?"

The minions went wild. This time Lucifer waited for them to calm down.

"I know…that I have been hard on you." He looked away and nodded.

The crowd responded with all kinds of responses, basically denying the truth.

"Yes, it's true. But I did it to prepare you for this momentous moment. As with all good things, we must fight for what is ours. And fight you will. Know that we outnumber them! Know that we have outsmarted them! Know that they fear us … as they should!"

The noise level was never higher.

"So," concluded Lucifer, "I say unto all of *thee*, go forth and reek havoc, my dogs of war!"

The army cheered and pounded the end of their pikes into the ground.

Lucifer raised both arms and laughed boisterously.

"Nice touch of Shakespeare there, my Lord," said Uriel.

"General, dispatch your army and leave no stone unturned."

"At once, my Lord!"

THE DOOR

Uriel opened his wings, drew his sword, leapt into the air and shouted, "Charge!" He then bolted into an open doorway—one of a thousand that would be used by the Devil's army.

The multitude of wingless minions got a glimpse of Heaven as they took off running and leapt through the doorway, crossed over and floated though the air, losing momentum the farther out they went. Eventually, they would stop and hang in midair, half way to their destination. To their surprise, only when another minion collided into them did they gain any momentum to move forward. Sometimes, they were struck by the business end of the spear or whatever kind of weapon the others were carrying.

*   *   *

This time both Richard and Allison would knock on the door, one knock each, followed by Michael who then said, "Junction." They then stepped back and let Michael open the door. It was totally different from when Richard first opened the bathroom door to Heaven. There were no angelic sentries guarding the doorway and the sky was in twilight. Even flakes of snow blew past the doorway. Heaven itself appeared dark and abandoned. Finally, there was the turbulence being caused by the hot air coming out of the opened doors meeting the cold air of Heaven.

"***Brrrrr!***" groaned Hamilton. "Who left the refrigerator open?"

"Why is it so cold?" asked Israel.

"This is Heaven?" asked Sparky.

"Where is everybody?" asked Thunder.

"Why is it so dark?" Daphne asked aloud, but got no reply.

"I don't like the looks of this," said Lomax.

Daphne turned to Dewey Mitchell. "Will you stay here with my daughter?" He nodded.

Michael drew his shinning broadsword, stepped off the floor and glided through the threshold with ease. Lomax followed, then Israel, Hamilton, Maggy, the boys and all the rest. They would find it odd and difficult as they floated about. Lomax found himself uncontrollably floating upside down and needed a helping hand to right himself.

"That was so weird," he told Israel who gave him the assist.

They all gazed in awe at the massive number of minions flowing out of the doors and gliding towards Heaven. To the

THE DOOR

mortals, they resembled a black cloud.

Lomax turned his attention to Archangel Michael. "Where are your troops? Your Praetorian Guard?"

Michael didn't answer. He appeared insecure and ill at ease. He rubbernecked, seemingly searching for something. *His Praetorians perhaps?*

Suddenly, Lucifer bolted out of one of the opened doors. For now on he would maintain his true form with his long red cape, combat attire and horns. "Yes, Michael? Where is God's army? Better yet, where is our dear Father?"

Uriel flew over to Lucifer just moments before a group of Angels, led by the Palace Lord Administrator, arrived on the scene. The Angels from this group shook the snow off their long flowing capes as they flew through the frosty air.

"Who are they?" asked Daphne.

"Can't you tell?" replied Lomax. "They're traitors."

"My Lord," said the Palace Lord Administrator to Lucifer, "word of your army's arrival has sent the population scurrying to the stars."

"And the Army of Light?" asked Lucifer.

"They, like the Trinity, have vacated, my Lord. Heaven is ours…I mean yours for the taking."

The Palace Lord Administrator turned to Uriel. "You can imagine my shock when I first heard that you had joined the cause."

"I guess I didn't want to end up like one of your museum pieces," replied Uriel.

"Wait a minute here," Lomax said to Michael, "you're giving up without a fight?"

Lucifer glanced over to Lomax. "For once I agree with you. But a victory is a victory no matter how you look at it." He glided closer to Michael, who raised his sword in a defensive manner. "Oh, Michael, is this anyway to treat a relative?"

An arc of electricity spewed forth from Michael's body and surrounded him for a second or two.

"Why aren't they moving?" asked Thunder, referring to the army of darkness.

Lucifer backed away from Michael, then spun round to gaze upon his army. His eyes narrowed as he realized that they weren't moving forward. Millions of them were still flying out of the doors in a steady stream and colliding with the ones who preceded them.

"It's rather obvious," said Lomax. He turned to the mountain of unopened doors that was behind the one that went to the Pilgrim house. "It was something Einstein said about gravity and the warping of time and space. Gravity is the ultimate force in the universe. Without it, you got nothing. No time, no space, no energy." He turned away and smiled. "Why do I get the idea that everything here is the complete opposite of what was? There's hardly any light! And what's the deal with this zero gravity and the snow?"

Daphne backhanded Lomax. "You talk too much!"

One of the ways Lucifer reacted when he was angry was to point his chin skyward. "Uriel, you reported that the oppressive gravity would be removed."

"And it has, brother."

"Oh, now I get it!" said Lomax. "Before, there was an 'oppressive' amount of gravity. No doubt a safeguard against attack, hence the need for wings. Now, there's no gravity. But without wings, how are you going to get around?" Lomax snapped his fingers and turned to Lucifer. "*Ah*, shucks! Your guys don't have any wings!"

Lucifer turned to Lomax and glared at him angrily. "I am growing tired of your insolence."

"Me too!" said Daphne. "Lomax, shut up!"

Lomax raised his hands in defeat.

Lucifer glided over to Uriel. "General, I order you to lead your army to their targets."

Uriel saluted the dark lord by giving the old Roman salute of slapping a fisted right hand against the chest. "Right away, my Lord!" He bolted across the open sky, circled the massive dark army, then returned in a matter of seconds. He stopped and hovered next to Michael.

"What are you doing?" asked Lucifer. "I just gave you a direct order."

"I hear and obey you, my Lord," replied Uriel, with a bow.

Lucifer stared at Uriel with an odd expression on his face.

Lomax chuckled. "How can someone so devious be so easily

THE DOOR

deceived?"

Lucifer started to growl, but he was interrupted by the sound of thousands of doors opening and thousands of winged Angels coming out, led by the Praetorian Guards.

Michael went off with them and engaged the dark army with their swords, spears and arrows. It wasn't much of a battle. The wingless minions were paralyzed by the lack of mobility, while God's army flew about, picking off their targets at will. This was the moment the Praetorians had trained and waited four hundred years for!

"No!" shouted Lucifer. "NO! *NO! NO!*"

Lucifer was enraged. He roared and spewed lightning bolts and tongues of fire in all directions. The squad of Praetorians who flew in to engage the dark master were blasted with lightning bolts and sent hurling far away. He blasted Michael several times with lightning bolts, giving him the thrashing of his spiritual life, shattering the Army Commander's shinny breastplate into a multitude of pieces and sending him hurling through the air. He ended up crashing against the mortals from Virginia and the sheer rock face of the cliff where Richard's door was implanted. He glowed for a time and even grimaced and moaned in pain. And there was fear painted on Michael's face. Hamilton saw it. But it was Uriel who received the brunt of Lucifer's vengeance. When Uriel came swooping in to intervene and rescue his brother and commanding officer, he was lashed with a long burst of lightning, set ablaze and sent hurling and screaming towards Heaven.

"If he can do that to an Archangel…" said Lomax, gesturing to Michael.

"Well," said Israel, "what do you expect? They're fighting the Devil!"

Thousands of God's soldiers and Praetorian Guards went racing in, only to be set on fire and blasted away by Lucifer.

"There's no stopping him!" said Sparky.

Lomax looked around at all the destruction Lucifer was causing. "I'll be damned!"

"You are," said Lucifer, his voice echoing from the distance. He then did something totally unexpected. He flew off and hurled a massive blast of electricity that exploded like a bomb near his dark army. The concussion wave from the blast sent them hurling towards Heaven.

"I think he's figured away around the zero gravity problem," said Sparky.

"It's the colliding hot and cold air masses that are enhancing his powers," said Thunder.

"Thanks for the weather report, Doc," said Lomax.

"And this is for failing me!" Lucifer shouted as he lashed out with a thunderbolt and struck the Palace Lord Administrator and the other traitors, incinerating them. When the smoke cleared, they resembled the other minions.

When the concussion wave reached the Junction, it drove the mortals back towards Richard's bathroom door.

Always the cool headed leader, Hamilton started shoving his boys, Maggy and the others through the doorway into Richard's bedroom. He then confronted a visibly weakened Michael who had stopped glowing.

"Well, Sergeant Major," said Michael, "once more into the breech?"

"Not today, General," said Hamilton, as he grabbed and pushed the archangel towards the bathroom door. Making the switch from weightlessness to gravity wasn't a pleasant experience. They all fell hard on the floor and it was difficult and tiring to get to their feet, especially Michael, who tried and fell down. Unknowingly, Michael's sword fell out of the scabbard and slid under Richard's bed.

Hamilton was the last to cross over.

THE DOOR

"The Door" courtesy of Tom Richardson
"The Northern Lights" courtesy of Bill Plaskon

Chapter Nineteen

THE DOOR

It was Diciembre who first noticed the arcs of electromagnetic energy flowing from the doors at the junction to Lucifer. "Look at this!" He pointed to the streaks of energy flowing from the doors at the Junction to Lucifer. "See how it flows?"

Almost everyone crawled back to the doorway.

"It looks like he's drawing his power directly from the doors!" said Hamilton.

"Which gets their energy from the Northern Lights," said Thunder.

"Which gets their energy directly from the sun," added Sparky.

"Limitless and enormous," said Diciembre.

"How do we fight something so powerful?" asked Israel.

"There's only one thing I know that is more powerful than the Northern Lights or the sun or even Lucifer," said Lomax.

"And what would that be?" asked Daphne.

Everyone, including Michael, who was lying on the floor, turned to Lomax to hear the answer.

But Lomax turned to Danvers and gave him a nod.

"The door...." said Danvers.

All the other humans in the room turned back to Michael to see his reaction to Danvers statement.

Archangel Michael raised an eyebrow and clapped his hands. "Figured it out, did you? Okay, now what?"

All eyes turned back to Lomax, who suddenly appeared not as confident or knowledgeable as before.

Hamilton went over to the doorway and looked out. He stood there, rubbing his chin.

"*Uh, oh,*" said Maggy. "He's thinking again...."

Hamilton turned around and pointed in the direction of the

westside of the basement. "We've got to get the door from the basement up to the second floor and through this doorway."

"It won't fit," said Daphne.

"We'll make it fit," replied Hamilton. "We're carpenters."

Lomax just had to make a comment. "Oh, this is just great! The future of the universe and all of humanity depending on the works of a carpenter!"

"Won't be the first time," said Hamilton, with a smile on his face. He then slapped his hands. "People, let's get to work!" He led the way out of the room. The others scrambled to follow them, leaving Daphne, Lomax and Michael in the bedroom.

Before she left, Daphne backhanded Lomax. "That was a real dumb thing to say!"

Lomax sighed as he reached out a hand to Michael. The Archangel took it and was helped to his feet. "Imagine the likes of me, helping someone like you."

"We shall see..." said the Archangel.

Hamilton was the first to reach the bottom step of the stairway in the basement. For a moment, he stopped and stared at the door he and Levi entombed in a block of concrete. He found a sledge-hammer and started pounding away at the concrete encasement.

It was Maggy who relieved her husband of the sledgehammer. "Let the boys do the work."

"Yes, *ma'am*."

The Hamilton boys took over with whatever tools they could find and made short work of it.

Hamilton gazed up at the bucksaw that was mounted in between two floor joists. It was the same one he and Levi used to cut the trees and mill the wood that was used to build this house. It was dusty and rusted, but still in good shape. With a little assistance from Michael, who glided to the ceiling and removed the mounts, the bucksaw was handed to Hamilton.

"What are you going to do with that?" asked Israel.

"We've got to get a double-sided church door up to Richard's room and through the bathroom doorway."

"You're going to saw holes in my house with that thing?" asked Israel.

"You mean my house?" said Levi, with a grin.

When the door was finally freed from its concrete tomb, it fell

THE DOOR

to the floor with a loud crash.

Something totally unexpected occurred at that precise moment. Dara went up to the door and reached out her hand to touch it. Her hand went right through it.

"Did you see that?" asked Daphne.

"Her hand passed right through it!" said Mitchell.

Lomax reached out to the door and his hand touched the wood. So did the six boys and Levi when they tried. When Mitchell and Daphne reached out to the door, their hands went right through it.

"I don't get it?" asked Lomax. "How is it my hand didn't pass through, but Dara's, Daphne's and Mitchell's did?"

"All of us have been through a door portal," said Danvers. He then pointed to Dara, Mary, Daphne and Mitchell, "except them."

"That proves it," said Sparky.

"Proves what?" asked Israel.

"We're out of phase with this reality and they're not."

"It's proton absorption," said Thunder. "Plain and simple. Every time you go through an active door…"

"…You receive a residual amount," said Sparky. "We absorbed these protons, but what about the door jams and walls in this house?"

"The protons are absorbed by the carbon in all living things," revealed Michael, "especially wood."

"Yes," said Diciembre, "like photosynthesis. But the wood on this door has been dead for over four hundred years." He turned to Thunder. "How can it absorb anything? Can you explain that, Doctor?"

"You're asking me?" she replied. "I threw away the science book on all of this a long time ago."

"Can we please stay focused on the main issue here?" asked Hamilton. "If the door is out of phase with this reality, then it should go right through the house walls. Correct?"

"Only the ones *out of phase* with this reality," said Michael. "The rest you'll have to cut through."

Israel pointed to the steel door at the top of the stairs. "You didn't say anything about steel…"

The pins were removed to the steel door and someone gave it a good kick to send it crashing on the floor of the foyer. The metal door jam followed.

THE DOOR

Sparky pulled the main switch to the housebreakers and turned off all electricity to the house. This allowed Hamilton and Fetch to use the bucksaw and cut a wide wedge into the wall wide enough to slide the door through. When Hamilton built the house, he used a lot of wood and gypsum and it took a lot of muscle to slice out a wedge in the wall. It took all six boys and all four adult men to lift the door onto the handrails of the banister, then push it up to the top of the basement's stairway and push and pull it through the hastily cut wedge in the wall. It crashed on the floor of the foyer. They then picked up the door, carried it across the foyer and laid it on the handrails to the second stairway. They then pushed the door up to the second floor. When they reached the second floor, they didn't stop their forward momentum. Growling like angry bears they charged towards Richard's bedroom and the door passed right through the wall and nearly passed clear through the bedroom before it stopped and mysteriously hovered in midair. The bottom edge of the door had passed through the house's exterior wall and was clearly visible outside of the house. The men and boys went into the bedroom.

"Now that's something you don't see everyday," said Mitchell.

When the women and children heard Mitchell's comment, they dashed up the stairway and made their way into Richard's bedroom.

Everyone stopped and stared at the hovering church door.

"Whatever we're going to do," said Mitchell, as he stared out the bedroom window at the street below, "we better do it fast before people outside start to taking notice of all this."

Each man assumed a position around the door and waited for Hamilton to give the order. "All together now," he said. "PUSH!" One and all gave the door a mighty shove towards the bathroom.

The door phased right through the bathroom's door jam and wall and floated out into the growing darkness. Almost immediately, the door was struck by powerful arcs of electricity from the other doors in The Junction.

"I'm not sure this was a good plan," said Diciembre. "Look at all the energy it's getting from the other doors."

"Good," said Lomax. "It's powering up. That's what we want."

Michael, still weakened, slowly glided into the bedroom, then

THE DOOR

laid down on the floor, next to the bathroom doorway. He was breathing hard as he watched the door float off. He smiled. "Ah, you mortals! You never cease to amaze me!"

"You all right, Prince?" Lomax asked him.

"Must be the gravity…of the situation," said Michael.

Meanwhile, Lucifer was fully engaged and totally engrossed in his one-sided battle, unleashing barrage after barrage of lightning bolts and powerful concussion waves that decimated the rank and file of Praetorian Guard units—sending them hurling off into wide expanse of the cosmos. Even though he was pre-occupied fighting off God's Angels, he noted the efforts of Lomax and the others and the presence of the door at the Junction. He shook his head. Whether it was in disbelief, discontent or some other emotion, he didn't indicate it at that time. There was no doubt about it, *victory was his for the taking!*

His mortal foes assembled by the opened bathroom doorway and stuck their heads through to see what was going on.

"He's still at it," said Lomax.

"You will never meet anyone more determined…" said Michael.

"I got news for you, Prince," said Lomax. "I meet that guy every morning when I looked in the mirror."

"But do you like who you see?"

Lomax thought it over and shook his head.

Israel uncharacteristically became impatient "Okay, now what?"

"We wait…" said Lomax

"Wait for what?" asked Israel.

 "For the door to knock."

"And then what?"

"Then, somebody goes out there and opens it."

"Do you have any idea what will happen then?" asked Maggy.

"Actually, I do. Unfortunately, it's the only way."

"He's right," said Sparky.

There was an upheaval of remarks from the others in the room.

"You're forgetting something," said Daphne. "Actually two things. You need for one or both of the children to be present—."

"—You mean out there?" asked Thunder. "Not with my kid you don't! I just got her back." She reached out and grabbed her

THE DOOR

daughter.

Lomax turned to Israel. "What about your son?"

Israel gestured to his son to come to him. "You up for this, Richard?"

Without hesitation he replied, "Yeah, dad."

"Me too," said Allison, with determination in her tone. She pushed away her mother's outstretched hand. "It's payback time!"

Thunder sighed as she turned to the other adults. "She gets that from me."

"What's the other thing we're forgetting?" asked Hamilton.

"Somebody has to knock on the door from the other side," said Danvers.

Freckles gulped. "You mean, from Hell?"

Lomax stared at Michael, who stared intently back at him. One studying the other. Neither expressed any emotions or reactions to what was being said by the others.

"There's nobody down there," said Moon. "They all *be* over *thar!*" He pointed to the dark cloud.

"You're wrong," said Diciembre. "Gabriel is still down there with those people."

Michael raised his hand and whispered. "Not so loud! He might hear you." He glanced out the doorway at Lucifer, looking for a reaction. When there wasn't one, he turned back and continued staring at Lomax.

Danvers lowered his head in shame. "They're in Hell because of me!"

"Wait," said Diciembre. "They're okay. He's protecting them. He's been doing it for four hundred years. He's got a cloak that makes them invisible."

"And how do you know that?" asked Mitchell.

"Gabriel grabbed me and pulled me in. The demons walked right passed us...otherwise they would have gotten me."

"Now why would God create a cloak for his Angels?" asked Lomax.

"Only Archangels have the power to cloak," revealed Michael.

Lomax smirked. "And I wonder who came up with the idea in the first place?"

Michael jerked a thumb at Lucifer.

"Figures? Can you send…you know who a message...to knock

THE DOOR

on the door?"

"Not while he's cloaked."

Lomax turned his gaze back to all the others. "Well, we're right back where we started from. Somebody is going to have to go down there and do it. Any volunteers?"

No one stepped forward, not even Danvers. It was the last place he wanted to go to. But Michael asked him anyway. "What about you, Nathaniel?"

Danvers cringed with fright. "Ask of me anything but that!"

"I said that your redemption would be costly..."

But Danvers looked away and shook his head.

"I'll go," announced Lomax.

"How would you get down there?" asked Israel, with concern in his tone. He did not like this idea at all.

"Through one of the doors the demons came through." Lomax gestured to the hundreds of opened doors in the junction. As he started to move towards the doorway, he was restrained by Michael's outstretched hand.

"You'll never make it," said Michael. "He's seen the door and he's waiting for *you* to try something...brave and foolish."

"Don't you mean stupid?" remarked Daphne.

Lomax pointed to himself. "Who, me?"

"Yes, Lomax, you." Michael then got to his feet. "Besides, it's not necessary for you to sacrifice yourself...*yet*."

"I don't like the way he said the word *'yet'*," said Daphne.

"Some people do the dumbest things at the most important times of their lives," Michael said to Lomax. "Let not the next few minutes be yours."

For Lomax it was like getting slapped across the face. "I should have jumped."

"I'll go," said Michael.

"You can't do both," said Mitchell, "knock on the door and then answer it."

"He's right," said Hamilton.

Suddenly, a familiar sound was heard. One of the doors in The Junction closed. It was followed by another, then another until all of them slammed shut.

"*Them* doors are closing!" said Red, as he gazed out the bathroom doorway.

THE DOOR

"Lucifer…" said Danvers.

"Yes," said Michael, "he's sealing off all the entrances and exits."

"Smart move," said Mitchell. "Now there's only one way in…or out." He gestured to the church door.

"Looks like you're going to need another plan, boy," Hamilton said to Lomax.

"Maybe not," said Lomax as he stared at Michael, studying him. "I need to roll back the tape to something you just said. *It's not necessary for you to sacrifice yourself.* Prince, there's something you're not telling us."

Michael reached out and covered Lomax's mouth with his hand. The Archangel once again gazed out the door to see if there was any reaction from Lucifer.

When Michael pulled his hand away, Lomax whispered, "You got that covered, don't you?"

Michael answered that question with a long, stone-faced stare. Then:

"Richard…Allison?" said Michael.

"Yes, my Prince?" replied Richard.

"Yes, my Prince?" replied Allison.

Michael reached across the threshold, grabbed a long leafy vine that grew next to the door. He gave it a powerful yank, pulling out the roots. After he brought the vines into the bedroom, he tied the ends around Richard and Allison waists, then handed the other ends to the Hamilton boys. He turned back to Richard and Allison. "When I wave to you, I want you both to cross the threshold and float out a few feet, but no further. Understand?"

Both children exchanged a glance. Nothing more needed to be said.

Michael turned to the Hamilton boys. "You're job is to pull them back in."

"When?" said Matthew.

Michael gave a smile. "Oh, you'll know."

"I just knew he was going to say that," said Matthew.

"Hold on here," Lomax said to Michael. "Are you thinking about going out there and answering that door by yourself?"

"Yes!"

"Well forget it. You're half beaten to death." In a move that

THE DOOR

completely surprised the Archangel and everyone in the room
Lomax said, "Besides, it's a double door. You'll need another set
of hands. I'll go with you."

"No!" said Danvers, with great concern in his voice. It
surprised Michael and especially Lomax. "You can't. Lomax,
you'll be sucked in…"

"…Along with everything else," added Allison.

"And all of them," said Richard, gesturing to the cloud of
minions in the distance.

"That's the plan, people!" said Hamilton.

"And it's a bad one because you'll end up in a place where
nobody gets out," Daphne said to Lomax.

Lomax gave a wink to Daphne. "Who me, *na!* Come on baby,
you know I'll find a way out." He turned to Michael, who was
shaking his head.

"He'll detect you the moment you cross this threshold," said
Daphne.

"Not," said Michael, "if we go together." The lower half of his
body became invisible, demonstrating to all the power of his cloak.

Even though Hamilton had fought in one major pitched battle
during the Civil War, he knew that he lacked the expertise and
experience to talk tactics and strategies with someone the likes of
Archangel Michael. On the other hand, he did suggest to General
Burbridge that the Union Army shift its tactics from marching
lumbering infantry forces into Southwest Virginia to the fast
moving and hard hitting cavalry. He also recommended the use of
diversionary tactics that General Stoneman used so proficiently
that he seized the towns of Bristol and Kingsport, Tennessee and
Saltville, Virginia without his forces firing a shot. So with a little
confidence in his tone he said, "You're going to have to cover a lot
of ground to reach that church door, cloaked or not. You're going
to need a diversion."

Michael gave it some thought and replied, "You got one in
mind?"

Hamilton looked away. His mind raced in search of one. But in
the end, he shook his head.

Maggy confronted her husband. "It's not so easy when you
don't know what's going to happen."

The Archangel reached out and put his arm around Lomax's

THE DOOR

shoulder. As he stepped off and crossed the threshold, Israel lunged forward and grabbed for Michael's cape and a wing and all three disappeared.

"No, wait!" Danvers rushed over to the doorway and looked around, but could not see Michael and Lomax and Israel. He backed off, breathing hard. "I should be doing this, not them. I am the cause of all of this."

When Danvers turned around, he spotted Michael's broadsword under Richard's bed. He rushed over to the bed and retrieved it.

Daphne recognized the broadsword. "That's Michael's!" She turned to the doorway. "Oh, no! He went out there without a weapon!"

"Move Daphne," said Danvers. When she got out of his way, he took off running, then let out a throaty battle cry as he crossed the threshold and leapt into the space between Richard's bathroom and the Lord of Darkness.

Meanwhile, Lucifer was unleashing a lightning bolt when he felt a presence passing behind him. "Whose that? Gabriel…? No—MICHAEL!" He ceased fire and whipped around, but saw or felt nothing further. It was then he heard Danver's yelp.

"Well, well, well, if it isn't the great traitor of the Puritans—welding a sword no less."

Danvers was going to strike at Lucifer with all his might, but suddenly an unseen force stopped him in mid-air and pulled away Michael's sword. He watched the broadsword continue to travel forward, then stop, flip end over end and then bolt towards him. The broadsword struck Danvers in the chest and passed through him until the point of the sword was sticking about two feet out from behind. He was then sent hurling at breakneck speed towards the rock face next to the bathroom door, where the point of the sword impacted. Danvers screamed in agony.

Maggy saw the whole thing and called out to her husband. "Ham, get my medical bag!" She then crossed the threshold and made her way to Danvers by pulling on the vines that grew on the rock face.

Hamilton stuck his head out of the bathroom doorway. "Maggy?" He then followed her to where Danvers was so firmly fastened into the rock face.

A stream of blood poured forth from Danver's chest and floated

THE DOOR

away. He appeared pale, light-headed and weak. The amount of blood being released from his wound seemed to diminish until at one point there was nothing more than a few drops.

"Hurry, Ham!" shouted Maggy.

Danvers smiled at her and shook his head. "No, Maggy," he said in a whisper. "It's over. At long last...."

Hamilton arrived a moment later with the medical bag. When Danvers reached out his hand, Hamilton took it.

"Ham, I was a good partner, wasn't I?" asked Danvers.

"The best. And John, you were my friend." Hamilton's eyes started to well up.

Danvers closed his eyes, exhaled and expired.

"This can't be happening," Maggy said to Hamilton. "The Devil can't kill."

They turned to Lucifer who started to glow like the Northern Lights.

"Finally," said Lucifer, "the power over life...and death."

"If you have that power," said Hamilton, "then bring life back to Danvers."

Lucifer laughed. "Oh, Ham. He is but the first to die. One down...seven billion to go!"

"The end of humanity," said Maggy.

Just then Michael de-cloaked. He was genuinely surprised to find Israel grasping at his uniform. The Archangel shoved each man off towards the door. He then turned towards Richard's bathroom door and gave a wave.

Both Richard and Allison crossed the threshold and hovered in midair as they held on to the leafy vines.

"Whatever you're thinking," Lucifer said to Michael as he glided towards the door, "it's not going to work."

Michael reached for his broadsword, but found the scabbard empty. His only recourse was to back away from Lucifer.

"Oh," replied Lomax, "and what would that be?" He diverted Lucifer's attention away form Michael.

"Do you take me for a fool?" thundered Lucifer. "I understand the power of the doors. Especially this one. That's why I made sure there's no one in Hell to knock on it." He waved his hand at his decimated minions floating aimlessly in the distance. "All of my followers are here."

THE DOOR

Israel turned to Lomax and said, "Maybe this wasn't such a good idea."

As Lucifer glided to within a few yards of the door, he put his hands behind his back so as to not appear threatening to anyone. "Oh, Michael, Michael, Michael. Where pray tell is our dear brother, Gabriel? When has he ever missed a good battle?" He jerked a thumb at the church door. "Or is he down there…getting ready to knock on the door?" He shook his head. "There is just one problem with that plan. I knew all along he's been there…watching and waiting. But *alas*, he won't be knocking on any doors. I can assure you of that."

"How?" asked Lomax.

"Before I left, I committed my best army to seize and detain him. He's not going anywhere."

"So," said Lomax, "some of your followers are still down there then?"

"Lomax!" said Michael.

"This guy just can't tell the truth," said Lomax. "Just a minute ago, he said there was no body down there. Now there's a whole army. So which *lie* is it, Your Highness?"

Lucifer sighed. "Lomax, you are beginning to annoy me. No wonder your wife complains to you…you know…in bed." Lucifer smirked.

Both Israel and Michael gave Lomax an odd look.

Lomax winced. "You know about that?" he whispered, not wanting to be heard by the others, especially the children and his wife.

He drew closer to Lomax. "I know everything! And I know that this war of the Angels is over and that I've won."

"Are you sure?" asked Lomax.

Lucifer turned slightly and gestured to the Praetorians who were floating aimlessly some distance away. "It's rather obvious, don't you think? No one can compete with my power." He raised his left hand and the thousands of doors that covered the mountain behind them surged with energy. In a flash, thousands of energy streams bolted to Lucifer's outstretched hand.

Both Lomax and Israel cringed. Lucifer's power was awesome.

"Join me!" said Lucifer.

"Who me?" asked Lomax, pointing to himself. "You talking to

THE DOOR

me?"

"Of course. I could use a resourceful man like yourself." He waved his arm towards Richard's bathroom door. "You above all the others on that miserable planet…remind me…of me!"

Lomax was taken aback by that compliment. "Really?" A cocky expression flashed across his face.

"Don't listen to him," said Michael.

Lucifer drew a little closer to Lomax and swept his arm in the direction of Heaven. "Look at it, Lomax. It's *ours* to rule."

"*Ours?* Why do you need me when you got all this power?"

"Because I think I need to change my ways. I need to be more giving and caring…"

Lomax made a face. "*Uh*, giving and caring is not exactly my forte."

Lucifer placed his hands on his chest and gazed skyward. "I want to be loved and worshiped."

Lomax tapped himself on the chest and gave a nod. "Loved and worshiped, now that I'm good at."

"Yeah, right!" shouted Daphne from the doorway.

Israel spoke up. "You want to be God?"

"I am God." Lucifer's tone was not so friendly.

Lomax snapped his fingers. "Wait! Hold the phone here! Don't you need to get rid of the old one first?"

"I already have. He's long gone!" He drew a little closer and really laid on the charm. "I want you to think about something."

"Who me?" asked Lomax.

"Yes, you! You're special! Besides, the number two spot is open." He pointed to Lomax, then to himself. "It could be you and me, Lomax. We could rule Heaven and earth together!"

Lomax was floored by the dark lord's offer. "***Gee!*** And here I thought you didn't like me!"

Diciembre stuck his head across the threshold and called out "Don't be a fool, Lomax!"

Lucifer instantly became enraged. His face and body turned blood red and he spun round and faced the bathroom door, pointing his right hand at it. Electromagnetic energy started to surge through his body as he got ready to lash out at Diciembre and the two children hanging next to the door.

Lomax had to think fast to save them. "I wouldn't let him upset you. Trust me, he's not worth it."

Lucifer hesitated, thought it over, then powered down. There was a big smile on his face as he spun round. "There. You see. I need you."

"Oh, come on," said Lomax, "the only thing you want…is this door!"

Lucifer's smile vanished. He then fired a massive bolt of lightning at the door. Lomax, Israel and Michael ducked behind it just in time. The door took the punishment and was unscathed.

"That was not wise," said Michael.

"Yeah," said Israel, "now you got him mad!"

Suddenly, the sky went completely and totally black as the sun that shined its golden rays on Heaven seemed to go dark.

"*Uh, oh!*" said Lomax. "Who turned out the lights?"

The only light being projected came from the arcs of electricity that surged through the dark lord's body. He started to laugh uproariously. "I, Lucifer am now the power and the light!"

Israel looked over to Michael, who now hung his head low. "This is not good."

Then it happened....

"Ham," said Maggy, "look at the sword! It's moving!"

The broadsword started to come out of Danver's chest as though someone was pulling on it. As soon as the sword was extracted, the blood that had seeped out streamed back into Danver's chest. A moment later, his eyes opened and he took a deep breath of air. To Maggy's amazement, the wound healed itself in a matter of seconds, without even leaving a scar. "Oh, dear…." He said to Maggy.

"Hey, everybody," shouted Hamilton, "Danvers is alive!"

"How'd that happen?" Lomax asked Lucifer.

Knock! Knock! It came from the church door. It surprised everyone—especially Lucifer.

"Hello!" said Lomax. "Avon calling!"

"I never thought I'd be happy to hear that sound again!" said Diciembre as he reached out to Allison. "Time for everybody to get inside!" He pulled in Allison, then Richard.

It took both Maggy and Hamilton to guide Danvers back into Richard's bedroom. Diciembre then helped them inside.

THE DOOR

Lucifer growled in anger. He raised his arms high and unleashed a steam of lightning bolts.

Diciembre closed the bathroom door just before the lightning bolts struck it.

Michael said to the two mortals, "Let's do it!" He climbed over the top of the door with Israel right behind him. They grabbed the left-side door handle, then looked over to Lomax.

As Lomax made his way to the front of the door a beautiful female Angel clad in a Praetorian uniform appeared next to him. He was instantly smitten. "Well, hello!"

"I'll help you!" she said as she reached for the door handle.

"Who are you?" asked Lomax.

"I'm Joan," she replied with a gorgeous smile. "Joan of Arc."

Lomax's face lit up. "Cool!"

"On the count of 3!" shouted Michael. "3, 2, 1! PULL!"

Lucifer saw the danger, bolted to The Junction and grabbed hold of one of the many doors.

The two mortals and two Angels pulled on the door handles and opened the old church door. There was a burst of bright light followed by an enormous vacuum brought on by the violent decompression of one dimension opening to another. The minion army—hundreds of millions strong—was pulled into the doorway, including the Palace Lord Administrator and the other traitors. The only object that resisted the powerful vacuum was Michael's broadsword, which hung in the air. There was no sound and it was over within seconds. The vacuum caused Richard's bathroom door to open, giving the mortals therein an opportunity to witness the event. The vacuum ceased when the atmosphere between the two dimensions equalized. There was one last burst of energy from the door before both angels and humans were sent flying off into the side of the mountain. When Lomax and Israel regained consciousness and opened their eyes, they noticed that the once impervious old Puritan church door was ablaze. The high reaching flames illuminated the area. They also realized that Lucifer was laying only a few feet away from them.

Hamilton and the others got to their feet and cheered. "It worked!" he said repeatedly.

"Yes, it did," said Diciembre. "Better yet, look! The door is burning!"

THE DOOR

Hamilton glanced over to Maggy. "You don't know how glad I am to see that!"

"This nightmare isn't over…yet," said Maggy.

Michael took flight and extended his hand to Israel. Lomax took Joan's and they were flown to the front side of the burning church door.

Lucifer followed them. He then realized that Michael wasn't in a weakened state anymore—if ever—when the Archangel raised his arm and his broadsword responded by shooting across the distance and into his hand. "It was all an act. Wasn't it?"

Lucifer started waving his arms and grimacing and sulking.

"What's he groaning about?" asked Lomax.

"Lucifer thinks Gabriel knocked on the door," replied Joan.

"If not Gabriel, then whom?" he roared. "**Tell me!**"

Israel spotted a shape approaching the door from the other side. "I think we're about to find out."

All eyes turned and focused on the souls of 19 people who came floating through of the flaming doorway.

"The Puritans?" asked Lucifer. "You mean I had them all along? But how...?" The answer came with the entrance of Archangel Gabriel. "Of course. So, it was *you* who knocked on the door?"

"Not I," replied Gabriel. His uniform was in tatters and his body armor was bent and shattered.

"Was it a good battle, brother?" Michael asked Gabriel.

Gabriel held up the broken sword and smiled. "Oh, the best!"

"If not you, then who?" asked Lucifer. He then brought a hand up to his face. "My best army couldn't detain him!"

"But they did, brother" said Gabriel. "One against so many. I may be good, but not that good."

"So then there was another? *Who?*"

But Gabriel didn't reply. He just grinned and joined up with Michael and Uriel, who suddenly appeared out of thin air none the worse for wear.

The urge to witness and be a part of the event overrode any fears the mortals may have had. One by one, they crossed over the threshold. For a short time they floated uncontrollably in the air, until a squad of Praetorians came swooping in and took hold of them.

THE DOOR

But of all the humans, no one showed more emotion than Danvers, who reached out to the nineteen Puritans and openly wept. "Please forgive me," he said repeatedly. A Praetorian brought him over to the Puritans.

"We have, Nathaniel," one of the Puritan woman replied. She then embraced him as did the others.

"Oh," said Lucifer, "this is pathetic! Please forgive me." He said mockingly. "Look at him cower to them. I COWER TO NO ONE! "

"Four hundred years in Hell and they forgive him," said Israel. "I don't know if I could do that."

Lucifer saw a chance to score some points. "I must say, that I too am moved by the warmth of emotions I have witnessed here." He turned to the three Archangels. "So much so, that I am willing to forgive you, my brothers for the thousands of centuries of depravation that I have known."

"That is rather good of you, brother," said Gabriel.

"God should be forgiving," said Lucifer. "Join with me, my brothers and we shall build a new Heaven…"

Lomax sighed. "*Ohhhh*, will you listen to this guy! You just don't get it, do you?"

Lucifer turned to Lomax and glared at him with red angry eyes.

"This was no battle," continued Lomax. "I've seen more action on a video game. No, all of this, the doors, Uriel the traitor, the absence of gravity and now the sun going dark was all part of an elaborate plan."

"To do what?" thundered Lucifer.

"Free the nineteen," replied Israel. He turned to Lomax. "Finally, that number makes sense."

Lucifer started to sweep his arms about and roar like a lion after a kill. "No! My victory is complete! I AM NOW GOD!"

"Oh, yeah?" asked Lomax, raising his right hand and gesturing to the dark sun. "It's kind of dark out here. You know, an old blind man recently told me, *'When everything goes completely black, just ask someone to turn the lights on'*. Well, I'm asking. How about some light?"

Lucifer turned to the darkening sun and waved his arms and released an enormous amount of lighting bolts into the air. But nothing happened.

THE DOOR

"I thought so," said Lomax. "Everything we have experienced here, up to this point, has been a diversion."

Michael, Uriel and Gabriel exchanged a glance and Lucifer saw it.

"Diversion?" asked Lucifer. "To do what?"

"I don't know," said Lomax, "but one of us is missing. Guess *He* needed a little time…alone…to do whatever." He elbowed Michael. "Right boys?"

Lucifer realized what Lomax was saying was true when rays of blinding golden light came forth from the other side of the burning church door. The intensity was such that the dark lord had to cover his eyes. ***"NOOOOOO!"***

God the Father slowly emerged from the double doorway in a ball of light that surged with energy. Only *His* face, chest and parts of *His* arms were visible to those who beheld *Him*. Only Lucifer had difficulty gazing upon *Him*. To everyone else a sense of gladness and peace ran through their bodies. *He* glided over to the nineteen Puritans and spent a moment with each, touching their faces and outstretched hands, whispering to them and blessing them.

Lucifer went crazy. "It should be me you should worship and love! Not HIM! I built all this!" He gestured to Heaven. "And I could destroy it just as easily….I…I…"

God turned and shot a look at Lucifer that silenced the fallen Angel. *He* then floated off, glancing to the mortals from Virginia and gave a respectful nod.

Hamilton made the sign of the cross.

"Why did you do that?" asked Maggy. "You're not Catholic."

"I am now!"

The three holy Archangels and Joan of Arc bowed to God and *He* responded in kind. When *He* swept past Lomax, *He* stopped suddenly, turned and placed a hand on the human's shoulder, but looked off in another direction.

He spoke a soft and pleasant voice. "I found your prayer…quite profound." *He* shot a parting glance to Lomax and gave a wink as *He* floated off.

Lomax being Lomax, he said, "Regards to Moses."

That made God grin.

The grin immediately evaporated when *He* confronted a

THE DOOR

cowering, whimpering Lucifer and held up a fisted hand. *His* fisted hand shook, as though *He* was trying to decide whether or not to strike his one time beloved Archangel.

Lucifer opened his eyes and saw the vibrating fist and the arcs of energy swirling all around it.

God's hand then became steady. The index finger was raised and *He* made it move to the left then to the right and then back again.

"Shame, shame," uttered Lomax. "You've been a bad boy."

Uriel flew over to the door, pointed his arms into the opening and unleashed a stream of white-hot fire into it. Suddenly, all the doors in the "Junction" that were connected to Hell blew open and spewed fire. It wasn't long before they disintegrated into ash. Lucifer's electromagnetic power source was no more. When flames came shooting out of the old Puritan church doorway, Uriel backed off and flew to God's side.

"Time for you to be my light again, Uriel, " said God.

"I was once your light," said Lucifer.

"Yes," replied God, in a low tone. "Once...."

God and Uriel bolted across the sky towards the darkening sun. There was a spectacular flash as the sun seemed to re-ignite, bathing Heaven and the surrounding area with golden rays of light. It was then the massive Army of God was seen, hovering over Heaven. Billions of winged Angels.

Suddenly, all of Heaven shook as gravity returned. Only the Angels remained aloft. Everything and everyone else landed gently onto the ground, with a few notable exceptions. Lucifer hit the ground hard and so did the church door.

The Angels of Heaven responded to their victory over evil with a round of uproarious cheering and play of trumpets.

The oppressive gravity was too powerful for even Lucifer. He flapped his wings as hard as he could to no avail. He was grounded. The door was severely damaged and totally engulfed in flames. He knew that he had lost and that it was time for him to go. But not until he listened and heard the multitude of Heavenly souls pray aloud the Lord's Prayer.

"Our Father, who art in Heaven, hallowed be thy name. Thy Kingdom come, thy will be done, on earth as it is in Heaven. Give us this day our daily bread. And forgive us our trespasses, as we

THE DOOR

forgive those who trespass against us. And lead us not into temptation, but deliver us from evil. For thine is the Kingdom, the power and the glory. Amen."

Daphne pursed her lips and blew a whistle in Lucifer's direction. "Hey, try to beat that!"

Lomax sighed. "Who's got the big mouth now, *huh?*"

Lucifer was not amused. He then called out. "I didn't win today, but I won't go home short handed. Come Nathaniel. You too Lomax."

"Oh, no!" said Daphne.

Danvers lowered his head and stepped off towards the dark lord. Several of the nineteen Pilgrims called out and reached out to him, but he knew that it was time for him to pay for his terrible sins.

"Excuse me," a man with a rich Boston accent called out.

Danvers recognized it. He lifted his head and spotted the former President walking towards him. The former President had wings, but preferred to walk to Danvers. "Mr. President?" They shook hands.

"Get away from him, he's mine!" boomed Lucifer.

The former President held up a transparent information pad. "I represent Mr. Pilgrim a.k.a. John Danvers in this matter."

"You're practicing law?" asked Danvers.

"Dick Nixon and I hung out a shingle some years ago, specializing in representing wayward souls." He gave his winning smile. "Like us."

"You're friends with Nixon?"

"We always were, except when we ran for President and now when there's a Duke and *H'vard* game." He glanced at his wrist-watch. "Oh, we better shove off. I've scheduled a hearing for you with Saint Peter and he doesn't like to be kept waiting."

"Are you representing Lomax too?" asked Lucifer.

Lomax gulped. So did Daphne.

"No," said the former President.

Lucifer smiled. "Then come, Lomax!" He even chuckled.

Lomax shot a glance to Daphne and Dara and his shoulders sank. "*Oh, no...*" **GAME OVER!**

Daphne screamed!

"Excuse me," said the former President. "Lomax isn't dead, besides...he was just blessed by the Almighty. So, he's not going

THE DOOR

anywhere, especially, not with you." He shot a glance to Lomax. "At least not today. As for tomorrow, well, that's up to him." It was a well-worded warning that Lomax recognized immediately.

Lomax got so excited that he rushed over to Daphne and Dara, threw his arms around them and kissed them like never before.

"I believe your business is done here," the former President said to Lucifer. "So be gone!"

Lucifer turned to Gabriel, Michael and Uriel. "You three did all of this…for them?" He pointed at the Puritans.

"For nineteen souls or for one," replied Gabriel. "It makes no difference to us." He raised his index finger mockingly to his former brother. "But that is where we differ with the likes of you."

Michael turned to his soldiers. "Praetorians, why are we here?"

"*For the Nineteen!*" they roared back.

"*For the Nineteen!*" others started to shout from far away. Before long, whole throngs were shouting it and the Praetorians and regular soldiers were pounding their spears against their shields in cadence with the chant.

Lucifer growled as he gave a last look to Lomax, then dove into the shooting flames of the door.

Seconds later, the flames consumed all of the old oak and the door turned to ash.

Hamilton and the others gazed up at the mountain and where there were thousands of doors, now trees abound. "Are all the doors gone?"

"Not all," replied Michael, in an assuring tone.

An Angel came forward and Danvers recognized her. "Oh, my goodness! It can't be?"

"Hello, John," she said as she went up to Danvers with her arms held out.

Danvers took her hands into his. "Can you find it in your heart to forgive me?"

Lomax pulled himself away from Daphne and Dara. "Mom? Is that you?"

"Yes, dear. It's me."

Lomax pointed his finger to his mother, then to Danvers. "You're my father? You!"

"Yes, Eddi. And that was the name I intended to give you."

"That's means…I'm a Pilgrim!" Lomax shot a glance to Israel.

THE DOOR

Danvers tossed him a set of keys. "There's a will in the bank deposit box. You're the silent partner now." He turned his gaze to Israel. "Work together you two."

"We will," said Israel with a smile.

"Good bye, son," said Lomax's mother. "I'll be seeing you."

Danvers offered his forearm to the lady and so did the former President. They then leisurely strolled off to Heaven.

THE DOOR

Epilog

IT'S PAYBACK TIME!

When Hamilton came down the stairway

to the foyer, the front door was out of phase. "Look! Do you see it?"

Maggy and the boys were excited.

"What does it mean, *pa?*" asked Moon.

Hamilton took Maggy by the hand. "It means we can go home now. But should we? We could stay here."

"No," said Dewey Mitchell. "You've got to go."

"All of you," added Sparky.

"Why?" asked Maggy.

"Because," said Sparky, "my great, grandfather was Fetch Hamilton."

Fetch did a double take. "What?"

"Mine," added Mitchell, "was Freckles Hamilton."

Freckles gasped. "I'm going to be a father? *Oh, no!*"

"Heck," said Mitchell, "half the town is kin to you people. You've got to go back!"

Hamilton turned to Maggy and smiled. "Do you know what they're saying, honey?"

Maggy smiled. "Grandchildren!" It was the one thing they always wanted and never thought they would have.

"Boys," said Hamilton, "let's go home!" He led the way back into the past.

When they got there, Joe was hoisting a sign over the entrance to the Hamilton property entrance. It read: *"The Lucky Seven Ranch."*

When the turboprop plane landed at the airport of Revelation Fiord,

THE DOOR

RCMP Inspector Seacrest was there to meet his daughter, Thunder and Sparky. After hugging and kissing both Thunder and his daughter, Seacrest shook Sparky's hand and thanked him.

But no one was happier to see Sparky than the mayor. "Thank God you've come back to us," he said. "After the door burnt up all of our satellites dishes got fried!"

"Oh, how terrible," said Sparky. He then turned to Thunder and said, "It's nice to know you're needed in this world."

Thunder kissed him on the lips and said, "Don't be working too late, *eh?*" She flashed her eyes at him.

"Mayor," said Sparky, "take me to the nearest dish! And hurry!"

Diciembre looked out the side window of the black SUV he was riding in and got a glimpse of the White House. He turned to Deputy Director Blackburn and said, "First time I've been invited to the White House. Well, I've been to Hell and back. This shouldn't be too bad."

Israel knocked on the front door and waited a moment. Don Beech opened the door. He was naked and there was a naked woman with him. Israel was shocked. "Don?"

"Hello Pilgrim."

"I think I owe you a barn."

"For-get-it. I'm-selling-the-damn-farm-and-get'n my-sorry-ass-back-to-Iowa!" He then slammed the door shut and let out a happy howl.

Dale Bonham and his wife were standing on the sidewalk, gazing at the plot of land where their house once stood. They were still in a state of shock. They were hurled out of one of the other doors in the Pilgrim house before all the doors were deactivated. They had been in limbo for seven years. Daphne and Mary and the kids went up to them.

"We lost everything," said Dale.

Daphne presented Dale with the keys to her house. "It's yours. We got the other."

"And you'll love the murals," said Mary, with a smile.

*   *   *

THE DOOR

The meeting took place in the dead of night and in an old abandoned wood frame house that no one had lived in for years. It was overgrown with vines and in a terrible shape. But it was a perfect location for a meth lab. Four police chiefs, wearing their uniforms and breath masks, walked out of the kitchen that served as a working lab and went into the living room. Toxic fumes filled the air. A pile of of currency covered the folding table. The ringleader was Dewey Mitchell's Police Chief and he held up a brief case.

"It belongs to Dewey," he said. "Time for some payback for all of our labs he shut down! His fingerprints are all over it. We'll fill it with cash and leave it right here. When our snitch calls this place in, of course no body will be here and that will be the end of Dewey Mitchell."

"How many years ago did we cook up this idea of becoming cops," said one of the other police chiefs, "to cover our tracks?"

"We've eliminated all of our competition and we're running the DEA in circles. Man, do we got it made!"

They let out a cheer!

Knock! Knock!

It came from the front door. It brought total silence from the four police chiefs.

"Don't open it," one chief said.

"Yeah," said another, "I've heard all kinds of stories about people who answer a knocking door and disappear."

"It's all bull." The Police Chief grabbed the doorknob, turned it and pulled. He was instantly blinded by powerful beams of light.

"Get your hands up where I can see them!" shouted a man. The man turned out to be a Drug Enforcement Agent (DEA) and he entered the room pointing an automatic pistol. Other pistol packing agents scrambled into the living room, wearing breath masks and disarmed the other chiefs.

The chiefs were taken outside and into an opening where the news media was setting up for a broadcast.

Marion's Police Chief pulled off his breath mask. "Stand down! We're conducting a crime investigation." Someone tried to handcuff the chief, but he resisted. "Don't you know who I am? I am the Police Chief! And lower your weapons! We're all cops here."

THE DOOR

When the DEA Agents lowered their weapons and put away their handcuffs, the chief thought he had pulled a fast one.

A bright light was focused on his face and a microphone shoved in front of his mouth by a local TV reporter. "Are you ready to make a statement chief?"

"Absolutely."

"Good. We go live in three seconds. Three, two, one. This is breaking news from Marion, Virginia, where the Police Chief is on the scene of another meth lab that was just discovered."

"This," said the chief, as he gestured to the other chiefs, "has been a joint operation between our four respective departments. Unfortunately, we've had to rely on ourselves to carry out this raid because one of our own is involved in the meth production in our towns. The good news is, we *got'em!* And we *got'em* good!" He gave a winning smile.

Someone started to clap. The lights and cameras were panned to Lomax, who was sitting on the hood of the chief's SUV with Dewey Mitchell, each holding a laptop that played separate DVD's. One laptop was showing the video recording of the break-in to Mitchell's house by the chief and two other chiefs and the other laptop was the unedited video and audio conversation of what just took place in the abandoned house.

While the four police chiefs watched the recordings, DEA Agents handcuffed them. One of the agents looked very much like Prince Michael.

"Wait a minute here!" shouted the Marion Police Chief. "We have rights!"

"Excuse me, sir. My name is Special Agent Michaels. And you are correct, sir. You do have rights. You have the right to shut up. Because anything that comes out of that filthy fat mouth of yours can and probably will be used in a court of law to put your sorry candy ass in prison. You have the right to be represented by a blood-sucking attorney. If you cannot afford one, after manufacturing and selling all this dope to our kids, then the state will be more than happy to provide you with an incompetent, paper pushing moron straight out of law school who couldn't defend the Virgin Mary let alone a piece of slime like yourself. Now, do you understand these rights?"

The police chief gave a nervous nod.

THE DOOR

Michaels started to turn away, but then stopped, pivoted on the soles of his shoes and went toe to toe with the police chief. "And as for payback, you sorry excuse for a public servant, don't you know ... payback ... is Hell...!"

THE DOOR

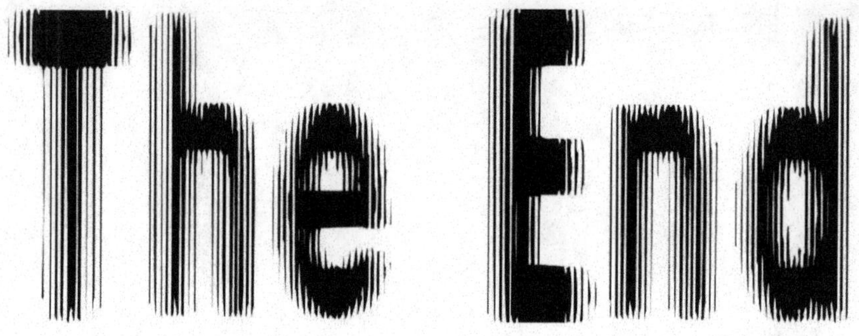

of
Richard de Montebello's

THE DOOR

Calling
An
Angel
A comedy...sort of
Richard de Montebello
Don't you just hate it when you call
Heaven and get a busy signal?